CARL HIAASEN

STORMY WEATHER

PAN BOOKS

First published 1995 by Alfred A. Knopf, Inc

First published in Great Britain 1995 by Pan Books
an imprint of Macmillan General Books
25 Eccleston Place, London SW1W 9NF
and Basingstoke

Associated companies throughout the world

ISBN 0 330 34615 6

The author gratefully acknowledges permission to quote from the song "Box of Rain",
lyrics by Robert Hunter. Copyright 1970 by Ice Nine Publishing Co.

1 3 5 7 9 8 6 4 2

A CIP catalogue record for this book is available from
the British Library

Typeset by CentraCet Limited, Cambridge
Printed by Mackays of Chatham plc, Chatham, Kent

STORMY
WEATHER

For Donna, Camille, Hugo and Andrew

Acknowledgements

For their expertise on the most esoteric subjects, I am deeply grateful to my good friends John Kipp (the finer points of skull collecting), Tim Chapman (the effects of canine shock collars on human volunteers) and Bob Branham (the care and handling of untamed South American coatimundis). I am also greatly indebted to my talented colleagues at the Miami *Herald*, whose superb journalism in the aftermath of Hurricane Andrew provided so much rich material for this novel.

C.H.

ONE

On August 23, the day before the hurricane struck, Max and Bonnie Lamb awoke early, made love twice and rode the shuttle bus to Disney World. That evening they returned to the Peabody Hotel, showered separately, switched on the cable news and saw that the storm was heading directly for the southeastern tip of Florida. The TV weatherman warned that it was the fiercest in many years.

Max Lamb sat at the foot of the bed and gazed at the color radar image—a ragged flame-colored sphere, spinning counter-clockwise toward the coast. He said, "Jesus, look at that."

A hurricane, Bonnie Lamb thought, on our honeymoon! As she slipped under the sheets, she heard the rain beating on the rental cars in the parking lot outside. "Is this part of it?" she asked. "All this weather?"

Her husband nodded. "We're on the edge of the edge."

Max Lamb seemed excited in a way that Bonnie found unsettling. She knew better than to suggest a sensible change of plans, such as hopping a plane back to La Guardia. Her new husband was no quitter; the reservations said five nights and six days, and by God that's how long they would stay. It was a special package rate; no refunds.

She said, "They'll probably close the park."

"Disney?" Max Lamb smiled. "Disney never closes. Not for plagues, famines, or even hurricanes." He rose to adjust the volume on the television. "Besides, the darn thing's three hundred miles away. The most we'll see up here is more rain."

Bonnie Lamb detected disappointment in her husband's tone.

1

Hands on his hips, he stood nude in front of the TV screen; his pale shoulder blades and buttocks were streaked crimson from a day on the water flumes. Max was no athlete, but he'd done fine on the river slide. Bonnie wondered if it had gone to his head, for tonight he affected the square-shouldered posture of a college jock. She caught him glancing in the mirror, flexing his stringy biceps and sizing up his own nakedness. Maybe it was just a honeymoon thing.

The cable news was showing live video of elderly residents being evacuated from condominiums and apartment buildings on Miami Beach. Many of the old folks carried cats or poodles in their arms.

"So," said Bonnie Lamb, "we're still doing Epcot tomorrow?"

Her husband didn't answer.

"Honey?" she said. "Epcot?"

Max Lamb's attention was rooted to the hurricane news. "Oh sure," he said absently.

"You remembered the umbrellas?"

"Yes, Bonnie, in the car."

She asked him to turn off the television and come to bed. When he got beneath the covers, she moved closer, nipped his earlobes, played her fingers through the silky sprout of hair on his bony chest.

"Guess what I'm not wearing," she whispered.

"Ssshhh," said Max Lamb. "Listen to that rain."

Edie Marsh headed to Dade County from Palm Beach, where she'd spent six months trying to sleep with a Kennedy. She'd had the plan all worked out, how she'd seduce a young Kennedy and then threaten to run to the cops with a lurid tale of perversion, rape and torture. She'd hatched the scheme while watching the William Kennedy Smith trial on Court TV and noticing the breathless relief with which the famous clan had received the acquittal; all of them with those fantastic teeth, beaming at the cameras but wearing an expression that Edie Marsh had seen more than a few times in her twenty-nine action-packed years—the look of those who'd dodged a bullet. They'd have no stomach for another scandal, not right away. Next time there'd be a mad stampede for the Kennedy family checkbook, in order to make the problem go away. Edie had it all figured out.

She cleaned out her boyfriend's bank account and grabbed the Amtrak to West Palm, where she found a cheap duplex apartment. She spent her days sleeping, shoplifting cocktail dresses and painting her nails. Each night she'd cross the bridge to the rich island, where she assiduously loitered at Au Bar and the other trendy clubs. She overtipped bartenders and waitresses, with the understanding that they would instantly alert her when a Kennedy, *any* Kennedy, arrived. In this fashion she had quickly met two Shrivers and a distant Lawford, but to Edie they would have been borderline fucks. She was saving her charms for a direct heir, a pipeline to old Joe Kennedy's mother lode. One of the weekly tabloids had published a diagram of the family tree, which Edie Marsh had taped to the wall of the kitchen, next to a Far Side calendar. Right away Edie had ruled out screwing any Kennedys-by-marriage; the serious money followed the straightest lines of genealogy, as did the scandal hunters. Statistically it appeared her best target would be one of Ethel and Bobby's sons, since they'd had so many. Not that Edie wouldn't have crawled nude across broken glass for a whack at John Jr., but the odds of *him* strolling unescorted into a Palm Beach fern bar were laughable.

Besides, Edie Marsh was nothing if not a realist. John Kennedy Jr. had movie-star girlfriends, and Edie knew she was no movie star. Pretty, sure. Sexy in a low-cut Versace, you bet. But John-John probably wouldn't glance twice. Some of those cousins, though, Bobby's boys—Edie was sure she could do some damage there. Suck 'em cross-eyed, then phone the lawyers.

Unfortunately, six grueling months of barhopping produced only two encounters with *Kennedy* Kennedys. Neither tried to sleep with Edie; she couldn't believe it. One of the young men even took her on an actual date, but when they returned to her place he didn't so much as grope her boobs. Just pecked her good night and said thanks for a nice time. The perfect goddamn gentleman, she'd thought. Just my luck. Edie had tried valiantly to change his mind, practically pinned him to the hood of his car, kissed and rubbed and grabbed him. Nothing! Humiliating is what it was. After the young Kennedy departed, Edie Marsh had stalked to the bathroom and studied herself in the mirror. Maybe there was wax in her ears or spinach in her teeth, something gross to put the guy off. But no, she looked fine. Furiously she peeled off her stolen dress, appraised her figure and thought: Did the little snot think he's too good for *this*? What a joke, that Kennedy charm. The kid had all the charisma of oatmeal. He'd bored her to death long before the lobster entrée arrived. She'd felt like hopping on the tabletop and shrieking at the top of her lungs: Who gives a shit about illiteracy in South Boston? Tell me about Jackie and the Greek!

That dismal evening, it turned out, was Edie's last shot. The summer went dead in Palm Beach, and all the fuckable Kennedys traveled up to Hyannis. Edie was too broke to give chase.

The hurricane on the TV radar had given her a new idea. The storm was eight hundred miles away, churning up the Caribbean, when she phoned a man named Snapper, who was coming off a short hitch for manslaughter. Snapper got his nickname because of a crooked jaw, which had been made that way by a game warden and healed poorly. Edie Marsh arranged to meet him at a sports bar on the beach. Snapper listened to her plan and said it was the nuttiest fucking thing he'd ever heard because (a) the hurricane probably won't hit here and (b) somebody could get busted for heavy time.

Three days later, with the storm bearing down on Miami, Snapper called Edie Marsh and said what the hell, let's check it out. I got a guy, Snapper said, he knows about these things.

The guy's name was Avila, and formerly he had worked as a building inspector for Metropolitan Dade County. Snapper and Edie met him at a convenience store on Dixie Highway in South Miami. The rain was deceptively light, given the proximity of the hurricane, but the clouds hung ominously low, an eerie yellow gauze.

They went in Avila's car, Snapper sitting next to Avila up front and Edie by herself in the back. They were going to a subdivision called Sugar Palm Hammocks: one hundred and sixty-four single-family homes platted sadistically on only forty acres of land. Without comment, Avila drove slowly through the streets. Many residents were outside, frantically nailing plywood to the windows of their homes.

"There's no yards," Snapper remarked.

Avila said, "Zero-lot lines is what we call it."

"How cozy," Edie Marsh said from the back seat. "What we need is a house that'll go to pieces in the storm."

Avila nodded confidently. "Take your pick. They're all coming down."

"No shit?"

"Yeah, honey, no shit."

Snapper turned to Edie Marsh and said, "Avila ought to know. He's the one inspected the damn things."

"Perfect," said Edie. She rolled down the window. "Then let's find something nice."

On instructions from the authorities, tourists by the thousands were bailing out of the Florida Keys. Traffic on northbound U.S. 1 was a wretched crawl, winking brake lights as far as the eye could see. Jack Fleming and Webo Drake had run out of beer at Big Pine. Now they were stuck behind a Greyhound bus halfway across the Seven Mile Bridge. The bus had stalled with transmission trouble. Jack Fleming and Webo Drake got out of the car—Jack's father's car—and started throwing empty Coors cans off the bridge. The two young men were still slightly trashed from a night at the Turtle Kraals in Key West, where the idea of getting stranded in a Force Four hurricane had sounded downright adventurous, a nifty yarn to tell the guys back at the Kappa Alpha house. The problem was, Jack and Webo had awakened to find themselves out of money as well as beer, with Jack's father expecting his almost-new Lexus to be returned . . . well, yesterday.

So here they were, stuck on one of the longest bridges in the world, with a monster tropical cyclone only a few hours away. The wind hummed across the Atlantic at a pitch that Jack Fleming and Webo Drake had never before heard; it rocked them on their heels when they got out of the car. Webo lobbed an empty Coors can toward the concrete rail, but the wind whipped it back hard, like a line drive. Naturally it then became a contest to see who had the best arm. In high school Jack Fleming had been a star pitcher, mainly sidearm, so his throws were not as disturbed by the gusts as those of Webo Drake, who had merely played backup quarterback for the junior varsity. Jack was leading, eight beer cans to six off the bridge, when a hand—an enormous brown hand—appeared with a wet slap on the rail.

Webo Drake glanced worriedly at his frat brother. Jack Fleming said, "Now what?"

A bearded man pulled himself up from a piling beneath the bridge. He was tall, with coarse silvery hair that hung in matted tangles to his shoulders. His bare chest was striped with thin pink abrasions. The man carried several coils of dirty rope under one arm. He wore camouflage trousers and old brown military boots with no laces. In his right hand was a crushed Coors can and a dead squirrel.

Jack Fleming said, "You a Cuban?"

Webo Drake was horrified.

Dropping his voice, Jack said: "No joke. I bet he's a rafter."

It made sense. This was where the refugees usually landed, in the Keys. Jack spoke loudly to the man with the rope: "*Usted Cubano?*"

The man brandished the beer can and said: "Usted un asshole?"

His voice was a rumble that fit his size. "Where do you dipshits get off," he said over the wind, "throwing your goddamn garbage in the water?" The man stepped forward and kicked out a rear passenger window of Jack's father's Lexus. He threw the empty beer can and the dead squirrel in the back seat. Then he grabbed Webo Drake by the belt of his jeans. "Your trousers dry?" the man asked.

Passengers in the Greyhound bus pressed their faces to the glass to see what was happening. Behind the Lexus, a family in a rented minivan could be observed locking the doors, a speedy drill they had obviously practiced before leaving the Miami airport.

Webo Drake said yes, his jeans were dry. The stranger said, "Then hold my eye." With an index finger he calmly removed a glass orb from his left socket and placed it carefully in one of Webo's pants pockets. "It loosed up on me," the stranger explained, "in all this spray."

Failing to perceive the gravity of the moment, Jack Fleming pointed at the shattered window of his father's luxury sedan. "Why the hell'd you do that?"

Webo, shaking: "Jack, it's all right."

The one-eyed man turned toward Jack Fleming. "I count thirteen fucking beer cans in the water and only one hole in your car. I'd say you got off easy."

"Forget about it," offered Webo Drake.

The stranger said, "I'm giving you boys a break because you're exceptionally young and stupid."

Ahead of them, the Greyhound bus wheezed, lurched and finally began to inch northward. The man with the rope opened the rear door of the Lexus and brushed the broken glass off the seat. "I need a lift up the road," he said.

Jack Fleming and Webo Drake said certainly, sir, that would be no trouble at all. It took forty-five minutes on the highway before they summoned the nerve to ask the one-eyed man what he was doing under the Seven Mile Bridge.

Waiting, the man replied.

For what? Webo asked.

Turn on the radio, the man said. If you don't mind.

News of the hurricane was on every station. The latest forecast put the storm heading due east across the Bahamas, toward a landfall somewhere between Key Largo and Miami Beach.

"Just as I thought," said the one-eyed man. "I was too far south. I could tell by the sky."

He had covered his head with a flowered shower cap; Jack Fleming noticed it in the rearview mirror, but withheld comment.

The young man was more concerned about what to tell his father regarding the busted window, and also about the stubborn stain a dead squirrel might leave on fine leather upholstery.

Webo Drake asked the one-eyed man: "What's the rope for?"

"Good question," he said, but gave no explanation.

An hour later the road spread to four lanes and the traffic began to move at a better clip. Almost no cars were heading south. The highway split at North Key Largo, and the stranger instructed Jack Fleming to bear right on County Road 905.

"It says there's a toll," Jack said.

"Yeah?"

"Look, we're out of money."

A soggy ten-dollar bill landed on the front seat between Jack Fleming and Webo Drake. Again the earthquake voice: "Stop when we reach the bridge."

Twenty minutes later they approached the Card Sound Bridge, which crosses from North Key Largo to the mainland. Jack Fleming tapped the brakes and steered to the shoulder. "Not here," said the stranger. "All the way to the top."

"The top of the bridge?"

"Are you deaf, junior?"

Jack Fleming drove up the slope cautiously. The wind was ungodly, jostling the Lexus on its springs. At the crest of the span, Jack pulled over as far as he dared. The one-eyed man retrieved his glass eye from Webo Drake and got out of the car. He yanked the plastic cap off his head and jammed it into the waistband of his trousers.

"Come here," the stranger told the two young men. "Tie me." He popped the eye into its socket and cleaned it in a polishing motion with the corner of a bandanna. Then he climbed over the rail and inserted his legs back under the gap, so he was kneeling on the precipice.

Other hurricane evacuees slowed their cars to observe the lunatic scene, but none dared to stop; the man being lashed to the bridge looked wild enough to deserve it. Jack Fleming and Webo Drake worked as swiftly as possible, given the force of the gusts and the rapidity with which their Key West hangovers were advancing. The stranger gave explicit instructions about how he was to be trussed, and the fraternity boys did what they were told. They knotted one end of the rope around the man's thick ankles and ran the other end over the concrete rail. After looping it four times around his chest, they cinched until he grunted. Then they threaded the rope under the rail and back to the ankles for the final knotting.

The product was a sturdy harness that allowed the stranger's arms to wave free. Webo Drake tested the knots and pronounced them tight. "Can we go now?" he asked the one-eyed man.

"By all means."

"What about the squirrel, sir?"

"It's all yours," the stranger said. "Enjoy."

Jack Fleming coasted the car downhill. At the foot of the bridge, he veered off the pavement to get clear of the traffic. Webo Drake found a rusty curtain rod in a pile of trash, and Jack used it to hoist the animal carcass out of his father's Lexus. Webo stood back, trying to light a cigaret.

Back on the bridge, under a murderous dark sky, the kneeling stranger raised both arms to the pulsing gray clouds. Bursts of hot wind made the man's hair stand up like a halo of silver sparks.

"Crazy fucker," Jack Fleming rasped. He stepped over the dead squirrel and threw the curtain rod into the mangroves. "You think he had a gun? Because that's what I'm telling my old man: Some nut with a gun kicked out the car window."

Webo Drake pointed with the cigaret and said, "Jack, you know what he's waiting for? That crazy idiot, he's waiting on the hurricane."

Although the young men stood two hundred yards away, they could see the one-eyed stranger grinning madly into the teeth of the rising wind. He wore a smile that blazed.

"Brother," Jack said to Webo, "let's get the hell out of here." The tollbooth was unmanned, so they blew through at fifty miles an hour, skidded into the parking lot of Alabama Jack's. There they used the one-eyed man's ten-dollar bill to purchase four cold cans of Cherry Coke, which they drank on the trip up Card Sound Road. When they were finished, they did not toss the empties from the car.

A noise awakened Bonnie Lamb. It was Max, snapping open a suitcase. She asked what in the world he was doing, fully dressed and packing his clothes at four in the morning. He said he wanted to surprise her.

"You're leaving me?" she asked. "After two nights."

Max Lamb smiled and came to the bed. "I'm packing for both of us."

He tried to stroke Bonnie's cheek, but she buried her face in the pillow, to block out the light. The rain was coming harder now, slapping horizontally against the windows of the high-rise hotel. She was glad her husband had come to his senses. They could do Epcot some other time.

She peered out of the pillow and said, "Honey, is the airport open?"

"I don't honestly know."

"Shouldn't you call first?"

"Why?" Max Lamb patted the blanket where it followed the curve of his wife's hips.

"We're flying home, aren't we?" Bonnie Lamb sat up. "That's why you're packing."

Her husband said no, we're not flying home. "We're going on an adventure."

"I see. Where, Max?"

"Miami."

"That's the surprise?"

"That's it." He tugged the covers away from her. "Come on, we've got a long drive—"

Bonnie Lamb didn't move. "You're serious."

"—and I want to teach you how to use the video camera."

She said, "I've got a better idea. Why don't we stay here and make love for the next three days. Dawn to dusk, OK? Tear the room to pieces. I mean, if it's adventure you want."

Max Lamb was up again, stuffing the suitcases. "You don't understand. This is a once-in-a-lifetime chance."

Right, Bonnie said, a chance to drown on our honeymoon. "I'd rather stay where it's warm and dry. I'll even watch *Emmanuelle2VI* on the Spectravision, like you wanted last night." This she regarded as a significant concession.

"By the time we get to Miami," said Max, "the dangerous part will be over. In fact, it's probably over already."

"Then what's the point?"

"You'll see."

"Max, I don't want to do this. Please."

He gave her a stiff, fatherly hug. She knew he was about to speak to her as if she were six years old. "Bonnie," Max Lamb said to his new wife. "My beautiful little Bonnie, now listen. Disney World we can do anytime. Anytime we want. But how often does a hurricane hit? You heard the weatherman, honey. 'The Storm of the Century,' he called it. How often does a person get to see something like that!"

Bonnie Lamb couldn't stand her husband's lordly tone. She couldn't stand it so much that she'd have done anything to shut him up.

"All right, Max. Bring me my robe."

He kissed her noisily on the forehead. "Thatta girl."

TWO

Snapper and Edie Marsh got two rooms at the Best Western in Pembroke Pines, thirty miles north of where the storm was predicted to come ashore. Snapper told the motel clerk that one room would be enough, but Edie said not on your damn life. The relationship had always been strictly business, Snapper being an occasional fence of women's wear and Edie being an occasional thief of same. Their new venture was to be another entrepreneurial partnership, more ambitious but not more intimate. Up front Edie alerted Snapper that she couldn't imagine a situation in which she'd have sex with him, even once. He did not seem poleaxed by the news.

She went to bed covering her ears, trying to shut out the hellish moan of the storm. It was more than she could bear alone. During the brief calm of the eye, she pounded on the door to Snapper's room and said she was scared half to death. Snapper said come on in, we're having ourselves a time.

Somewhere in the midst of a hurricane, he'd found a hooker. Edie was impressed. The woman clutched a half-empty bottle of Barbancourt between her breasts. Snapper had devoted himself to vodka; he wore a Marlins cap and red Jockey shorts, inside out. Candles gave the motel room a soft, religious lighting. The electricity had been out for two hours.

Edie Marsh introduced herself to the prostitute, whom Snapper had procured through a telephone escort service. Here was a dedicated employee! thought Edie.

The back side of the storm came up, a roar so unbearable that the three of them huddled like orphans on the floor. The candles flickered madly as the wind sucked at the windows. Edie could see the walls breathing—Christ, what a lousy idea this was! A large painting of a pelican fell, grazing one of the hooker's ankles. She cried out softly and gnawed at her artificial fingernails. Snapper kept to the vodka. Occasionally his free hand would turn up like a spider on Edie's thigh. She smashed it, but Snapper merely sighed.

By dawn the storm had crossed inland, and the high water was falling fast. Edie Marsh put on a conservative blue dress and dark nylons, and pinned her long brown hair in a bun. Snapper wore the only suit he owned, a slate pinstripe he'd purchased two years earlier for an ex-cellmate's funeral; the cuffed trousers stopped an inch shy of his shoetops. Edie chuckled and said that was perfect.

They dropped the prostitute at a Denny's restaurant and took the Turnpike south to see what the hurricane had done. Traffic was bumper-to-bumper lunacy, fire engines and cop cars and ambulances everywhere. The radio said Homestead had been blown off the map. The governor was sending the National Guard.

Snapper headed east on 152nd Street but immediately got disoriented. All traffic signals and street signs were down; Snapper couldn't find Sugar Palm Hammocks. Edie Marsh became agitated. She kept repeating the address aloud: 14275 Noriega Parkway. One-four-two-seven-five. Tan house, brown shutters, swimming pool, two-car garage. Avila had guessed it was worth $185,000.

"If we don't hurry," Edie told Snapper, "if we don't get there soon—"

Snapper instructed her to shut the holy fuck up.

"Wasn't there a Dairy Queen?" Edie went on. "I remember him turning at a Dairy Queen or something."

Snapper said, "The Dairy Queen is gone. *Every* goddamn thing is gone, case you didn't notice. We're flying blind out here."

Edie had never seen such destruction; it looked like Castro had nuked the place. Houses without roofs, walls, windows. Trailers and cars crumpled like foil. Trees in the swimming pools. People weeping, Sweet Jesus, and everywhere the plonking of hammers and the growling of chain saws.

Snapper said they could do another house. "There's only about ten thousand to choose from."

"I suppose."

"What's so special about 1-4-2-7-5?"

"It had personality," Edie Marsh said.

Snapper drummed his knuckles on the steering wheel. "They all look the same. All these places, exactly the same."

His gun lay on the seat between them.

"Fine," said Edie, unsettled by the change of plans, the chaos, the grim dripping skies. "Fine, we'll find another one."

Max and Bonnie Lamb arrived in Dade County soon after daybreak. The roads were slick and gridlocked. The gray sky was growling with TV helicopters. The radio said two hundred thousand homes were seriously damaged or destroyed. Meanwhile the Red Cross was pleading for donations of food, water and clothing.

The Lambs exited the Turnpike at Quail Roost Drive. Bonnie was stunned by the devastation; Max himself was aglow. He held the Handycam on his lap as he steered. Every two or three blocks, he slowed to videotape spectacular rubble. A flattened hardware store. The remains of a Sizzler steak house. A school bus impaled by a forty-foot pine.

"Didn't I tell you?" Max Lamb was saying. "Isn't it amazing!"

Bonnie Lamb shuddered. She said they should stop at the nearest shelter and volunteer to help.

Max paid no attention. He parked in front of an exploded town house. The hurricane had thrown a motorboat into the living room. The family—a middle-aged Latin man, his wife, two little girls—stood in a daze on the sidewalk. They wore matching yellow rain slickers.

Max Lamb got out of the car. "Mind if I get some video?"

The man numbly consented. Max photographed the wrecked building from several dramatic angles. Then, stepping through the plaster and broken furniture and twisted toys, he casually entered the house. Bonnie couldn't believe it: He walked right through the gash that was once the front door!

She apologized to the family, but the man said he didn't mind; he'd need pictures anyway, for the insurance people. His daughters began to sob and tremble. Bonnie Lamb knelt to comfort them. Over her shoulder she caught sight of her husband with the camera at his eye, recording the scene through a broken window.

Later, in the rental car, she said: "That was the sickest thing I ever saw."

"Yes, it's very sad."

"I'm talking about you," Bonnie snapped.

"What?"

"Max, I want to go home."

"I bet we can sell some of this tape."

"Don't you dare."

Max said: "I bet we can sell it to C-SPAN. Pay for the whole honeymoon!"

Bonnie closed her eyes. What had she done? Was her mother right about this man? Latent asshole, her mother had whispered at the wedding. Was she right?

At dusk Edie Marsh swallowed two Darvons and reviewed the plan with Snapper, who was having second thoughts. He seemed troubled at the idea of waiting weeks for the payoff. Edie said there wasn't much choice, the way insurance worked. Snapper said he planned to keep his options open, just the same. Edie Marsh took it to mean he'd bug out on a moment's notice.

They had picked a house in a flattened development called Turtle Meadow, where the hurricane had peeled away all the roofs. Snapper said it was probably one of Avila's routes. He said Avila had bragged of inspecting eighty new homes a day without leaving the truck. "Rolling quotas," is what Avila called them. Snapper allowed that Avila wasn't much of a roof inspector, as he was deathly afraid of heights and therefore refused to take a ladder on his rounds. Consequently, Avila's roof certifications were done visually, from a vehicle, at speeds often exceeding thirty-five miles an hour. Snapper said Avila's swiftness and trusting attitude had made him a favorite among the local builders and contractors, especially at Christmastime.

Scanning the debris, Edie Marsh said Avila was damn lucky not to be in jail. That's why he quit when he did, Snapper explained. The bones told him it was time. That, and a grand jury.

Bones? said Edie.

You don't want to know, Snapper said. Honestly.

They were walking along the sidewalk, across the street from the house they had chosen on the drive-by that morning. Now the neighborhood was pitch black except for the erratic flicker of flashlights and the glow of a few small bonfires. Many families had abandoned the crumbled shells of their homes for nearby motels, but a few men had stayed to patrol against looters. The men wore pinched tense expressions and carried shotguns. Snapper was glad to be white and wearing a suit.

The house he and Edie Marsh had chosen wasn't empty, dark or quiet. A bare light bulb had been strung from the skeletal remains of the roof, and the gray-blue glow of a television set pulsed against the plaster. These luxuries were explained by the rumble of a portable generator. Edie and Snapper had seen a fat man gassing it up earlier in the day.

The street was either Turtle Meadow Lane or Calusa Drive, depending on which of the fallen street signs was accurate. The number "15600" was sprayed in red paint on an outside wall of the house, as was the name of the insurance company: "Midwest Casualty."

A big outfit, Edie noted. She'd seen the commercials on television; the company's symbol was a badger.

"A badger?" Snapper frowned. "The fuck does a badger have to do with insurance?"

"I dunno." Edie's mouth was dry. She felt sleepy. "What does a cougar have to do with cars? It's just advertising is all."

Snapper said, "The only thing I know about badgers is they're stubborn. And the last goddamn thing we need's a stubborn insurance company."

Edie said, "For heaven's sake—"

"Let's find another house."

"No!" Weaving slightly, she crossed the street toward 15600.

"You hear me?" Snapper called, then started after her.

Edie wheeled in the driveway. "Let's do it!" she said. "Right now, while it's quiet."

Snapper hesitated, working his jaw like a dazed boxer.

"Come on!" Edie tugged her hair out of the bun and mussed it into a nest in front of her face. Then she hitched her dress and raked her fingernails up both thighs, tearing tracks in her nylons.

Snapper checked to make sure none of the neighborhood vigilantes were watching. Edie picked a place on the driveway and stretched out, facedown. Using two broken roof trusses, Snapper did a superb job setting the scene. Edie was pinned.

From under the debris, she said, "Blood would help."

Snapper kicked a nail toward her left hand. "Take it easy."

Edie Marsh held her breath and scratched the point of the nail from her elbow to her wrist. It hurt like a bitch. She wiped her arm across one cheek to smear the blood for dramatic effect. On cue, Snapper began shouting for help. Edie was impressed; he sounded damn near sincere.

Max Lamb congratulated himself for stocking up on video supplies before they drove down from Orlando. Other tourists had not come so prepared for the hurricane and could be seen foraging through luggage in a manic search for spare tapes and batteries. Meanwhile, pausing only to reload, Max Lamb was compiling dramatic footage of a historic natural disaster. Even if C-SPAN wasn't interested, his friends in New York would be. Max was a junior account executive at a medium-sized advertising firm, and there were many persons whom he yearned to impress. Max was handy with the Sony, but it wouldn't hurt to seek professional assistance; he knew of a place on East Fiftieth Street that edited home videos and, for a small extra charge, added titles and credits. It would be perfect! Once Bonnie settled down, Max Lamb would ask her about throwing a cocktail party where they could screen the hurricane tapes for his clients and his colleagues at the agency.

Max trotted with predatory energy from one wrecked home-stead to another, the video camera purring in his hand. He was so absorbed in recording the tragedy that he forgot about his wife, who had stopped following three blocks ago. Max had wanted to show Bonnie how to use the camera so he could pose amid hurricane debris; she'd told him she would rather swallow a gallon of lye.

For editing purposes, Max Lamb kept a mental inventory of his best shots. He had plenty of rubble scenes, and felt the need to temper the visual shock with moments of poignancy—vignettes that would capture the human toll, spiritual as well as physical.

A mangled bicycle grabbed Max's attention. The hurricane had wrapped it, as snug as a wedding band, around the trunk of a coconut palm. A boy no older than eight was trying to remove the bike. Max dropped to one knee and zoomed in on the youngster's face as he tugged grimly on the bent handlebars. The boy's expression was dull and cold, his lips pressed tight in concentration.

Max thought: He's in shock. Doesn't even know I'm here.

The youngster didn't seem to care that his bicycle was destroyed beyond repair. He simply wanted the tree to give it back. He pulled and pulled with all his might. The empty eyes showed no sign of frustration.

Amazing, Max Lamb thought as he peered through the view-finder. *Amazing*.

Something jostled his right arm, and the boy's image in the viewfinder shook. A hand tugged at Max's sleeve. Cursing, he looked up from the Handycam.

It was a monkey.

Max Lamb pivoted on one heel and aimed the camera at the scrawny animal. Through the viewfinder he saw that the monkey had come through the storm in miserable shape. Its auburn fur was matted and crusty. A bruise as plump as a radish rose from the bridge of its broad velvet nose. The shoe-button eyes were squinty and ringed with milky ooze.

Swaying on its haunches, the monkey bared its gums in a woozy yawn. Listlessly it began to paw at its tail.

"See what we have here—a wild monkey!" Max narrated, for the benefit of future viewers. "Just look at this poor little fella. . . ."

From behind him, a flat voice: "Better watch it, mister." It was the boy with the broken bicycle.

Max, the Handycam still at his eye, said, "What's the matter, son?"

"Better watch out for that thing. My dad, he had to shoot one last night."

"Is that right?" Max smiled to himself. Why would anyone shoot a monkey?

"They're real sick. That's what my dad said."

"Well, I'll certainly be careful," said Max Lamb. He heard footsteps as the strange boy ran off.

Through the viewfinder, Max noticed the monkey's brow was twitching oddly. Suddenly it was airborne. Max lowered the camera just as the animal struck his face, knocking him backward. Miniature rubbery fingers dug at Max's nostrils and eyes. He cried out fearfully. The monkey's damp fur smelled awful.

Max Lamb began rolling in the dirt as if he were on fire. Screeching, the wiry little creature let go. Max sat up, scrubbing his face with the sleeves of his shirt. The stinging told him he'd been scratched. For starters he would require a tetanus booster, and then something more potent to counteract the monkey germs.

As he rose to his feet, Max heard chittering behind the palm tree. He was poised to run, until he spotted the monkey loping with an addled gait in the opposite direction. It was dragging something by a strap.

Max Lamb was enraged. The damn thing was stealing his Handycam! Idiotically he gave pursuit.

An hour later, when Bonnie Lamb went looking for her husband, he was gone.

Two uniformed Highway Patrol troopers stood in the rain at the top of the bridge. One was a tall, powerfully built black man. The other officer was a woman of milky smooth complexion and medium height, with a bun of reddish-brown hair. Together they leaned against the concrete rail and stared down a long length of broken rope, dangling in the breeze over the choppy brown water.

Five motorists had phoned on their cellulars to report that a crazy man was tied to the Card Sound Bridge. That was only hours before the hurricane, when every police officer within fifty miles had been busy evacuating the sane. Nobody had time for jumpers, so nobody checked the bridge.

The black trooper had been sent to Miami all the way from Liberty County, in northern Florida, to help clear traffic for the rescue convoys. At the command center he'd caught a glimpse of the incident notation in the dispatch log—"White male, 40–50 yrs old, 190–220 lbs, gray hair/beard, possible psych. case"—and decided to sneak down to North Key Largo for a look. Technically he was assigned to Homestead, but in the post-storm chaos it was easy to roam and not be missed. He had asked the other trooper to ride with him, and even though she was off duty she'd said yes.

Now motorists crossing the steep bridge braked in curiosity at the sight of the two troopers at the top. *What're they looking at, Mom? Is there a dead body in the water?*

Raindrops trickled from the brim of the black trooper's Stetson as he gazed across Biscayne Bay, leaden and frothy after the dreadful storm. He reached over the rail and hauled up the soggy rope. After examining the end of it, he showed the rope to the other trooper and said, with a weariness: "That's my boy."

The rope hadn't snapped in the hurricane. It had been cut with a knife.

THREE

Tony Torres sat in what remained of his living room and sipped what remained of his Chivas. He found it amusing that his "Salesman of the Year" award had survived the hurricane; it was all that remained hanging on the rain-soaked walls. Tony Torres recalled the party two months earlier, when they'd given him the cheap laminated plaque. It was his reward for selling seventy-seven double-wide house trailers, eighteen more than any other salesman in the history of PreFab Luxury Homes, formerly Tropic Trailers, formerly A-Plus Affordable Homes, Ltd. In the cutthroat world of mobile-home sales, Tony Torres had become a star. His boss had presented the Chivas and a thousand-dollar bonus along with the plaque. They'd paid a waitress to dance topless on a table and sing "For He's a Jolly Good Fellow."

Oh well, Tony Torres thought. Life's a fucking roller coaster. He stroked the stock of the shotgun that lay across his globe-shaped lap, and remembered things he wished he didn't. For instance, that bullshit in the sales pitch about U.S. government safety regulations . . .

The Steens had questioned him thoroughly about hurricanes. So had the Ramirezes and the pain-in-the-ass Stichlers. So had Beatrice Jackson, the widow, and her no-neck son. Tony Torres always said what he'd been coached to say, that PreFab Luxury Homes built state-of-the-art homes guaranteed to withstand high winds. Uncle Sam set the specs. It's all there in the brochure!

So Tony's customers secured their mortgages and bought up the double-wides, and then the hurricane came and blew them away. All seventy-seven. The trailers imploded, exploded, popped off the tiedowns and took off like fucking aluminum ducks. Not one of the damn things made it through the storm. One minute they were pleasant-looking middle-class dwellings, with VCRs and convertible sofas and baby cribs . . . and the next minute they were shrapnel. Tony Torres had driven to the trailer park to see for himself. The place looked like a war zone. He was about to get out of the car when somebody recognized him—old man Stichler, who began spluttering insanely and hurling jagged debris at the salesman. Tony drove off at a high rate of speed. Later he learned that the widow Jackson was found dead in the wreckage of the trailer court.

Tony Torres was unfamiliar with remorse, but he did feel a stab of sorrow. The Chivas took care of that. How was I to know? he thought. I'm a salesman, not a goddamn engineer.

The more Tony drank, the less sympathy he retained for his customers. They goddamn well *knew*. Knew they were buying a tin can instead of a real house. Knew the risks, living in a hurricane zone. These were grown-ups, Tony Torres told himself. They made a choice.

Still, he anticipated trouble. The shotgun was a comfort. Unfortunately, anybody who wanted to track him down had only to look in the Dade County phone book. Being a salesman meant being available to all of humanity.

So let 'em come! Tony thought. Any moron customers got a problem, let 'em see what the storm did to *my* house. They get nasty, I turn the matter over to Señor Remington here.

Shouts rousted Tony Torres from the sticky embrace of his BarcaLounger. He took the gun and a flashlight to the front of the house. Standing in the driveway was a man with an unfortunate pin-striped suit and a face that appeared to have been modified with a crowbar.

"My sister!" the man exclaimed, pointing at a pile of busted lumber.

Tony Torres spotted the prone form of a woman under the trusses. Her eyes were half closed, and a fresh streak of blood colored her face. The woman groaned impressively. The man told Tony to call 911 rightaway.

"First tell me what happened," the salesman said.

"Just look—part of your damn roof fell down on her!"

"Hmmm," said Tony Torres.

"For Christ's sake, don't just stand there."

"Your sister, huh?" Tony walked up to the woman and shined the flashlight in her eyes. The woman squinted reflexively, raising both hands to block out the light.

Tony Torres said, "Guess you're not paralyzed, darling."

He tucked the flashlight under one arm and raised the shotgun toward the man. "Here's the deal, sport. The phones are blown, so we won't be calling 911 unless you got a cellular in your pants, and that looks more like a pistol to me. Second of all, even if we *could* call 911 we'll be waiting till Halloween. Every ambulance from here to Key West is busy because of the storm. Your 'sister' should've thought of that before her accident—"

"What the hell you—"

Tony Torres took the pistol from the man's waist. "Third of all," the salesman said, "my damn roof didn't fall on nobody. Those trusses came off the neighbor's house. That would be Mister Leonel Varga, next door. My own personal roof is lying in pieces somewhere out in the Everglades, is my guess."

From beneath the lumber, the woman said: "Shit, Snapper." The man shot her a glare, then looked away.

Tony Torres said: "I'm in the business of figuring people out quick. That's what a good salesman does. And if she's your sister, sport, then I'm twins with Mel Gibson."

The man with the crooked jaw shrugged.

"Point is," Tony said, "she ain't really hurt. You ain't really her brother. And whatever fucked-up plan you had for ripping me off is now officially terminated."

The man scowled bitterly. "Hey, it was *her* idea."

Tony ordered him to lift the wooden trusses off his partner. When the woman got up, the salesman noticed she was both attractive and intelligent-looking. He motioned with the shotgun.

"Both of you come inside. Hell, inside is pretty much outside, thanks to that goddamn storm. But come in, anyhow, 'cause I'd love to hear your story. I could use a laugh."

The woman smoothed the front of her dress. "We made a bad mistake. Just let us go, OK?"

Tony Torres smiled. "That's funny, darling." He swung the Remington toward the house and pulled the trigger. The blast tore a hole the size of a soccer ball in the garage door.

"Hush," said the drunken salesman, cupping a hand to one ear. "Hear that? Dead fucking silence. Shoot off a twelve-gauge and nobody cares. Nobody comes to see. Nobody comes to help. Know why? Because of the hurricane. The whole place is a madhouse!"

The man with the crooked jaw asked, more out of curiosity than concern: "What is it you want with us?"

"I haven't decided," said Tony Torres. "Let's have a drinky poo."

A week before the hurricane, Felix Mojack died of a viper bite to the ankle. Ownership of his failing wildlife-import business passed to a nephew, Augustine. On the rainy morning he learned of his uncle's death, Augustine was at home practicing his juggling. He had all the windows open, and the Black Crowes playing on the stereo. He was barefoot and wore only a pair of royal-blue gym shorts. He stood in the living room, juggling in time to the music. The objects that he juggled were human skulls; he was up to five at once. The faster Augustine juggled, the happier he was.

On the kitchen table was an envelope from Paine Webber. It contained a check for $21,344.55. Augustine had no need for or interest in the money. He was almost thirty-two years old, and his life was as simple and empty as one could be. Sometimes he deposited the Paine Webber dividends, and sometimes he mailed them off to charities, renegade political candidates or former girlfriends. Augustine sent not a penny to his father's defense lawyers; that was the old man's debt, and he could damn well settle it when he got out of prison.

Augustine's juggling was a private diversion. The skulls were artifacts and medical specimens he'd acquired from friends. When he had them up in the air—three, four, five skulls arcing fluidly from hand to hand—Augustine could feel the full rush of their faraway lives. It was inexplicably and perhaps unwholesomely exhilarating. Augustine didn't know their names, or how they'd lived or died, but from touching them he drew energy.

In his spare time Augustine read books and watched television and hiked what was left of the Florida wilderness. Even before he became wealthy—when he worked on his father's fishing boat, and later in law school—Augustine nursed an unspecific anger that he couldn't trace and wasn't sure he should. It manifested itself in the occasional urge to burn something down or blow something up—a high-rise, a new interstate highway, that sort of thing.

Now that Augustine had both the time and the money, he found himself without direction for these radical sentiments, and with no trustworthy knowledge of heavy explosives. Out of guilt, he donated large sums to respectable causes such as the Sierra Club and the Nature Conservancy. His ambition to noble violence remained a harmless fantasy. Meanwhile he bobbed through life's turbulence like driftwood.

The near-death experience that made Augustine so rich had given him zero insight into a grand purpose or cosmic destiny. Augustine barely remembered the damn Beechcraft going down. Certainly he saw no blinding white light at the end of a cool tunnel, heard no dead relatives calling to him from heaven. All he recalled of the coma that followed the accident was an agonizing and unquenchable thirst.

After recovering from his injuries, Augustine didn't return to the hamster-wheel routine of law school. The insurance settlement financed a comfortable aimlessness that many young men would have found appealing. Yet Augustine was deeply unhappy. One night, in a fit of depression, he violently purged his bookshelves of all genius talents who had died too young. This included his treasured Jack London.

Typically, Augustine was waiting for a woman to come along and fix him. So far, it hadn't happened.

One time a dancer whom Augustine was dating caught him juggling his skulls in the bedroom. She thought it was a stunt designed to provoke a reaction. She told him it wasn't funny, it was perverted. Then she moved to New York. A year or so later, for no particular reason, Augustine sent the woman one of his dividend checks from Paine Webber. She used the money to buy a Toyota Supra and sent Augustine a snapshot of herself, smiling and waving in the driver's seat. Augustine wondered who'd taken the picture and what he'd thought of the new car.

Augustine had no brothers and sisters, his mother was in Nevada and his father was in the slammer. The closest relative was his uncle Felix Mojack, the wildlife importer. As a boy, Augustine often visited his uncle's small cluttered farm out in the boondocks. It was more fun than going to the zoo, because Felix let Augustine help with the animals. In particular, Felix encouraged his nephew to familiarize himself with exotic snakes, as Felix himself was phobic (and, it turned out, fatally incompetent) when it came to handling reptiles.

After Augustine grew up, he saw less and less of his busy uncle. Progress conspired against Felix; development swept westward, and zoning regulations forced him to move his operation repeatedly. Nobody, it seemed, wished to build elementary schools or shopping malls within walking distance of caged jungle cats and wild cobras. The last time Felix Mojack was forced to relocate his animals, Augustine gave him ten thousand dollars for the move.

At the time of Felix's death, the farm inventory listed one male African lion, three cougars, a gelded Cape buffalo, two Kodiak bears, ninety-seven parrots and macaws, eight Nile crocodiles, forty-two turtles, seven hundred assorted lizards, ninety-three snakes (venomous and nonvenomous) and eighty-eight rhesus monkeys.

The animals were kept on a nine-acre spread off Krome Avenue, not far from the federal prison. The day after the funeral, Augustine drove out to the place alone. He had a feeling that his uncle ran a loose operation, and a tour of the facility corroborated his suspicion. The fencing was buckled and rusty, the cages needed new hinges, and the concrete reptile pits hadn't been drained and cleaned in months. In the tar-paper shed that Felix had used for an office, Augustine found paperwork confirming his uncle's low regard for U.S. Customs regulations.

It came as no surprise that Felix had been a smuggler; rather, Augustine was grateful that his uncle's choice of contraband had been exotic birds and snakes, and not something else. Wildlife, however, presented its own unique challenges. While bales of marijuana required no feeding, bears and cougars did. Lean and hungry was a mild description of the illegal menagerie; Augustine was appalled by the condition of some of the animals and presumed their deterioration was a result of his uncle's recent financial troubles. Fortunately, the two young Mexicans who worked for Felix Mojack graciously agreed to help out for a few days after his death. They stocked the freezers with raw meat for the large carnivores, bought boxloads of feed for the parrots and monkeys, and restocked on white mice and insects for the reptiles.

Meanwhile Augustine scrambled to locate a buyer for the animals, somebody qualified to take good care of them. Augustine was so preoccupied with the task that he didn't pay enough attention to news reports of a tropical storm intensifying in the Caribbean. Even when it bloomed into a hurricane, and Augustine saw the weather bulletin on television, he assumed it would do what most storms did in late summer—veer north, away from South Florida, on the prevailing Atlantic steering currents.

Once it became clear that the hurricane would strike southern Dade County with a direct hit, Augustine had little time to act. He was grimly aware what sustained one-hundred-mile-per-hour winds would do to his dead uncle's shabby farm. He spent the morning and afternoon on the telephone, trying to find a secure location for the animals. Interest invariably dropped off at the mention of a Cape buffalo. At dusk Augustine drove out to fasten tarps and tie-downs on the cages and pens. Sensing the advancing storm, the bears and big cats paced nervously, growling in agitation. The parrots were in a panic; the frenetic squawking attracted several large hawks to the nearby pines. Augustine stayed two hours and decided it was hopeless. He sent the Mexicans home and drove to a nearby Red Cross shelter to wait out the storm.

When he returned at dawn, the place was destroyed. The fencing was strewn like holiday tinsel across the property. The corrugated roofing had been peeled off the compound like a sardine tin. Except for a dozen befuddled turtles, all his uncle's wild animals had escaped into the scrub and marsh and, inevitably, the Miami suburbs. As soon as phone service was restored, Augustine notified the police what had happened. The dispatcher laconically estimated it would be five or six days before an officer could be spared, because everybody was working double shifts after the hurricane. When Augustine asked how far a Gaboon viper could travel in five or six days, the dispatcher said she'd try to send somebody out there sooner.

Augustine couldn't just sit and wait. The radio said a troop of storm-addled monkeys had invaded a residential subdivision off Quail Roost Drive, only miles from the farm. Augustine immediately loaded the truck with his uncle's dart rifle, two long-handled nooses, a loaded .38 Special, and a five-pound bag of soggy monkey chow.

He didn't know what else to do.

Canvassing the neighborhood in search of her husband, Bonnie Lamb encountered the dull-eyed boy with the broken bicycle. His description of the tourist jerk with the video camera fit Max too well.

"He ran after the monkey," the boy said.

Bonnie Lamb said, "What monkey?"

The boy explained. Bonnie assessed the information calmly. "Which way did they go?" The boy pointed. Bonnie thanked him and offered to help pry his bicycle off the tree. The boy turned away, so she walked on.

Bonnie was puzzled by the monkey story, but most of the questions clouding her mind concerned Max Lamb's character. How could a man wander off and forget about his new wife? Why was he so fascinated with the hurricane ruins? How could he so cruelly intrude on the suffering of those who lived here?

During two years of courtship, Max had never seemed insensitive. At times he could be immature and self-centered, but Bonnie had never known a man who wasn't. In general, Max was a responsible and attentive person; more than just a hard worker, an achiever. Bonnie appreciated that, as her two previous boyfriends had taken a casual approach to the concept of full-time employment. Max impressed her with his seriousness and commitment, his buoyant determination to attain professional success and financial security. At thirty, Bonnie was at a point in life where she liked the prospect of security; she was tired of worrying about money, and about men who had none. Beyond that, she truly found Max Lamb attractive. He wasn't exceptionally handsome or romantic, but he was sincere—boyishly, completely, relentlessly sincere. His earnestness, even in bed, was endearing. This was a man Bonnie thought she could trust.

Until today, when he started acting like a creep.

The predawn expedition to Miami seemed, at first, a honeymoon lark—Max's way of showing his bride that he could be as wild and impulsive as her old boyfriends. Against her best instincts, Bonnie played along. She felt sure that seeing the hurricane's terrible destruction would end Max's documentary ambitions, that he'd put down the camera and join the volunteer relief workers, who were arriving by the busload.

But he didn't. He kept taping, becoming more and more excited, until Bonnie Lamb could no longer bear it. When he asked her to operate the camera while he posed on an overturned station wagon, Bonnie nearly slugged him. She quit tagging after Max because she didn't want to be seen with him. Her own husband.

In one gutted house she spotted an old woman, her mother's age, stepping through splintered bedroom furniture. The woman was calling the name of a pet kitten, which had disappeared in the storm. Bonnie Lamb offered to help search. The cat didn't turn up, but Bonnie did find the old woman's wedding album, beneath a shattered mirror. Bonnie cleared the broken glass and retrieved the album, damp but not ruined. Bonnie opened it to the date of inscription: December 11, 1949. When the old woman saw the album, she broke down in Bonnie's arms. With a twinge of shame, Bonnie glanced around to make sure that Max wasn't secretly filming them. Then she began to cry, too.

Later, resolved to confront her husband, Bonnie Lamb went to find him. If he refused to put away that stupid camera, she would demand the keys to the rental car. It promised to be the first hard test of the new marriage.

Two hours passed with no sign of Max, and Bonnie's anger dissolved into worry. The tale told by the boy with the broken bicycle ordinarily would have been comical, but Bonnie took it as further evidence of Max's reckless obsession. He was afraid of animals, even hamsters, a condition he blamed on an unspecified childhood trauma; to boldly pursue a wild monkey was definitely out of character. On the other hand, Max loved that damn Handycam. More than once he'd reminded Bonnie that it had cost seven hundred dollars, mail order from Hong Kong. She could easily envision him chasing a seven-hundred-dollar investment down the street. She could even envision him strangling the monkey for it, if necessary.

Another squall came, and Bonnie cursed mildly under her breath. There wasn't much left standing, in the way of shelter. She felt a shiver as the raindrops ran down her neck, and decided to return to the rental car and wait for Max there. Except she wasn't sure where the car was parked—without street signs or mailboxes, every block of the destroyed subdivision looked the same. Bonnie Lamb was lost.

She saw the helicopters wheeling overhead, heard the chorus of sirens in the distance, yet on the streets of the neighborhood there were no policemen, no soldiers, no proper authority to which a missing husband could be reported. Exhausted, Bonnie sat on a curb. To keep dry, she tried to balance a large square of plywood over her head. A gust of wind got under the board and pulled Bonnie over backward; as she went down, a corner of the board struck her sharply on the forehead.

She lay there stunned for several moments, staring at the

muddy sky, blinking the raindrops from her eyes. A man appeared, standing over her. He wore a small rifle slung on one shoulder.

"Let me help," he said.

Bonnie Lamb allowed him to lift her from the wet grass. She noticed her blouse was soaked, and shyly folded her arms across her breasts. The man retrieved the plywood board and braced it at a generous angle against a concrete utility pole. There he and Bonnie Lamb took shelter from the slashing rain.

The man was in his early thirties, with good shoulders and tanned, strong-looking arms. He had short brown hair, a sharp chin and friendly blue eyes. He wore Rockport hiking shoes, which gave Bonnie a sense of relief. She couldn't imagine a psychopathic sex killer choosing Rockports.

"Do you live around here?" she asked.

The man shook his head. "Coral Gables."

"Is the gun loaded?"

"Sort of," the man said, without elaborating.

"My name is Bonnie."

"I'm Augustine."

"What are you doing out here?" she asked.

"Believe it or not," he said, "I'm looking for my monkeys."

Bonnie Lamb smiled. "What a coincidence."

Max Lamb woke up with a headache that was about to get worse. He found himself stripped to his underwear and bound to a pine tree. The tall man with the glass eye, the man who'd snatched him off the street as if he were a wayward toddler, was thrashing and flopping in a leafy clearing by the campfire. When the impressive seizure ended, the kidnapper gathered himself in a lotus position. Max Lamb noticed a thick black collar around the man's neck. In one hand he held a shiny cylinder that reminded Max of a remote control for a model car. The cylinder had a short rubber antenna and three colored buttons.

The one-eyed man was mumbling: "Too much juice, too much . . ." He wore a cheap plastic shower cap on his head. Max would have assumed he was a street person, except for the teeth; the kidnapper displayed outstanding orthodontics.

He seemed unaware that his captive was observing him. Deliberately the man extended both legs to brace himself, inhaled twice deeply, then pushed a red button on the remote-control cylinder. Instantly his body began to jerk like an enormous broken puppet. Max Lamb watched helplessly as the stranger writhed through the leaves toward the fire. His boots were in the flames when the fit finally ended. Then the man rose with a startling swiftness, stomping his huge feet until the soles cooled.

One hand went to his neck. "By God, that's better."

Max Lamb concluded it was a nightmare, and shut his eyes. When he opened them again, much later, he saw that the campfire was freshly stoked. The one-eyed kidnapper crouched nearby; now his neck was bare. He was feeding Oreo cookies to the larcenous monkey, which appeared to be regaining its health. Max was more certain than ever that what he'd witnessed earlier was a dream. He felt ready to assert himself.

"Where's my camera?" he demanded.

The kidnapper stood up, laughing through his wild beard. "Perfect," he said. "'Where's my camera?' That's just perfect."

In a hazardously patronizing tone, Max Lamb said: "Let me go, pardner. You don't *really* want to go to jail, do you?"

"Ha," the stranger said. He reached for the shiny black cylinder.

A bolt of fire passed through Max Lamb's neck. He shuddered violently and gulped for breath. His tongue tasted of hot copper. Crimson spears of light punctured the night. Max warbled in fear.

"Shock collar," the kidnapper explained, unnecessarily. "The TriTronics 200. Three levels of stimulation. Range of one mile. Rechargeable nickel-cadmium batteries. Three-year warranty."

Max felt it now, stiff leather against the soft skin of his throat.

"State of the art," said the stranger. "You a bird hunter?"

Max mouthed the word "no."

"Well, trust me. Field trainers swear by these gizmos. Dogs get the message real quick, even Labs." The stranger twirled the remote control like a baton. "Me, I couldn't put one of these on an animal. Fact, I couldn't even try it on *you* without testing it myself. That's what a big old softy I am."

The kidnapper scratched the crown of the monkey's head. The monkey hopped back and bared its tiny teeth, which were flecked black with Oreo crumbs. The kidnapper laughed.

Max Lamb, quavering: "Keep it away from me!"

"Not an animal person, huh?"

"What is it you want?"

The stranger turned toward the fire.

Max said, "Is it money? Just take whatever I've got."

"Jesus, you're thick." The stranger pushed the red button, and Max Lamb thrashed briefly against his ropes. The monkey skittered away, out of the firelight.

Max looked up to see the psycho, taping him with the video camera! "Say cheese," the stranger said, aiming the Handycam with his good eye.

Max Lamb reddened. He felt spindly and pale in his underwear.

The man said, "I might send this up to Rodale and Burns. What d'you think—for the office Christmas bash? 'How I Spent My Florida Vacation,' starring Max Leo Lamb."

Max sagged. Rodale and Burns was the Madison Avenue advertising agency where he worked. The lunatic had been through his billfold.

"They call me Skink," the kidnapper said. He turned off the Handycam and carefully capped the lens. "But I prefer 'captain.'"

"Captain what?"

"Obviously you were impressed by the hurricane." The stranger packed the video camera in a canvas sleeve. "Myself, I was disappointed. I was hoping for something more ... well, biblical."

Max Lamb said, as respectfully as possible: "It looked pretty bad to me."

"You hungry?" The kidnapper brought a burlap sack to the tree where his prisoner was tied.

"Oh God," said Max Lamb, staring inside the bag. "You can't be serious."

FOUR

Filling the BarcaLounger like a stuffed tuna, Tony Torres encouraged Edie Marsh and Snapper to reveal the details of their aborted scam. Facing a loaded shotgun, they complied.

Snapper gestured sourly toward Edie, who said: "Simple. I fake a fall in your driveway. My 'brother' here threatens to sue. You freak out and offer us money."

"Because you guys know," Tony said, slapping a mosquito on his blubbery neck, "I'll be getting quite a wad of dough on account of the hurricane. Insurance dough."

"Exactly," Edie Marsh said. "Your place is wrecked, last thing you need is a lawsuit. So Snapper says here's an idea: Soon as your hurricane money comes in, cut us a piece and we call it even."

Tony Torres sucked his teeth in amusement. "How big a piece, darling?"

"Whatever we could take you for."

"Ah," said Tony.

"We figured you'd just factor us in the insurance claim. Jack up your losses by a few grand, who'd ever know?"

"Beautiful," Tony said.

"Oh yeah," said Snapper, "fucking genius. Look how good it worked."

He and Edie sat with their backs to the living-room wall; Snapper with his long legs drawn up, Edie's straight out, kneecaps pressed together. A picture of innocence, Tony Torres thought. The runs in her stockings were a nifty touch.

The carpet was sodden from the storm, but Edie Marsh didn't

complain. Snapper felt the wetness creeping through the seat of his dress trousers—the annoyance was sufficient that he might kill Tony Torres, if the opportunity presented itself.

Deep in thought, the salesman slurped at a sweaty bottle of imported beer. He'd offered his captives a quart of warm Gatorade, which they'd refused without comment. A humid breeze blew through the fractures in the walls and rocked the bare sixty-watt bulb on its beam. Edie Marsh tilted her head and saw a spray of stars where Tony's ceiling had once been. The noise from the portable generator gave Snapper an oppressive headache.

Eventually, Tony Torres said: "You understand there's no law to speak of. The world's upside down, for the time being."

"You could kill us and get clean away with it. That's what you mean," Snapper said.

Edie looked at him. "You're a tremendous help."

Tony indicated that he preferred not to shoot them. "But here's my thinking," he said. "Tomorrow, maybe the day after, somebody from Midwest Casualty will come see about the house. I expect he'll say it's a total loss, unless he's blind as a bat. Anyway, the good news: I happen to own the place free and clear. Paid it off last March." Tony paused to stifle a burp. "I was having a good run at the office, so what the hell. I paid the mortgage off."

Edie Marsh said: "Salesman of the Year." She had noticed the plaque.

"Mister," Snapper interjected, "you got somethin' I can put under my ass? The rug's all wet. A newspaper maybe?"

"Oh, I think you'll live," said the salesman. "Anyhow, since the bank don't own the house, all the insurance comes to me. As I say, there's the good news. The bad news is, half belongs to my wife. Her name's on the deed."

Snapper asked where she was. Tony Torres said she'd run off three months ago with a parapsychology professor from the university. He said they'd gotten into crystal healing and moved to Eugene, Oregon.

"In a VW van!" he scoffed. "But she'll be back for her cut. Of that there's no doubt. Neria will return. See where I'm headed?"

"Yeah," said Snapper. "You want us to kill your wife."

"Jesus, what a one-track mind you got. No, I don't want you to *kill* my wife." The salesman appealed to Edie Marsh. "You get it, don't you? Before they cut a check, the insurance company is gonna need both signatures. Me and the missus. And I also believe the adjuster might want to chat face-to-face. What'd you say your name was?"

"Edie."

"OK, Edie, you wanna be an actress here's your chance. When the man from Midwest Casualty shows up, you be Neria Torres. My loving wife." Tony smirked at the notion. "Well?"

Edie Marsh asked what was in it for her, and Tony Torres said ten grand. Edie said she'd have to think about it, which took about one one-hundredth of a second. She needed money.

"What about me?" Snapper asked.

Tony said, "I always wanted a bodyguard."

Snapper grunted skeptically. "How much?"

"Ten for you, too. It's more than fair."

Snapper admitted it was. "Why," he asked, with a trace of scorn, "do *you* need a bodyguard?"

"Some customers got really pissed off at me. It's a long boring story."

Edie Marsh said, "How pissed off?"

"I don't intend to find out," said Tony Torres. "Once I get the check, I'm gone."

"Where?"

"None a your damn business."

Middle America was what Tony had in mind. A handsome two-story house with a porch and a fireplace, on three-quarters of an acre outside Tulsa. What appealed to Tony about Middle America was the absence of hurricanes. There were tornadoes galore, but nobody expected any man-made structure (least of all, a trailer home) to withstand the terrible force of a tornado. Nobody would blame a person if the double-wides he sold blew to pieces, because that was the celestial nature of tornadoes. Tony Torres figured he would be safe from disgruntled customers in Tulsa.

Snapper said, "I'm gonna be a bodyguard, I'll need my gun."

Tony smiled. "No you won't. That face of yours is enough to scare the piss out of most mortal men. Which is perfect, because the people who're mad at me, they don't actually need to be shot. They just need to be scared. See where I'm headed?"

He took a length of bathroom pipe and smashed Snapper's pistol to pieces.

Edie Marsh said, "I've got a question, too."

"Well, bless your heart."

"What happens if your wife shows up?"

"We got probably six, seven days of breathing room," Tony Torres said. "However long it takes to drive that old van back from Oregon. See, Neria won't fly. She's terrified of planes."

Snapper remarked that money was known to make a person drive faster than usual, or overcome a fear of flying. Tony said he wasn't worried. "The radio said State Farm and Allstate are writing settlements already. Midwest won't be far behind—see, no company wants to look stingy in a national disaster."

Edie asked Tony Torres if he intended to hold them prisoner. He gave a great slobbering laugh and said hell, no, they could vamoose anytime they pleased. Edie stood and announced she was returning to the motel. Snapper rose warily, never taking his eyes off the shotgun.

He said to Tony: "Why are you doing this? Lettin' us walk out of here."

"Because you'll be back," the salesman said. "You most certainly will. I can see it in your eyes."

"Really?" Edie said, tartly.

"Really, darling. It's what I do for a living. Read people." The Naugahyde hissed as Tony Torres hoisted himself up from the BarcaLounger. "I need to take a leak," he declared. Then, with a hoot: "I'm sure you can find your way out!"

On the slow drive back to Pembroke Pines, Edie Marsh and Snapper mulled the options. Both of them were broke. Both recognized the post-hurricane turmoil as a golden opportunity. Both agreed that ten thousand dollars was a good week's work.

"Trouble is," Edie said, "I don't trust that asshole. What is it he sells?"

"Trailer homes."

"Good Lord."

"Then let's walk away," Snapper said, without conviction. "Try the slip-and-fall on somebody else."

Edie contemplated the ugly, self-inflicted scratch on her arm. Posing under a pile of lumber had been more uncomfortable than she'd anticipated. She wasn't eager to try it again.

"I'll coast with this jerkoff a day or two," she told Snapper. "You do what you want."

Snapper configured his crooked jaws into the semblance of a grin. "I know what you're thinkin'. I ain't no salesman, but I can read you just the same. You're thinkin' they's more than ten grand in this deal, you play it right. If *we* play it right."

"Why not." Edie Marsh pressed her cheek against the cool glass of the car's window. "It's about time my luck should change."

"*Our* luck," Snapper said, both hands tight on the wheel.

Augustine helped Bonnie Lamb search for her husband until nightfall. They failed to locate Max, but along the way they came upon an escaped male rhesus. It was up in a grapefruit tree, hurling unripened fruit at passing humans. Augustine shot the animal with a tranquilizer dart, and it toppled like a marionette. Augustine was dismayed to discover, stapled in one of its ears, a tag identifying it as property of the University of Miami.

He had captured somebody else's fugitive monkey.

"What now?" asked Bonnie Lamb, reasonably. She reached out to pet the stunned animal, then changed her mind. The rhesus studied her through dopey, half-closed eyes.

"You're a good shot," she said to Augustine.

He wasn't listening. "This isn't right," he muttered. He carried the limp monkey to the grapefruit tree and propped it gently in the crook of two boughs. Then he took Bonnie back to his truck. "It'll be dark soon," he said. "I forgot to bring a flashlight."

They drove through the subdivision for fifteen minutes until Bonnie Lamb spotted the rental car. Max wasn't there. Somebody had pried the trunk and stolen all the luggage, including Bonnie's purse.

Damn kids, Augustine said. Bonnie was too tired to cry. Max had the car keys, the credit cards, the money, the plane tickets. "I need to find a phone," she said. Her folks would wire some money.

Augustine drove to a police checkpoint, where Bonnie Lamb reported her husband missing. He was one of many, and not high on the list. Thousands who'd escaped their homes in the hurricane were being sought by worried relatives. For relief workers, reuniting local families was a priority; tracking wayward tourists was not.

A bank of six phones had been set up near the checkpoint, but the lines were long. Bonnie found the shortest one and settled in for a wait. She thanked Augustine for his help.

"What will you do tonight?" he asked.

"I'll be OK."

Bonnie was startled to hear him say: "No you won't."

He took her by the hand and led her to the pickup. It occurred to Bonnie that she ought to be afraid, but she felt illogically safe with this total stranger. It also occurred to her that panic would be a normal reaction to a husband's disappearance, but instead she felt an inappropriate calmness and lucidity. Probably just exhaustion, she thought.

Augustine drove back to the looted rental car. He scribbled a note and tucked it under one of the windshield wipers. "My phone number," he told Bonnie Lamb. "In case your husband shows up later tonight. This way he'll know where you are."

"We're going to your place?"

"Yes."

In the darkness, she couldn't see Augustine's expression. "It's madness out here," he said. "These idiots shoot at anything that moves."

Bonnie nodded. She'd been hearing distant gunfire from all directions. *Dade County is an armed camp.* That's what their travel agent had warned them. Death Wish Tours, he'd called it. *Only a fool would set foot south of Orlando.*

Crazy Max, thought Bonnie. What had possessed him?

"You know why my husband came down here?" she said. "Know what he was doing when he got lost? Taking video of the wrecked houses. And the people, too."

"Why?" Augustine asked.

"Home movies. To show his pals back North."

"Jesus, that's—"

"Sick," Bonnie Lamb said. "'Sick' is the word for it."

Augustine said nothing more. Slowly he worked his way toward the Turnpike. The futility of the monkey hunt was evident; Augustine realized that most of his dead uncle's wild animals were irretrievable. The larger mammals would inevitably make their presence known—the Cape buffalo, the bears, the cougars—and the results were bound to be unfortunate. Meanwhile the snakes and crocodiles probably were celebrating freedom by copulating merrily in the Everglades, ensuring for their species a solid foothold in a new tropical habitat. Augustine felt it was morally wrong to interfere. An escaped cobra had as much natural right to a life in Florida as did all those retired garment workers from Queens. Natural selection would occur. The test applied to Max Lamb as well, but Augustine felt sorry for his wife. He would set aside his principles and help find her missing husband.

He drove using the high beams because there were no street lights, and the roads were a littered gauntlet of broken trees and utility poles, heaps of lumber and twisted metal, battered appliances and gutted sofas. They saw a Barbie dollhouse and a canopy bed and an antique china cabinet and a child's wheelchair and a typewriter and a tangle of golf clubs and a cedar hot tub, split in half like a coconut husk—Bonnie said it was as if a great supernatural fist had snatched up a hundred thousand lives and shaken the contents all over creation.

Augustine was thinking more in terms of a B-52 raid.

"Is this your first one?" Bonnie asked.

"Technically, no." He braked to swerve around a dead cow, bloated on the center line. "I was conceived during Donna—least that's what my mother said. A hurricane baby. That was 1960. Betsy I can barely remember because I was only five. We lost a few lime trees, but the house held up fine."

Bonnie said, "That's kind of romantic. Being conceived in the middle of a hurricane."

"My mother said it made perfect sense, considering how I turned out."

"And how *did* you turn out?" Bonnie asked.

"Reports differ."

Augustine edged the truck into a line of storm traffic crawling up the northbound ramp to the Turnpike. A rusty Ford with a crooked Georgia license plate cut them off. The car was packed with itinerant construction workers who'd been on the road for several days straight, apparently drinking the whole time. The driver, a shaggy blond with greenish teeth, leered and yelled an obscenity up at Bonnie Lamb. With one hand Augustine reached behind his seat and got the small rifle. Bracing it against the doorpost, he fired a tranquilizer dart cleanly into the belly of the redneck driver, who yipped and pitched sideways into the lap of one of his pals.

"Manners," said Augustine. He gunned the truck, nudging the stalled Ford off the pavement.

Bonnie Lamb thought: God, what am I doing?

They broke camp at midnight—Max Lamb, the rhesus monkey and the man who called himself Skink. Max was grateful that the man had allowed him to put on his shoes, because they walked for hours in pitch darkness through deep swamp and spiny thickets. Max's bare legs stung from the scratches and itched from the bug bites. He was terribly hungry but didn't complain, knowing the man had saved him the rump of the dead raccoon that was boiled for dinner. Max wanted no part of it.

They came to a canal. Skink untied Max's hands, unbuckled the shock collar and ordered him to swim. Max was halfway across when he saw the blue-black alligator slide out of the sawgrass. Skink told him to quit whimpering and kick; he himself swam with the rejuvenated monkey perched on his head. One huge hand held Max's precious Sony and the remote control for the dog collar high above the water.

After scrabbling ashore, Max said, "Captain, can we rest?"

"Ever seen a leech before? 'Cause there's a good one on your cheek."

After Max Lamb finished flaying himself, Skink retied his wrists and refastened the dog collar. Then he sprayed him down with insect repellent. Max croaked out a thank-you.

"Where are we?" he asked.

"The Everglades," Skink replied. "More or less."

"You promised I could call my wife."

"Soon."

They headed west, trudging through palmettos and pinelands shredded by the storm. The monkey scampered ahead, foraging wild berries and fruit buds.

Max said: "Are you going to kill me?"

Skink stopped walking. "Every time you ask that stupid question, you're going to get it." He set the remote on the weakest setting.

"Ready?"

Max Lamb clenched his lips. Skink stung him with a light jolt. The tourist twitched stoically. Soon they came to a Miccosukee village, which was not as badly damaged as Max Lamb would have imagined. Since the Indians were awake, cooking food, Max assumed it would soon be dawn. In open doorways the children gathered shyly to look at the two strange white men: Skink with his brambly hair, ill-fitting eye and mangy monkey, Max Lamb in his dirty underwear and dog collar.

Skink stopped at a wooden house and spoke quietly to a Miccosukee elder, who brought out a cellular phone. As he untied Max's hands, Skink warned: "One call is all you get. He says the battery's running low."

Max realized that he didn't know how to reach his wife. He had no idea where she was. So he called their apartment in New York and spoke to the answering machine: "Honey, I've been kidnapped—"

"Abducted!" Skink broke in. "Kidnapping implies ransom, Max. Don't fucking flatter yourself."

"OK, 'abducted.' Honey, I've been abducted. I can't say very much except I'm fine, all things considered. Please call my folks, and also call Pete up at Rodale about the Bronco billboard project. Tell him the race car should be red, not blue. The file's on my desk. . . . Bonnie, I'm not sure who's got me, or why, but I guess I'll find out soon enough. God, I hope you pick up this message—"

Skink snatched the phone. "I love you, Bonnie," he said. "Max forgot to tell you, so I will. Bye now."

They ate with the Miccosukees, who declined Skink's offer of boiled coon but generously shared helpings of fried panfish, yams, cornmeal muffins and citrus juice. Max Lamb ate heartily but, mindful of the electric dog collar, said little. After breakfast, Skink tied him to a cypress post and disappeared with several men of the tribe. When he returned, he declared it was time to leave.

Max said, "Where's my stuff?" He was worried about his billfold and clothes.

"Right here." Skink jerked a thumb toward his backpack.

"And my Sony?"

"Gave it to the old man. He's got seven grandchildren, so he'll have a ball."

"What about my tapes?"

Skink laughed. "He loved 'em. That monkey attack was something special. Max, lift your arms." He spritzed the prisoner with more bug juice.

Max Lamb, somberly: "That Handycam retails for about nine hundred bucks."

"It's not like I gave it away. I traded."

"For what?"

Skink chucked him on the shoulder. "I'll bet you've never been on an airboat."

"Oh no. Please."

"Hey, you wanted to see Florida."

It wasn't easy being a black Highway Patrol trooper in Florida. It was even harder if you were involved intimately with a white trooper, the way Jim Tile was involved with Brenda Rourke.

They'd met at a training seminar about the newest gadgets for clocking speeders. In the classroom they were seated next to each other. Jim Tile liked Brenda Rourke right away. She had a sane and healthy outlook on the job, and she made him laugh. They traded stories about freaky traffic stops, lousy pay and the impossible FHP bureaucracy. Because he was black, and few fellow officers were, Jim Tile rarely felt comfortable in a roomful of state troopers. But he felt fine next to Brenda Rourke, partly because she was a minority, too; the Highway Patrol employed even fewer women than blacks or Latins.

During one session, a buzz-cut redneck shot a rat-eyed look at Jim Tile to remind him that Trooper Rourke was a white girl, and that still counted for plenty in parts of Florida. Jim Tile didn't get up and move; he kept his seat beside Brenda. It took the cracker trooper only about two hours to quit glaring.

At the lunch break, Jim Tile and Brenda Rourke went to an Arby's. She was worried about her upcoming transfer to South Florida; Jim Tile couldn't say much to allay her fears. She said she was studying Spanish, in preparation for road duty in Miami. The first phrase she'd learned was: *Sale del carro con las manos arriba.* Out of the car with your hands up!

At the time, Jim Tile held no romantic intentions. Brenda Rourke was a nice person, that was all. He never even asked if she had a boyfriend. A few months later, when he was down in Dade County for a trial, he ran into her at FHP headquarters. Later they went to dinner and then to Brenda's apartment, where they were up until three in the morning, chatting, of all things—initially out of nervousness, and later out of an easy intimacy. The trial lasted six days, and every night Jim Tile found himself back at Brenda's place. Every morning they awakened exactly as they'd fallen asleep—her head in the crook of his right shoulder, his feet hanging off the short bed. He'd never felt so peaceful. After the trial ended and Jim Tile returned to North Florida, he and Brenda took turns commuting for long weekends.

He wasn't much of a talker, but Brenda could drag it out of him. She especially liked to hear about the time he was assigned to guard the governor of Florida—not just any governor, but the one who'd quit, disappeared and become a legendary recluse. Brenda had been in high school, but she remembered when it happened. The newspapers and TV had gone wild. "Mentally unstable," was what her twelfth-grade civics teacher had said of the runaway governor.

When Jim Tile had heard that, he threw back his head and laughed. Brenda would sit cross-legged on the carpet, her chin in her hands, engrossed by his stories of the one they now called Skink. Out of loyalty and prudence, Jim Tile didn't mention that he and the man had remained the closest of friends.

"I wish I'd met him," Brenda had said, in the past tense, as if Skink were dead. Because Jim Tile had, perhaps unconsciously, made it sound like he was.

Now, two years later, it seemed that Brenda's improbable wish might come true. The governor had surfaced in the hurricane zone.

On the ride back from Card Sound, she asked: "Why would he tie himself to a bridge during a storm?" It was the logical question.

Jim Tile said, "He's been waiting for a big one."

"What for?"

"Brenda, I can't explain. It only makes sense if you know him."

She said nothing for a mile or two, then: "Why didn't you tell me that you two still talk?"

"Because we seldom do."

"Don't you trust me?"

"Of course." He pulled her close enough to steal a kiss.

She pulled away, a spark in her pale-blue eyes. "You're going to try to find him. Come on, Jim, be straight with me."

"I'm afraid he's got a loose wire. That's not good."

"This isn't the first time, is it?"

"No," said Jim Tile, "it's not the first time."

Brenda brought his hand to her lips and kissed his knuckles lightly. "It's OK, big guy. I understand about friends."

FIVE

When they got to Augustine's house, Bonnie Lamb called her answering machine in New York. She listened twice to Max's message, then replayed it for Augustine.

"What do you think?" she asked.

"Not good. Is your husband worth a lot of money?"

"He does all right, but he's no millionaire."

"And his family?"

Bonnie said her husband's father was quite wealthy. "But I'm sure Max wasn't foolish enough to mention it to the kidnappers."

Augustine made no such assumption. He heated tomato soup for Bonnie and put clean linens on the bed in the guest room. Then he went to the den and called a friend with the FBI. By the time he got off the phone, Bonnie Lamb had fallen asleep on the living-room sofa. He carried her to the spare room and tucked her under the covers. Then he went to the kitchen and fixed two large rib-eye steaks and a baked potato, which he washed down with a cold bottle of Amstel.

Later he took a long hot shower and thought about how wonderful Mrs Lamb—warm and damp from the rain and sweat—had smelled in his arms. It felt good to have a woman in the house again, even for just a night. Augustine wrapped himself in a towel and stretched out on the hardwood floor in front of the television. He flipped back and forth between local news broadcasts, hoping not to see any of his dead uncle's wild animals running amok, or Mrs Lamb's husband being loaded into a coroner's wagon.

At midnight Augustine heard a cry from the guest room. He correctly surmised that Mrs Lamb had discovered his skull collection. He found her sitting up, the covers pulled to her chin. She was gazing at the wall.

"I thought it was a dream," she said.

"Please don't be afraid."

"Are they real?"

"Friends send them to me," Augustine said, "from abroad, mostly. One was a Christmas present from a fishing guide in Islamorada." He wasn't sure what Bonnie Lamb thought of his hobby, so he apologized for the fright. "Some people collect coins. I'm into forensic artifacts."

"Body parts?"

"Not fresh ones—artifacts. Believe it or not, a good skull is hard to come by."

That was the line that usually sent them bolting for the door. Bonnie didn't move.

"Can I look?"

Augustine took one from a shelf. She inspected it casually, as if it were a cantaloupe in a grocery store. Augustine smiled; he liked this lady.

"Male or female?" Bonnie turned the skull in her hands.

"Male, late twenties, early thirties. Guyanese, circa 1940. Came from a medical school in Texas."

Bonnie asked why the lower jaw was missing. Augustine explained that it fell off when the facial muscles decayed. Most old skulls were found without the mandible.

Lifting it by the eye sockets, Bonnie returned the spooky relic to its place on the wall. "How many have you got up there?"

"Nineteen."

She whistled. "And how many are women?"

"None," said Augustine. "They're all young males. So you've got nothing to worry your pretty head about."

She rolled her eyes at the joke, then asked: "Why all males?"

"To remind me of my own mortality."

Bonnie groaned. "You're one of *those*."

"Other times," Augustine said, "when I'm sure my life has

47

gone to hell, I come in here and think about what happened to these poor bastards. It improves my outlook considerably."

She said, "Well, that makes about as much sense as everything else. Can I take a shower?"

Later, over coffee, he told her what the FBI man had said. "They'll treat your husband's disappearance as a kidnapping when there's a credible ransom demand. And he stressed the word 'credible.'"

"But what about the message on the machine? That other man's voice cutting in?"

"Of course they'll listen to it. But I've got to warn you, they're shorthanded right now. Lots of agents got hit hard by the storm, so they're out on personal leave."

Bonnie was exasperated by the lack of interest in Max's plight. Augustine explained that restless husbands often used natural disasters as a cover to flee their wives. Precious manpower and resources were wasted tracking them to the apartments, condominiums and houseboats of their respective mistresses. Consequently, post-hurricane reports of missing spouses were now received with chilly skepticism.

Bonnie Lamb said, "For God's sake, we just got married. Max wouldn't take off on a stunt like that."

Augustine shrugged. "People get cold feet."

She leaned across the kitchen table and took a swing at him. Augustine blocked the punch with a forearm. He told Mrs Lamb to settle down. Her cheeks were flushed and her eyes shone.

Augustine said, "I meant we can't rule out anything."

"But you heard that man on the answering machine!"

"Yeah, and I'm wondering why a serious kidnapper would be such a smartass. 'Don't flatter yourself, Max.' And then the guy gets on the line and says, 'I love you, Bonnie.' Just to needle your husband, see? Make him feel like shit." Augustine poured more coffee for both of them. He said, "There's something damn strange about it. That's all I'm saying."

Bonnie Lamb had to agree. "To leave his voice all over a telephone tape—"

"Exactly. The guy's either incredibly stupid, or he's got brass balls—"

"Or he just doesn't care," Bonnie said.

"You picked up on that, too."

"It's scary."

Augustine said, "I'm not so sure."

"Don't start again. Max is *not* faking this!"

"That stuff about having you call Pete at Rodale, the Bronco billboard—was he talking in code or what? Because some maniac kidnaps *me*, the last thing I'm worried about is keeping up with my ad accounts. What I'm worried about is saving my hide."

Bonnie looked away. "You don't know Max, what a workaholic he is."

Augustine pushed back from the table. Normally he wasn't wild about women who punched for no good reason.

"What do we do now?" She held the cup with both hands, shaking slightly. "You heard the man's tone."

"Yeah, I did."

"Let's agree he's not your average kidnapper. What is he?"

Augustine shook his head. "How would I know, Mrs Lamb?"

"It's Bonnie." She stood up, perfectly calm now, tightening the sash on the robe he'd loaned her. "Maybe together we can figure him out."

Augustine emptied his coffee in the sink. "I think we both need some sleep."

On the way back to Tony Torres's house, Edie Marsh asked Snapper if he had a stopwatch.

"Why?"

"Because I want to put a clock on this jerk," she said, "see how long it takes before he tries to screw me."

Snapper, who had daydreamed of doing the same thing, said: "I give him two days before he makes a move."

"I give him two hours," Edie said.

"So what'll you do? Ten grand's ten grand."

Edie said, "You better be joking. I'd shove hot daggers in my eyes before I'd let that pig touch me." It was a long bleak slide from dating a Kennedy to fucking a mobile-home salesman.

"What if he don't let up?" asked Snapper.

"Then I walk."

"Yeah, but—"

"Hey," Edie said, "you want the money so bad, *you* fuck him, OK? I think the two of you'd make a very cute couple." ·

Snapper didn't press the issue. He'd already hatched a backup plan, in case the Torres deal fell apart. Avila was in a happy mood when he'd called the motel. Apparently the *santería* saints had informed him he could become very rich by starting his own roofing business. The saints had pointed out that the hurricane left two hundred thousand people without shelter, and that many of these poor folks were so desperate to get their houses repaired that they wouldn't think of asking to see a valid contractor's license, which of course Avila did not possess.

"But you're afraid of heights," Snapper had reminded him.

"That's where you come in," Avila had said. "I'm the boss, you're the foreman. All we need is a crew."

"Meaning you won't be joining us up on the roof with the boiling tar in the hot sun."

"Jesus, Snap, somebody's got to handle the paperwork. Somebody's got to write up the contracts."

Snapper had inquired about the split. Avila said guys he knew were charging fifteen grand per roof, a third of it up front. He said some home owners were offering cash, to speed the job. Avila said there was enough work around to keep them busy for two years.

"Thanks to you," Snapper had said.

Avila failed to see irony in the fact that corruptly incompetent building inspections were a chief reason that so many roofs had blown off in the storm, and that so much new business was now available for incompetent roofers.

"You guys plan it this way?" Snapper had asked.

"Plan what?"

Snapper didn't trust Avila as far as he could spit, but the roofing option was something to consider if Torres went sour.

The trailer salesman also happened to be in sunny spirits when Snapper and Edie Marsh arrived. He was sprawled, shirtless, in a chaise on the front lawn. He wore Bermuda shorts and monogrammed socks pulled high on his hairy shins. The barrel of the shotgun poked out from a stack of newspapers on his lap. When Edie Marsh and Snapper got out of the car, Tony clapped his hands and exclaimed: "I knew you'd be back!"

"A regular Nostradamus," said Edie. "Is the electricity up yet? We picked up some stuff for the refrigerator."

Tony reported that the power remained off, and the portable generator had run out of gas overnight. He was storing food in two large Igloo coolers, packed with ice he'd purchased from gougers for twenty dollars a bag. The good news: Telephone service had been restored.

"And I got through immediately to Midwest Casualty," Tony said. "They're sending an adjuster today or tomorrow."

Edie thought: Too good to be true. "So we wait?"

"We wait," Tony said. "And remember, it's Neria. N-e-r-i-a. Middle initial, G as in Gómez. What'd you buy?"

"Tuna sandwiches," Snapper replied, "cheese, eggs, ice cream, Diet Sprite and stale fucking Lorna Doones. There wasn't much to choose from." He iced the groceries, found a pool chair and took a position upwind of the sweaty Tony Torres. The sky had cleared and the summer sun blazed down, but it was pointless to look for shade. There wasn't any; all the trees in Turtle Meadow were leveled.

Tony complimented Edie Marsh for costuming herself as an authentic housewife—jeans, white Keds, a baggy blouse with the sleeves turned up. His only complaint was the sea-green scarf in her hair. He said, "Silk is a little much, considering the circumstances."

"Because it clashes with those gorgeous Bermudas of yours?" Edie glared at Tony Torres as if he were a maggot on a wedding cake. She was disinclined to remove the scarf, which was one of her favorites. She had boosted it from a Lord & Taylor's in Palm Beach.

"Suit yourself," said Tony. "Point is, details are damn important. It's the little things people notice."

"I'll try and keep that in mind."

Snapper said, "Hey, Mister Salesman of the Year, can we run the TV off that generator?"

Tony said sure, if they only had some gasoline.

Snapper tapped his wristwatch and said, "Sally Jessy comes on in twenty minutes. Men who seduce their daughter-in-law's mother-in-law."

"No shit? We could siphon your car." Tony pointed at the rubble of his garage. "There's a hose in there someplace."

Snapper went to find it. Edie Marsh said it was a lousy idea to siphon fuel from the car, since they might be needing speedy transportation. Snapper winked and told her not to worry. Off he went, ambling down the street, the garden hose coiled on his left shoulder.

Edie expropriated the pool chair. Tony Torres perked up. "Scoot closer, darling."

"Wonderful," she said, under her breath.

The salesman fanned himself with the Miami *Herald* sports pages. He said, "It just now hit me: Men who steal their daughter-in-law's mother-in-law. That's pretty funny! He don't look like a comedian, your partner, but that's a good one."

"Oh, he's full of surprises." Edie leaned back and closed her eyes. The sunshine felt good on her face.

The hurricane had transformed the trailer court into a sprawling aluminum junkyard. Ira Jackson found Lot 17 because of the bright yellow tape that police had roped around the remains of the double-wide mobile home where his mother, Beatrice, had died. After identifying her body at the morgue, Ira Jackson had driven directly to Suncoast Leisure Village, to see for himself.

Not one trailer had made it through the storm.

From the debris, Ira Jackson pulled his mother's Craftmatic adjustable bed. The mattress was curled up like a giant taco shell. Ira Jackson crawled inside and lay down.

He recalled, as if it were yesterday, the morning he and his mother met with the salesman to close the deal. The man's name was Tony. Tony Torres. He was fat, gassy and balding, yet extremely self-assured. Beatrice Jackson had been impressed with his pitch.

"*Mister Torres says it's built to go through a hurricane.*"

"*I find that hard to believe, Momma.*"

"*Oh yes, Mister Jackson, your mother's right. Our prefabricated homes are made to withstand gusts up to one hundred twenty miles per hour. That's a U.S. government regulation. Otherwise we couldn't sell 'em!*"

Ira Jackson was in Chicago, beating up some scabs for a Teamsters local, when he'd heard about the hurricane headed for South Florida. He'd phoned his mother and urged her to move to a Red Cross shelter. She said it was out of the question.

"I can't leave Donald and Marla," she told her son.

Donald and Marla were Mrs Jackson's beloved miniature dachshunds. The hurricane shelter wouldn't allow pets.

So Ira's mother had stayed home out of loyalty to her dogs and a misplaced confidence that the mobile-home salesman had told the truth about how safe it was. Donald and Marla survived the hurricane by squeezing under an oak credenza and sharing a rawhide chew toy to pass the long night. A neighbor had rescued them the next morning and taken them to a vet.

Beatrice Jackson was not so lucky. Moments after the hurricane stripped the north wall off her double-wide, she was killed by a flying barbecue that belonged to one of her neighbors. The imprint of the grill remained visible on her face, peaceful as it was, lying in the Dade County morgue.

Beatrice's death had no effect whatsoever on the mood of her dachshunds, but her son was inconsolable. Ira Jackson raged at himself for letting his mother buy the trailer. It had been his idea for her to move to Florida—but that's what guys in his line of work did for their widowed mothers; got them out of the cold weather and into the sunshine.

God help me, Ira Jackson thought, tossing restively on the mechanical mattress. I should've held off another year. Waited till I could afford to put her in a condo.

That cocksucker Torres. *A-hundred-twenty-mile-per-hour gusts.* What kind of scum would lie to a widow?

"Excuse me!"

Ira Jackson bolted upright to see a gray-haired man in a white undershirt and baggy pants. Skin and bones. Wire-rimmed eyeglasses that made him look like a heron. In one arm he carried a brown shopping bag.

"Have you seen an urn?" he asked.

"Jesus, what?"

"A blue urn. My wife's ashes. It's like a bottle."

Ira Jackson shook his head. "No, I haven't seen it." He rose to his feet. He noticed that the old man was shaking.

"I'm going to kill him," he said angrily.

Ira Jackson said, "Who?"

"That lying sonofabitch who sold me the double-wide. I saw him here after the hurricane, but he took off."

"Torres?"

"Yeah." The old man's cheeks colored. "I'd murder him, swear to God, if I could."

Ira Jackson said, "You'd get a medal for it." Humoring the guy, hoping he'd run out of steam and go away.

"Hell, you don't believe me."

"Sure I do." He was tempted to tell the old man to quit worrying, Señor Tony Torres would be taken care of. Most definitely. But Ira Jackson knew it would be foolish to draw attention to himself.

The old man said: "My name's Levon Stichler. I lived four lots over. Was it your mother that died here?"

Ira Jackson nodded.

Levon Stichler said, "I'm real sorry. I'm the one found her two dogs—they're at Dr Tyler's in Naranja."

"She'd appreciate that, my mother." Ira Jackson made a mental note to pick up the dachshunds before the vet's office closed.

The old man said, "My wife's ashes blew away in the hurricane."

"Yeah, well, if I come across a blue bottle—"

"What the hell could they do to me?" Levon Stichler wore a weird quavering smirk. "For killing him, what could they do? I'm seventy-one goddamn years old—what, life in prison? Big deal. I got nothing left anyhow."

Ira Jackson said, "I was you, I'd put it out of my mind. Scum like Torres, they usually get what they deserve."

"Not in my world," said Levon Stichler. But the widow Jackson's son had taken the wind out of his sails. "Hell, I don't know how to find the sonofabitch anyhow. Do you?"

"Wouldn't have a clue," Ira Jackson said.

Levon Stichler shrugged in resignation, and returned to the heap that once was his home. Ira Jackson watched him poking through the rubble, stooping every so often to examine a scrap. All around the trailer court, other neighbors of the late Beatrice Jackson could be seen hunched and scavenging, picking up pieces.

Her son opened his wallet, which contained: six hundred dollars cash, a picture of his mother taken in Atlantic City, three fake driver's licenses, a forged Social Security card, a stolen Delta Airlines frequent flyer card, and numerous scraps of paper with numerous phone numbers from the 718 area code. The wallet also held a few legitimate business cards, including one that said:

Antonio Torres
Senior Sales Associate
PreFab Luxury Homes
(305) 555-2200

The trailer salesman had jotted his home number on the back of the business card. Ira Jackson kicked through his mother's storm-soaked belongings until he found a Greater Miami telephone directory. The salesman's home number matched the one belonging to an A. R. Torres at 15600 Calusa Drive. Ira Jackson tore the page from the phone book. Carefully he folded it to fit inside his wallet, with the other important numbers.

Then he drove his fraudulently registered Coupe de Ville to a convenience store, where he purchased a Rand McNally road map of Dade County.

SIX

The vagabond monkey chose to forgo the airboat experience. Max Lamb was given no choice. The one-eyed man strapped him to the passenger seat and off they went at fifty miles an hour, skimming the grass, cattails and lily pads. For a while they followed a canal that paralleled a two-lane highway; Max could make out the faces of motorists gaping at him in his underwear. It didn't occur to him to signal for help; the electrified dog collar had conditioned total passivity.

Riding high in the driver's perch, the man who called himself Skink sang at the top of his lungs. It sounded like "Desperado," an old Eagles tune. The familiar melody surfed above the ear-splitting roar of the airboat's engine; more than ever, Max Lamb believed he was in the grip of a madman.

Soon the airboat made a wide turn away from the road. It plowed a liquid trail through thickening marsh, the sawgrass hissing against the metal hull. The hurricane had bruised and gouged the swamp; smashed cypresses and pines littered the waters. Skink stopped singing and began to emit short honks and toots that Max Lamb assumed to be either wild bird calls or a fearsome attack of sinusitis. He was afraid to inquire.

At noon they stopped at a dry hammock, its once-lush branches now skeletal from the storm. Skink tied the airboat to a knuckled stand of roots. Evidence of previous campfires reassured Max Lamb that other humans had been there before. The kidnapper didn't bother to tie him; there was no place to run. With Skink's permission, Max put on his clothes to protect himself from the

56

horseflies and mosquitoes. When he complained of being thirsty, Skink offered his own canteen. Max took a tentative swallow.

"Coconut milk?" he asked, hopefully.

"Something like that."

Max suggested that wearing the shock collar was no longer necessary. Skink whipped out the remote control, pushed the red button and said: "If you've got to ask, then it's still necessary."

Max jerked wordlessly on the damp ground until the pain stopped. Skink caught a mud turtle and made soup for lunch. Tending the fire, he said, "Max, I'll take three questions."

"Three?"

"For now. Let's see how it goes."

Max warily eyed the remote. Skink promised there would be no electronic penalty for dumb queries. "So fire away."

Max Lamb said, "All right. Who are you?"

"My name is Tyree. I served in the Vietnam conflict, and later as a governor of this fair state. I resigned because of disturbing moral and philosophical conflicts. The details would mean nothing to you."

Max Lamb failed to mask his disbelief. "You were governor? Come off it."

"Is that question number two?"

Impatiently, Max fingered the dog collar. "No, the second question is: Why me?"

"Because you made a splendid target of yourself. You with your video camera, desecrating the habitat."

Max Lamb got defensive. "I wasn't the only one taking pictures. I wasn't the only tourist out there."

"But you were the one I saw first." Skink poured hot soup into a tin cup and handed it to his sulking prisoner. "A hurricane is a holy thing," he said, "but you treated it as an amusement. Pissed me off, Max."

Skink lifted the pot off the hot coals and tipped it to his lips. Steam wisped from his mouth, fogging his glass eye. He put the pot down and wiped the turtle drippings from his chin. "I was tied up on a bridge," he said, "watching the storm roll out of the ocean. God, what a thing!"

He stepped toward Max Lamb and lifted him by the shirt, causing Max to drop the soup he had not touched.

Skink hoisted him to eye level and said: "Twenty years I waited for that storm. We were so close, so goddamn close. Two or three degrees to the north, and we're in business. . . ."

Max Lamb dangled in the stranger's iron clasp. Skink's good eye glistened with a furious, dreamy passion. "You're down to one question," he said, returning Max to his feet.

After settling himself, Max asked: "What happens now?"

Skink's stormy expression dissolved into a smile. "What happens now, Max, is that we travel together, sharing life's lessons."

"Oh." Max's eyes cut anxiously to the airboat.

The governor barked a laugh that scattered a flock of snowy egrets. He tousled his prisoner's hair and said, "We go with the tides!"

But a despairing Max Lamb couldn't face the prospect of true adventure. Now that it seemed he would not be murdered, he was burdened by another primal concern: *If I don't get back to New York, I'm going to lose my job.*

Edie Marsh was daydreaming about teak sailboats and handsome young Kennedys when she felt the moist hand of Tony Torres settle on her left breast. She cracked an eyelid and sighed.

"Quit squeezing. It's not a tomato."

"Can I see?" Tony asked.

"Absolutely not." But she heard the squeaky shift of weight as the salesman edged the chaise closer.

"Nobody's around," he said, fumbling with her buttons. Then an oily laugh: "I mean, you *are* my wife."

"Jesus." Edie felt the sun on her nipples and looked down. Well, there they were—the pig had undone her blouse. "Don't you understand English?"

Tony Torres contentedly appraised her breasts. "Yeah, darling, but who's got the shotgun."

"That's so romantic," Edie Marsh said. "Threaten to shoot me—there's no better way to put a girl in the mood. Fact, I'm all wet just thinking about it." She pushed his hand away and rebuttoned her blouse. "Where's my shades," she muttered.

Tony cradled the Remington across his belly. Sweat puddled at his navel. He said, "You *will* think about it. They all do."

"I think about cancer, too, but it doesn't make me horny." To Edie, the only attractive thing about Tony Torres was his gold Cartier wristwatch, which was probably engraved in such a gaudy way that it could not be prudently fenced.

He asked her: "Have you ever been with a bald man?"

"Nope. You ever seen venereal warts?"

The salesman snorted, turning away. "Somebody's in a pissy mood."

Edie Marsh dug the black Ray-Bans out of her purse and disappeared behind them. The shotgun made her nervous, but she resolved to stay cool. She tried to shut out the summer glare, the ceaseless drone of chain saws and dump trucks, and the rustle of Tony Torres reading the newspaper. The warmth of the sun made it easy for Edie Marsh to think of the duned shores at the Vineyard, or the private beaches of Manalapan.

Her reverie was interrupted by footsteps on the sidewalk across the street. She hoped it was Snapper, but it wasn't. It was a man walking two small dachshunds.

Edie felt Tony's hand on hers and heard him say, "Darling, would you squirt some Coppertone on my shoulders?"

Quickly she rose from the chair and crossed the road. The man was watching his dachshunds pee on the stem of a broken mailbox. He held both leashes in one hand, loosely. There was a melancholy slump to his shoulders that should have disappeared with the approach of a pretty woman, but did not.

Edie Marsh told him the dogs were adorable. When she stooped to pet them, the dachshunds simultaneously rolled over and began squirming like worms on a griddle.

"What're their names?"

"Donald and Marla," the man replied. He wasn't tall, but he was built like a furnace. He wore a peach knit shirt and khaki slacks. He said to Edie: "You live at that house?"

She saw Tony Torres eyeing them from the chaise. She asked

the stranger if he was from the Midwest Casualty insurance company. He motioned sarcastically toward the dogs and said, "Sure. And my associates here are from Merrill Lynch."

The dachshunds were up, wagging their butts and licking at Edie's bare ankles. The man jerked his double chin toward Tony Torres and said, "You related to him? A wife or sister maybe."

"Please," Edie Marsh said, with an exaggerated shudder.

"OK, then I got some advice. Take a long fucking walk."

Edie's mind began to race. She looked in both directions down the street, but didn't see Snapper.

The man said, "The hell you waiting for?" He handed her the two leashes. "Go on, now."

Augustine awoke to the smell of coffee and the sounds of a married woman fixing breakfast in his kitchen. It seemed a suitable time to assess the situation.

His father was in prison, his mother was gone, and his dead uncle's wild animals had escaped among unsuspecting suburbanites. Augustine himself was free, too, in the truest and saddest sense. He had absolutely no personal responsibilities. How to explain such a condition to Bonnie Lamb?

My father was a fisherman. He ran drugs on the side, until he was arrested near the island of Andros.

My mother moved to Las Vegas and remarried. Her new husband plays tenor saxophone in Tony Bennett's orchestra.

My most recent ex-girlfriend was a leg model for a major hosiery concern. She saved her modeling money and bought a town house in Brentwood, California, where she fellates only circumcised movie agents, and the occasional director.

But what about you? Mrs Lamb will ask. What do you do for a living?

I read my bank statements.

And Mrs Lamb will react with polite curiosity, until I explain about the airplane accident.

It happened three years ago while flying back from Nassau after visiting my old man in Fox Hill Prison. I didn't realize the pilot was drunk until he T-boned the twin Beech into the fuselage of a Coast Guard helicopter, parked inside a hangar at the Opa-Locka airport.

Afterwards I slept for three months and seventeen days in the intensive care unit of Jackson Hospital. When I awoke, I was rich. The insurance carrier for the charter-air service had settled the case with an attorney whom I did not know and to this day have never met. A check for eight hundred thousand dollars appeared, and much to my surprise, I invested it wisely.

And Mrs Lamb, if I'm reading her right, will then say: So what is it you *do*?

Honestly, I'm not certain. . . .

The conversation, over bacon and French toast, didn't go precisely as Augustine had anticipated. At the end of his story, Bonnie Lamb looked over the rim of her coffee cup and asked: "Is that where you got the scar—from the plane crash?"

"Which scar?"

"The Y-shaped one on your lower back."

"No," said Augustine, guardedly. "That's something else." He made a mental note not to walk around without a shirt.

Later, clearing the kitchen table, Bonnie asked about his father.

"Extradited," Augustine reported, "but he much prefers Talladega to the Bahamas."

"Are you two close?"

"Sure," said Augustine. "Only seven hundred miles."

"How often do you go to see him?"

"Whenever I want to get angry and depressed."

Augustine often wished that the plane crash had wiped out his memory of that last visit at Fox Hill Prison, but it hadn't. They were supposed to talk about the extradition, about lining up a half-decent lawyer in the States, about maybe cutting a deal with prosecutors so that the old man might actually get out before the turn of the century.

But Augustine's father wanted to talk about something else when his son came to see him. He wanted a favor.

—Bollock, you remember Bollock? He owes me a piece of a shipment.

—The answer is no.

—Come on, A.G. I got lawyers to pay. Take Leaker and Ape along. They'll handle Bollock. Not the money, though. That I want in your hands only.

—Dad, I don't believe this. I just don't believe it. . . .

—Hey, go down to Nassau harbor. See what they done to my boat! Ape says they stripped the radar and all the electric.

—So what. You didn't know how to use it anyway.

—Listen, wiseass, I was taking fire. It was the middle of the goddamn night.

—Still, it's not easy to park a sixty-foot long-liner in nine inches of water. How exactly did you manage that?

—Watch your tone, son!

—Grown man, hangin' out with guys called Leaker and Ape. Look where it got you.

—A.G., I'd love to keep strollin' down memory lane, but the guard says we're outta time. So will you do it? Go see Henry Bollock down on Big Pine. Get my slice and stick it in the Caymans. What's the harm?

—Pathetic.

—What?

—I said, you're pathetic.

—So I'll take that as a "no," you won't do this for me?

— Jesus Christ.

—You disappoint me, boy.

—And I'm proud of you, too, Dad. I bust my buttons every time your name comes up.

And Augustine recalled thinking, as he sat in the Beechcraft on the runway at Nassau: He's hopeless, my old man. He won't learn. He'll get out of prison and go right back to it.

A son looks a man square in the eye and calls him pathetic, *pathetic*, any other father would curse or cry or take a punch at the kid. Not mine. By God, not when there's drug money needs collecting. So how about it, A.G.?

Fuck him, thought Augustine. Not because of what he'd done or what he'd been hauling, but because his stupid selfish greed had outlived the crime. Fuck him, Augustine thought, because it's hopeless. He was supposed to raise me, goddammit, I wasn't supposed to raise him.

And then the plane took off.

And then the plane went down.

And nothing was ever the same about the way Augustine saw the world, or his place in it. Sometimes he wasn't sure if it was the accident that had changed him, or the visit with his father at Fox Hill Prison.

At FBI headquarters, Bonnie Lamb spent an hour talking with maddeningly polite agents. One of them dialed her answering machine and dubbed Max's queer kidnap message. They urged her to notify the Bureau as soon as she received a credible ransom demand. Then, and only then, would a kidnap squad take over the case. The agents instructed Bonnie to check her machine often and be careful not to erase any tapes. They expressed no strong views about whether she ought to remain in Miami and search for her husband, or return to New York and wait.

The agents let Bonnie Lamb borrow a private office, where she tried with no luck to reach Max's parents, who were traveling in Europe. Next Bonnie phoned her own parents. Her mother sounded sincere in her alarm; her father, as usual, sounded helpless. He half-heartedly offered to fly to Florida, but Bonnie said it wasn't necessary. All she could do was wait for Max or the kidnapper to call again. Bonnie's mother promised to FedEx some cash and an eight-by-ten photograph of Max, for the authorities.

Bonnie Lamb's last call was to Peter Archibald at the Rodale & Burns advertising agency in Manhattan. Max Lamb's colleague was shocked at Bonnie's news, but vowed to maintain the confidentiality requested by the FBI. When Bonnie passed along her husband's frantic instructions about the cigaret billboard, Peter Archibald said: "You married a real trouper, Bonnie."

"Thank you, Peter."

Augustine took her to a fish house for lunch. She ordered a gin-and-tonic, and said: "I want your honest opinion about the FBI guys."

"OK. I think they had problems with the tape."

"Max didn't sound scared enough."

"Possibly," Augustine said, "and, like I mentioned, he seemed a little too worried about the Marlboro account."

"It's Broncos," Bonnie corrected. From the way she winced at the gin, Augustine could tell she wasn't much of a drinker. "So they blew me off as a jilted wife."

"Not at all. They started a file. They're the best darn file-starters in the world. Then they'll send your tape to the audio lab. They'll probably even make a few phone calls. But you saw how deserted the place was—half their agents are home cleaning up storm damage."

She said, angrily, "The world doesn't stop for a hurricane."

"No," Augustine said, "but it wobbles like a sonofabitch. I'm having the shrimp, how about you?"

Mrs Lamb didn't speak again until they were in the pickup truck, heading south to the hurricane zone. She asked Augustine to stop at the county morgue.

He thought: She couldn't have gotten this brainstorm *before* lunch.

Snapper had neither the ambition nor the energy to be a predator in the classic criminal mold. He saw himself strictly as a canny opportunist. He wouldn't endeavor to commit a first-degree felony unless the moment presented itself. He believed in serendipity, because it suited his style of minimal exertion.

He heard the kids coming long before he saw them. The souped-up Cherokee blasted Snoop Doggy Dogg through the neighborhood, rattling the few windows that the hurricane had not broken. The kids drove by once, circled the block, and cruised past again.

Snapper smiled to himself, thinking: It's the damn pinstripes. They think I'm carrying money.

He kept walking. When the Cherokee came around a third time, the rap music had been turned off. Stupid, Snapper thought. Why not take out a billboard: Watch us mug this guy!

As the Jeep rolled up behind him, Snapper stepped to the side and slowed his pace. He slipped Tony Torres's garden hose off his shoulder and carried it coiled in front of him. The Cherokee came alongside. One of the kids was hanging out the passenger window. He waved a chrome-plated pistol at Snapper.

"Hey, mud-fuckah," the kid said.

"Good mornin'," said Snapper. He deftly looped a coil of the garden hose around the kid's head and jerked him out of the truck. When the kid hit the pavement, he dropped the gun. Snapper picked it up. He stepped on the kid's chest and, with one hand, began twisting the hose tightly on the kid's throat.

The other muggers piled out of the Cherokee with the intention of rescuing their friend and killing the butt-ugly geek in the shiny suit, but the plan changed when they saw who had the pistol. Then they ran.

Snapper waited until the kid on the ground was almost unconscious before loosening the hose. "I need to borrow some gas," said Snapper, "to watch Sally Jessy."

The kid sat up slowly and rubbed his neck, which bled from the place where his three gold chains had cut into his flesh. He wore a tank top to show off the tattoos on his left biceps—a gang insignia and the nickname "Baby Raper."

Snapper said, "Baby, you got a gas can?"

"Fuck no." The kid answered in a raw whisper.

"Too bad. I'll have to take the whole truck."

"I don't care. Ain't mine."

"Yeah, that was my hunch."

The kid said, "Man, wus wrong wid yo face?"

"Excuse me?"

"I axed what's wrong wid yo mud-fuckin face."

Snapper went in the Cherokee and removed the Snoop Doggy Dogg compact disc from the stereo. He used the shiny side of the CD like a small mirror, pretending to admire himself in it.

"Looks fine to me," he said, after several moments.

The kid smirked. "Sheeeiiit."

Snapper put the pistol to the kid's temple and ordered him to get on his belly. Then he yanked the mugger's pants down to his ankles.

A Florida Power and Light cherry picker came steaming down the street. The kid shouted for help, but the driver kept going.

Twisting to look over his shoulder, Baby Raper saw Snapper hold the CD up to the sky, like a chrome communion wafer.

Snapper said: "Worst fuckin' excuse for music I ever heard."

"Man, whatcha gone do wid dat?"

"Guess."

Ira Jackson stood with his back to the sun. Tony Torres squinted, shielding his brow with one hand.

The salesman said: "Do I remember you? Course I remember you."

"My mother was Beatrice Jackson."

"I said I remember."

"She's dead."

"So I heard. I'm very sorry." Stretched in the chaise, Tony Torres felt vulnerable. He raised both knees to give himself a brace for the shotgun.

Ira Jackson asked Tony if he remembered anything else. "Such as what you promised my mother about the double-wide being as safe as a regular CBS house?"

"Whoa, sport, I said no such thing." Tony Torres was itching to get to his feet, but that was a major project. One wrong move, and the flimsy patio chair could collapse under his weight. "'Government approved,' is what I told you, Mister Jackson. Those were my exact words."

"My mother's dead. The double-wide went to pieces."

"Well, it was one hellacious hurricane. The Storm of the Century, they said on TV." Tony was beginning to wonder if this dumb ape didn't see the Remington aimed at his dick. "We're talking about a major natural disaster, sport. Look how it wrecked these houses. *My* house. Hell, it blew down the entire goddamn Homestead Air Force Base! There's no hiding from something like that. I'm sorry about your mother, Mister Jackson, but a trailer's a trailer."

"What happened to the tie-downs?"

Oh Christ, Tony thought. Who knew enough to look at the fucking tie-downs? He struggled to appear indignant. "I've got no idea what you're talking about."

Ira Jackson said, "I found two of 'em hanging off a piece of the double-wide. Straps were rotted. Augers cut off short. No anchor disks—this shit I saw for myself."

"I'm sure you're mistaken. They passed inspection, Mister Jackson. Every home we sold passed inspection." The confidence was gone from the salesman's tone. He was uneasy, arguing with a faceless silhouette.

"Admit it," Ira Jackson said. "Somebody cut the damn augers to save a few bucks on installation."

"Keep talkin' that way," warned Tony Torres, "and I'll sue your ass for slander."

Even before it was made a specified condition of his parole, Ira Jackson had never possessed a firearm. In his many years as a professional goon, it had been his experience that men who brandished guns invariably got shot with one. Ira Jackson favored the more personal touch afforded by crowbars, aluminum softball bats, nunchaku sticks, piano wire, cutlery, or gym socks filled with lead fishing sinkers. Any would have done the job nicely on Tony Torres, but Ira Jackson had brought nothing but his bare fists to the salesman's house.

"What is it you want?" Tony Torres demanded.

"An explanation."

"Which I just gave you." Tony's eyes watered from peering into the sun's glare, and he was growing worried. Edie the Ice Maiden had disappeared with Ira Jackson's dogs—what the hell was *that* all about? Were they in on something? And where was the freak in the bad suit, his so-called bodyguard?

Tony said to Ira Jackson: "I think it's time for you to go." He motioned with the shotgun toward the street.

"This is how you treat dissatisfied customers?"

A jittery laugh burst from the salesman. "Sport, you ain't here for no refund."

"You're right." Ira Jackson was pleased by the din of the neighborhood—hammers, drills, saws, electric generators. All the folks preoccupied with putting their homes back together. The noise would make it easier to cover the ruckus, if the mobile-home salesman tried to put up a struggle.

Tony Torres said, "You think I don't know to use this twelve-gauge, you're makin' a big mistake. Check out the hole in that garage door."

Ira Jackson whistled. "I'm impressed, Mister Torres. You shot a house."

Tony's expression hardened. "I'm counting to three."

"My mother was hit by a damn barbecue."

"*One!*" the salesman said. "Every second you look more like a looter, mister."

"You promised her the place was safe. All those poor people—how the hell do you sleep nights?"

"*Two!*"

"Relax, you fat fuck. I'm on my way." Ira Jackson turned and walked slowly toward the street.

Tony Torres took a deep breath; his tongue felt like sandpaper. He lowered the Remington until it rested on one of his kneecaps. He watched Beatrice Jackson's son pause in the driveway and kneel as if tying a shoe.

Craning to see, Tony shouted: "Move it, sport!"

The cinder block caught him by surprise—first, the sheer weight of it, thirty-odd pounds of solid concrete; second, the fact that Ira Jackson was able to throw such a hefty object, shot-putter style, with such distressing accuracy.

When it struck the salesman's chest, the cinder block knocked the shotgun from his hands, the beer from his bladder and the breath from his lungs. He made a sibilant exclamation, like a water bed rupturing.

So forceful was the cinder block's impact that it doubled Tony Torres at the waist, causing the chaise longue to spring on him like an oversized mousetrap. The moans he let out as Ira Jackson dragged him to the car were practically inaudible over the chorus of his neighbors' chain saws.

SEVEN

The Dade County Medical Examiner's Office was quiet, neat and modern—nothing like Bonnie Lamb's notion of a big-city morgue. She admired the architect's thinking; the design of the building successfully avoided the theme of violent homicide. With its brisk and clerical-looking layout, it could have passed for the regional headquarters of an insurance company or a mortgage firm, except for the dead bodies in the north wing.

A friendly secretary brought coffee to Bonnie Lamb while Augustine spoke privately to an assistant medical examiner. The young doctor remembered Augustine from a week earlier, when he had come to claim his uncle's snakebitten remains. The medical examiner was intrigued to learn from Augustine that the tropical viper that had killed Felix Mojack now roamed free. He E-mailed a memorandum to Jackson Memorial, alerting the emergency room to requisition more antivenin, just in case. Then he took a Xeroxed copy of Bonnie Lamb's police report down the hall.

When he returned, the medical examiner said the morgue had two unidentified corpses that loosely matched the physical description of Max Lamb. Augustine relayed the news to Bonnie.

"You up for this?" he asked.

"If you go with me."

It was a long walk to the autopsy room, where the temperature seemed to drop fifteen degrees. Bonnie Lamb took Augustine's hand as they moved among the self-draining steel tables, where a half-dozen bodies were laid out in varying stages of dissection. The room gave off a cloying odor, the sickly-sweet commingling of chemicals and dead flesh. Augustine felt Bonnie's palm go cold. He asked her if she was going to faint.

"No," she said. "It's just . . . God, I thought they'd all be covered with sheets."

"Only in the movies."

The first John Doe had lank hair and sparse, uneven sideburns. He was the same race and age, but otherwise bore no resemblance to Max Lamb. The dead man's eyes were greenish blue; Max's were brown. Still, Bonnie stared.

"How did he die?"

Augustine asked: "Is it Max?"

She shook her head sharply. "But tell me how he died."

With a Bic pen, the young medical examiner pointed to a dime-sized hole beneath the dead man's left armpit. "Gunshot wound," he said.

Augustine and Bonnie Lamb followed the doctor to another table. Here the cause of death was no mystery. The second John Doe had been in a terrible accident. He was scalped and his face pulverized beyond recognition. A black track of autopsy stitches ran from his breast to his pelvis.

Bonnie stammered, "I don't know, I can't tell—"

"Look at his hands," the medical examiner said.

"No wedding ring," Augustine observed.

"Please. I want her to look," the medical examiner said. "We remove the jewelry for safekeeping."

Bonnie dazedly circled the table. The bluish pallor of the dead man's skin made it difficult to determine his natural complexion. He was built like Max—narrow shoulders, bony chest, with a veined roll of baby fat at the midsection. The arms and legs were lean and finely haired, like Max's. . . .

"Ma'am, what about the hands?"

Bonnie Lamb forced herself to look, and was glad she did. The hands were not her husband's; the fingernails were grubby and gnawed. Max believed religiously in manicures and buffing.

"No, it's not him." She spoke very softly, as if trying not to awaken the man with no face.

The doctor wanted to know if her husband had any birthmarks. Bonnie said she hadn't noticed, and felt guilty—as if she hadn't spent enough time examining the details of Max's trunk and extremities. Couldn't most lovers map their partner's most intimate blemishes?

"I remember a mole," she said in a helpful tone, "on one of his elbows."

"Which elbow?" asked the medical examiner.

"I don't recall."

"Like it matters," said Augustine, restlessly. "Check both his arms, OK?"

The doctor checked. The dead man's elbows had no moles. Bonnie turned away from the body and laid her head against Augustine's chest.

"He was driving a stolen motorcycle," the doctor explained, "with a stolen microwave strapped to the back."

Augustine sighed irritably. "A hurricane looter."

"Right. Smacked a lumber truck doing eighty."

"*Now* he tells us," said Bonnie Lamb.

The wash of relief didn't hit her until she was back in Augustine's pickup truck. *It wasn't Max at the morgue, because Max is still alive. This is good. This is cause to be thankful.* Then Bonnie began to tremble, imagining her husband gutted like a fish on a shiny steel tray.

When they returned to the neighborhood where Max Lamb had vanished, they found the rental car on its rims. The hood stood open and the radiator was gone. Augustine's note on the windshield wiper was untouched—a testament, he remarked, to the low literacy rate among car burglars. He offered to call a wrecker.

"Later," Bonnie said, tersely.

"That's what I meant. Later." He locked the truck and set the alarm.

They walked the streets for nearly two hours, Augustine with the .38 Special wedged in his belt. He thought Max Lamb's abductor might have holed up, so they checked every abandoned house in the subdivision. Walking from one block to the next, Bonnie struck up conversations with people who were patching their battered homes. She hoped one of them would remember seeing Max on the morning after the hurricane. Several residents offered colorful accounts of monkey sightings, but Bonnie spoke with no one who recalled the kidnapping of a tourist.

Augustine drove her to the Metro police checkpoint, where she contacted a towing service and the rental-car agency in Orlando. Then she made a call to the apartment in New York to get her messages. After listening for a minute, she pressed the pound button on the telephone and handed the receiver to Augustine.

"Unbelievable," she said.

It was Max Lamb's voice on the line. The static was so heavy he could have been calling from Tibet:

"Bonnie, darling, everything's OK. I don't believe my life's in danger, but I can't say when I'll be free. It's too hairy to explain over the phone—uh, hang on, he wants me to read something. Ready? Here goes:

"'I have nothing to do with the creaking machinery of humanity—I belong to the earth! I say that lying on my pillow and I can feel the horns sprouting from my temples.'"

After a scratchy pause: "Bonnie, honey, it sounds worse than it is. Please don't tell my folks a thing—I don't want Dad all worked up for no reason. And please call Pete and, uh, ask him to put me down for sick leave, just in case this situation drags out. And tell him to stall the sixth floor on the Bronco meeting next week. Don't forget, OK? Tell him under no circumstances should Bill Knapp be brought in. It's still my account. . . ."

Max Lamb's voice dissolved into fuzzy pops and echoes. Augustine hung up. He walked Bonnie back to the pickup.

She got in and said, "This is making me crazy."

"We'll call again from my house and get it on tape."

"Oh, I'm sure it'll jolt the FBI into action. Especially the poetry."

"Actually I think it's from a book."

"What does it mean?" she asked.

Augustine reached across her lap and placed the .38 Special in the glove compartment. "It means," he said, "your husband probably isn't as safe as he thinks."

*

By and large, the Highway Patrol troopers based in northern Florida were not overjoyed to learn of their temporary reassignment to southern Florida. Many would have preferred Beirut or Somalia. The exception was Jim Tile. A trip to Miami meant precious time with Brenda Rourke, although working double shifts in the hurricane zone left them scarcely enough energy to collapse in each other's arms.

Jim Tile hadn't counted on an intrusion by the governor, but it wasn't totally surprising. The man worshipped hurricanes. Ignoring his presence would have been selfish and irresponsible; the trooper didn't take the friendship that lightly, nor Skink's capacity for outstandingly rash behavior. Jim Tile had no choice but to try to stay close.

In the age of political correctness, a large black man in a crisply pressed police uniform could move at will through the corridors of white-cracker bureaucracy and never once be questioned. Jim Tile took full advantage in the days following the big storm. He mingled authoritatively with Dade County deputies, Homestead police, firefighters, Red Cross volunteers, National Guardsmen, the Army command and antsy emissaries of the Federal Emergency Management Agency. Between patrol shifts, Jim Tile helped himself to coffee and A-forms, 911 logs, computer printouts and handwritten incident reports—he scanned for nothing in particular; just a sign.

As it happened, though, madness flowed rampant in the storm's wake. Jim Tile leafed through the paperwork, and thought: My Lord, people are cracking up all over town.

The machinery of rebuilding doubled as novel weapons for domestic violence. Thousands of hurricane victims had stampeded to purchase chain saws for clearing debris, and now the dangerous power tools were being employed to vent rage. A gentleman with a Black & Decker attempted to truncate a stubborn insurance adjuster in Homestead. An old woman in Florida City used a lightweight Sears to silence a neighbor's garrulous pet cockatoo. And in Sweetwater, two teenaged gang members successfully detached each other's arms (one left, one right) in a brief but spectacular duel of stolen Homelites.

If chain saws ruled the day, firearms ruled the night. Fearful of looters, vigilant home owners unloaded high-caliber semiautomatics at every rustle, scrape and scuff in the darkness. Preliminary casualties included seven cats, thirteen stray dogs, two opossums and a garbage truck, but no actual thieves. Residents of one rural neighborhood wildly fired dozens of rounds to repel what they described as a troop of marauding monkeys—an episode that Jim Tile dismissed as mass hallucination. He resolved to limit his investigative activities to daytime hours, whenever possible.

Nearly all the missing persons reported to authorities were locals who had fled the storm and lost contact with concerned relatives up North. Most turned up safe at shelters or in the homes of neighbors. But one case caught Jim Tile's attention: a man named Max Lamb.

According to the information filed by his wife, the Lambs drove to Miami on the morning after the hurricane struck. Mrs Lamb told police that her husband wanted to see the storm damage. The trooper wasn't surprised—the streets were clogged with out-of-towners who treated the hurricane zone as a tourist attraction.

Mr Max Lamb had left his rental car, in pursuit of video. It seemed improbable to Jim Tile that anybody from Manhattan could get lost on foot in the flat simple grid of a Florida subdivision. The trooper's suspicions were heightened by another incident, lost deep in the stack of files.

A seventy-four-year-old woman had called to say she had witnessed a possible assault. It was summarized in two short paragraphs, taken over the telephone by a dispatcher:

"Caller reports suspicious subject running along 10700 block of Quail Roost Drive, carrying another subject over his shoulder. Subject One is described as w/m, height and weight unknown. Subject Two is w/m, height and weight unknown.

"Caller reports Subject B appeared to be resisting, and was possibly nude. Subject A reported to be carrying a handgun with a flashing red light (??). Search of area by Units 2334 and 4511 proved negative."

Jim Tile knew of no pistols with blinking red lights, but most hand-held video cameras had one. From a distance, a frightened elderly person might mistake a Sony for a Smith & Wesson.

Maybe the old woman had witnessed the abduction of Mr Max Lamb. Jim Tile hoped not. He hoped the Quail Roost sighting was just another weird Dade County roadside altercation and not the act of his volatile swamp-dwelling friend, who was known to hold ill-mannered tourists in low esteem.

The trooper made a copy of Mrs Lamb's report and slipped it in his briefcase along with several others. When he had some free time, he'd try to interview her.

There was only twenty minutes left for lunch with Brenda, before both of them had to start another shift. Being able to see her, even briefly, was well worth the ordeal of working the batty streets of South Florida.

Jim Tile was most displeased, therefore, to personally witness the hijacking of a Salvation Army truck while he was driving to the Red Lobster restaurant where Brenda waited. The trooper was obliged to give chase, and by the time it was over he'd missed his luncheon date.

As he disarmed and handcuffed the truck hijacker, Jim Tile wondered aloud why anybody with half a brain would use a MAC-10 to steal a truck full of secondhand clothes. The young man said his original intention was to spray-paint a gang insignia on the side of the Salvation Army truck, but before he could finish his tagging the driver took off. The young man explained that he'd had no choice, as a matter of self-respect, but to pull his sub-machine gun and, yo, steal the motherfucking truck.

As Trooper Jim Tile assisted the talkative hijacker into the cage of his patrol car, he silently vowed to redouble his efforts to persuade Brenda Rourke to transfer out of this hellhole called Miami, to a more civilized hellhole where they could work together.

Snapper was proud of how he'd acquired the Jeep Cherokee, but Edie Marsh showed no interest in his conquest.

"What's the story?" Snapper pointed at the dachshunds.

"Donald and Marla," Edie said, annoyed. The animals were pulling her back and forth across Tony Torres's front yard and peeing with wild abandon. Edie was amazed at the power in their stubby Vienna-sausage legs.

"By the way," she said, straining against the leashes, "it took that asshole all of three minutes before he grabbed my tits."

"Big deal, so you win the bet."

"Take these damn dogs!"

Snapper backed away. Numerous encounters with police German shepherds had left him with permanent scars, physical and mental. Over the years, Snapper had become a cat person.

"Just let 'em go," he said to Edie.

The moment she dropped the leashes, the two dachshunds curled up at her feet.

"Beautiful," Snapper said with a grunt. "Hey, look what I found." He flashed the chrome-plated pistol he'd taken from the gangsters. Palming the cheap gun, he noticed the chambers were empty. "Damn spades," he said, heaving it into the murky swimming pool.

Edie Marsh told Snapper about the tough guy with the New York accent who came for Tony Torres. "You picked a peachy time to disappear," she added.

"Shut the fuck up."

"Well, Tony's gone. Even his damn beach chair. Figure it out yourself."

"Shit."

"He won't be back," Edie said gravely. "Not in one piece, anyway."

A concrete block occupied the spot where Tony's chaise had been. Snapper cursed his rotten timing. The ten grand was history. Even in the unlikely event that the salesman returned, he'd never pay. Snapper had fucked up big-time; he wasn't cut out to be a bodyguard.

He said, "I don't guess you got a new plan."

A siren drowned Edie's reply, which she punctuated with a familiar hand gesture. An ambulance came speeding down Calusa Drive. Snapper figured it was carrying Baby Raper to the hospital, for some unusual surgery. Snapper wouldn't be surprised to read about it in a medical journal someday.

He spotted Tony Torres's Remington shotgun, broken into pieces on the driveway. Snapper thought: It's definitely time to abort the mission. Tomorrow he'd call Avila about the roofer's gig.

"I'll give you a lift," he said to Edie Marsh, "but not those damn dogs."

"Jesus, I can't just leave 'em here."

"Suit yourself." Snapper scooped three Heinekens from Tony's ice cooler, got in the souped-up Cherokee and drove off without so much as a wave.

Edie Marsh tethered Donald and Marla to a sprinkler in the backyard. Then she entered the ruined shell of the salesman's house, to check for items of value.

Skink ordered Max Lamb to disrobe and climb a tree. Max did as he was told. It was a leafless willow; Max sat carefully on a springy limb, his bare legs dangling. Beneath him Skink paced, fulminating. In one hand he displayed the remote-control unit for the electronic training collar.

"You people come down here—fucking yupsters with no knowledge, no appreciation, no *interest* in the natural history of the place, the ancient sweep of life. Disney World—Christ, Max, that's not Florida!" He pointed an incriminating finger at his captive. "I found the ticket stubs in your wallet, Tourist Boy."

Max was rattled; he'd assumed everybody liked Disney World. "Please," he said to Skink, "if you shock me now, I'll fall."

Skink pulled off his flowered cap and knelt by the dead embers of the campfire. Max Lamb was acutely worried. Coal-black mosquitoes swarmed his pale plump toes, but he didn't dare slap at them. He was afraid to move a muscle.

All day the kidnapper's spirits had seemed to improve. He'd even taken Max to a rest stop along the Tamiami Trail, so Max could call New York and leave Bonnie another message. While Max waited for the pay phone, Skink had dashed onto the highway to collect a fresh roadkill. His mood was loose, practically convivial. He sang during the entire airboat ride back to the cypress hammock; later he merely chided Max for not knowing that Neil Young had played guitar for Buffalo Springfield.

Max Lamb believed himself to be blessed with a winning personality, a delusion that led him to assume the kidnapper had grown fond of him. Max felt it was only a matter of time before he'd be able to shmooze his way to freedom. He put no stock in Skink's oral biography, and regarded the man as an unbalanced but moderately intelligent derelict; in short, a confused soul who could be won over with a thoughtful, low-key approach. And wasn't that an advertiser's forte—winning people over? Max believed he was making progress, too, with tepid conversation, pointless anecdotes and the occasional self-deprecatory joke. Skink certainly acted calmer, if not serene. Three hours had passed since he'd last triggered the canine shock collar; an encouraging lull, from Max's point of view.

Now, for reasons unknown, the one-eyed brute was seething again. To Max Lamb, he announced: "Pop quiz."

"On what?"

Skink rose slowly. He tucked the remote control in a back pocket. With both hands he gathered his wild hair and knotted it on one side of his head, above the ear—a misplaced mop of a ponytail. Then he removed his glass eye and polished it with spit and a crusty bandanna. Max became further alarmed.

"Who was here first," Skink asked, "the Seminoles or the Tequestas?"

"I, uh—I don't know." Max gripped the branch so hard that his knuckles turned pink.

Skink, replacing the artificial eyeball, retrieving the remote control from his pocket: "Who was Napoleon Bonaparte Broward?"

Max Lamb shook his head, helplessly. Skink shrugged. "How about Marjory Stoneman Douglas?"

"Yes, yes, wait a minute." The willow limb quivered under Max's nervous buttocks. "She wrote *The Yearling*!"

Moments later, regaining consciousness, he found himself in a fetal ball on a mossy patch of ground. Both knees were scraped from the fall. His throat and arms still burned from the dog collar's jolt. Opening his eyes, Max saw the toes of Skink's boots. He heard a voice as deep as thunder: "I should kill you."

"No, don't—"

"The arrogance of coming to a place like this and not knowing—"

"I'm sorry, captain."

"—not caring to learn—"

"I told you, I'm in advertising."

Skink slipped a hand under Max Lamb's chin. "What do you believe in?"

"For God's sake, it's my honeymoon." Max was on the slippery ledge of panic.

"What do you stand for? Tell me that, sir."

Max Lamb cringed. "I can't."

Skink chuckled bitterly. "For future reference, you got your Marjories mixed up. Rawlings wrote *The Yearling*; Douglas wrote *River of Grass*. I got a hunch you won't forget."

He cleaned the bloody scrapes on Max's legs and told him to put on his clothes. His confidence fractured, Max dressed in arthritic slow motion. "Are you ever going to let me go?"

Skink seemed not to have heard the question. "Know what I'd really like," he said, stoking a new fire. "I'd like to meet this bride of yours."

"That's impossible," Max said, hoarsely.

"Oh, nothing's impossible."

Among the stream of outlaws who raced south in the feverish hours following the hurricane was a man named Gil Peck. His plan was to pass himself off as an experienced mason, steal what he could in the way of advance deposits, then haul ass back to Alabama. The scam had worked flawlessly against victims of Hurricane Hugo in South Carolina, and Gil Peck was confident it would work in Miami, too.

He arrived in a four-ton flatbed carrying a small but authentic-looking load of red bricks, which he'd ripped off from an unguarded construction site in Mobile—a new cancer wing for a pediatric hospital. Gil Peck had caught the festive groundbreaking on TV. That afternoon he'd backed up the flatbed, helped himself to the bricks and driven nonstop to South Florida.

So far, business was booming. Gil Peck had collected almost twenty-six hundred dollars in cash from half a dozen desperate home owners, all of whom expected him to return the following Saturday morning with his truckload of bricks. By then, of course, Gil Peck would be northbound and gone.

By day he worked the hustle, by night he scavenged hurricane debris. The big flatbed conveyed an air of authority, and no one questioned its presence. Even after curfew, the National Guardsmen waved him through the flashing barricades.

Many valuables had survived the storm's thrashing, and Gil Peck became an expert at mining rubble. An inventory of his two-day bounty included: a bagel toaster, a Stairmaster, a silver tea set, three offbrand assault rifles, a Panasonic cellular telephone, two pairs of men's golf spikes, a waterproof kilogram package of hashish, a brass chandelier, a scuba tank, a gold class ring from the University of Miami (1979), a set of police handcuffs, a collection of rare Finnish pornography, a Michael Jackson hand puppet, an unopened bottle of 100-milligram Darvocets, a boxed set of Willie Nelson albums, a Loomis fly rod, a birdcage and twenty-one pairs of women's bikini-style panties.

Exploring the demolished remains of a mobile-home park, Gil Peck was a happy fellow. There was a bounce to his step as he followed the yellow beam of the flashlight from one ruin to another. Thanks to the Guard, the Highway Patrol and the Dade County police, Gil Peck was completely alone and unmolested in the summer night; free to plunder.

And what he spied in the middle of a shuffleboard court made his greedy heart flutter with joy: a jumbo TV dish. The hurricane undoubtedly had uprooted it from some millionaire's estate and tossed it here, for Gil Peck to salvage. With the flashlight he traced the outer parabola and found one small dent. Otherwise the eight-foot satellite receiver was in top condition.

Gil Peck grinned and thought: Man, I must be living right. A dish that big was worth a couple-grand, easy. Gil Peck thought it might fit nicely in his own backyard, behind the chicken coops. He envisioned free HBO for the rest of his natural life.

He walked around to the other side to make sure there was no additional damage. He was shocked by what his flashlight revealed: Inside the TV dish was a dead man, splayed and mounted like a butterfly.

The dead man was impaled on the cone of the receiver pipe, but it wasn't the evil work of the hurricane. His hands and feet had been meticulously bound to the gridwork in a pose of crucifixion. The dead man himself was obese and balding, and bore no resemblance to the Jesus Christ of Gil Peck's strict Baptist upbringing. Nonetheless, the sight unnerved the bogus mason to the point of whimpering.

He switched off the flashlight and sat on the shuffleboard court to steady himself. Stealing the TV saucer obviously was out of the question; Gil Peck was working up the nerve to swipe the expensive watch he'd spotted on the crucified guy's left wrist.

Except for kissing his grandmother in her casket, Gil Peck had never touched a corpse before. Thank God, he thought, the guy's eyes are closed. Gingerly Gil Peck climbed into the satellite dish, which rocked under the added weight. Holding the flashlight in his mouth, he aimed the beam at the dead man's gold Cartier.

The clasp on the watchband was a bitch. Rigor mortis contributed to the difficulty of Gil Peck's task; the crucified guy refused to surrender the timepiece. The more Gil Peck struggled with the corpse, the more the TV saucer rolled back and forth on its axis, like a top. Gil Peck was getting dizzy and mad. Just as he managed to slip a penknife between the taut skin and the watchband, the dead man expelled an audible blast of postmortem flatulence. The detonation sent Gil Peck diving in terror from the satellite dish.

Edie Marsh paid a neighbor kid to siphon gas from Snapper's abandoned car and crank up Tony Torres's portable generator.

Edie gave the kid a five-dollar bill that she'd found hidden with five others inside a toolbox in the salesman's garage. It was a pitiful excuse for a stash; Edie was sure there had to be more.

At dusk she gave up the search and planted herself in Tony's BarcaLounger, a crowbar at her side. She turned up the volume of the television as loudly as she could stand, to block out the rustles and whispers of the night. Without doors, windows or a roof, the Torres house was basically an open campsite. Outside was black and creepy; people wandered like spirits through the unlit streets. Edie Marsh had the jitters, being alone. She gladly would have fled in Tony's huge boat of a Chevrolet, if it hadn't been blocked in the driveway by Snapper's car, which Edie would have gladly swiped if only Snapper hadn't taken the damn keys with him. So she was stuck at the Torres house until daybreak, when it might be safe for a woman to travel on foot with two miniature dachshunds.

She planned to get out of Dade County before anything else went wrong. The expedition was a disaster, and Edie blamed no one but herself. Nothing in her modest criminal past had prepared her for the hazy and menacing vibe of the hurricane zone. Everyone was on edge; evil, violence and paranoia ripened in the shadows. Edie Marsh was out of her league here. Tomorrow she'd hitch a ride to West Palm and close up the apartment. Then she'd take the Amtrak home to Jacksonville, and try to make up with her boyfriend. She estimated that reconciliation would require at least a week's worth of blow jobs, considering how much she'd stolen from his checking account. But eventually he'd take her back. They always did.

Edie Marsh was suffering through a TV quiz show when she heard a man's voice calling from the front doorway. She thought: Tony! The pig is back.

She grabbed the crowbar and sprung from the chair. The man at the door raised his arms. "Easy," he said.

It wasn't Tony Torres. This person was a slender blond with round eyeglasses and a tan briefcase and matching Hush Puppy shoes. In one hand he carried a manila file folder.

"What do you want?" Edie held the crowbar casually, as if she carried it at all times.

"Didn't mean to scare you," the man said. "My name is Fred Dove. I'm with Midwest Casualty."

"Oh." Edie Marsh felt a pleasant tingle. Like the first time she'd met one of the young Kennedys.

With a glance at the file, Fred Dove said, "Maybe I've got the wrong street. This is 15600 Calusa?"

"That's correct."

"And you're Mrs Torres?"

Edie smiled. "Please," she said, "call me Neria."

EIGHT

Bonnie and Augustine were cutting a pizza when Augustine's FBI friend stopped by to pick up the tape of Max Lamb's latest message. He listened to it several times on the cassette player in Augustine's living room. Bonnie studied the FBI man's expression, which remained intently neutral. She supposed it was something they worked on at the academy.

When he finished playing the tape, the FBI agent turned to Augustine and said, "I've read it somewhere. That 'creaking machinery of humanity.'"

"Me, too. I've been racking my brain."

"God, I can just see 'em up in Washington, giving it to a crack team of shrinks—"

"Or cryptographers," Augustine said.

The FBI man smiled. "Exactly." He accepted a hot slice of pepperoni for the road, and said good night.

Augustine asked Bonnie a question at which the agent had only hinted: Was it conceivable that Max Lamb could have written something like that himself?

"Never," she said. Her husband was into ditties and jingles, not metaphysics. "And he doesn't read much," she added. "The last book he finished was one of Trump's autobiographies."

It was enough to convince Augustine that Max Lamb wasn't being coy on the phone; the mystery man was feeding him lines. Augustine didn't know why. The situation was exceedingly strange.

Bonnie took a shower. She came out wearing a baby-blue flannel nightshirt that Augustine recognized from a long-ago relationship. Bonnie had found it hanging in a closet.

"Is there a story to go with it?" she asked.

"A torrid one."

"Really?" Bonnie sat beside him on the sofa, at a purely friendly distance. "Let me guess: Flight attendant?"

Augustine said, "Letterman's a rerun."

"Cocktail waitress? Fashion model?"

"I'm beat." Augustine picked up a book, a biography of Lech Wałesa, and flipped it open to the middle.

"Aerobics instructor? Legal secretary?"

"Surgical intern," Augustine said. "She tried to cut out my kidneys one night in the shower."

"That's the scar on your back? The Y."

"At least she wasn't a urologist." He closed the book and picked up the channel changer for the television.

Bonnie said, "You cheated on her."

"Nope, but she thought I did. She also thought the bathtub was full of centipedes, Cuban spies were spiking her lemonade, and Richard Nixon was working the night shift at the Farm Store on Bird Road."

"Drug problem?"

"Evidently." Augustine found a Dodgers game on ESPN and tried to appear engrossed.

Bonnie Lamb asked to see the scar closely, but he declined. "The lady had poor technique," he said.

"She use a real scalpel?"

"No, a corkscrew."

"My God."

"What is it with women and scars?"

Bonnie said, "I knew it. You've been asked before."

Was she flirting? Augustine wasn't sure. He had no point of reference when it came to married women whose husbands recently had disappeared.

"How's this," he said. "You tell me all about your husband, and maybe I'll show you the damn scar."

"Deal," said Bonnie Lamb, tugging the nightshirt down to cover her knees.

Max Lamb met and fell in love with Bonnie Brooks when she was an assistant publicist for Crespo Mills Internationale, a leading producer of snack and breakfast foods. Rodale & Burns had won the lucrative Crespo advertising account, and assigned Max Lamb to develop the print and radio campaign for a new cereal called Plum Crunchies. Bonnie Brooks flew in from Crespo's Chicago headquarters to consult.

Basically, Plum Crunchies were ordinary sugar-coated corn-flakes mixed with rock-hard fragments of dried plums—that is to say, prunes. The word "prune" was not to appear in any Plum Crunchies publicity or advertising, a corporate edict with which both Max Lamb and Bonnie Brooks wholeheartedly agreed. The target demographic was sweet-toothed youngsters aged fourteen and under, not constipated senior citizens.

On only their second date, at a Pakistani restaurant in Greenwich Village, Max sprung upon Bonnie his slogan for Crespo's new cereal: *You'll go plum loco for Plum Crunchies!*

"With p-l-u-m instead of p-l-u-m-b on the first reference," he was quick to explain.

Though she personally avoided the use of lame homonyms, Bonnie told Max the slogan had possibilities. She was trying not to dampen his enthusiasm; besides, he was the expert, the creative talent. All she did was bang out press releases.

On a napkin Max Lamb crudely sketched a jaunty, cockeyed mynah bird that was to be the cereal-box mascot for Plum Crunchies. Max said the bird would be colored purple ("like a plum!") and would be named Dinah the Mynah. Here Bonnie Brooks felt she should speak up, as a colleague, to remind Max Lamb of the many other cereals that already used bird logos (Froot Loops, Cocoa Puffs, Kellogg's Corn Flakes, and so on). In addition, she gently questioned the wisdom of naming the mynah bird after an aging, though much-beloved, TV singer.

Bonnie: "Is the bird supposed to be a woman?"

Max: "The bird has no particular gender."

Bonnie: "Well, do mynahs actually eat plums?"

Max: "You're adorable, you know that?"

He was falling for her, and she was falling (though a bit less precipitously) for him. As it turned out, Max's bosses at Rodale & Burns liked his slogan but hated the concept of Dinah the Mynah. The executives of Crespo Mills concurred. When the new cereal finally debuted, the box featured a likeness of basketball legend Patrick Ewing, slam-dunking a giddy cartoon plum. Surveys later revealed that many customers thought it was either an oversized grape or a prune. Plum Crunchies failed to capture a significant share of the fruited-branflake breakfast market and quietly disappeared forever from the shelves.

Bonnie and Max's long-distance romance endured. She found herself carried along by his energy, determination and self-confidence, misplaced as it often was. While Bonnie was bothered by Max's tendency to judge humankind strictly according to age, race, sex and median income, she attributed his cold eye to indoctrination by the advertising business. She herself had become cynical about the brain activity of the average consumer, given Crespo's worldwide success with such dubious food products as salted doughballs, whipped olive spread and shrimp-flavored popcorn.

In the early months of courtship, Max invented a game intended to impress Bonnie Brooks. He bet that he could guess precisely what model of automobile a person owned, based on his or her demeanor, wardrobe and physical appearance. The skill was intuitive, Max told Bonnie; a gift. He said it's what made him such a canny advertising pro. On dates, he'd sometimes follow strangers out of restaurants or movie theaters to see what they were driving. "Ha! A Lumina—what'd I tell ya? The guy had midsize written all over him!" Max would chirp when his guess was correct (which was, by Bonnie's generous reckoning, about five percent of the time). Before long, the car game grew tiresome and Bonnie Brooks asked Max Lamb to stop. He didn't take it personally; he was a hard man to insult. This, too, Bonnie attributed to the severe environment of Madison Avenue.

While Bonnie's father was amiably indifferent to Max, her mother was openly unfond of him. She felt he tried too hard, came on too strong; that he was trying to sell himself to Bonnie the same way he sold breakfast cereal and cigarets. It wasn't that Bonnie's mother thought Max Lamb was a phony; just the opposite. She believed he was exactly what he seemed to be—completely goal-driven, every waking moment. He was no different at home than he was at the office, no less consumed with attaining success. There was, said Bonnie's mother, a sneaky arrogance in Max Lamb's winning attitude. Bonnie thought it was an odd criticism, coming from a woman who had regarded Bonnie's previous boyfriends as timid, unmotivated losers. Still, her mother had never used the term "asshole" to describe Bonnie's other suitors. That she pinned it so quickly on Max Lamb nagged painfully at Bonnie until her wedding day.

Now, with Max apparently abducted by a raving madman, Bonnie fretted about something else her mother had often mentioned, a trait of Max's so obvious that even Bonnie had acknowledged it. Augustine knew what she was talking about.

"Your husband thinks he can outsmart anybody."

"Unfortunately," Bonnie said.

"I can tell from the phone tapes."

"Well," she said, fishing for encouragement, "he's managed to make it so far."

"Maybe he's learned when to keep his mouth shut." Augustine stood up and stretched his arms. "I'm tired. Can we do the scar thing some other time?"

Bonnie Lamb laughed and said sure. She waited until she heard the bedroom door shut before she phoned Pete Archibald at his home in Connecticut.

"Did I wake you?" she asked.

"Heck, no. Max said you might be calling."

Bonnie's words stuck in her throat. "You—Pete, you talked to him?"

"For about an hour."

"When?"

"Tonight. He's all frantic that Bill Knapp's gonna snake the

Bronco cigaret account. I told him not to worry, Billy's tied up with the smokeless division on some stupid rodeo tour—"

"Pete, never mind all that. Where did Max call from?"

"I don't know, Bon. I assumed he'd spoken to you."

Bonnie strained to keep the hurt from her voice. "Did he tell you what happened?"

On the other end, Pete Archibald clucked and ummmed nervously. "Not all the gory details, Bonnie. Everybody—least all the couples I know—go through the occasional bedroom drama. Fights and whatnot. I don't blame you for not giving me the real story when you called before."

Bonnie Lamb's voice rose. "Peter, Max and I aren't fighting. And I *did* tell you the real story." She caught herself. "At least it was the story Max told me."

After an uncomfortable pause, Pete Archibald said, "Bon, you guys work it out, OK? I don't want to get in the middle."

"You're right, you're absolutely right." She noticed that her free hand was balled in a fist and she was rocking sideways in the chair. "Pete, I won't keep you. But maybe you could tell me what else Max said."

"Shop talk, Bonnie."

"For a whole hour?"

"Well, you know your husband. He gets rolling, you know what he's like."

Maybe I don't, Bonnie thought.

She said good-bye to Pete Archibald and hung up. Then she went to Augustine's room and knocked on the door. When he didn't answer, she slipped in and sat lightly on the corner of the bed. She thought he was asleep, until he rolled over and said: "Not a good night for the skull room, huh?"

Bonnie Lamb shook her head and began to cry.

Edie Marsh gave it her best shot. For a while, the plan went smoothly. The man from Midwest Casualty took meticulous notes as he followed her from room to room in the Torres house. Many of the couple's belongings had been pulverized beyond recognition, so Edie began embellishing losses to inflate the claim. She lovingly described the splintered remains of a china cabinet as a priceless antique that Tony inherited from a great-grandmother in San Juan. Pausing before a bare bedroom wall, she pointed to the nails upon which once hung two original (and very expensive) watercolors by the legendary Jean-Claude Jarou, a martyred Haitian artist whom Edie invented off the top of her head. A splintered bedroom bureau became the hand-hewn mahogany vault that had yielded eight cashmere sweaters to the merciless winds of the hurricane.

"Eight sweaters," said Fred Dove, glancing up from his clipboard. "In Miami?"

"The finest Scottish cashmeres—can you imagine? Ask your wife if it wouldn't break her heart."

Fred Dove took a small flashlight from his jacket and went outside to evaluate structural damage. Soon Edie heard barking from the backyard, followed by emphatic human profanities. By the time she got there, both dachshunds had gotten a piece of the insurance man. Edie led him inside, put him in the BarcaLounger, rolled up his cuffs and tended his bloody ankles with Evian and Ivory liquid, which she salvaged from the kitchen.

"I'm glad they're not rottweilers," said Fred Dove, soothed by Edie's ministrations with a soft towel.

Repeatedly she apologized for the attack. "For what it's worth, they've had all their shots," she said, with no supporting evidence whatsoever.

She instructed Fred Dove to stay in the recliner and keep his feet elevated, to slow the bleeding. Leaning back, he spotted Tony Torres's Salesman of the Year plaque on the wall. "Pretty impressive," Fred Dove said.

"Yes, it was quite a big day for us." Edie beamed, a game simulation of spousely pride.

"And where's Mister Torres tonight?"

Out of town, Edie replied, at a mobile-home convention in Dallas. For the second time, Fred Dove looked doubtful.

"Even with the hurricane? Must be a pretty important convention."

"It sure is," said Edie Marsh. "He's getting another award."

"Ah."

"So he *had* to go. I mean, it'd look bad if he didn't show up. Like he wasn't grateful or something."

Fred Dove said, "I suppose so. When will Mister Torres be returning to Miami?"

Edie sighed theatrically. "I just don't know. Soon, I hope."

The insurance man attempted to lower the recliner, but it kept springing to the sleep position. Finally Edie Marsh sat on the footrest, enabling Fred Dove to climb out. He said he wanted to reinspect the damage to the master bedroom. Edie said that was fine.

She was rinsing the bloody towel in a sink when the insurance man called. She hurried to the bedroom, where Fred Dove held up a framed photograph that he'd dug from the storm rubble. It was a picture of Tony Torres with a large dead fish. The fish had a mouth the size of a garbage pail.

"That's Tony on the left," Edie said with a dry, edgy laugh.

"Nice grouper. Where'd he catch it?"

"The ocean." Where else? thought Edie.

"And who's this?" The insurance man retrieved another frame off the floor. The glass was cracked, and the picture was puckered from storm water. It was a color nine-by-twelve, mounted inside gold filigree: Tony Torres with his arm around the waist of a petite but heavy-breasted Latin woman. Both of them wore loopy champagne smiles.

"His sister Maria," Edie blurted, sensing the game was about to end.

"She's in a wedding gown," Fred Dove remarked, with no trace of sarcasm. "And Mister Torres is wearing a black tuxedo and tails."

Edie said, "He was the best man."

"Really? His hand is on her bottom."

"They're very close," said Edie, "for a brother and sister." The words trailed off in defeat.

Fred Dove's shoulders stiffened, and his tone chilled. "Do you happen to have some identification? A driver's license would be good. Anything with a current photograph."

Edie Marsh said nothing. She feared compounding one felony with another.

"Let me guess," said the insurance man. "All your personal papers were lost in the hurricane."

Edie bowed her head, thinking: This can't be happening again. One of these days I've got to catch a break. She said, "Shit."

"Pardon?"

"I said 'shit.' Meaning, I give up." Edie couldn't believe it—a fucking *wedding* picture! Tony and the unfaithful witch he planned to rip off for half the hurricane money. Too bad Snapper bolted, she thought, because this was ten times better than Sally Jessy.

"Who are you?" Fred Dove was stern and official.

"Look, what happens now?"

"I'll tell you exactly what happens—"

At that moment, the electric generator ran out of gasoline, dying with a feeble series of burps. The lightbulb went dim and the television went black. The house at 15600 Calusa became suddenly as quiet as a chapel. The only sound was a faint jingle from the backyard, where the two dachshunds squirmed to pull free of their leashes.

In the darkness, Fred Dove reached for his flashlight. Edie Marsh intercepted his wrist and held on to it. She decided there was nothing to lose by trying.

"What are you doing?" the insurance man asked.

Edie brought his hand to her mouth. "What's it worth to you?"

Fred Dove stood as still as a statue.

"Come on," Edie said, her tongue brushing his knuckles, "what's it worth?"

The insurance man, in a shaky whisper: "What's *what* worth—not calling the police? Is that what you mean?"

Edie was smiling. Fred Dove could tell by the feel of her lips and teeth against his hand.

"What's this house insured for?" she asked.

"Why?"

"One twenty? One thirty?"

"One forty-one," said Fred Dove, thinking: Her breath is so *unbelievably* soft.

Edie switched to her sex-kitten voice, the one that had failed to galvanize the young Palm Beach Kennedy. "One forty-one? You sure, Mister Dove?"

"The structure, yes. Because of the swimming pool."

"Of course." She pressed closer, wishing she weren't wearing a bra but suspecting it didn't much matter. Poor Freddie's brakes were already smoking. She feathered her eyelashes against his neck and felt him bury his face in her hair.

The insurance man labored to speak. "What is it you want?"

"A partner," Edie Marsh replied, sealing the agreement with a long blind kiss.

Sergeant Cain Darby took his weekends with the National Guard as seriously as he took his regular job as a maximum-security-prison guard. Although he would have preferred to remain in Starke with the armed robbers and serial killers, duty called Cain Darby to South Florida on the day after the hurricane struck. Commanding Darby's National Guard unit was the night manager of a Days Inn, who sternly instructed the troops not to fire their weapons unless fired upon themselves. From what Cain Darby knew of Miami, this scenario seemed not entirely improbable. Nonetheless, he understood that a Guardsman's chief mission was to maintain order in the streets, assist needy civilians and prevent looting.

The unit's first afternoon was spent erecting tents for the homeless and unloading heavy drums of fresh drinking water from the back of a Red Cross trailer. After supper, Cain Darby was posted to a curfew checkpoint on Quail Roost Drive, not far from the Florida Turnpike. Darby and another Guardsman, the foreman of a paper mill, took turns stopping the cars and trucks. Most drivers had good excuses for being on the road after curfew — some were searching for missing relatives, others were on their way to a hospital, and still others were simply lost in a place they no longer recognized. If questions arose about a driver's alibi, the paper-mill foreman deferred judgment to Sergeant Darby, due to his law-enforcement experience. Common violators were TV crews, sightseers, and teenagers who had come to steal. These cars Cain Darby interdicted and sent away, to the Turnpike ramp.

At midnight the paper-mill foreman returned to camp, leaving Sergeant Darby alone at the barricade. He dozed for what must have been two hours, until he was startled awake by loud snorting. Blearily he saw the shape of a large bear no more than thirty yards away, at the edge of a pine glade. Or maybe it was just a freak shadow, for it looked nothing like the chubby black bears that Cain Darby routinely poached from the Ocala National Forest. The thing that he now *thought* he was seeing stood seven feet at the shoulders.

Cain Darby closed his eyes tightly to clear the sleep. Then he opened them again, very slowly. The huge shape was still there, a motionless phantasm. Common sense told him he was mistaken— they don't grow thousand-pound bears in Florida! But that's sure what it looked like. . . .

So he raised his rifle.

Then, from the corner of his eye, he spotted headlights barreling down Quail Roost Drive. He turned to see. Somebody was driving toward the roadblock like a bat out of hell. Judging by the rising chorus of sirens, half the Metro police force was on the chase.

When Cain Darby spun back toward the bear, or the shape that *looked* like a bear, it was gone. He lowered the gun and directed his attention to the maniac in the oncoming truck. Cain Darby struck an erect military pose in front of the candy-striped barricades—spine straight, legs apart, the rifle held at a ready angle across the chest.

A half mile behind the truck was a stream of flashing blue and red lights. The fugitive driver seemed undaunted. As the headlights drew closer, Sergeant Darby hurriedly weighed his options. The asshole wasn't going to stop, that much was clear. By now the man had (unless he was blind, drunk or both) seen the soldier standing in his path.

Yet the vehicle was not decelerating. If anything, it was gaining speed. Cain Darby cursed as he dashed out of the way. If there was one thing he found intolerable, it was disrespect for a uniform, whether it belonged to the Department of Corrections or the National Guard. So he indignantly cranked off a few rounds as the idiot driver smashed through the barricade.

No one was more stunned than Cain Darby to see the speeding truck overshoot the Turnpike ramp and plunge full speed into a drainage canal; no one except the driver, Gil Peck. The sound of gunfire had destroyed his ragged reflexes, particularly his ability to locate the brake pedal. He couldn't believe some peckerwood Guardsman was shooting at him.

What did not surprise Gil Peck, considering his heavy cargo of stolen bricks, was how swiftly the flatbed sunk in the warm brown water. He squeezed through the window, swam to shore and began weeping at his own foul luck. All his hurricane booty was lost, except for the package of hash, which bobbed to the surface at the precise moment the first police car arrived.

Yet the drugs weren't the most serious of Gil Peck's legal concerns. As he was being handcuffed, he declared: "I didn't kill him!"

"Kill who?" the officer asked.

"The guy, you know. The guy at the trailer park." Gil Peck assumed that's why the cops were chasing him—they'd found the body of the crucified man.

But they hadn't. Gil Peck's nausea worsened. He should've kept his damn mouth shut. Now it was too late. Pink and blue bikini panties began to float up, like pale jellyfish, from the bed of the sunken truck.

The officer said: "What guy at what trailer park?"

Gil Peck told him about the dead man impaled in the TV dish. As other policemen arrived, Gil Peck repeated the story, and also his impassioned denials of guilt. One of the officers asked Gil Peck if he would take them to the body, and he agreed.

After the paramedics checked him for broken bones, the thief was toweled off and deposited in the back-seat cage of a Highway Patrol car. The trooper at the wheel was a large black man in a

Stetson. On the way to the trailer court, Gil Peck delivered yet another excited monologue about his innocence.

"If you didn't do it," the trooper cut in, "why'd you run?"

"Scared, man." Gil Peck shivered. "You should see."

"Oh, I can't wait," the trooper said.

"You a Christian, sir?"

It was amazing, thought the trooper, how quickly the handcuffs induced spiritual devoutness. "Anyone read you your rights?" he asked the truck driver.

Gil Peck thrust his face to the mesh of the cage. "If you're a Christian, you gotta believe what I'm sayin'. It wasn't me that crucified the poor fucker."

But Jim Tile hoped with all his Christian heart that it was. Because the other prime suspect was someone he didn't want to arrest, unless there was no choice.

NINE

Skink eavesdropped leisurely while Max Lamb made two calls. The phone booth was at a truck stop on Krome Avenue, the fringe of the Everglades. Longbeds overloaded with lumber, sheet glass and tar paper streamed south in ragged convoys to the hurricane zone. Nobody glanced twice at the unshaven man on the phone, despite the collar around his neck.

When Max Lamb hung up, Skink grabbed his arm and led him to the airboat, beached on the bank of a muddy canal. Skink ordered him to lie in the bow, and there he remained for two hours, his cheekbone vibrating against the hull. The howl of the aviation engine filled his ears. Skink was no longer singing harmony. Max Lamb wondered what he'd done to further annoy his abductor.

They stopped once. Skink left the airboat briefly and returned with a large cardboard box, which he set in the bow next to Max. They traveled until dusk. When Skink finally lifted him to his knees, Max was surprised to see the Indian village. They didn't stay long enough for Max to negotiate the return of his video camera. Skink borrowed a station wagon, put the box in the back, and buckled his prisoner on the passenger side. There was no sign of the monkey, and for that Max Lamb was grateful.

Skink put on the shower cap and started the car. Max needed to pee but was afraid to ask. He was no longer confident that he could talk his way out of the kidnapping.

"Is something wrong?" he asked.

Skink shot him a stony look. "I remember your wife from the hurricane video. Hugging two little Cuban girls."

"Yes, that was Bonnie."

"Beautiful woman. You zoomed in on her face."

"Can we stop the car," Max interrupted, squirming, "just for a minute?"

Skink kept his eyes on the road. "Your bride's got a good heart. That much is obvious from the video."

"A saint," Max agreed. He jammed both hands between his legs; he'd tie his dick in a Windsor before he'd wet himself in front of the governor.

"Why she's with you, I can't figure. It's a real puzzler," Skink said. He braked the car sharply. "Why didn't you try to phone her tonight? You call your buddy in New York. You call your folks in Milan-fucking-Italy. Why not Bonnie?"

"I don't know where she is. That damn answering machine—"

"And the crap about you and her having a fight—"

"I didn't want Peter to worry," Max said.

"Well, God forbid." Skink jammed the transmission into Park and flung himself out the door. He reappeared in the beam of the headlights, a hoary apparition crouched on the pavement. Max Lamb craned to see what he was doing.

Skink strolled back to the station wagon and tossed a dead opossum on the seat next to Max, who gasped and recoiled. A few miles later, Skink added a truck-flattened coachwhip snake to the evening's menu. Max forgot about his bladder until they made camp at an abandoned horse barn west of Krome.

The horses were gone, scattered by the storm; the owners had come by to retrieve the saddles and tack, and to scatter feed in case any of the animals returned. Max Lamb stood alone in the musky darkness and relieved himself torrentially. He considered running, but feared he wouldn't survive a single night alone in nature. In Max's mind, all Florida south of Orlando was an immense swamp, humidly teeming with feral beasts. Some had claws and poisonous fangs, some drove airboats and feasted on roadkill. They were all the same to Max.

Skink appeared at his side to announce that dinner soon would be served. Max followed him into the stables. He asked if it was wise to make a campfire inside a barn. Skink replied that it was extremely dangerous, but cozy.

Max Lamb was impressed that the odor of horseshit could not be vanquished by a mere Force Four hurricane. On a positive note, the fragrance of dung completely neutralized the aroma of boiled opossum and pan-fried snake. After supper Skink stripped to his boxer shorts and did two hundred sit-ups in a cloud of ancient manure dust. Then he retrieved the large cardboard box from the car and brought it inside the barn. He asked Max if he wanted a cigaret.

"No, thanks," Max said. "I don't smoke."

"You're kidding."

"Never have," Max said.

"But you sell the stuff—"

"We do the advertising. That's it."

"Ah," Skink said. "Just the advertising." He picked his trousers off the floor and went through the pockets. Max Lamb thought he was looking for matches, but he wasn't. He was looking for the remote control to the shock collar.

When Max regained his senses, he lay in wet moldering hay. His eyeballs were jumping in their sockets, and his neck felt tingly and hot. He sat up and said, "What'd I do?"

"Surely you believe in the products you advertise."

"Look, I don't smoke."

"You could learn." With a pocketknife, Skink opened the cardboard box. The box was full of Bronco cigarets, probably four dozen cartons. Max Lamb failed to conceal his alarm.

The kidnapper asked how he could be sure of a product until he tested it himself. Grimly Max responded: "I also do the ads for raspberry-scented douche, but I don't use the stuff."

"Careful," said Skink, brightly, "or you'll give me another brainstorm." He opened a pack of Broncos. He tapped one out and inserted it between Max's lips. He struck a match on the wall of the barn and lit the cigaret.

"Well?"

Max spit out the cigaret. "This is ridiculous."

Skink retrieved the soggy Bronco and replaced it in Max's frowning mouth. "You got two choices," he said, fingering the remote control, "smoke or be smoked."

Reluctantly Max Lamb took a drag on the cigaret. Immediately he began to cough. It worsened as Skink tied him upright to a post. "You people are a riddle to me, Max. Why you come down here. Why you act the way you do. Why you live such lives."

"For God's sake—"

"Shut up now. Please."

Skink dug through the backpack and took out a Walkman. He chose a damp corner of the barn and put on the headphones. He lighted what appeared to be a joint, except it didn't smell like marijuana.

"What's that?" Max asked.

"Toad." Skink took a hit. After a few minutes, his good eye rolled back in his head and his neck went limp.

Max Lamb went through the Broncos like a machine. Whenever Skink opened an eye, he tapped a finger to his neck—a menacing reminder of the shock collar. Max smoked and smoked. He was finishing number twenty-three when Skink shook out of the stupor and rose.

"Damn good toad." He plucked the Bronco from Max's mouth.

"I feel sick, captain."

Skink untied him and told him to rest up. "Tomorrow you're going to leave a message for your wife. You're going to arrange a meeting."

"What for?"

"So I can observe the two of you together. The chemistry, the starry eyes, all that shit. OK?"

Skink went outside and crawled under the station wagon, where he curled up and began to snore. Max coughed himself to sleep in the barn.

Bonnie Lamb awoke in Augustine's arms. Her guilt was diluted by the observation that he was wearing jeans and a T-shirt. She didn't remember him dressing during the night, but obviously he had. She was reasonably sure that no sex had occurred; plenty of tears, yes, but no sex.

Bonnie wanted to pull away without waking him. Otherwise there might be an awkward moment, the two of them lying there embraced. Or maybe not. Maybe he'd know exactly what not to say. Clearly he was experienced with crying women, because he was exceptionally good at hugging and whispering. When she found herself thinking about how nice he smelled, Bonnie knew it was time to sneak out of bed.

As she'd hoped, Augustine had the good manners to pretend to stay asleep until she was safely in the kitchen, making coffee.

When he walked in, she felt herself blush. "I'm so sorry," she blurted, "for last night."

"Why? Did you take advantage of me?" He went to the refrigerator and took out a carton of eggs. "I'm a heavy sleeper," he said. "Easy prey for sex-crazed babes."

"Especially newlyweds."

"Oh, they're the worst," said Augustine. "Ravenous harlots. You want scrambled or fried?"

"Fried." She sat at the table. She tore open a packet of NutraSweet and managed to miss the coffee cup entirely. "Please believe me. I don't usually sleep with strange men."

"Sleeping is fine. It's the screwing you want to watch out for." He was peeling an orange at the sink. "Relax, OK? Nothing happened."

Bonnie smiled. "Can I at least say thanks, for being a friend."

"You're very welcome, Mrs Lamb." He glanced over his shoulder. "What's so funny?"

"The jeans."

"Don't tell me there's a hole."

"No. It's just—well, you got up in the middle of the night to put them on. It was a sweet gesture."

"Actually, it was more of a precaution." The eggs sizzled when Augustine dropped them into the hot pan. "I'm surprised you even noticed," he said, causing Bonnie to redden once more.

In the middle of breakfast, the phone rang. It was the Medical

Examiner's Office—another John Doe was being hauled to the county morgue. The coroner on duty wanted Bonnie to stop by for a look. Augustine said she'd call him back. He put the phone down and told her.

"Can they make me go?"

"I don't think so."

"Because it's not Max," Bonnie said. "Max is too busy talking to Rodale and Burns."

"A white male is all they said. Apparent homicide."

The last word hung in the air like sulfur. Bonnie put down her fork. "It can't be him."

"Probably not," Augustine agreed. "We don't have to go."

She got up and went to the bathroom. Soon Augustine heard the shower running. He was washing the dishes when she came out. She was dressed. Her wet hair was brushed back, and she'd found the intern's rose lipstick in the medicine chest.

"I guess I need to be sure," she said.

Augustine nodded. "You'll feel better."

Snapper's real name was Lester Maddox Parsons. His mother named him after a Georgia politician best known for scaring off black restaurant customers with an ax handle. Snapper's mother believed Lester Maddox should be President of the United States and the whole white world; Snapper's father leaned toward James Earl Ray. When Snapper was barely seven years old, his parents took him to his first Ku Klux Klan rally; for the occasion, Mrs Parsons dressed her son in a costume sewn from white muslin pillowcases; she was especially proud of the pointy little hood. The other Klansmen and their wives fawned over Lester, remarking on the youngster's handsome Southern features—baffling praise, because all that was visible of young Lester were his beady brown eyes, peeping through the slits of his sheet. He thought: I could be a Negro, for all they know!

Still, the boy enjoyed Klan rallies because there was great barbecue and towering bonfires. He was disappointed when his family stopped attending, but he couldn't argue with his parents' reason for quitting. They referred to it as The Accident, and Lester would never forget the night. His father had gotten customarily shitfaced and, when the climactic moment came to light the cross, accidentally ignited the local Grand Kleagle instead. In the absence of a fire hose, the frantic Klansmen were forced to save their blazing comrade by spritzing him with well-shaken cans of Schlitz beer. Once the fire was extinguished, they placed the charred Kleagle in the bed of Lester's father's pickup and drove to the hospital. Although the man survived, his precious anonymity was lost forever. A local television crew happened to be outside the emergency room when the Kleagle—hoodless, his sheet in scorched tatters—arrived. Once his involvement in the Klan was exposed on TV, the man resigned as district attorney and moved upstate to Macon. Lester's father blamed himself, a sentiment echoed in harsher terms by the other Klansmen. Morale in the local chapter further deteriorated when a newspaper revealed that the young doctor who had revived the dying Kleagle was a black man, possibly from Savannah.

The Parsonses decided to leave the Klan while it was still their choice to do so. Lester's father joined a segregated bowling league, while his mother mailed out flyers for J. B. Stoner, another famous racist who periodically ran for office. Politics bored young Lester, who turned his pubescent energies to crime. He dropped out of school on his fourteenth birthday, although his preoccupied parents didn't find out for nearly two years. By then the boy's income from stealing backhoes and bulldozers was twice his father's income from repairing them. The Parsonses strove not to know what their son was up to, even when it landed him in trouble. Lester's mother worried that the boy had a mean streak; his father said all boys do. Can't get by otherwise in this godfor-saken world.

Lester Maddox Parsons was seventeen when he got his nick-name. He was hot-wiring a farmer's tractor in a peanut field when a game warden snuck up behind him. Lester dove from the cab and took a punch at the man, who calmly reconfigured Lester's face with the butt of an Ithaca shotgun. He sat in the county jail for three days before a doctor came to examine his jaw, which was approximately thirty-six degrees out of alignment. That it healed at all was a minor miracle; Snapper was spitting out snips of piano wire until he was twenty-two years old.

The Georgia prison system taught the young man an important lesson: It was best to keep one's opinions about race mingling to oneself. So when Avila introduced Snapper to the roofing crew, Snapper noted (but did not complain) that two of the four workers were as black as the tar they'd be mixing. The third roofer was a muscular young *Marielito* with the number "69" tattooed elegantly inside his lower lip. The fourth roofer was a white crackhead from Santa Rosa County who spoke a version of the English language that was utterly incomprehensible to Snapper and the others. Although each of the roofers owned long felony rap sheets, Snapper couldn't say that his feelings toward the crew approached anything close to kinship.

Avila sat the men down for a pep talk.

"Thanks to the hurricane, there's a hundred fifty thousand houses in Dade County need new roofs," he began. "Only a damn fool couldn't make money off these poor bastards."

The plan was to line up the maximum number of buyers and perform the minimum amount of actual roofing. By virtue of owning a suit and tie, Snapper was assigned the task of bullshitting potential customers through the fine print of the "contract," then collecting deposits.

"People are fucking desperate for new roofs," Avila said buoyantly. "They're getting rained on. Fried from the sun. Eat up by bugs. Faster they get a roof on their heads, the more they'll pay." He raised his palms to the sky. "Hey, do they really care about price? It's insurance money, for Christ's sake."

One of the roofers inquired how much manual labor would be involved. Avila said they should repair a small section on every house. "To put the people's minds at ease," he explained.

"What's a 'small' section?" the roofer demanded.

Another said, "It's fucking August out here, boss. I know guys that dropped dead of heatstroke."

Avila reassured the men they could get by with doing a square, maybe less, on each roof. "Then you can split. Time they figure out you won't be back, it's too late."

The crackhead mumbled something about contracting licenses. Avila turned to Snapper and said, "They ask about our license, you know what to do."

"Run?"

"*Exactamente!*"

Snapper wasn't pleased with his door-to-door role in the operation, particularly the odds of encountering large pet dogs. He said to Avila: "Sounds like too much talking to strangers. I hate that shit. Why don't you do the contracts?"

"Because I inspected some of these goddamn houses when I was with building-and-zoning."

"The owners don't know that."

Chango had warned Avila to be careful. Chango was Avila's personal *santería* deity. Avila had thanked him with a turtle and two rabbits.

"I'm keeping low," Avila told Snapper. "B-and-Z's got snitches all over the damn county. Somebody recognizes my face, we're screwed."

Snapper wasn't sure if Avila was paranoid or purely lazy. "So where will you be exactly," he said, "when we're out on a job? Maybe some air-conditioned office." He heard the roofers snicker, a hopeful sign of solidarity.

But Avila was quick to assert his authority. "Job? This isn't no 'job,' it's an act. You boys aren't here 'cause you can mop tar. You're here 'cause you look like you can."

"What about me?" Snapper goaded. "How come *I* was hired?"

"Because we couldn't get Robert Redford." Avila stood up to signal the end of the meeting. "Snap, why the hell you *think* you got hired? So people would be sure to pay. *Comprende?* One look at that fucked-up face, and they know you mean business."

Maybe an ordinary criminal would've taken it as a compliment. Snapper did not.

*

All the mattresses in Tony Torres's house were soaked from the storm, so Edie Marsh had sex with the insurance man on the BarcaLounger. It was a noisy and precarious endeavor. Fred Dove was nervous, so Edie had to assist him each step of the way. Afterwards he said he must've slipped a disk. Edie was tempted to remark that he hadn't moved enough muscles to slip anything; instead she told him he was a stallion in technique and proportion. It was a strategy that seldom failed. Fred Dove contentedly fell asleep with his head on her shoulder and his legs snagged in the footrest, but not before promising to submit a boldly fraudulent damage claim for the Torres house and split the check with Edie Marsh.

An hour before dawn, Edie heard a terrible commotion in the backyard. She couldn't rise to investigate because she was pinned beneath the insurance man in the BarcaLounger. Judging from the tumult outside, Donald and Marla had gone rabid. The confrontation ended in a flurry of plaintive yips and a hair-raising roar. Edie Marsh didn't move until the sun came up. Then she stealthily roused Fred Dove, who panicked because he'd forgotten to phone his wife back in Omaha. Edie told him to hush up and put on his pants.

She led him to the backyard. The only signs of the two miniature dachshunds were limp leashes and empty collars. The Torres lawn was torn to shreds. Several large tracks were visible in the damp gray soil; deep raking tracks, with claws.

Fred Dove's left Hush Puppy fit easily one of the imprints. "Good Lord," he said, "and I wear a ten and a half."

Edie Marsh asked what kind of wild animal would make such a track. Fred Dove said it looked big enough to be a lion or a bear. "But I'm not a hunter," he added.

She said, "Can I come stay with you?"

"At the Ramada?"

"What—they don't allow women?"

-"Edie, we shouldn't be seen together. Not if we're going through with this."

"You expect me to stay out here alone?"

"Look, I'm sorry about your dogs—"

"They weren't my goddamn dogs."

"Please, Edie."

With his round eyeglasses, Fred Dove reminded her of a serious young English teacher she'd known in high school. The man had worn Bass loafers with no socks and was obsessed with T. S. Eliot. Edie Marsh had screwed the guy twice in the faculty lounge, but he'd still given her a C on her final exam because (he claimed) she'd missed the whole point of "J. Alfred Prufrock." The experience had left Edie Marsh with a deep-seated mistrust of studious-looking men.

She said, "What do you mean, *if* we go through with this? We made a deal."

"Yes," Fred Dove said. "Yes, we did."

As he followed her into the house, she asked, "How soon can you get this done?"

"Well, I could file the claim this week—"

"Hundred percent loss?"

"That's right," replied the insurance man.

"A hundred and forty-one grand. Seventy-one for me, seventy for you."

"Right." For somebody about to score the windfall of a lifetime, Fred Dove was subdued. "My concern, again, is Mister Torres—"

"Like I told you last night, Tony's in some kind of serious jam. I doubt he'll be back."

"But didn't you say Mrs Torres, the real Mrs Torres, might be returning to Miami—"

"That's why you need to hurry," Edie Marsh said. "Tell the home office it's an emergency."

The insurance man pursed his lips. "Edie, every case is an emergency. There's been a hurricane, for God's sake."

Impassively, she watched him finish dressing. He spent five full minutes trying to smooth the wrinkles out of his sex-rumpled Dockers. When he asked to borrow an iron, Edie reminded him there was no electricity.

"How about taking me to breakfast," she said.

"I'm already late for an appointment in Cutler Ridge. Some

poor old man's got a Pontiac on top of his house." Fred Dove kissed Edie on the forehead and followed up with the obligatory morning-after hug. "I'll be back tonight. Is nine all right?"

"Fine," she said. Tonight he'd undoubtedly bring condoms—one more comic speed bump on the highway to passion. She made a mental note to haul one of Tony's mattresses out in the sun to dry; another strenuous session in the BarcaLounger might put poor Freddie in traction.

"Bring the claim forms," she told him. "I want to see everything."

He jotted a reminder on his clipboard and slipped it into the briefcase.

"Oh yeah," Edie said. "I also need a couple gallons of gas from your car."

Fred Dove looked puzzled.

"For the generator," she explained. "A hot bath would be nice . . . since you won't let me share your tub at the Ramada."

"Oh, Edie—"

"And maybe a few bucks for groceries."

She softened up when the insurance man took out his wallet. "That's my boy." She kissed him on the neck and ended it with a little bite, just to prime the pump.

"I'm scared," he said.

"Don't be, sugar. It's a breeze." She took two twenties and sent him on his way.

TEN

On the drive to the morgue, Augustine and Bonnie Lamb heard a news report about a fourteen-foot reticulated python that had turned up in the salad bar of a fast-food joint in Perrine.

"One of yours?" Bonnie asked.

"I'm wondering." It was impossible to know if the snake had belonged to Augustine's dead uncle; Felix Mojack's handwritten inventory was vague on details.

"He had a couple big ones," Augustine said, "but I never measured the damn things."

Bonnie said, "I hope they didn't kill it."

"Me, too." He was pleased that she was concerned for the welfare of a primeval reptile. Not all women would be.

"They could give it to a zoo," she said.

"Or turn it loose at the county commission."

"You're bad."

"I know," Augustine said. As legal custodian of the menagerie, he felt a twinge of responsibility for Bonnie Lamb's predicament. Without a monkey to chase, her husband probably wouldn't have been abducted. Maybe the culprit was one of Uncle Felix's rhesuses, maybe not.

Without reproach, Bonnie asked: "What'll you do if one of those critters kills a person?"

"Pray it was somebody who deserved it."

Bonnie was appalled. Augustine said, "I don't know what else to do, short of a safari. You know how big the Everglades are?"

They rode in silence for a while before Bonnie said: "You're right. They're free, and that's how it ought to be."

"I don't know how anything *ought* to be, but I know how it is. Hell, those cougars could be in Key Largo by now."

Bonnie Lamb smiled sadly. "I wish I was."

Before entering the chill of the Medical Examiner's Office, she put on a baggy ski sweater that Augustine had brought for the occasion. This time there were no preliminaries to the viewing. The same young coroner led them directly to the autopsy room, where the newly murdered John Doe was the center of attention. The corpse was surrounded by detectives, uniformed cops, and an unenthusiastic contingent of University of Miami medical students. They parted for Augustine and Bonnie Lamb.

A ruddy, gray-haired man in a lab coat stood at the head of the steel table. He nodded cordially and took a step back. Holding her breath, Bonnie lowered her eyes to the corpse. The man was potbellied and balding. His olive skin was covered from shoulder to toe with sprouts of shiny black hair. In the center of the chest was a gaping, raspberry-hued wound. His throat was a necklace of bruises that looked very much like purple fingerprints.

"It's not my husband," Bonnie Lamb said.

Augustine led her away. A tall black policeman followed.

"Mrs Lamb?"

Bonnie, on autopilot, kept moving.

"Mrs Lamb, I need to speak with you."

She turned. The policeman was broadly muscled and walked with a hitch in his right leg. He wore a state trooper's uniform and held a tan Stetson in his huge hands. He seemed as relieved to be out of the autopsy room as they were.

Augustine asked if there was a problem. The trooper suggested they go someplace to talk.

"About what?" Bonnie asked.

"Your husband's disappearance. I'm running down a few leads, that's all." The trooper's manner was uncharacteristically informal for a cop in uniform. He said, "Just a few questions, folks. I promise."

Augustine didn't understand why the Highway Patrol would

take an interest in a missing-person case. He said, "She's already spoken to the FBI."

"This won't take long."

Bonnie said, "If you've got something new, anything, I'd like to hear about it."

"I know a great Italian place," the trooper said.

Augustine saw that Bonnie had made up her mind. "Is this official business?" he asked the trooper.

"Extremely unofficial." Jim Tile put on his hat. "Let's go eat," he said.

In the mid-1970s, a man named Clinton Tyree ran for governor of Florida. On paper he seemed an ideal candidate, a bold fresh voice in a cynical age. He was a rare native son, handsome, strapping; an ex-college football sensation and a decorated veteran of Vietnam. On the campaign trail, he could talk smart in Palm Beach or play dumb in the Panhandle. The media were dazzled because he spoke in complete sentences, spontaneously and without index cards. Best of all, his private past was uncluttered by slimy business deals, the intricacies of which taxed the comprehension of journalists and readers alike.

Clinton Tyree's only political liability was a five-year stint as an English professor at the University of Florida, a job that historically would have marked a candidate as too thoughtful, educated and broad-minded for state office. But, in a stunning upset, voters forgave Clint Tyree's erudition and elected him governor.

Naively the Tallahassee establishment welcomed the new chief executive. The barkers, pimps and fast-change artists who controlled the legislature assumed that, like most of his predecessors, Clinton Tyree dutifully would slide into the program. He was, after all, a local boy. Surely he understood how things worked.

But behind the governor's movie-star smile was the incendiary fervor of a terrorist. He brought with him to the capital a passion so deep and untainted that it was utterly unrecognizable to other politicians; they quickly decided that Clinton Tyree was a crazy man. In his first post-election interview, he told *The New York Times* that Florida was being destroyed by unbridled growth, overdevelopment and pollution, and that the stinking root of those evils was greed. By way of illustration, he cited the Speaker of the Florida House for possessing "the ethics of an intestinal bacterium," merely because the man had accepted a free trip to Bangkok from a Miami Beach high-rise developer. Later Tyree went on radio urging visitors and would-be residents to stay out of the Sunshine State for a few years, "so we can gather our senses." He announced a goal of Negative Population Growth and proposed generous tax incentives for counties that significantly reduced human density. Tyree couldn't have caused more of an uproar had he been preaching satanism to preschoolers.

The view that the new governor was mentally unstable was reinforced by his refusal to accept bribes. More appallingly, he shared the details of these illicit offers with agents of the Federal Bureau of Investigation. In that manner, one of the state's richest and most politically connected land developers got shut down, indicted and convicted of corruption. Clearly Clinton Tyree was a menace.

No previous governor had dared to disrupt the business of paving Florida. For seventy glorious years, the state had shriveled safely in the grip of those most efficient at looting its resources. Suddenly this reckless young upstart was inciting folks like a damn communist. Save the rivers. Save the coasts. Save the Big Cypress. Where would it end? *Time* magazine put him on the cover. David Brinkley called him a New Populist. The National Audubon Society gave him a frigging medal. . . .

One night, in a curtained booth of a restaurant called the Silver Slipper, a pact was made to stop the madman. His heroics in Southeast Asia made him immune to customary smear tactics, so the only safe alternative was to neutralize him politically. It was a straightforward plan: No matter what the new governor wanted, the legislature and cabinet would do the opposite—a voting pattern to be ensured by magnanimous contributions from bankers, contractors, real estate brokers, hoteliers, farm conglomerates and other special-interest groups that were experiencing philosophical differences with Clinton Tyree.

The strategy succeeded. Even the governor's fellow Democrats felt sufficiently threatened by his reforms to abandon him without compunction. Once it became clear to Clint Tyree that the freeze was on, he slowly began to come apart. Each defeat in the legislature hit him like a sledge. His public appearances were marked by bilious oratory and dark mutterings. He lost weight and let his hair grow. During one cryptic press conference, he chose not to wear a shirt. He wrote acidulous letters on official stationery, and gave interviews in which he quoted at length from Carl Jung, Henry Thoreau and David Crosby. One night the state trooper assigned to guard the governor found him creeping through a graveyard; Clinton Tyree explained his intention was to dig up the remains of the late Napoleon Bonaparte Broward, the governor who had first schemed to drain the Everglades. Tyree's idea was to distribute Governor Broward's bones as souvenirs to visitors in the capitol rotunda.

Meanwhile the ravaging of Florida continued unabated, as did the incoming stampede. A thousand fortune-seekers took up residence in the state every day, and there was nothing Clint Tyree could do about it.

So he quit, fled Tallahassee on a melancholy morning in the back of a state limousine, and melted into the tangled wilderness. In the history of Florida, no governor had ever before resigned; in fact, no elected officeholder had made such an abrupt or eccentric exit from public life. Journalists and authors hunted the missing Clinton Tyree but never caught up with him. He moved by night, fed off the road, and adopted the solitary existence of a swamp rattler. Those who encountered him knew him by the name of Skink, or simply "captain," a solemn hermitage interrupted by the occasional righteous arson, aggravated battery or highway sniping.

Only one man held the runaway governor's complete trust— the Highway Patrol trooper who had been assigned to guard him during the gubernatorial campaign and later had come to work at the governor's mansion; the same trooper who was driving the limousine on the day Clinton Tyree disappeared. It was he alone who knew the man's whereabouts, kept in touch and followed his movements; who was there to help when Clinton Tyree went around the bend, which he sometimes did. The trooper had been there soon after his friend lost an eye in a vicious beating; again after he shot up some rental cars in a roadside spree; again after he burned down an amusement park.

Some years were quieter than others.

"But he's been waiting for this hurricane," Jim Tile said, twirling a spoonful of spaghetti. "There's cause to be concerned."

Augustine said: "I've heard of this guy."

"Then you understand why I need to talk to Mrs Lamb."

"Mrs Lamb," Bonnie said, caustically, "can't believe what she's hearing. You think this lunatic's got Max?"

"An old lady in the neighborhood saw a man fitting the governor's description carrying a man fitting your husband's description. Over his shoulder. Buck naked." Jim Tile paused to allow Mrs Lamb to form a mental picture of the scene. He said, "I don't know about the lady's eyesight, but it's worth checking out. You mentioned a tape you made—the kidnapper's voice."

"It's back at the house," said Augustine.

"Would you mind if I listened to it?"

Bonnie said, "This is ludicrous, what you're saying—"

"Humor me," said Jim Tile.

Bonnie pushed away her plate of lasagna, half eaten. "What's your interest?"

"He's my friend. He's in trouble," the trooper said.

"All I care about is Max."

"They're both in danger."

Bonnie demanded to know about the fat man in the morgue. The trooper said he'd been strangled and impaled on a TV satellite dish. The motive didn't appear to be robbery.

"Did your 'friend' do that, too?"

"They're talking to some dumb goober from Alabama, but I don't know."

To Bonnie, it was all incredible. "You did say 'impaled'?"

"Yes, ma'am." The trooper didn't mention the mock crucifixion. Mrs Lamb was plenty upset already.

Through clenched teeth she said, "This place is insane."

Jim Tile was in full agreement. Tiredly he looked at Augustine. "I'm just tracking down a few leads."

"Come on back to the house. We'll play that tape for you."

Ira Jackson's intention had been to kill the mobile-home salesman and then drive home to New York and arrange his mother's funeral. To his dismay, the murder of Tony Torres left him restless and unfulfilled. Driving through the gutted hurricane zone, Ira Jackson realized what a pitifully insignificant little fuck Tony Torres had been. South Florida was crawling with guys who cheerfully sold death traps to widows. The evidence was plain: Ira Jackson knew shitty construction when he saw it, and he saw it everywhere. Homes in one subdivision came out of the storm with scarcely a shingle out of place; across the street, an equally high-priced development was obliterated, every house blown to pieces.

A goddamn disgrace, Ira Jackson thought. This was exactly the kind of thing that gave corruption a bad name. He recalled the cocky proclamation of Tony Torres: *Every home I've sold passed inspection.*

Undoubtedly it was true. Dade County's code inspectors were as culpable for the destruction as schmuck salesmen like Torres. To Ira Jackson's experienced eye, the substandard construction was too widespread to be explained by mere incompetence; a blind man would have red-tagged some of those cardboard subdivisions. Inspectors most certainly had been paid off with cash, booze, dope, broads, or all of the above. It happened in Brooklyn, too, but Brooklyn didn't get many hurricanes.

Ira Jackson angrily thought of the tie-downs that were supposed to anchor his late mother's double-wide trailer. Someone from the county should have noticed the rotted straps; someone should have examined the augers, to make sure they hadn't been sawed off. Ira Jackson wondered who that someone was, and how much he'd been bribed not to do his job.

He drove to the Metro building-and-zoning department to find out.

Snapper had sweated through his cheap suit. Mr Nathaniel Lewis was giving him a hard time about the deposit. Out in the truck, the phony roofers were drinking warm beer and arguing about sports.

"Four thousand down is totally out of line," Nathaniel Lewis was saying.

"All depends on how soon you want a roof. I figured you's in a hurry."

"Sure we're in a hurry. Just look at this place."

Snapper agreed that the house was in terrible shape; the Lewises had cut up plastic garbage bags and tacked them to the bare beams, to keep out the rain. "Look," said Snapper, "everybody's roof got blown away. Our phone's ringing off the hook. Four grand puts you top of the list. Priority One."

Nathaniel Lewis was sharper than Snapper preferred. "If your phone's ringin' off the hook, how is it you come knockin' on my door like some damn Jehovah. And how is it your crew's sittin' on their butts in the truck, if they's so much work to be done?"

"They're on a break," Snapper lied. "We're doing that duplex two blocks over. Save on gas money if we pick up a few more jobs in the neighborhood."

Lewis said, "Three down—and that's only if you start right away."

"We can handle that."

The crew ascended the skeleton of Lewis's roof. Snapper didn't have to tell the men to take their time; that came naturally. Avila had said it was important to make lots of noise, like legitimate roofers, so the black guys staged a truss-hammering contest, with the Latin guy as referee. The white crackhead was left to cut plywood for the decking.

Snapper waited in the cab of the truck, which smelled like stale Coors and marijuana. Mercifully the sky darkened after about an hour, and a hard thunderstorm broke loose. While the roofers scrambled to load the truck, Snapper told Nathaniel Lewis they'd return first thing in the morning. Lewis handed him a cashier's check for three thousand dollars. The check was made out to Fortress Roofing, Avila's bogus company. Snapper thought it was a very amusing name.

He got in the stolen Jeep Cherokee and headed south. The crew followed in the truck. Avila had advised Snapper to move around, don't stay in one area. A smart strategy, Snapper agreed. They made it to Cutler Ridge ahead of the weather. Snapper found an expensive ranch-style house sitting on two acres of pinelands. Half the roof had been torn off by the hurricane. A Land Rover and a black Infiniti were parked in the tiled driveway.

Jackpot, Snapper thought.

The lady of the house let him in. Her name was Whitmark, and she was frantic for shelter. She'd been scouting the rain clouds on the horizon, and the possibility of more flooding in the living room had sent her dashing to the medicine chest. The "roofing foreman" listened to Mrs Whitmark's woeful story:

The pile carpet already was ruined, as was Mr Whitmark's state-of-the-art stereo system, and of course mildew had claimed all the drapery, the linens and half her winter evening wardrobe; the Italian leather sofa and the cherry buffet had been moved to the west wing, but—

"We can start this afternoon," Snapper cut in, "but we need a deposit."

Mrs Whitmark asked how much. Snapper pulled a figure out of his head: seven thousand dollars.

"You take cash, I assume."

"Sure," Snapper said, trying to sound matter-of-fact, like all his customers had seven grand lying around in cookie jars.

Mrs Whitmark left Snapper alone while she went for the money. He raised his eyes to the immense hole in the ceiling. At that moment, a sunbeam broke through the bruised clouds, flooding the house with golden light.

Snapper shielded his eyes. Was this a sign?

When Mrs Whitmark returned, she was flanked by two blackand-silver German shepherds.

Snapper went rigid. "Mother of Christ," he murmured.

"My babies," said Mrs Whitmark, fondly. "We don't have a problem with looters. Do we, sugars?" She stroked the larger dog under its chin. On command, both of them sat at her feet. They cocked their heads and gazed expectantly at Snapper, who felt a spasm in his colon.

His hands trembled so severely that he was barely able to write up the contract. Mrs Whitmark asked what had happened to his face. "Did you fall off a roof?"

"No," he said curtly. "Bungee accident."

Mrs Whitmark gave him the cash in a scented pink envelope. "How soon can you start?"

Snapper promised that the crew would return in half an hour. "We'll need to pick up some lumber. It's a big place you've got here."

Mrs Whitmark and her guard dogs accompanied Snapper to the front door. He kept both hands jammed in his pockets, in case one of the vicious bastards lunged for him. Of course, if they were trained like police K-9s, they wouldn't bother with his hands. They'd go straight for the balls.

"Hurry," Mrs Whitmark said, scanning the clouds with dilated pupils. "I don't like the looks of this sky."

Snapper walked to the truck and gave the crew the bad news. "She didn't go for it. Says her husband's already got a roofer lined up for the job. Some company from Palm Beach, she said."

"Thank God," said one of the black guys, yawning. "I'm beat, boss. How about we call it a day?"

"Fine by me," said Snapper.

Jim Tile rewound the tape and played it again.

"*Honey, I've been kidnapped—*"

"*Abducted! Kidnapping implies ransom, Max. Don't fucking flatter yourself. . . .*"

Bonnie Lamb said, "Well?"

"It's him," the trooper said.

"You're sure?"

"*I love you, Bonnie. Max forgot to tell you, so I will. Bye now. . . .*"

"Oh yeah," said Jim Tile. He popped the cassette out of the tape deck.

Bonnie asked Augustine to call his agent friend at the FBI. Augustine said it wasn't such a hot idea.

The trooper agreed. "They'll never find him. They don't know where to look, they don't know how."

"But you do?"

"What will probably happen," Jim Tile said, "is the governor will keep your husband until he gets bored with him."

"Then what?" Bonnie demanded. "He kills him?"

"Not unless your husband tries something stupid."

Augustine thought: We might have a problem.

The trooper told Bonnie Lamb not to panic; the governor wasn't irrational. There were ways to track him, make contact, engage in productive dialogue.

Bonnie excused herself and went to take some aspirin. Augustine walked outside with the trooper. "The FBI won't touch this," Jim Tile said, keeping his voice low. "There's no ransom demand, no interstate travel. It's hard for her to understand."

Augustine observed that Max Lamb wasn't helping matters, calling New York to check on his advertising accounts. "Not exactly your typical victim," he said.

Jim Tile got in the car and placed his Stetson on the seat. "I'll get back with you soon. Meanwhile go easy with the lady."

Augustine said, "You don't think he's crazy, do you."

The trooper laughed. "Son, you heard the tape."

"Yeah. I don't think he's crazy, either."

"'Different' is the word. Seriously different." Jim Tile turned up the patrol car's radio to hear the latest hurricane dementia. The Highway Patrol dispatcher was directing troopers to the intersection of U.S. 1 and Kendall Drive, where a truck loaded with ice had overturned. A disturbance had erupted, and ambulances were on the way.

"Lord," Jim Tile said. "They're murdering each other over ice cubes." He sped off without saying good-bye.

Back in the house, Augustine was surprised to find Bonnie Lamb sitting next to the kitchen phone. At her elbow was a notepad upon which she had written several lines. He was struck by the elegance of her handwriting. Once, he'd dated a woman who dotted her *i*'s with perfect tiny circles; sometimes she drew happy faces inside the circles, sometimes she drew frowns. The woman had been a cheerleader for her college football team, and she couldn't get it out of her system.

Bonnie Lamb's handwriting bore no trace of retired cheerleader. "Directions," she replied, waving the paper.

"Where?"

"To see Max and this Skink person. They left directions on my machine."

She was excited. Augustine sat next to her. "What else did they say?"

"No police. No FBI. Max was very firm about it."

"And?"

"Four double-A batteries and a tape of *Exile on Main Street*. Dolby chrome oxide, whatever that means. And a bottle of pitted green olives, no pimientos."

"This would be the governor's shopping list?"

"Max hates green olives." Bonnie Lamb put her hand on Augustine's arm. "What do we do? You want to hear the message?"

"Let's go talk to them, if that's what they want."

"Bring your gun. I'm serious." Her eyes flashed. "We can kidnap Max from the kidnapper. Why not!"

"Settle down, please. When's the meeting?"

"Midnight tomorrow."

"Where?"

When she told him, he looked discouraged. "They'll never show. Not there."

"You're wrong," Bonnie Lamb said. "Where's that gun of yours?"

Augustine went to the living room and switched on the

television. He channel-surfed until he found a Monty Python rerun; a classic, John Cleese buying a dead parrot. It never failed to make Augustine laugh.

Bonnie sat beside him on the sofa. When the Monty Python sketch ended, he turned to her and said, "You don't know a damn thing about guns."

ELEVEN

Max Lamb awoke to these words: "You need a legacy."

He and Skink had bummed a ride in the back of a U-Haul truck. They were bucking down U.S. Highway One among two thousand cans of Campbell's broccoli cheese soup, which was being donated to hurricane victims by a Baptist church in Pascagoula, Mississippi. What the shipment lacked in variety it made up for in Christian goodwill.

"This," said the kidnapper, waving at the soup boxes, "is what people do for each other in times of catastrophe. They give help. You, on the other hand—"

"I said I was sorry."

"—you, Max, arrive with a video camera."

Max Lamb lit a cigaret. The governor had been in a rotten mood all day. First his favorite Stones tape broke, then the batteries crapped out in his Walkman.

Skink said, "The people who gave this soup, they went through Camille. Please assure me you know about Camille."

"Another hurricane?"

"A magnificent shitkicker of a hurricane. Max, I believe you're making progress."

The advertising man sucked apprehensively on the Bronco. He said, "You were talking about getting a boat."

Skink said, "Everyone ought to have a legacy. Something to be remembered for. Let's hear some of your slogans."

"Not right now."

"I never see TV anymore, but some commercials I remember." The kidnapper pointed at the canyon of red-and-white soup cans. " 'M'm, m'm good!' That was a classic, no?"

Unabashedly Max Lamb said, "You ever hear of Plum Crunchies? It was a breakfast cereal."

"A cereal," said Skink.

" 'You'll go plum loco for Plum Crunchies!' "

The kidnapper frowned. From his camo trousers he produced a small felt box of the type used by jewelry stores. He opened it and removed a scorpion, which he placed on his bare brown wrist. The scorpion raised its fat claws, pinching the air in confusion. Max stared incredulously. The skin on his neck heated beneath the shock collar. He drew up his legs, preparing to spring from the truck if Skink tossed the awful creature at him.

"This little sucker," Skink said, "is from Southeast Asia. Recognized him right away." With a pinkie finger, he stroked the scorpion until it arched its venomous stinger.

Max Lamb asked how a Vietnamese scorpion got all the way to Florida. Skink said it was probably smuggled by importers. "Then, when the hurricane struck, Mortimer here made a dash for it. I found him in the horse barn. Remember Larks? 'Show us your Larks!' "

"Barely." Max was a kid when the Lark campaign hit TV.

Skink said: "That's what I mean by legacy. Does anyone remember who thought up Larks? But the Marlboro man, Christ, that's the most successful ad campaign in history."

It was a fact. Max Lamb wondered how Skink knew. He noticed that the scorpion had become tangled in the gray-blond hair on the captain's arm.

"What are you going to do with it?" Max asked.

No answer. He tried another strategy. "Bonnie is deathly afraid of insects."

Skink scooped the scorpion into the palm of one hand. "This ain't no insect, Max. It's an arachnid."

"Bugs is what I meant, captain. She's terrified of all bugs." Max was speaking for himself. Icy needles of anxiety pricked at his arms and legs. He struggled to connect the kidnapper's scorpion sympathies with his views of the Marlboro man. What was the psychopath trying to say?

"Can she swim, your Bonnie? Then she'll be fine." The governor popped the scorpion in his cheek and swallowed with an audible gulp.

"Oh Jesus," said Max.

After a suitable pause, Skink opened his mouth. The scorpion was curled placidly on his tongue, its pincers at rest.

Max Lamb stubbed out the Bronco and urgently lit another. He leaned his head against a crate of soup cans and said a silent prayer: Dear God, don't let Bonnie say anything to piss this guy off.

Avila's career as a county inspector was unremarkable except for the six months when he was the target of a police investigation. The cops had infiltrated the building department with an under-cover man posing as a supervisor. The undercover man noticed, among a multitude of irregularities, that Avila was inspecting new roofs at a superhuman rate of about sixty a day, without benefit of a ladder. A surveillance team was put in place and observed that Avila never bothered to climb the roofs he was assigned to inspect. In fact, he seldom left his vehicle except for a regular two-hour buffet lunch at a nudie bar in Hialeah. It was noted that Avila drove past construction sites at such an impractical speed that contractors frequently had to jog after his truck in order to deliver their illicit gratuities. The transactions were captured with crystal clarity on videotape.

When the police investigation became public, a grand jury convened to ponder the filing of felony indictments. To give the appearance of concern, the building-and-zoning department reas-signed Avila and several of his crooked colleagues to duties that were considered low-profile and menial, a status confirmed by the relatively puny size of the bribes. In Avila's case, he was relegated to inspecting mobile homes. It was a job for which he had no qualifications or enthusiasm. Trailers were trailers; to Avila, nothing but glorified sardine cans. The notion of "code enforcement" at a trailer park was oxymoronic; none of them, Avila knew, would survive the feeblest of hurricanes. Why go to the trouble of tying the damn things down?

But he made a show of logging inspections, taking what modest graft the mobile-home dealers would toss his way—fifty bucks here and there, a bottle of Old Grand-dad, porno tapes, an eight-ball of coke. Avila wasn't worried about police surveillance on his beat. Authorities were concerned with protecting the upwardly mobile middle-class home buyer; nobody gave a shit what happened to people who bought trailers.

Except men like Ira Jackson, whose mother lived in one.

With the exception of the bus depot in downtown Guatemala City, the Dade County building department was the most disorganized and institutionally indifferent place that Ira Jackson had ever seen. It took ninety minutes to find a clerk who admitted to fluency in English, and another hour to get his hands on the documents for the Suncoast Leisure Village trailer park. Under the circumstances, Ira Jackson was mildly surprised that the file still existed. From what he saw, others were vanishing by the carload. Realizing the hurricane would bring scandal to the construction industry, developers, builders and compromised inspectors were taking bold steps to obscure their own roles in the crimes. As Ira Jackson elbowed his way to an empty chair, he recognized—amid the truly aggrieved—faces of the copiously guilty: brows damp, lips tight, eyes pinched and fretful. They were men who feared the prospect of public exposure, massive lawsuits or prison.

If only it were true, thought Ira Jackson. Experience had taught him otherwise. Bozos who rob liquor stores go to jail, not rich guys and bureaucrats and civil servants.

Ira Jackson thumbed through the trailer-court records until he found the name of the man who had botched the inspection of his mother's double-wide. He fought his way to the file counter and cornered a harried-looking clerk, who informed him that Mr Avila no longer was employed by Dade County.

Why not? Ira Jackson asked.

Because he quit, the clerk explained; started his own business. Since Ira Jackson was already agitated, the clerk saw no point in revealing that Avila's resignation was part of a plea-bargain agreement with the State Attorney's Office. That was a private matter that Mr Avila himself should share with Mr Jackson, if he so desired.

Ira Jackson said, "You got a current address, right?"

The clerk said it was beyond his authority to divulge that information. Ira Jackson reached across the counter and rested his hand, very lightly, on the young man's shoulder. "Listen to me, Paco," he said. "I'll come to your home. I'll harm your family. You understand? Even your pets."

The clerk nodded. "Be right back," he said.

Snapper was more annoyed than afraid when he saw the flashing blue lights in the rearview. He'd figured the Jeep Cherokee was already hot when he swiped it from the gangster rappers; he didn't figure the cops would be looking for it so soon. Not with all the hurricane emergencies.

Pulling to the side of the road, he wondered if Baby Raper had blabbed when he got to the hospital. No doubt the kid was ticked when Snapper retrofitted that compact disc up his ass, like a big shiny suppository.

But why would the cops care about *that*? Snapper thought: Maybe it's got nothing do with the gangster rapper or the stolen Jeep. Maybe it's just my driving.

The cop who stopped him was a female Highway Patrol trooper. She had pleasant features and pretty pale-blue eyes that reminded Snapper of a girl he'd tried to date back in Atlanta, some sort of turbocharged Catholic. The lady trooper's dark hair was pulled up under her hat, and she wore a gold wedding band that cried out for pawning. The holster appeared oversized and out of place on her hip. She shined a light in the Jeep and asked to see Snapper's driver's license.

"I left my wallet at home."

"No identification?"

"'Fraid not." For effect, he patted his pockets.

"What's your name?"

"Boris," said Snapper. He loved Boris and Natasha, from the old Rocky and Bullwinkle TV show.

"Boris what?" the trooper asked.

Snapper couldn't spell the cartoon Boris's last name, so he said, "Smith. Boris J. Smith."

The trooper's pale eyes seemed to darken, and the tone of her voice flattened. "Sir, I clocked you at seventy in a forty-five-mile-per-hour zone."

"No kidding." Snapper felt relieved. A stupid speeding ticket! Maybe she'd write him up without running the tag.

The trooper said: "It's against the law to operate a motor vehicle in Florida without a valid license. You're aware of that."

OK, Snapper thought, *two* tickets. Big fucking deal. But he noticed she wasn't calling him "Mister Smith."

"You're also aware that it's illegal to give false information to a law-enforcement officer?"

"Sure." Snapper cursed to himself The bitch wasn't buying it.

"Stay in your vehicle, please."

In the mirror, Snapper watched the flashlight bobbing as the trooper walked back to her car. Undoubtedly she intended to call in the license plate on the Cherokee. Snapper felt his shoulders tighten. He had as much chance of explaining the stolen vehicle as he did explaining the seven thousand dollars in his suit.

He saw two choices. The first was to flee the scene, which was guaranteed to result in a chase, a messy crash and an arrest on numerous nonbondable felonies.

The second choice was to stop the lady trooper before she got on the radio. Which is what he did.

Some cons wouldn't hit a woman, but Snapper was neutral on the issue. A cop was a cop. The trooper spotted him coming but, encumbered by the steering wheel, had difficulty pulling that enormous Smith & Wesson out of its holster. She managed to get the snap undone, but by then it was good-night-nurse.

He took the flashlight, the gun and the wedding band, and left the trooper lying unconscious by the side of the road. Speeding away, he noticed a smudge of color on one of his knuckles.

Makeup, it looked like.

He didn't feel shame, regret or anything much at all.

Edie Marsh was beginning to appreciate the suffering of real hurricane victims. It rained three times during the day, leaving dirty puddles throughout the Torres house. The carpets squished underfoot, green frogs vaulted from wall to wall, and mosquitoes were hatching in one of the bathroom sinks. Even after the cloudbursts stopped, the exposed beams dripped for hours. Combined with the cacophony of neighborhood hammers and chain saws, the racket was driving Edie nuts. She walked outside and called halfheartedly for the missing dachshunds, an exercise that she abandoned swiftly after spying a fat brown snake. Edie's scream attracted a neighbor, who took a broom and scared the snake away. Then he inquired about Tony and Neria.

They're out of town, said Edie Marsh. They asked me to watch the place.

And you are . . . ?

A cousin, Edie replied, knowing she looked about as Latin as Goldie Hawn.

As soon as the neighbor left, Edie hurried into the house and stationed herself in Tony's recliner. She turned up the radio and laid the crowbar within arm's reach. When darkness came, the hammering and sawing stopped, and the noises of the neighborhood changed to bawling babies, scratchy radios and slamming doors. Edie began worrying about looters and rapists and the unknown predator that had slurped poor Donald and Marla like Tic Tacs. By the time Fred Dove showed up, she was a basket of nerves.

The insurance man brought a corsage of gardenias. Like he was picking her up for the prom!

Edie Marsh said, "You can't be serious."

"What's wrong? I couldn't find roses."

"Fred, I can't stay here anymore. Get me a room."

"Everything's going to be fine. Look, I brought wine."

"Fred?"

"And scented candles."

"Yo, Fred!"

"What?"

Edie steered him to a soggy sofa and sat him down. "Fred, this is business, not romance."

He looked hurt.

"Sweetie," she said, "we had sexual intercourse exactly one time. Don't worry, there's every chance in the world we'll do it again. But it isn't love and it isn't passion. It's a financial partnership."

The insurance man said, "You seduced me."

"Of course I did. And you were fantastic."

As Fred Dove's ego reinflated, his posture improved.

"But no more flowers," Edie scolded, "and no more wine. Just get me a room at the damn Ramada, OK?"

The insurance man solemnly agreed. "First thing tomorrow."

"Look at this place, honey. No roof. No glass in the windows. It's not a house, it's a damn cabana!"

"You're right, Edie, you can't stay here. I'll rejigger the expense account."

She rolled her eyes. "Fred, don't be so anal. We're about to rip off your employer for a hundred and forty-one thousand bucks, and you're pitching a hissy fit over a sixty-dollar motel room. Think about it."

"Please don't get angry."

"You've got the claim papers?"

"Right here."

After scanning the figures, Edie Marsh felt better. She plucked the gardenias from the corsage and arranged them in a coffeepot, which was full of lukewarm rainwater. She opened the bottle of Chablis, and they toasted to a successful venture. After four glasses, Edie felt comfortable enough to ask what the insurance man planned to do with his cut of the money.

"Buy a boat," Fred Dove said, "and sail to Bimini."

"What about wifey?"

"Who?" said Fred Dove. They laughed together. Then he asked Edie Marsh how she was going to spend her seventy-one grand.

"Hyannis Port," she said, without elaboration.

Later, when the Chablis was gone, Edie dragged a dry mattress into the living room, turned off the lightbulb and lit one of Fred Dove's candles, which smelled like malted milk. As Edie took off her clothes, she heard Fred groping inside his briefcase for a rubber. He tore the foil with his teeth and pressed the package into her hand.

Even when she was sober, condoms made Edie laugh. When drunk she found them downright hilarious, the silliest contraptions imaginable. For tonight Fred Dove had boldly chosen a red one, and Edie was no help whatsoever in putting it on. Neither, for that matter, was Fred. Edie's tittering had pretty well shattered the mood, undoing all the good work of the wine.

Flat on his back, the insurance man turned his head away. Edie Marsh slapped his legs apart and knelt between them. "Don't you quit on me," she scolded. "Pay attention, sweetie. Come on." Firmly she took hold of him.

"Could you just—?"

"No." It was always bad form to giggle in the middle of a blow job, and Fred Dove was the sort who'd never recover, emotionally. "Focus," she instructed him. "Remember how good it was last night."

Edie had gotten the condom partially deployed when she heard the electric generator cut off. Out of fuel, she figured. It could wait; Fred Jr was showing signs of life.

She heard a soft click, and suddenly the insurance man's festively crowned penis was illuminated in a circle of bright light. Edie Marsh let go and sat upright. Fred Dove, his eyes shut tightly in concentration, said, "Don't stop now."

In the front doorway stood a man with a powerful flashlight.

"Candles," he said. "That's real fuckin' cozy."

Fred Dove's chest stopped moving, and one hand fumbled for his eyeglasses. Edie Marsh got up and folded her arms across her breasts. She said, "Thanks for knocking, asshole."

"I came back for my car." Snapper played the light up and down her body.

"It's in the driveway, right where you left it."

"What's the hurry," said Snapper, stepping into the house.

Bonnie Lamb went to Augustine's room at one-thirty in the morning. She climbed under the sheets without brushing against him even slightly. It wasn't easy, in a twin bed.

She whispered, "Are you sleeping?"

"Like a log."

"Sorry."

He rolled over to face her. "You need a pillow?"

"I need a hug."

"Bad idea."

"Why?"

"I'm slightly on the naked side. I wasn't expecting company."

"Apology number two," she said.

"Close your eyes, Mrs Lamb." He got up and pulled on a pair of loose khakis. No shirt, she observed, unalarmed. He slipped under the covers and held her. His skin was warm and smooth against her cheek, and when he moved she felt a taut, shifting wedge of muscle. Max's physical topography was entirely different, but Bonnie pushed the thought from her mind. It wasn't fair to compare hugging prowess. Not now.

She asked Augustine if he'd ever been married. He said no.

"Engaged?"

"Three times."

Bonnie raised her head. "You're kidding."

"Unfortunately not." In the artificial twilight, Augustine saw she was smiling. "This amuses you?"

"Intrigues me," she said. "Three times?"

"They all came to their senses."

"We're talking about three different women. No repeats?"

"Correct," said Augustine.

"I've got to ask what happened. You don't have to answer, but I've got to ask."

"Well, the first one married a successful personal-injury lawyer—he's doing class-action breast-implant litigation; the second one started an architecture firm and is currently a mistress to a Venezuelan cabinet minister; and the third one is starring on a popular Cuban soap opera—she plays Miriam, the jealous schizophrenic. So I would say," Augustine concluded, "that each of them made a wise decision by ending our relationship."

Bonnie Lamb said, "I bet you let them keep the engagement rings."

"Hey, it's only money."

"And you still watch the soap opera, don't you?"

"She's quite good in it. Very convincing."

Bonnie said, "What an unusual guy."

"You feeling better? My personal problems always seem to cheer people up."

She put her head down. "I'm worried about tomorrow, about seeing Max again."

Augustine told her it was normal to be nervous. "I'm a little antsy myself."

"Will you bring the gun?"

"Let's play it by ear." He seriously doubted if the governor would appear, much less deliver Bonnie's husband.

"Are you scared?" When she spoke, he could feel her soft breath on his chest.

"Restless," he said, "not scared."

"Hey."

"Hey what?"

"You getting excited?"

Augustine shifted in embarrassment. What did she expect? He said, "My turn to apologize."

But she didn't move. So he took a slow quiet breath and tried to focus on something else . . . say, Uncle Felix's fugitive monkeys. How far had they scattered? How were they coping with freedom?

Augustine's self-imposed pondering was interrupted when Bonnie Lamb said: "What if Max is different now? Maybe something's happened to him."

Augustine thought: Something's happened, all right. You can damn sure bet on it.

But what he told Bonnie was: "Your husband's hanging in there. You wait and see."

TWELVE

Skink said, "Care for some toad?"

The shock collar had done its job; Max Lamb was unconditionally conditioned. If the captain wanted him to smoke toad, he would smoke toad.

"It's an offer, not a command," Skink said, by way of clarification.

"Then no, thanks."

Max Lamb squinted into the warm salty night. Somewhere out there, Bonnie was searching. Max was neither as anxious nor as hopeful as he should have been, and he wondered why; his reaction to practically every circumstance was muted, as if key brain synapses had been cauterized by the ordeal of the kidnapping. For instance, he had failed to raise even a meek objection at the Key Biscayne golf course, where they'd stopped to free the Asian scorpion. Skink had tenderly deposited the venomous bug in the cup on the eighteenth green. "The mayor's favorite course," he'd explained. "Call me an optimist." Max had stood by wordlessly.

Now they were on a wooden stilt house in the middle of the bay. Skink dangled his long legs off the end of a dock, which was twisted and buckled like a Chinese parade dragon. The hurricane had sucked the wooden pilings from their holes. Most of the other stilt houses were shorn at the stems, but this one had outlasted the storm, though barely. It lurched and creaked in the thickish breeze; Max Lamb suspected it was sinking with the tide. Skink said the house belonged to a man who'd retired on disability from the State

Attorney's Office. The man recently had married a beautiful twelve-string guitarist and moved to the island of Exuma.

Under a swinging lantern, Skink lighted another exotic-smelling joint; marijuana and French onion soup, thought Max Lamb. Something strong and cheesy.

"The toad itself is toxic," Skink explained. "*Bufo marinus.* A South American import—overran the local species. Sound familiar?" He took a long sibilant drag. "The glands of Señor Bufo perspire a milky sap that can kill a full-grown Doberman in six minutes flat."

To Max, it didn't sound like a substance that one should be inhaling.

"There's a special process," Skink said, "of extraction." He took another huge hit.

"What does it do, this toad sap?"

"Nothing. Everything. What all good drugs do, I suppose. Psychoneurotic roulette." Skink's chin dropped to his chest. His good eye fluttered and closed. His breathing rose to a startling volume; the exhalations sounded like the brakes of a subway train. For fifteen minutes Max Lamb didn't make a move; the notion to escape never occurred to him, such was the Pavlovian influence of the collar.

In the interval of enforced suspension, Max's thoughts drifted to Bill Knapp up at Rodale. The scheming viper undoubtedly had his sights on Max's corner office, with its partially obstructed but nonetheless energizing view of Madison Avenue. Each day lost to the ambivalent kidnapper was a potential day of advancement for Billy the Backstabber; Max Lamb was burning to return to the agency and crush the devious little fucker's ambitions. Brutal humiliation was called for, and Max hoped he was up to the task. Darkly he imagined Billy Knapp a jobless, wifeless, homeless, toothless wretch, hunched over a can of Sterno in a wintry alley, sucking on a moist spliff laced with poisonous toad sweat . . .

When Skink snapped awake, he coughed hard and flipped the butt of the dead joint into the storm-silted water. Not far from the house, the broken mast of a submerged sailboat protruded from the waves. Skink pointed at the ghostly wreck but said nothing. His leathery finger stayed in the air for an exceptionally long time.

"Tell me," he said to Max Lamb, "the most breathtaking place you've ever seen."

"Yellowstone Park. We took a bus tour."

"Good God."

"So what?"

"Outside Yellowstone they've got a grizzly-bear theme park. Did you go? I mean, some truly sad cases—no claws, no testicles. They're about as wild as goddamn hamsters, but tourists line up to see 'em. Deballed grizzly bears!"

Rapidly Skink shook his head back and forth, as if trying to roust a bumblebee from his ear. Max Lamb wasn't sure how the conversation had gone so far astray. He did not share the madman's compassion for the altered grizzly bears; removing the claws seemed an entirely sensible procedure, liability-wise, for a public amusement park. But Max knew there was no percentage in arguing. He remained quiet as Skink withdrew into a heap on the planks of the spavined deck. The kidnapper trembled and heaved and cried out names that Max Lamb didn't recognize. A half hour later he was up, scouting the starlit horizons.

"You all right?" Max asked.

Skink nodded soberly. "The down side of toad. I do apologize."

"Are you sure Bonnie can find us out here?"

"Why in the name of God would you marry a woman who can't follow simple directions."

"But it's so dark—"

The trip to Stiltsville had frightened Max Lamb beyond exclamation—full throttle, no running lights, a wet nasty chop in an open skiff. Infinitely more harrowing than the airboat. The hurricane had turned the bay into a spectral gauntlet of sunken yachts, trawlers, cabin cruisers and runabouts. On the way out, Skink had removed his glass eye and pressed it, for safekeeping, into the palm of Max's right hand. Max had clenched it as if it were the Hope diamond.

"Your wife," Skink was saying, "will surely hook up with somebody who knows the way."

"I could use a cigaret. Please, captain."

Skink groped in his coat until he came up with a fresh pack. He tossed it, along with a lighter, to his captive.

Max Lamb was embarrassed that he'd so quickly become hooked on the infamously harsh Broncos. Around the agency they were jokingly known as Bronchials, such was their killer reputation with anti-smoking zealots. Max attributed his hazardous new habit to severe stress, not a weakness of character. In the advertising business it was essential to remain immune from the base appetites that tyrannized the average consumer.

Skink said: "What else have you to show for yourself?"

"I'm not sure what you mean."

"Slogans, tiger. Besides the Plum Crispies."

"Crunchies," said Max, tightly.

The dock shimmied as Skink rose to his feet. Max braced himself against a half-rotted beam. There was nowhere to go; the old man who ferried them across the bay had snatched Skink's fifty dollars and hastily aimed the skiff back toward the mainland.

Skink swung the lantern around and around his head. Caught in the erratic strobe, Max said, "All right, captain, here's one: 'That fresh good-morning feeling, all day long.'"

"Product name?"

"Intimate Mist."

"No!" The lantern hissed as Skink put it down.

Max tried not to sound defensive. "It's a feminine hygiene item. Very popular."

"The raspberry rinse! Sweet Jesus, I thought you were joking. This is the sum of your life achievements—*douche* jingles?"

"No," Max snapped. "Soft drinks, gasoline additives, laser copiers—I've worked on plenty of accounts." He wondered what had impelled him to mention the Intimate Mist campaign. Was it an unconscious act of masochism, or carelessness caused by fatigue?

Skink sat heavily on the porch, which was canted at an alarming angle toward the bay. "I do hear a boat," he said.

Max stared curiously across the water. He heard nothing but the slap of waves and the scattered piping of seagulls. He asked, "What happens now?"

There was no reply. Max Lamb saw, in the yellow flicker of the lantern, a smile cross the crazy man's face.

"You seriously don't want any ransom?"

"I didn't say that. *Money* is what I don't want."

"Then what?" Max flicked his cigaret into the water. "Tell me what the hell it's all about. I'm sick of this game, I really am!"

Skink was amused by the display of anger. Maybe there was hope for the precious little bastard. "What I want," he said to Max Lamb, "is to spend some time with your wife. She intrigues me."

"In what way?"

"Clinically. Anthropologically. What in the world does she see in you? How do you two fit?" Skink gave a mischievous wink. "I like mysteries."

"If you touch her—"

"What a brave young stud!"

Max Lamb took two steps toward the madman, but froze when Skink raised a hand to his own throat. *The collar!* Max felt a hot sizzle shoot from his scalp down the length of his spine. Instantly he foresaw himself hopping like a puppet. Had he known that the battery in the Tri-Tronics remote control had been dead for the past six hours, it wouldn't have softened his reaction. He was a slave to his subconscious. He had come to understand that the anticipation of pain was more immobilizing than the pain itself—though the knowledge didn't help him.

When Max settled down, Skink assured him he had no carnal interest in his wife. "Christ, I'm not trying to get laid; I'm trying to figure out man's place in the food chain." His long arms swept an arc across the stars. "A riddle of the times, Tourist Boy. Five thousand years ago we're doodling on the walls of caves. Today we're writing odes to fruit-flavored douche."

"It's a job," Max Lamb replied petulantly. "Get over it."

Skink yawned like a gorged hyena. "That's a damn big engine

coming. I hope your Bonnie wasn't foolish enough to call the police."

"I warned her not to."

Skink went on: "My opinion about your wife will be shaped by how she handles this situation. Whom she brings. Her attitude. Her composure."

Max Lamb asked Skink if he had a gun. Skink clicked his tongue against his front teeth. "See the running lights?"

"No."

"Toward Key Biscayne. Over there."

"Oh, yeah."

"Two engines, it sounds like. I'm guessing twin Mercs."

Somebody aboard the boat had a powerful spotlight. It swept back and forth across the flats of Stiltsville. As the craft drew nearer, the white light settled on the porch of the stilt house. Skink seemed unconcerned.

He began to remove toads from his pockets; gray, jowly, scowling, lump-covered toads, some as large as Idaho potatoes. Max Lamb counted eleven. Skink lined them up side by side at his feet. Max had nothing to add to the scenario, perhaps it was all a dream, beginning with the mangy hurricane monkey, and soon he'd awaken in bed with Bonnie. . . .

The pudgy Bufo toads began to squirm and huff and pee. Skink rebuked them with a murmur. When the beam of the speedboat's spotlight hit them, the toads blinked their moist globular eyes and jumped toward it. One by one they leaped off the dock and plopped into the water. Skink hooted mirthfully. "South, boys! To Havana, San Juan, wherever the hell you came from!"

Max watched the toads disappear; some kicked for the depths, others bobbed on the foamy crests of waves. Max didn't know what would happen to them, nor did he care. They were just ugly toads, and barracudas could devour them, as far as he was concerned. His only interest was in drawing a lesson from the episode, one that might be employed to handle the cyclopean kidnapper.

But Skink already seemed to have forgotten about the Bufos.

Once more he was rhapsodizing about the hurricane. "Look at Cape Florida, every last tree flattened—forest to moonscape in thirty blessed minutes!"

"The boat—"

"You ponder that."

"It's flashing a light at us—"

"The gorgeous fury inside that storm. And you with your video camera." Skink sighed disappointedly. "'Sin is a thing that writes itself across a man's face.' Oscar Wilde. I don't expect you've read him."

Max's silence affirmed it.

"Well, I've been waiting," said Skink, "to see it written across your face. Sin."

"What I did was harmless, OK? Maybe a bit insensitive, but harmless. You've made your point, captain. Let me go now."

The speedboat was close enough to see it was metallic blue with a white jagged stripe, like a lightning bolt, along the hull. Two figures were visible at the console.

"There she is," said Max.

"And no cops." Skink waved the boat in.

One of the figures moved to the bow and tossed a rope. Skink caught it and tied off. As soon as the rope came tight, the twin outboards went quiet. The current nudged the stern of the boat against the pilings, into the lantern's penumbra.

Max Lamb saw that it was Bonnie on the bow. When he called her name, she stepped to the dock and hugged him in a nurselike fashion, consoling him as if he were a toddler with a skinned knee. Max received the attention with manly reserve; he was conscious of being watched not only by his captor but by Bonnie's male escort.

Skink smiled at the reunion scene, and slipped back into the shadows of the stilt house. The driver of the boat made no move to get out. He was young and broad-shouldered, and comfortable on the open water. He wore a pale-blue pullover, cutoffs and no shoes. He seemed unaffected by navigating a pitch-black bay mined with overturned hulls and floating timbers.

From the darkness, Skink asked the young man for his name.

"Augustine," he answered.

"You have the ransom?"

"Sure do."

Bonnie Lamb said: "Don't worry, he's not the police."

"I can see that," came Skink's voice.

The boat driver stepped to the gunwale. He handed Bonnie a shopping bag, which she gave to her husband, who handed it to the kidnapper in the shadows.

Max Lamb said: "Bonnie, honey, the captain wants to talk to you. Then he'll let me go."

"I'm considering it," Skink said.

"Talk to me about what?"

The driver of the boat reached inside the console and came out with a can of beer. He took a swallow and leaned one hip against the steering wheel.

Bonnie Lamb asked her husband: "What's that on your neck?" It looked like some appalling implement of bondage; she'd seen similar items in the display windows of leather shops in Greenwich Village.

Skink came into the light. "It's a training device. Lie down, Max."

Bonnie Lamb studied the tall, disheveled stranger. He was all the state trooper had promised, and more. In size he appeared capable of anything, yet Bonnie felt in no way threatened.

"Max, now!" the kidnapper said to her husband.

Obediently Max Lamb lay prone on the wooden dock. When Skink told him to roll over, like a dog, he did.

Bonnie was embarrassed for her husband. The kidnapper noticed, and apologized. He instructed Max to get up.

The shopping bag contained everything Skink had demanded. Within moments the new batteries were inserted in the Walkman, and "Tumbling Dice" was spilling out of his earphones. He opened the jar of green olives and poured them into his gleaming bucket of a mouth.

Bonnie Lamb asked Max what in God's name was going on.

"Later," he whispered.

"Tell me now!"

"She deserves to know," the kidnapper interjected, spraying olive juice. "She's risking her life, being out here with a nutcase like me."

Bonnie Lamb had dressed for a boat ride—blue slicker, jeans and deck shoes. Good stuff but practical, Skink noticed, none of that catalog nonsense from California. He pulled off the earphones and complimented Bonnie for her common sense. Then he instructed her husband to remove the shock collar and toss it in the sea.

Max's hands quavered at his neck. Skink told him to go ahead, dammit, off with it! Max's lips tightened in determination, but he couldn't make himself touch it. Finally it was his wife who stepped forward, unhooked the clasp and removed the Tri-Tronics dog trainer. She examined it in the light of the lantern.

"Sick," she said to Skink, and set the collar on the dock.

From his jacket he took a videotape cassette. He tossed it to Bonnie Lamb, who caught it with both hands. "Your hubbie's home movies from the hurricane. Talk about sick."

Bonnie wheeled and threw the cassette into the bay.

The girl had fire! Skink liked her already. Nervously Max lighted a cigaret.

His wife wouldn't have been more repulsed had he jabbed a hypodermic full of heroin in his arm. She said, "Since when do you smoke?"

"If you put the collar back on him," Skink volunteered helpfully, "I can teach him to quit."

Max Lamb told Skink to get on with it. "You said you wanted to talk to her, so talk."

"No, I said I wanted to spend time with her."

Bonnie turned toward the barefoot young man at the helm of the striped speedboat. He apparently had nothing to say. His demeanor was casual, almost bored.

"Where," Bonnie asked the kidnapper, "did you want to spend time? And doing what?"

"Not what you think," Max Lamb cut in.

Skink put on his plastic shower cap. "The hurricane has set me on a new rhythm. I feel it ticking."

He put his hands on Bonnie's shoulders, gently moving her to Max's side. From the governor's shadow she felt his stare. He was studying them, her and Max, like they were lab rats. Then she heard him mutter: "I still don't see how."

Tersely Bonnie said, "Just tell us what you want."

"Watch it," Max advised. "He's been smoking dope."

Skink looked away, toward the ocean. "No offense, Mrs Lamb, but your husband has put me sorely off the human race. A feminine counterpoint would be nice."

Bonnie was surprised by a pleasurable shiver, gooseflesh rising on her neck. The stranger's voice was soothing and hypnotic, a wild broad river; she could have listened to him all night. Mad is what he was, demonstrably mad. But his story fascinated her. Once a governor, the trooper had said. Bonnie longed to know more.

Yet here was her husband, exhausted, sunburned, emotionally sapped. She ought to tend to him. Poor Max had been through hell.

"I only want to talk," the kidnapper said.

"All right," Bonnie told him, "but just for a little while."

He cupped a hand to his mouth. "You, Augustine! Take Mister Lamb to safety. He needs a shower and a shave and possibly a stool softener. Return at dawn for his wife."

Skink grabbed Max under the arms and lowered him to the speedboat. He cut the line with a pocketknife, pushing the bow away from the sagging stilt house. He flung one arm around Bonnie and with the other began to wave. As the boat drifted out of the lantern's glow, Skink saw a third figure rise in the stern of the boat—where had *he* been hiding? Then the young man at the wheel brought a rifle to his shoulder.

"Damn," said Skink, pushing Bonnie Lamb from the line of fire.

Something stung him fiercely, spinning him clockwise and down. He was still spinning when he hit the warm water, and wondering why his arms and legs weren't working, wondering why he hadn't heard a shot or seen a muzzle flash, wondering if perhaps he was already dead.

THIRTEEN

Late on the night of August 27, with a warm breeze at his back and nine cold Budweisers in his belly, Keith Higstrom decided to go hunting. His friends declined to accompany him, as Keith was as clumsy and unreliable a shooter as he was a drunk.

Truthfully there wasn't much to hunt in South Florida, the wild game having long ago fled or died. However, the hurricane had dispersed throughout the suburbs an exotic new quarry: livestock. Mile upon mile of ranch posts in rural Dade County had been uprooted, freeing herds of cattle and horses to explore vistas beyond their mucky flooded pastures. Motivated more by dull hunger than by native inquisitiveness, the animals began appearing in places where they were not customarily encountered. One such place was Keith Higstrom's neighborhood, a subdivision of indistinguishable clam-colored houses, stacked twenty deep and twenty-five across and bordered on every side by bankrupt strip shopping malls.

It was here Keith Higstrom had spent his childhood. His father's family had moved to Miami from northern Minnesota in the early 1940s bringing an affinity for long guns and an appetite for the great outdoors. An impressionable boy, Keith had listened to hunting yarns his entire life—timber wolves and trophy black bears in the north woods, white-tailed deer and wild turkeys in the Florida scrub. The head of an eight-point buck, stoic but marble-eyed, hung over the Higstrom dinner table; the tawny pelt of a prized panther was tacked spread-eagle on the west wall of the den. At age five, Keith began collecting in leatherbound volumes each edition of *Outdoor Life, Field & Stream* and *Sports Afield*. His most treasured possession was an autographed photo of the famous Joe Foss, standing over a dead grizzly. At age six, young Keith got a Daisy popgun, a BB pistol at age nine, a pellet rifle at age eleven, and his first .22 at thirteen.

Yet ... even plinking beer cans at the local rock pit, the boy displayed an unfailing lack of proficiency with firearms. His father was more than slightly disappointed. Young Keith was a pure menace with a gun. Practice brought no improvement, nor did experimenting with different styles of weapons. Scopes didn't help. Tripods didn't help. Recoil cushions didn't help. Even goddamn breathing exercises didn't help.

Often these father–son target practices disintegrated into sulking and tears until the elder Higstrom relented, allowing young Keith to fire a few rounds with a twelve-gauge Mossberg, just so he could have the experience of hitting *something*. Clearly the family lineage of crack dead-eye shots had come to a sorry end. Keith's father returned from these outings looking pale and shaken, although he said nothing to Keith's mother about what he'd witnessed at the rock pit.

Fortunately, by the time Keith was old enough to go out hunting, there was practically nothing left to shoot in Miami except for rats and low-flying seagulls. Every autumn, Keith badgered his father into taking him to the Big Cypress Swamp or private hunting camps in the Everglades, where the deer were chased into high water by airboats and shot at point-blank range. The elder Higstrom dreaded these excursions and found no sport in the killing, but his son couldn't have been happier had he been lobbing grenades at crippled fawns.

It was on one such miserable morning that Keith Higstrom's father swore off hunting forever. They were riding a tank-sized swamp buggy in hot pursuit of a scraggly, half-senile bobcat. Suddenly Keith began firing wildly at an object high in the sky—a bald eagle, it turned out, a federally protected species. The attempted felony was not consummated, due to the young man's shaky aim, but in the fever of the moment he managed to blow off his father's left ear.

Deafened, blood-drenched, writhing facedown in Everglades marl, the elder Higstrom experienced a peculiar catharsis, an unexpected soothing of the soul, as if a cool white sheet were slowly being drawn over his head. Yes, his injury was terrible, and the deafness would (if he came clean about it) cost him his job as an air traffic controller. On the other hand, he could never again be forced to go hunting with his excitable son!

Keith Higstrom couldn't duck responsibility for the accident, nor the guilt that went with it. His father recovered from the gunshot wound, and was kind enough not to bring it up more than once or twice a day. Before long, Keith's remorse gave way to an unspoken resentment, for he perceived that his father was using the missing ear as an excuse to avoid their weekend expeditions. A plastic surgeon had attached a durable polyurethane facsimile to the left side of the elder Higstrom's head, while a high-tech hearing aid had restored the old man's auditory capacity to eighty-one percent of what it was before the Everglades mishap. Yet he stubbornly refused to pick up a gun. Doctor's orders, he squawked.

For Keith, outdoor companionship was increasingly hard to come by. His friends always seemed to have prior commitments whenever Keith invited them to go hunting. Frustrated and restless, he spent long sullen weekends cleaning his guns and watching videotapes of his favorite *American Sportsman* episodes. Whenever his trigger finger got itchy, he'd drive out the Tamiami Trail and park by the canal. As soon as darkness fell, Keith would load a double-barrel shotgun, strap on a headlamp and stalk along the shoreline. His usual targets were turtles and opossums; anything faster or smarter generally eluded him.

Shortly after the hurricane, Keith Higstrom noticed four dairy cows and a palomino mare grazing on his neighbor's front lawn. Everyone on the block was gathered on the sidewalk, laughing and taking pictures; a light moment of relief in the otherwise somber aftermath of the storm. That night, drinking with his buddies at an Irish bar on Kendall Drive, Keith asked: "How much does a cow weigh?"

One of Keith's friends said, "I give up, Higstrom. How much does a cow weigh?"

"It's not a joke. More than an elk? Because I got cows loose on my street."

One of his friends said, "From the hurricane."

"Yeah, but how big do you figure? More than a mulie?" Keith Higstrom drained his Budweiser and stood up. "Let's go hunting, boys."

"Sit down, Higstrom."

"You pussies coming or not?"

"Have another beer, Keith."

With a burp, he charged out the door. He drove home, slipped into the den, and removed his grandfather's old .30-06 from the maple gun cabinet. He dropped a box of bullets, and giggled drunkenly when nobody woke up. He pulled on his boots and his mail-order camo jumpsuit, strapped on the headlamp, and went looking for a cow to shoot.

They were no longer grazing in his neighbor's front yard. Dropping into an exaggerated half crouch, Keith Higstrom weaved down the block. He felt light as a feather, lethal as a snake. The rifle was slick and magnificent in his hands. His plan was to tie the dead cow on the front fender of his Honda Civic and drive all the way back to Kendall, back to the Irish bar where his chickenshit pals were drinking. Keith Higstrom chuckled in advance at the spectacle.

For cover he used mounds of hurricane debris, shuffling noisily from one to another. The street was empty and black and shadowless; the homes on the north side still had no electricity. Passing the Ullmans' house, Keith Higstrom heard something in the backyard—deep raspy snorting. He thought it might be the runaway palomino. As he snuck around the corner of the garage, the beam of Keith Higstrom's headlamp illuminated a pair of glistening indigo eyes, as large as ashtrays.

"God damn," he exclaimed.

An enormous animal stood next to the Ullmans' half-drained swimming pool. The light from Keith's headlamp played up and down its blue-black flanks. This was no ordinary cow. For starters, it was as big as a tractor. Its sharp horns were lavishly curved and downslung, upside down from those of domestic American stock.

Keith Higstrom knew exactly what he was looking at. Hadn't he watched Jimmy Dean and Curt Gowdy shoot one of the very same majestic bastards on *The American Sportsman*? But that was in Africa, for Christ's sake. Not Miami, Florida.

It occurred to Keith that he might be suffering the effects of too much alcohol, that the gigantic oval-eyed ungulate glaring at him was merely a Budweiser-enhanced Angus.

Then it snorted again, expelling twin strings of dewy snot. The animal lowered its head and, with hooves the size of laundry irons, decisively pawed a trench in the Ullmans' newly replanted Bermuda sod.

"Shit on a biscuit," Keith Higstrom said, raising his grandfather's rifle. "That's a Cape buffalo!"

He fired and, naturally, missed. Twice.

The gunshots awakened Mr Ullman, a banker by trade and a recent arrival from Copenhagen, who looked out the bedroom window just in time to see a tremendous bull galloping across his yard with a thrashing young American impaled on its rack. Mr Ullman quickly telephoned the police and informed them, as urgently as his newly acquired English would allow, that an "unlucky cowboy is being perforated seriously." Eventually the police figured out what Mr Ullman was trying to say.

Two hours later, a police dispatcher phoned Augustine's house with a message: His dead uncle's missing Cape buffalo, identified by an ear tag, had turned up in the produce aisle of a storm-gutted supermarket. Unfortunately, there was trouble. The dispatcher requested that Augustine call Animal Control as soon as possible.

Augustine didn't check his answering machine for several hours, because he was out on Biscayne Bay with Bonnie Lamb.

They had borrowed the speedboat from one of Augustine's friends, an airline pilot. The pilot owed Augustine a favor from a long-ago divorce, when Augustine had let him bury $45,000 worth of gold Krugerrands behind Augustine's garage, to conceal them from his future ex-wife's private investigator. After the divorce litigation ended, the airline pilot was left with nothing but the hidden stash of coins. He immediately depleted them on a ninety-one-pound fashion model, who later abandoned him at a five-star hotel in Morocco. Although years had passed, the pilot never forgot Augustine's act of friendship in a time of personal crisis.

The speedboat was on a trailer at a marina in North Miami Beach, untouched by the hurricane. Augustine and Bonnie Lamb met Jim Tile there. His eyes were red and his voice was raw. He told them that a close friend, a female trooper, had been savagely beaten by a car thief, and that he would have preferred to be out on road patrol, hunting for the gutless low-life sonofabitch.

As distracted as he was, Jim Tile also seemed visibly anxious about the boat trip. Even in the dark, the bay looked rough and tricky. Oddly, Bonnie Lamb wasn't worried. Maybe it was the way Augustine handled himself behind the wheel; steering casually with two fingers as he aimed, with his free hand, the spotlight. Smoothly he weaved around massive tree limbs and wind-split lumber and ghostly capsized hulls. The scary ride temporarily took Jim Tile's mind off the image of Brenda on an ambulance stretcher. . . .

Bonnie was anticipating her first sight of the man called Skink. She kept thinking about the bloodied corpse in the morgue— impaled on a TV dish, the trooper had said. Was Skink the killer? To hear the trooper tell it, the ex-governor was not a nut of the certifiable, Mansonesque strain. Rather, he was launched on a mission: a reckless doomed mission, boisterously outside the law. Bonnie was intrigued by bold eccentrics. She wasn't afraid of Skink, not with the trooper and Augustine at her side. In an odd way, although she'd never admit it, she looked forward to confronting the kidnapper almost as much as to reuniting with her husband. . . .

Now Jim Tile and Augustine were struggling to drag the unconscious man over the gunwale of the speedboat. His clothes were soaked, adding to his considerable bulk. Bonnie Lamb tried to help. Augustine got a silvery handful of the man's hair, the trooper had him by the belt loops, Bonnie dug her fingers in the tongues of his boots—and finally the kidnapper was on the deck, vomiting seawater.

From the bow came a whine of disgust: Max Lamb, arms folded, face pinched, sucking a Bronco cigaret. Bonnie turned back to the tranquilized stranger. The trooper knelt beside him. With a handkerchief he cleaned the foul splatter off Skink's face; the glass eye needed special attention.

Augustine said, "He's breathing."

A volcanic cough, and then: "I saw lobsters big as Sonny Liston." Skink raised his head.

Jim Tile said, "Be still now."

"My Walkman!"

"We'll get you a new one. Now lie still."

Skink lowered his head with a sharp clunk. Humming, he shut both eyes.

Bonnie Lamb asked, "What do we do with him?"

Max laughed acidly. "He's going to jail, what'd you think?"

Bonnie looked at Augustine, who said, "It's up to Jim. He's the law."

The trooper had a thermos open, trying to get some hot coffee into his groggy friend. Bonnie put her hands under the kidnapper's head to help him drink. Augustine went to the console and started the boat. Over the noise of the engines, Bonnie asked Jim Tile if she should sit with the man during the ride back, in case he got ill again. The trooper leaned close and in a low voice said: "He's all right now. Go check on your husband."

"OK," Bonnie said. She was glad for the darkness, so the trooper couldn't see her blush. Neither could Max.

The conversation between Gar Whitmark and his wife was not a loving one. That she had handed seven thousand cash to a band of crooked roofers was infuriating enough; that she had failed to ask the name of the one taking the money was unforgivably stupid. The only clue in tracking the thieves was the piece of yellow paper that had been given by the phony roofing foreman to Mrs Whitmark, the yellow paper intended to double as a receipt and an estimate, the yellow paper that Mrs Whitmark had instantly misplaced.

Gar Whitmark's anger had another facet. He was by trade a builder of residential subdivisions, and was therefore personally familiar with every honest, competent roofer in Dade County. The list was not voluminous, but from it Gar Whitmark had intended to select the crew that would rebuild the roof of his gutted home. He'd left messages with a half-dozen companies, and had explained (repeatedly) to his wife that it would take time to line up the job. The hurricane had launched a drooling Klondike stampede among roofers—the best ones were swamped with emergency work and likely would be engaged for months to come. Meanwhile out-of-towners were pouring into Miami by the truckload; some were capable and experienced, some were hapless and inept, and many were gypsy impostors. All arrived to find boundless opportunity.

The typical hurricane victim, frantic for shelter, was forced to trust his instincts when choosing a roof builder. Unfortunately, the instincts of the typical hurricane victim in such matters were not acute. Gar Whitmark, however, had the twin advantages of knowing the cast of characters and possessing the clout to divert the best of them to his own pressing needs. With little trouble he located a top-notch roofer who agreed to put all other contracts aside to tackle Gar Whitmark's roof (Whitmark being one of the most prolific home builders—and employers of roofing contractors—in all South Florida). However, the craftsman whom Whitmark selected first had to replace two other roofs: his own, and that of his wife's mother.

Gar Whitmark gave the man seven days to patch up the family roofs. The delay proved unbearable for Mrs Whitmark, whose roaring anxiety at the chance of more rain-stained Chippendales was no match for her customary palliative dosages of sedatives, muscle relaxants, sleep aids and mood elevators. To Mrs Whitmark, the unexpected appearance of willing roofers at the door had been a godsend. She thought her husband would be grateful for her initiative—it would be one less problem for him to worry about, what with all the nasty threats of negligence suits from customers whose Whitmark Signature homes had disintegrated like soggy cardboard in the hurricane.

Standing in the living room, the rain beating a tattoo on his blue-veined forehead, Gar Whitmark instructed his wife to immediately locate the goddamn receipt or estimate or whatever the goddamn so-called foreman had called it. After an hour's search, the crucial yellow paper turned up neatly folded in Mrs Whitmark's high-school yearbook; Gar Whitmark couldn't imagine why his wife had put it there, or how she found it. Nor could she explain it herself—her brain was too jumbled by the hurricane.

The receipt bore the name of "Fortress Roofing," which brought a bitter cackle from Gar Whitmark. At least the scammers had a sense of irony! Gar Whitmark dialed the number and got an answering machine. He hung up and called the director of the county building-and-zoning department, who owed his job to seven of the county commissioners, who owed their jobs to Gar Whitmark's generous campaign contributions. As Gar Whitmark anticipated, the building director expressed shock and alarm that a fraud was perpetrated on Gar Whitmark's wife, and promised a thorough criminal investigation.

No, he hadn't ever heard of Fortress Roofing—but he'd damn sure find out who was behind it.

Sooner the better, said Gar Whitmark, toweling the rainwater from his stinging scalp, which bristled with fifty pink-stemmed, freshly implanted hair plugs.

Fifteen minutes later, the building director phoned back to report, mournfully, that Fortress Roofing had never obtained a valid Dade County contractor's license and was therefore an unknown outlaw entity.

In a fury, Gar Whitmark began contacting roofers he knew—some honest, some not. The name Fortress struck a note with one or two, who said they'd recently lost crew to the new company. The sonofabitch owner, they said, was an ex-inspector named Avila. Dirty as they come, the roofers warned.

Gar Whitmark knew Avila quite well, having successfully bribed him for many years. All those times Gar Whitmark's subcontractors had slipped booty to the greedy bastard! Cash, booze, porn—Avila had a taste for the hard stuff; girl-on-girl, if Gar Whitmark remembered correctly.

He called his secretary, whose fingers swiftly punched up a

highly confidential computer file of corrupt and/or corruptible officials in Dade, Broward, Palm Beach, Lee and Monroe Counties. It was a lengthy roster, alphabetized for convenience. Avila's name and unlisted home phone number winked fatefully at the bottom of the first screen.

Gar Whitmark waited until three in the morning before phoning.

"This is your old friend Gar Whitmark," he said. "Your crew of gypsy fakers hit my wife for seven grand. My wife is not well, Avila. If I don't see my money by tomorrow morning, you'll be in the county jail by tomorrow night. And I will arrange for you to share a cell with Paul Pick-Percy."

The threat brutally jarred Avila wide awake. Paul Pick-Percy was a notorious cannibal. Currently he awaited trial on charges of killing and eating his landlord, who had neglected to repair a leaky ball cock in Paul Pick-Percy's toilet tank. Recently Paul Pick-Percy had also been found guilty of killing and eating a tardy cable-TV repairman and a rude tollbooth attendant.

Avila said: "Seven thousand? Mister Whitmark, I swear to God I don't know nothing about this."

"Suit yourself—"

"Wait, now hold on. . . ." Avila sat upright in bed. "Tell me supposedly what happened, OK?"

"There is no fucking 'supposedly.' " Gar Whitmark related his wife's pitiable tale.

"And the truck was ours, you're sure?"

"I'm holding the receipt, dipshit. 'Fortress Roofing' is what it says."

Avila grimaced. "Who signed it?"

Gar Whitmark said the signature was illegible. "My wife said the guy had a fucked-up jaw made him look like a moray eel. Plus he wore a bad suit."

"Shit," Avila said. Exactly what he'd feared.

"Is this ringing a bell?" Gar Whitmark's sarcasm was heavy and ominous.

Avila sagged against the headboard of his bed. "Sir, you'll get your money back first thing."

"Damn straight. And a new roof as well."

"What?"

"You heard me, noodle dick. The seven grand your people stole, plus you're picking up the bill when my new roof gets done. By real roofers."

Avila's stomach pitched. Gar Whitmark probably lived in a goddamn ranch house way down south, with all the other millionaires. Avila figured he'd be looking at twenty thousand, easy, for a new roof job. He said, "That ain't really fair."

"You'd rather do dinner with Chef Pick-Percy?"

"Aw, Christ, Mister Whitmark."

"I didn't think so."

Avila got out of bed and went to the backyard to round up two roosters, which he took to the garage for beheading. He hoped the sacrifice would be favorably received. After a short scuffle, the deed was done. Avila dripped the warm blood into a plastic pail filled with pennies, bleached cat bones and turtle shells. The pail was placed at the feet of a ceramic statue of Chango, the saint of lightning and fire. The child-sized statue wore a robe, colored beads and a gold-plated crown. Kneeling in beseechment, Avila raised his blood-flecked arms toward the heavens and asked Chango to please strike Snapper dead as a fucking doornail for screwing up the roofer scam.

Avila wasn't sure the ceremony would work. He was relatively new to the study of *santería* and, characteristically, hadn't bothered to research it thoroughly. Avila had begun dabbling in the blood practices when he first learned the authorities were investigating him for bribery; several cocaine dealers of his acquaintance swore that *santería* worship had kept them out of jail, so Avila figured there was nothing to lose by trying. In Hialeah he conferred with a genuine *santero* priest, who offered to teach him the secrets of the religion, rooted in ancient Afro-Cuban customs. The history was infinitely too deep and mystical for Avila, and soon he grew impatient with the lessons.

All he really wanted, he explained to the *santero*, was the ability to put curses on his enemies. Lethal curses.

The priest wailed and told him to get lost. But Avila went home convinced that, from the mumbo jumbo he'd seen, he could teach himself the basics of hexing. For his deity Avila picked the saint Chango, because he liked the macho name. For his first target he chose the county prosecutor leading the investigation against corrupt building inspectors.

Pennies were easy to come by, as were old animal bones; Avila's grandmother lived four blocks from a pet cemetery in Medley. Obtaining blood was the biggest obstacle for Avila, who had no zeal for performing live sacrifices. The first few times, he tried pleasing Chango by sprinkling the coins and bones with steak juices and homemade bouillon. Nothing happened. Evidently the *santería* saints preferred the fresh stuff.

One rainy Sunday afternoon, Avila bought himself a live chicken. His wife was cooking a big dinner for the cousins, so she banished Avila from the kitchen. He put a Ginsu knife in his back pocket and smuggled the victim to the garage. As soon as Avila began spreading newspapers on the floor, the chicken sensed trouble. Avila was astounded that a puny five-pound bird could make such a racket or put up such spirited resistance. The crudely staged sacrifice eventually was completed, but Avila emerged scratched, pecked and smeared with bloody feathers. So was his wife's cream-colored Buick Electra. Her ear-splitting tirade caused the cousins to forgo dessert and head home early.

Two days later, the magic happened. The prosecutor targeted by Avila's chicken curse fell and dislocated a shoulder in the shower. At the time, he was in the company of an athletic prostitute named Kandi, who was thoughtful enough not only to call 911 but to make herself available for numerous press interviews. Given the media uproar, the State Attorney suggested that the fallen prosecutor take an indefinite leave of absence.

The corruption investigation wasn't derailed, merely reassigned. Nevertheless, Avila was convinced that the *santería* spell was a success. Later attempts to replicate the results proved fruitless (and messy), but Avila blamed his own inexperience, plus a lack of suitable facilities. Perhaps, during the sacrifices, he was chanting the wrong phrases, or chanting the right phrases in the wrong order. Perhaps he was performing the ceremonies at a bad time of day for the mercurial Chango. Or perhaps Avila was simply using inferior poultry.

While he ended up plea-bargaining with the replacement prosecutor, Avila's faith in the witchcraft of bones and blood remained unshaken. He decided Snapper's transgression was heinous enough to merit the offering of two chickens instead of one. If that didn't work, he'd invest in a billy goat.

The roosters did not succumb quietly, the clamor awakening Avila's wife, aunt and mother. The women burst into the garage to find Avila singing Spanish gibberish to his cherished ceramic statue. Avila's wife instantly spied red droplets and a waxen fragment of chicken beak on the left front fender of her Electra, and savagely took to striking her husband with a garden rake.

On the other side of Dade County, Snapper dozed peacefully in a dead man's Naugahyde recliner. He felt no pain from the supernatural hand of Chango, nor did he feel the hateful glare of Edie Marsh, who was stretched out on the mildewed carpet and trussed to a naked insurance man.

FOURTEEN

As the candles melted to lumps, Snapper's shadow flickered and shrunk on the pale bare walls. His profile reminded Edie Marsh of a miniature tyrannosaurus.

For laughs, he refused to let Fred Dove remove the red condom.

"That's mean," Edie said.

"Well, I'm one mean motherfucker," Snapper proclaimed. "You don't believe me, there's a lady cop in the hospital you should see."

When he yawned, the misaligned mandible waggled horizontally, then appeared to disengage altogether from his face. He looked like a snake trying to swallow an egg.

Edie said, "What is it you want?"

"You know damn well." Snapper held the flashlight on Fred Dove's retreating cock. "Where'd you find a red rubber?" he asked. "Mail order, I bet. Looks like a Santy Claus hat."

From the floor, the insurance man gave a disconsolate whimper. Edie leaned her head against the small of his back. Snapper had positioned them butt-to-butt, binding their hands with a curtain sash. In Fred Dove's briefcase Snapper found the business cards and policy folders from Midwest Casualty. From that it was easy to figure out—Edie on her knees, and so on. Snapper marveled at the exquisite timing of his entrance.

He said, "Fair is fair. A three-way split."

"But you took off!" Edie objected. "You left me here with that asshole Tony."

Snapper shrugged. "I changed my mind. I'm allowed. So how much money we talkin' about?"

"Fuck you," said Edie Marsh.

Without leaving the recliner, Snapper cocked one leg and kicked her in the side of the head. The sound of the blow was sickening. Edie moaned but didn't cry.

"For God's sake." Fred Dove's voice cracked, as if he were the one who'd been clobbered.

Snapper said, "Then tell me how much."

"Don't you dare." Edie was woozy, but sharply she dug both elbows into Fred Dove's ribs.

"I'm waiting," said Snapper.

Edie felt the insurance man stiffen against the ropes. Then she heard him say: "A hundred forty-one thousand dollars."

"Moron!" Edie hissed.

"But you won't get a dime," Fred Dove warned Snapper, "without me and Edie."

"That a fact?"

"Yes, sir."

"Not a goddamn cent," Edie agreed, "because guess who's getting the settlement check. *Missus* Neria Torres. Me."

Snapper aimed the flashlight on Edie's face, which bore a puffy salmon imprint of his shoe. "Sweetie," he said, "it's hard to sign a check if you're in a body cast. Understand?"

She turned away from the harsh light and silently cursed her lousy taste in convicts.

Fred Dove said to Snapper: "You ought to untie us."

"Well, listen to Santy Claus!"

Edie's pulse jackhammered in her temples. "You know what it is, Fred? Snapper's jealous. See, it's not about the insurance money. It's that I was going to make love to you—"

"Haw!" Snapper exclaimed.

"—and he knows," Edie went on, "he knows I wouldn't do it with him for all the money in Fort Knox!"

Snapper laughed. Nudging Fred Dove with a toe, he said, "Don't kid yourself, bubba. She'd fuck a syphilitic porky-pine, she thought there was a dollar in it."

"Nice talk," Edie said. God Almighty, her head hurt.

The insurance man fought to steady his nerves. He was flabbergasted to find himself in the middle of something so ugly, complicated and dangerous. Only hours ago the arrangement seemed foolproof and exciting: a modestly fraudulent claim, a beautiful and uninhibited co-conspirator, a wild fling in an abandoned hurricane house.

A bright-red condom seemed appropriate.

Then out of nowhere appeared this Snapper person, a hard-looking sort and an authentic criminal, judging by what Fred Dove had seen and heard. The insurance man didn't want such a violent character for a third partner. On the other hand, he didn't want to die or be harmed seriously enough to require hospitalization. Blue Cross would demand facts, as would Fred Dove's wife.

So he offered Snapper forty-seven thousand dollars. "That's how it splits three ways."

Snapper swung the flashlight to Fred Dove's face. He said, "You figured that up in your head? No pencil and paper, that's pretty good."

Yeah, thought Edie Marsh. Thank you, Dr Einstein.

Fred Dove said to Snapper: "Do we have a deal?"

"Fair is fair." He rose from the BarcaLounger and made his way to the garage. Within moments the portable generator belched to life. Snapper returned to the living room and turned on the solitary lightbulb. Then, kneeling beside Fred Dove and Edie Marsh, he cut the curtain sash off their wrists.

"Let's go eat," he said. "I'm fuckin' starved."

Fred Dove rose shakily. He modestly locked his hands in front of his crotch. "I'm taking this thing off," he declared.

"The rubber?" Snapper gave him a thumbs-up. "You do that." He glanced at Edie, who made no effort to cover her breasts or anything else. She eyed Snapper in a dark poisonous way.

He said, "That's how you goin' to Denny's? Fine by me. Maybe we'll get a free pie."

Wordlessly Edie walked behind the Naugahyde recliner, picked up the crowbar she'd left there, took two steps toward Snapper, and swung at him with all her strength. He went down squalling.

Weapon in hand, Edie Marsh straddled him. Her damp and tangled hair had fallen to cover the bruised half of her face. To Fred Dove, she looked untamed and dazzling and alarmingly capable of homicide. He feared he was about to witness his first.

Edie inserted the sharp end of the crowbar between Snapper's deviated jawbones, pinning his bloodless tongue to his teeth.

"Kick me again," she said, "and I'll have your balls in a blender."

Fred Dove snatched his pants and his briefcase, and ran.

They returned the borrowed speedboat to the marina and went back to Coral Gables. With great effort they carried the man known as Skink into Augustine's house.

Max Lamb was unnerved by the wall of grinning skulls, but said nothing as he made his way down the hall to the shower. Augustine got on the telephone to sort out what had happened with his dead uncle's Cape buffalo. Bonnie fixed a pot of coffee and took it to the guest room, where the governor was recovering from the animal dart. He and Jim Tile were talking when Bonnie walked in. She wanted to stay and listen to this improbable stranger, but she felt she was intruding. The men's conversation was serious, held in low tones. She heard Skink say:

"Brenda's a strong one. She'll make it."

Then, Jim Tile: "I've tried every prayer I know."

As Bonnie slipped out the door, she encountered Max, sucking on a cigaret as he emerged from the bathroom. She resolved to be forbearing about her husband's odious new habit, which he blamed on the battlefield stress of the abduction.

She followed him to the living room and sat beside him on the sofa. There, in sensational detail, he described the torture he'd received at the hands of the one-eyed misfit.

"The dog collar," Bonnie Lamb said.

"That's right. Look at my neck." Max opened the top buttons of his shirt, which he'd borrowed from Augustine. "See the burns? See?"

Bonnie didn't notice any marks, but nodded sympathetically. "So you definitely want to prosecute."

"Absolutely!" Max Lamb detected doubt in his wife's voice. "Christ, Bonnie, he could've murdered me."

She squeezed his hand. "I still don't understand why—why he did it in the first place."

"With a fruitcake like that, who knows." Max Lamb purposely didn't mention Skink's disgust with the hurricane videos; he remembered that Bonnie felt the same way.

She said, "I think he needs professional help."

"No, sweetheart, he needs a professional jail." Max lifted his chin and blew smoke at the ceiling.

"Honey, let's think about this—"

But he pulled away from her, bolting for the phone, which Augustine had just hung up. "I'd better call Pete Archibald," Max Lamb said over his shoulder, "let everyone at Rodale know I'm OK."

Bonnie Lamb got up and went to the guest room. The governor was sitting upright in bed, but his eyes were half shut. His ragged beard was finely crusted with ocean salt. Jim Tile, his Stetson tucked under one arm, stood near the window.

Bonnie poured each of them another cup of coffee. "How's he feeling?" she whispered.

Skink's good eye blinked open. "Better," he said, thickly.

She set the coffeepot on the bedstand. "It was monkey tran-quilizer," she explained.

"Never to be combined with psychoactive drugs," said Skink, "particularly toad sweat."

Bonnie looked at Jim Tile, who said, "I asked him."

"Asked me what?" Skink rasped.

"About the dead guy in the TV dish," the trooper said. Then, to Bonnie: "He didn't do it."

"Though I do admire the style," said Skink.

Bonnie Lamb did a poor job of masking her doubt. Skink peered sternly. "I didn't kill that fellow, Mrs Lamb. But I damn sure wouldn't tell you if I had."

"I believe you. I do."

The governor finished the coffee and asked for another cup. He told Bonnie it was the best he'd ever tasted. "And I like your boy," he said, gesturing toward the wall of skulls. "I like what he's done with the place."

Bonnie said: "He's not my boy. Just a friend."

Skink nodded. "We all need one of those." With difficulty he rolled out of bed and began stripping off his wet clothes. Jim Tile led him to the shower and started the water. When the trooper returned, carrying the governor's plastic cap, he asked Bonnie Lamb what her husband intended to do.

"He wants to prosecute." She sat on the edge of the bed, listening to the shower run.

Augustine came into the room and said, "Well?"

"I can arrest him tonight," Jim Tile told Bonnie, "if your husband comes to the substation and files charges. What happens then is up to the State Attorney."

"You'd do that—arrest your own friend?"

"Better me than a stranger," the trooper said. "Don't feel bad about this, Mrs Lamb. Your husband's got every right."

"Yes, I know." Prosecuting the governor was the right thing— a person couldn't be allowed to run around kidnapping tourists, no matter how offensively they behaved. Yet Bonnie was saddened by the idea of Skink's going to jail. It was naive, she knew, but that's how she felt.

Jim Tile was questioning Augustine about the skulls on the wall. "Cuban voodoo?"

"No, nothing like that."

"Nineteen is what I count," the trooper said. "I won't ask where you got 'em. They're too clean for homicides."

Bonnie Lamb said, "They're medical specimens."

"Whatever you say." After twenty years of attending head-on collisions, Jim Tile had a well-earned aversion to human body parts. "Specimens it is," he said.

Augustine removed five of the skulls from the shelves and lined them up on the hardwood floor, at his feet. Then he picked up three and began to juggle.

The trooper said, "I'll be damned."

As he juggled, Augustine thought about the drunken young fool who tried to shoot his uncle's Cape buffalo. What a sad, dumb way to die. Fluidly he snatched a fourth skull off the floor and put it in rotation; then the fifth.

Bonnie Lamb found herself smiling at the performance in spite of its creepiness. The governor emerged from the shower in a cloud of steam, naked except for a sky-blue towel around his neck. His thick silver hair sent snaky tails of water down his chest. He used a corner of the towel to dab the condensation off his glass eye. He beamed when he saw Augustine's juggling.

Jim Tile felt dizzy, watching the skulls fly. Max Lamb appeared in the doorway. His expression instantly changed from curiosity to revulsion, as if a switch had been flipped inside his head. Bonnie knew what he was going to say before the words left his lips: "You think *this* is funny?"

Augustine continued juggling. It was unclear whether he, or the governor's nudity, was the object of Max Lamb's disapproval.

The trooper said, "It's been a long night, man."

"Bonnie, we're leaving." Max's tone was patronizing and snarky. "Did you hear me? Playtime is over."

She was infuriated that her husband would speak to her that way in front of strangers. She stormed from the room.

"Oh, Max?" Skink, wearing a sly smile, touched a finger to his own throat. Max Lamb's neck tingled the old Tri-Tronics tingle. He jumped reflexively, banging against the door.

From the backpack Skink retrieved Max's billfold and the keys to the rental car. He dropped them in Max's hand. Max mumbled a thank-you and went after Bonnie.

Augustine stopped juggling, catching the skulls one by one. Carefully he returned them to their place on the wall.

The governor tugged the towel from his neck and began drying his arms and legs. "I like that girl," he said to Augustine. "How about you?"

"What's not to like."

"You've got a big decision to make."

"That's very funny. She's married."

"Love is just a kiss away. So the song says." Playfully Skink seized Jim Tile by the elbows. "Tell me, Officer. Am I arrested or not?"

"That's up to Mister Max Lamb."

"I need to know."

"They're talking it over," Jim Tile said.

"Because if I'm not bound for jail, I'd dearly love to go find the bastard who beat up your Brenda."

For a moment the trooper seemed to sag under the weight of his grief. His eyes welled up, but he kept himself from breaking down.

Skink said, "Jim, please. I live for opportunities like this."

"You've had enough excitement. We all have."

"You, son!" the governor barked at Augustine. "You had enough excitement?"

"Well, they just shot my water buffalo at a supermarket—"

"Ho!" Skink exclaimed.

"—but I'd be honored to help." The skull juggling had left Augustine energetic and primed. He was in the mood for a new project, now that Bonnie's husband was safe.

"You think about what I said," Skink told Jim Tile. "In the meantime, I'm damn near hungry enough to eat processed food. How about you guys?"

He charged toward the door, but the trooper blocked his path. "Put on your pants, captain. Please."

The corpse of Tony Torres lay unclaimed and unidentified in the morgue. Each morning Ira Jackson checked the *Herald*, but in the reams of hurricane news there was no mention of a crucified mobile-home salesman. Ira Jackson took this as affirmation of Tony Torres's worthlessness and insignificance; his death didn't rate one lousy paragraph in the newspaper.

Ira Jackson turned his vengeful attentions toward Avila, the inspector who had corruptly rubber-stamped the permits for the late Beatrice Jackson's trailer home. Ira Jackson believed Avila was as culpable as Tony Torres for the tragedy that had claimed the life of his trusting mother.

Early on the morning of August 28, Ira Jackson drove to the address he'd pried from the reluctant clerk at the Metro building department. A woman with a heavy accent answered the front door. Ira Jackson asked to speak to Señor Avila.

"He bissy eng de grotch."

"Please tell him it's important."

"Hokay, but he berry bissy."

"I'll wait," said Ira Jackson.

Avila was scrubbing rooster blood off the whitewalls of his wife's Buick when his mother announced he had a visitor. Avila swore and kicked at the bucket of soap. It had to be Gar Whitmark, harassing him for the seven grand. What did he expect Avila to do—rob a fucking bank!

But it wasn't Whitmark at the door. It was a stocky middle-aged stranger with a chopped haircut, a gold chain around his neck and a smudge of white powder on his upper lip. Avila recognized the powder as doughnut dust. He wondered if the guy was a cop.

"My name is Rick," said Ira Jackson, extending a pudgy scarred hand. "Rick Reynolds." When the man smiled, a smear of grape jelly was visible on his bottom row of teeth.

Avila said, "I'm kinda busy right now."

"I was driving by and saw the truck." Ira Jackson pointed. "Fortress Roofing—that's you, right?"

Avila didn't answer yes or no. His eyes flicked to his truck at the curb, and the Cadillac parked behind it. The man wasn't a cop, not with a flashy car like that.

"The storm tore off my roof. I need a new one ASAP."

Avila said, "We're booked solid. I'm really sorry."

He hated to turn down a willing sucker, but it would be suicidal to run a scam on someone who knew where he lived. Especially someone with forearms the size of fence posts.

Avila made a mental note to move the roofing truck off the street, to a place where passersby couldn't see it.

Ira Jackson licked the doughnut sugar from his lip. "I'll make it worth your while," he said.

"Wish I could help."

"How's ten thousand sound? On top of your regular price."

Try as he might, Avila couldn't conceal his interest. The guy had a New York accent; they did things in a big way up there.

"That's ten thousand cash," Ira Jackson added. "See, it's my grandmother, she lives with us. Ninety years old and suddenly it's raining buckets on her head. The roof's flat-out gone."

Avila feigned compassion. "Ninety years old? Bless her heart." He stepped outside and closed the door behind him. "Problem is, I've got a dozen other jobs waiting."

"Fifteen thousand," Ira Jackson said, "if you move me to the top of the list."

Avila rubbed his stubbled chin and eyed the visitor. How often, he thought, does fifteen grand come knocking at the door? A rip-off was out of the question, but another option loomed. Radical, to be sure, but do-able: Avila could build the man a legitimate, complete roof. Use the cash to settle up with Gar Whitmark. Naturally the crew would piss and moan, spoiled bastards. Properly installing a roof was a hard, hot, exhausting job. Perhaps desperate times called for honest work.

"I see," remarked Ira Jackson, "your place came through the hurricane pretty good."

"We were a long way from the eye, thank God."

"Thank God is right."

"Where exactly do you live, Mister Reynolds? Maybe I can squeeze you on the schedule."

"Fantastic."

"I'll send a man out for an estimate," Avila said. Then he remembered there was no man to send; the thieving Snapper had skipped.

Ira Jackson said, "I'd prefer it was you personally."

"Sure, Mister Reynolds. How about tomorrow first thing?"

"How about right now? We can ride in my car."

Avila couldn't think of a single reason not to go, and fifteen thousand reasons why he should.

When Max Lamb put down the phone, his face was gray and his mouth was slack. He looked as if he'd been diagnosed with a terminal illness. The reality was no less grave, as far as the Rodale & Burns agency was concerned. On the other end of the line, easygoing Pete Archibald had sounded funereal and defeated. The news from New York was bad indeed.

The National Institutes of Health had scheduled a press conference to further enumerate the health hazards of cigaret smoking. Ordinarily the advertising world would scarcely take notice, so routine and predictable were these dire outcries. No matter how harrowing the medical revelations, the impact on retail cigaret sales seldom lasted more than a few weeks. This time, though, the government had used sophisticated technology to test specific brands for concentrations of tars, nicotine and other assorted carcinogens. Broncos rated first; Bronco Menthols rated second, Lady Broncos third. Epidemiologically, they were the most lethal products in the history of tobacco cultivation. Smoking a Bronco, in the lamentably quotable words of one wiseass NIH scientist, was "only slightly safer than sucking on the tailpipe of a Chevrolet Suburban."

Details of the NIH bombshell had quickly leaked to Durham Gas Meat & Tobacco, manufacturer of Broncos and other fine products. The company's knee-jerk response was a heated threat to cancel its advertising in all newspapers and magazines that intended to report the government's findings. That bombastically idiotic maneuver, Max Lamb knew, would itself become front-page headlines if sane heads didn't prevail. Max had to get back to New York as soon as possible.

When he told his wife, she said: "Right now?"

As if she didn't understand the gravity of the crisis.

"In my business," Max explained impatiently, "this is a flaming 747 full of orphans, plowing into a mountainside."

"Is it true about Broncos?"

"Probably. That's not the problem. They can't start yanking their ads; there's serious money at stake. Double-digit millions."

"Max."

"What?"

"Please put out that damn cigaret."

"Jesus, Bonnie, listen to yourself."

They were sitting in wicker chairs on Augustine's patio. It was three or four in the morning. Inside the house, Neil Young played on the stereo. Through the French doors Bonnie Lamb saw Augustine in the kitchen. He noticed she was watching, and shot her a quick shy smile. The black trooper and the one-eyed governor were standing over the stove; it smelled like they were frying bacon and ham.

Max Lamb said, "We'll catch the first plane." He stubbed out his Bronco and flipped the butt into a birdbath.

"What about *him*?" Bonnie cut her eyes toward the kitchen window, where Skink could be seen breaking eggs at the sink. She said to Max, "You wanted to file charges, didn't you? Put him in jail where he belongs."

"Honey, there's no time. After the NIH mess blows over, we'll fly back and take care of that maniac. Don't worry."

Bonnie Lamb said, "If they let him go now . . ." She finished the sentence in her head.

If they let him go now, they'll never find him again. He'll vanish like a ghost in the swamp. And wouldn't that be a darn shame.

Bonnie bewildered herself with such sentiment. What's wrong with me? The man abducted and abused my husband. Why don't I want to see him punished?

"You're right," she said to Max. "You should go back to New York as soon as you can."

With a frown, he reached over and lightly smacked a mosquito on her arm. "What does that mean—you're not coming?"

"Max, I'm not up for a plane trip this morning. My stomach's in knots."

"Take some Mylanta."

"I did," Bonnie lied. "Maybe it was the boat ride."

"You'll feel better later."

"I'm sure I will."

He said he'd get her a room near the airport. "Take a long nap," he suggested, "and catch an evening flight."

"Sounds good."

Poor Max, she thought. He hasn't got a clue.

FIFTEEN

Bonnie Brooks's father worked in the circulation department of the Chicago *Tribune*, and her mother was a buyer for Sears. They had an apartment in the city and a summer cabin on the boundary waters in Minnesota. Bonnie, an only child, had mixed memories of family vacations. Her father was an unadventurous fellow for whom the northern wilderness held no allure. Because he couldn't swim and was allergic to deerflies, he avoided the lakes. Instead he stayed in the cabin and assembled model airplanes; classic German Fokkers were his passion. The tedious hobby was made more so by her father's chronic ham-fistedness, which turned the simplest glue job into high drama. Bonnie and her mother stayed out of the way, to avoid being blamed for disturbing his concentration.

While her father toiled over the model planes, Bonnie's mother paddled her across the wooded lakes in an old birch canoe. Bonnie remembered those happy mornings—trailing her fingertips in the chilly water, feeling the sunlight warm the back of her neck. Her mother was not the stealthiest of paddlers, but they saw their share of wildlife—deer, squirrels, beavers, the occasional moose. Bonnie recalled asking, more than once, why her folks had bought the cabin if her father was so averse to the outdoors. Her mother always explained: "It was either here or Wisconsin."

Bonnie Brooks attended Northwestern University and, to her father's puzzlement, majored in journalism. Soon she embarked on her first serious romance, with a divorced adjunct professor who claimed to have won prizes for his reportage of the Vietnam War. The absence of plaques in the professor's office Bonnie naively attributed to modesty. For Christmas she decided to surprise him with a framed, laminated copy of his front-page scoop about the mining of Haiphong harbor. Yet when Bonnie searched the college's microfilm of the San Francisco *Chronicle*, for whom her lover had supposedly worked, she found not a single bylined story bearing his name. Demonstrating the blood instincts of a seasoned reporter, she contacted the newspaper's personnel department and (using harmless subterfuge) was able to determine that the closest her heroic seducer had ever come to Southeast Asia was the copy desk of the *Chronicle*'s Seattle bureau.

Bonnie Brooks acted decisively. First she dumped the jerk, then she got him fired from the university. Subsequent boyfriends were more loyal and forthcoming, but what they lacked in dishonesty they made up for with indolence. Bonnie's mother grew tired of cooking them meals and deflecting their halfhearted offers to help dry the dishes. She couldn't wait for her daughter to graduate from school and find herself a grown-up man.

Good or bad, jobs in journalism were hard to come by. Like many of her classmates, Bonnie Brooks wound up writing publicity blurbs and press releases. She went to work first for the City of Chicago Parks Department and then for a baby-food company that was eventually purchased by Crespo Mills Internationale. There Bonnie was promoted to the job of assistant corporate publicist. The title was attached to a salary that ten tough years in most city newsrooms wouldn't have earned. As for the writing, it was as elementary as it was unsatisfying. In addition to pabulums and breakfast cereals, Crespo Mills manufactured whipped condiment spreads, peanut butter, granola bars, cookies, crackers, trail mix, flavored popcorn, bread sticks and three styles of croutons. In no time, Bonnie Brooks ran out of appetizing adjectives. Attempts at lyrical originality were discouraged by her Crespo supervisors; during one especially dreary streak, she was required to use the word "tasty" in fourteen consecutive press releases. When Max Lamb asked her to marry him and move to New York, Bonnie didn't hesitate to quit her job.

Max could take only a few days off from work, so they decided to take their honeymoon at Disney World—a corny choice, but

Bonnie figured anything was better than Niagara Falls. She knew that a waterfall, no matter how grandiose, wouldn't hold Max's interest. Neither, it turned out, did Mickey Mouse. Two days at the Magic Kingdom and Max was as antsy as a cat burglar.

Then the hurricane blew in, and he just *had* to go see. . . .

Bonnie had wanted to stay in Orlando, stay cuddled under the scratchy motel sheets and make love while the rain drummed on the windows. Why wasn't that enough for him?

She'd almost asked that very question as they sat in the dark on Augustine's patio after the adventure in Stiltsville. And later, on the way to the airport. And again, standing at the Delta gate, when he'd hugged her in a loose and distracted way, his hair and shirt reeking of cigarets.

But Bonnie hadn't asked. The moment wasn't right; he was a man with a purpose. A grown-up man, just like her mother wanted her to find. Except her mother thought Max was an asshole. Her father, well, he thought Max Lamb was a fine young fella. He thought all Bonnie's boyfriends had been fine young fellas.

She wondered what her father would think of her now, on the way to a hospital, scrunched in the front seat of a pickup truck between a one-eyed, toad-smoking kidnapper and a plane-crash survivor who juggled skulls.

Brenda Rourke's head was fractured in three places, and one of her cheeks needed reconstruction. She was bleeding under the right temporal bone, but doctors had managed to stanch it. A plastic surgeon had repaired a U-shaped gash on her forehead, stitching the loose flap above the hairline.

Bonnie Lamb had never seen such terrible wounds. Even the governor seemed shaken. Augustine fastened his eyes on his shoetops—the sounds and smells of the hospital were too familiar. He felt parched.

Jim Tile held both of Brenda's hands in one of his own. Her eyes were open but unfocused; she had no sense of anyone besides Jim at her bedside. She was trying to talk through the drugs and the pain; he leaned closer to listen.

After a while he straightened, announcing in a low, angry voice, "The bastard stole her ring. Her mother's wedding ring."

Skink slipped from the room so quietly that Bonnie and Augustine didn't notice immediately. There was no trace of him outside the door, but a rush of blue and white uniforms attracted them to the end of the hall. The governor was in the nursery, strolling among the newborns. He carried an infant in the crook of each arm. The babies slept soundly, and he studied them with profound sadness. To Bonnie Lamb he appeared harmless, despite the rebellious beard and the grubby combat pants and the army boots. A trio of husky orderlies conferred at a water fountain; apparently a negotiation had already been attempted, with poor results. Calmly Jim Tile entered the nursery and returned the infants to their glass cribs.

Nobody intervened when the trooper led Skink out of the hospital, because it looked like a routine arrest; another loony street case hauled to the stockade: Jim Tile, his arm around the madman, walking him briskly down the maze of pale-green corridors; the two of them talking intently; Bonnie and Max dodging wheelchairs and gurneys and trying to keep up.

When they reached the parking lot, Jim Tile said he had to go to work. "The President's coming, and guess who gets to clear traffic."

He folded a piece of paper into Skink's hand and got into the patrol car. Wordlessly Skink settled in the bed of Augustine's pickup and lay down. His good eye was fixed on the clouds, and his arms were folded across his chest.

Augustine asked Jim Tile: "What do we do with him?"

"That's entirely up to you." The trooper sounded exhausted.

Bonnie Lamb asked about Brenda Rourke. Jim Tile said the doctors expected her to pull through.

"What about the guy who did it?"

"They haven't caught him," the trooper replied, "and they won't." He strapped on the seat belt, locked the door, adjusted his sunglasses. "Place used to be something special," he said absently. "Long, long time ago."

A feral cry rose from the bed of the pickup truck. Jim Tile

blinked over the rims of his shades. "It was nice meeting you, Mrs Lamb. You and your husband do what's right. The captain, he'll understand."

Then the trooper drove off.

On the way to the airport hotel, where Max Lamb had reserved a day room for her, Bonnie slid across the front seat and rested her cheek on Augustine's shoulder. He was dreading this part, saying good-bye. It was always easier as a bitter cleaving, when suitcases snapped shut, doors slammed, taxis screeched out of the driveway. He checked the dashboard clock—less than three hours until her flight.

Through the back window of the truck, Bonnie saw that Skink had pulled the flowered cap over his face and drawn himself into a loose-jointed variation of a fetal curl.

She said, "I wonder what's on that piece of paper."

"My guess," said Augustine, "it's either a name or an address."

"Of what?"

"It's just a guess," he said, but he told her anyway.

That night he didn't have to say good-bye, because Bonnie Lamb didn't go home to New York. She canceled her flight and returned to Augustine's house. Her phone messages for Max were not returned until after midnight, when she was already asleep in the skull room.

Shortly after noon on August 28, the telephone in Tony Torres's kitchen started ringing.

Snapper told Edie Marsh to get it.

"*You* get it," she said.

"Real funny."

Snapper couldn't walk; the blow from the crowbar had messed up his right leg. He was laid out in the BarcaLounger with his knee packed in three bags of ice, which Edie had purchased for fifty dollars on Quail Roost Drive from some traveling bandit in a fish truck. The fifty bucks came out of Snapper's big score against the Whitmarks. He didn't tell Edie Marsh how much money remained in his pocket. He also didn't mention the trooper's gun in the Cherokee, in the event she blew her top again.

The phone continued ringing. "Answer it," Snapper said. "Maybe it's your Santy Claus boyfriend."

Edie picked up the phone. On the other end, a woman's voice said: "Hullo?"

Edie hung up. "It wasn't Fred," she said.

"The fuck was it?"

"I didn't ask, Snapper. We're not supposed to be here, remember?" She said it sounded like long distance.

"What if it's the insurance company? Maybe the check's ready."

Edie said, "No. Fred would tell me."

Snapper hacked out a laugh. "Fred's gone, you dumb twat. You scared him off!"

"How much you wanna bet."

"Right, he can't stay away, you're such a fantastic piece a ass."

"You can't even imagine," Edie said, showing some tongue. Maybe she wasn't hot enough for a young Kennedy, but she was the best thing young Mr Dove had ever seen. Besides, he couldn't back out of the deal now. He'd already put in for the phony claim.

Again the phone rang. Edie Marsh said, "Shit."

"For Christ's sake, gimme a hand." Snapper writhed irritably on the BarcaLounger. "Come on!"

Bracing a forearm on Edie's shoulder, he hobbled to the kitchen. She plucked the receiver off the hook and handed it to him.

"Yo," Snapper said.

"Hullo?" A woman. "Tony, is that you?"

"Hmmphrr," answered Snapper, cautiously.

"It's me. Neria."

Who? Frigid drops from the ice pack dripped down Snapper's injured leg. The purple kneecap felt as if it were about to burst, like a rotten mango. Edie pressed close, trying to hear what the caller was saying.

"Tony, I been tryin' to get through for days. What's with the house?"

Then Snapper remembered: The wife! Tony Torres had said her name was Miriam or Neria, some Cuban thing. He'd also said she'd be coming back for her cut of the insurance.

"Bad connection," Snapper mumbled into the receiver.

"What's going on? I call next door and Mister Varga, he said the hurricane totaled our house and now there's strangers living there. Some woman, Tony. You hear me? And Mister Varga said you shot a hole in the garage. What the hell's going on down there?"

Snapper held the receiver at arm's length, like it was a stick of dynamite. His bottom jaw shoveled in and out; the joints of his face made a popping sound that gave Edie the creeps.

"Tony?" squeaked the voice on the telephone.

Edie took it from Snapper's hand and said, "I'm very sorry. You've got the wrong number." Then she hung up.

At first all Snapper could say was, "Goddamn."

"The wife?"

"Yeah. Goddamn."

Edie Marsh helped him pogo to the chair. The ice crunched as he sat down. "Where's your Santy Claus boyfriend live?"

"Some Ramada."

"Goddamn. We don't got much time."

Edie said, "Where's Mrs Torres? Is she here in Miami?"

"Hell if I know. Get me to the car."

"I've got some more bad news. The dogs came back this morning."

"The wiener dogs?"

"We can't just leave them here. They need to be fed."

With both hands Snapper choked his throbbing leg and said, "Never again. I swear to Christ."

"Oh yeah," Edie Marsh said, "like this is some fun picnic for me. Here, give me your arm."

Avila's new customer took the Turnpike south. Before long the Cadillac was pinned in traffic—construction trucks, eighteen-

wheelers, Army convoys, ambulances, sightseers, National Guardsmen, and hundreds of queasy insurance adjusters, all heading into
the hurricane zone. Ground Zero.

"Looks like a bombing range," said the man calling himself
Rick Reynolds.

"Sure does. Where's your house?"

"We got a ways yet." As the car inched along, the man turned
up the radio: Rush Limbaugh, making wisecracks about the wife
of some candidate. Avila didn't think the jokes were all that funny,
but the man chuckled loyally. After the program ended, a news
report announced that the President of the United States was flying
to Miami to see the storm damage firsthand.

"Great," said Avila. "You think traffic sucks now, just wait."

The man said, "Yeah, one time I got stuck behind Reagan's
motorcade in the Holland Tunnel. Talk about a fuck story—two
hours we're breathing fumes."

Avila inquired how long the man had been in Dade County.
Couple months, he answered. Moved down from New York.

"And I never saw nuthin' like this."

Avila said, "Me, neither."

"I don't get it. Some houses go down like dominoes, some
don't lose a shingle. How's that happen?"

Avila checked his wristwatch. He wondered if the guy had the
fifteen grand on him, or maybe in the trunk of the car. He glanced
in the back seat: a crumpled road map and two empty Mister
Donut boxes.

The man said, "My guess is somebody got paid off. There's no
other way to make sense of it."

Avila kept his eyes ahead. "This ain't New York," he said.
Finally the traffic started to move.

The customer said a trailer park not far from his neighborhood
got blown to smithereens. "Old lady was killed," he said.

"Man, that's rough."

"Wonderful old lady. But every single trailer got destroyed,
every damn one."

Avila said, "Storm of the century."

"No, but here's the thing. The tie-downs on those mobile

177

homes was rotted out. The augers was sawed off. Anchor disks missing. Now you tell me some inspector didn't get greased."

Avila shifted uncomfortably. "Straps rot fast in this heat. How much farther?"

"Not long."

The customer picked up Krome Avenue to 168th Street. There he turned back east and drove for a mile to a subdivision called Fox Hollow, which had eroded to more or less bare foundations in the hurricane. The man parked in front of the skeletal remains of a small tract home.

Avila got out of the Cadillac and said, "God, you weren't kidding."

The roof of the house was totally blown away; gables, beams, trusses, everything. Avila was stunned that Mr Reynolds was allowing his family to remain in such an unprotected structure. Avila followed him inside, stepping over the wind-flattened doors. The place looked abandoned except for the kitchen, where a pack of stray dogs fought over rancid hamburger in the overturned refrigerator. Avila's customer grabbed an aluminum baseball bat and chased the mongrels off.

Peeking into the flooded bedrooms, Avila saw no sign of the customer's family. Immediately he felt the whole day go sour. Just to be sure, he said, "So where's your ninety-year-old grandmother?"

"Dead and buried," Ira Jackson replied, slapping the bat in the palm of one hand, "on beautiful Staten Island."

As the man from New York prepared to nail him to a pine tree, Avila concluded that Snapper was responsible for hiring the attacker.

Clearly the plan was to murder Avila and take control of his crooked roofers. Where was the mighty fist of Chango? Avila wondered grimly. Had the double-chicken sacrifice misfired?

Then the man from New York explained himself—who he was, what had happened to his mother, and why Avila must die a horrible drawn-out death. At first Avila pleaded innocence, feigning outrage at the fate of Beatrice Jackson. Soon he realized that the survival skills so essential to a county bureaucrat—the ability on a moment's notice to shift blame, dodge responsibility and misplace crucial paperwork—were of no use to him now.

Avila reasoned it was better to tell the truth than to have it tortured out of him. So, out of sheer bladder-shriveling fear, he confessed to Ira Jackson.

Yes, it was he who'd been assigned to approve the mobile homes at Suncoast Leisure Village. And yes, he'd failed to perform thorough and timely inspections. And—yes, yes! God forgive me!—he'd taken bribes to overlook code violations.

"Didn't you see those goddamn rotten straps?" demanded Ira Jackson, who was making a crucifix with fallen roof beams.

"No," Avila admitted.

"The augers?"

"No, I swear."

"Never even checked?" Ira Jackson pounded ferociously with a hammer.

"I didn't see them," Avila said morosely, "because I never drove out there."

Ira Jackson's hammer halted in midair. Avila, who was lashed to a broken commode in a bathroom, lowered his eyes in a pantomime of shame. That's when he saw that the toilet bowl was alive with bright-green frogs and mottled brown snakes, splashing beneath him in fetid water.

With a shiver he said, "I never went to the trailer park. The guy sent me the money—"

"How much?"

"Fifty bucks a unit. He sent it to the office, so I figured what the hell, why waste gas? Instead of driving all the way down there, I . . ." Here Avila caught himself. It seemed unnecessary to reveal that he'd played golf on the afternoon he was supposed to inspect Suncoast Leisure Village.

". . . I didn't go."

"You're shittin' me."

"No. I'm very, very sorry."

The expression on Ira Jackson's face caused Avila to reevaluate his decision to be candid. Evidently the doughnut man intended to torture him, no matter what. Ira Jackson bent over the crucifix and went back to work.

Raising his voice over the racket, Avila said, "Christ, if I knew what he was doing with those trailers, he never woulda got permits. You gotta believe me, there's no amount of money would make me take a pass on cut augers. No way!"

"Shut up." Ira Jackson carried the cross to the backyard and began nailing it to the trunk of a pine. It had been a tall lush tree until the hurricane sheared off the top thirty feet; now it was merely a bark-covered pole.

With each plonk of the hammer, Avila's spirits sank. He said a prayer to Chango, then tried a "Hail Mary" in the wan hope that traditional Catholic entreaty would be more potent in staving off a crucifixion.

As the man from New York dragged him to the tree, Avila cried, "Please, I'll do anything you want!"

"OK," said Ira Jackson, "I want you to die."

He positioned Avila upright against the cross and wrapped duct tape around his ankles and wrists to minimize the squirming. Avila shut his eyes when he saw the doughnut man snatch up the hammer. The moment the cold point of the nail punctured his palm, Avila emitted a puppy yelp and fainted.

When he awoke, he saw that Chango had answered his prayers with a fury.

SIXTEEN

At nine sharp on the morning of August 31, an attractive brunette woman carrying two miniature dachshunds walked into a Hialeah branch of the Barnett Bank and opened an account under the name of "Neria G. Torres."

For identification, the woman provided an expired automobile registration and a handful of soggy mail. The bank officer politely requested a driver's license or passport, any document bearing a photograph. The woman said her most personal papers, including driver's license, were washed away by the hurricane. As the bank officer questioned her more closely, the woman became distraught. Soon her little dogs began to bark plangently; one of them squirted from her arms and dashed in circles around the lobby, nipping at other customers. To quiet the scene, the banker agreed to accept the woman's auto registration as identification. His own aunt had lost all her immigration papers in the storm, so Mrs Torres's excuse seemed plausible. To open the account she gave him one hundred dollars cash, and said she'd be back in a few days to deposit a large insurance check.

"You're lucky they settled so fast," the banker remarked. "My aunt's having a terrible time with her company."

The woman said her homeowner policy was with Midwest Casualty. "I've got a *great* insurance man," she added.

Later, when Edie Marsh told the story to Fred Dove, he reacted with the weakest twitch of an ironic smile. Under the woeful circumstances, it was as good as a cartwheel.

Edie, Snapper and the two noisy wiener dogs had moved into

his room at the Ramada. No other accommodations were available for a radius of sixty miles, because the hotels were jammed full of displaced families, relief volunteers, journalists, construction workers and insurance adjusters. Fred Dove felt trapped. His fear of getting arrested for fraud was now compounded by a fear that his wife would call the motel room, then Edie Marsh or Snapper would answer the phone and the wiener dogs would start howling, leaving Fred Dove to invent an explanation that no sensible woman in Omaha, Nebraska, would ever accept.

"Cheer up," Edie told him. "We're all set at the bank."

"Good," he said in a brittle tone.

The long tense weekend had abraded the insurance man's nerves—Snapper, gimping irritably around the small motel room, slugging down vodka, threatening to blast the yappy dachshunds with a massive black handgun he claimed to have stolen from a police officer.

No wonder I'm edgy, thought Fred Dove.

To deepen the gloom, sharing the cramped room with Snapper and the dogs left the insurance man no opportunity for intimacy with Edie Marsh. Not that he could have availed himself of a sexual invitation; the withering effect of Snapper's previous coital interruption endured, as Snapper continued to tease Fred Dove about the red condom.

Also looming large was the question of Edie's aptitude for violence—a disconcerting vision of the crowbar episode was scorched into Fred Dove's memory. He worried that she or Snapper might endeavor to murder each other at any moment.

Edie stretched out next to him on the bed. "You're miserable," she observed.

"Yes indeed," said the insurance man.

With his bum leg elevated, Snapper was stationed in an armchair three and one half feet from the television screen. Every so often he would take a futile swipe at Donald or Marla, and tell them to shut the holy fuck up.

"Sally Jessy," Edie whispered. Fred Dove sighed.

On the TV, a woman in a dreadful yellow wig was accusing her gap-toothed white-trash husband of screwing her younger sister. Instead of denying it, the husband said damn right, and it was the best nooky I ever had. Instantly the sister, also wearing a dreadful wig and lacking in teeth, piped up to say she couldn't get enough. Sally Jessy exhaled in weary dismay, the studio audience hooted, and Snapper let out a war whoop that set off the dogs once again.

"If the phone rings," Fred Dove said, "please don't answer."

Edie Marsh didn't need to ask why.

"You got any kids?" she asked.

The insurance man said he had two, a boy and a girl. He thought Edie might follow up and ask about their ages, what grades they were in, and so on. But she showed no interest.

She said, "Cheer up, OK? Think about your cruise to Bimini."

"Look, I was wondering—"

Snapper, growling over one shoulder: "You two mind? I'm tryin' to watch the fuckin' show."

Edie signaled for Fred Dove to follow her to the bathroom. He perked up, anticipating a discreet blow job or something along those lines.

But Edie only wanted a quiet place to chat. They perched their butts on the edge of the bathtub. She stroked his hand and said, "Tell me, sugar. What's on your mind?"

"OK, the company sends me the check—"

"Right."

"I give it to you," said Fred Dove, "and you deposit it in the bank."

"Right."

"And then?"

Edie Marsh answered with exaggerated clarity, like a school-teacher coaxing an exceptionally dull-witted pupil. "*Then*, Fred, I go back to the bank in a couple days and cut *three* separate cashier's checks for forty-seven thousand *each*. Just like we agreed."

Undeterred by the condescension, he said: "Don't forget the hundred dollars I gave you to open the account."

Edie let go of his hand and brushed it, like a cockroach, off her lap. Lord, what an anal dweeb! "Yes, Freddie, I'll make absolutely sure your check says forty-seven thousand *one hundred*. OK? Feel better?"

The insurance man grunted unhappily. "I won't feel better till it's over."

Edie Marsh didn't inform Fred Dove about the phone call from the real Neria Torres. She didn't want to spook him out of the scam.

"The best part about this deal," she said, "is that nobody's in a position to screw anyone else. You've got shit on me, I've got shit on you, and we've both got plenty of shit on Snapper. That's why it's going down so clean."

Fred Dove said, "That gun of his scares me to death."

"Not much we can do. The asshole digs guns."

Outside, Donald and Marla began scratching at the bathroom door in the frenetic manner of deranged badgers.

"Let's get out there," Edie Marsh said, "before Snapper loses it."

"This is nuts!"

Edie mechanically guided Fred Dove's head to her bosom. "Don't you worry," she said, and he was momentarily transported to a warm, fragrant valley, where no harm could ever come.

Then, on the other side of the door, a gun went off, the dachshunds bayed and Snapper bellowed profanely.

"Jesus!" Edie exclaimed.

The insurance man burrowed in her cleavage. "What're we going to do?" he asked, desolately.

Avila thought: I'm either dead or dreaming.

Because it should hurt worse than this, being nailed to a cross. Even if it's only one hand, it should hurt like a mother. I ought to be screaming at the top of my lungs, instead of just hanging here with a dull ache. Hanging like a wet flag and staring at . . .

It *must* be a dream.

Because they don't have lions in Florida. And that's what that monster is, a full-grown African lion. King of the motherfucking jungle. So real you can see the red-brown stains on its mouth. So real you can smell its piss. So real you can hear the dead man's spine dear God Almighty being crunched in its fangs.

The lion was eating the doughnut man.

Avila was frozen in the pose of a scarecrow. He was afraid to blink. Between bites, the big cat would glance up, yawn, lick its paws, shake the gnats off its mane. Avila noticed a blue tag fastened to one of its ears, but that wasn't important.

The important thing was: He definitely wasn't dreaming. The lion was real. Clearly it was sent to save his life.

And not by the Catholic God—Catholics had no expertise in the summoning of demonic jungle beasts. No, it was a funkier, more mystical deity who had answered Avila's plea from the cross.

Gracias, Chango! *Muchas gracias*.

When I get home, Avila promised his *santería* guardian, I shall make an offering worthy of royalty. Chickens, rabbits. Perhaps I'll even spring for a goat.

In the meantime, Avila implored, please make the lion go away so I can get this fucking nail out of my hand!

The big cat dined leisurely, no more than fifteen yards from the pine tree. Ira Jackson's hammer lay where he'd dropped it, at Avila's feet. From marks on the ground, it appeared that the doughnut man had been jumped from behind, swiftly done in, and dragged to the dry weedy patch where the lion now sat, possessively attending the disemboweled, disarticulated corpse. Ira Jackson's gold chain dangled like spaghetti from the cat's whiskered maw. It disappeared with a flick of the tongue.

Avila's knowledge of lion eating habits was sketchy, but he couldn't believe the animal could still be hungry after devouring the substantial Mr Jackson. Despite the worsening pain in his hand, Avila remained rock steady against the cross until the lion quit munching and nodded off.

Slowly Avila turned his head to examine the nasty puncture. His palm was striped with congealed blood. The nail had penetrated the tough fleshy web between the second and third fingers, which wiggled feebly at Avila's silent bidding. A moral victory, of sorts—Ira Jackson had failed to break any major bones.

Keeping a close watch on the snoozing lion, and moving with

glacial deliberation, Avila tugged his good hand free of the duct tape. Slowly he reached across and began to work the nail loose from the punctured palm. The undertaking caused less agony than he'd anticipated; perhaps Chango had anesthetized him as well.

Luckily, the wood of the makeshift crucifix was soft. In less than a minute the nail pulled out, and Avila's hand fell free, with only a modest geyser of blood. He inserted the hand forcefully between his shaking knees, and bit his lower lip to stifle a cry. The lion did not stir. The exhaust of its snore fluttered the bright remains of Ira Jackson's sports shirt, which clung like a lobster bib to the big cat's throat.

While the beast slept, Avila unwrapped the sticky tape from his ankles. As he furtively inched clear of the pine tree, his eyes fell on a partially masticated chunk of bone—a wee remnant of the doughnut man, but a potent talisman for future *santería* rites.

Avila pocketed the moist prize and stole away.

Skink chose to spend the night in the back of the pickup truck. Shortly after ten, Augustine emerged from the house with a hot Cuban sandwich and two bottles of beer. Skink winked appreciatively and sat up. He finished the sandwich in four huge bites, guzzled the beer and said: "So she stayed."

"I don't know why."

"Because she's never seen the likes of you."

"Or you," said Augustine.

"And because her husband behaved poorly."

Augustine slouched against the fender. "She's here, and I'm glad about it. Which makes me quite the model of rectitude—a woman on her honeymoon, for Christ's sake."

Skink arched a tangled eyebrow. "A new low?"

"Oh yes."

"Her decision, son. Don't beat yourself up."

Anxiety, not guilt, gnawed at Augustine. On his present course, he would very soon fall in love with Mrs Max Lamb. How much fragrant late-night snuggling could a man endure? And Bonnie was an ardent snuggler, even in platonic mode. Augustine was racked with worry. He had no chance whatsoever, not with her hair smelling like bougainvilleas, not with that velvet slope of neck, not with those denim-blue eyes. He couldn't recall being with a woman who felt so *right*, nestled in his embrace. Even her slumbering snorts and sniffles soothed him—that's how hard he was falling.

It's just a kiss away. Like Mick and Keith said.

A newly married woman. Brilliant.

Unconsciously Augustine found himself gazing at the window of the guest room. Soon Bonnie's shadow crossed behind the drapes. Then the lights went off.

Skink poked him sharply. "Settle down. Nothing'll happen unless she wants it to." He stood in the bed of the pickup for a series of twisting calisthenics, accompanied by preternaturally asthmatic grunts. That went on for twenty full minutes under the stars. Augustine watched without interrupting. Afterwards Skink sat down heavily, rocking the truck.

Pointing at the remaining beer, he said: "You gonna drink that?" 'Help yourself."

"You're a patient young man."

"I've got nothing but time," Augustine said. Why rush the guy?

Skink threw back his head and tilted the beer bottle until it was empty. Pensively he said: "You never know how these things'll play out."

"Doesn't matter, captain. I'm in."

"OK. Here." He handed Augustine the scrap of paper that Jim Tile had given him at the hospital. On the paper, the trooper had written:

black Jp. Cherokee
BZQ-42F

Augustine was impressed that Brenda Rourke remembered the license tag, or anything else, after the hideous beating.

Skink said, "The plate's stolen. No surprise there."

"The driver?"

"White non-Latin male, late thirties. Deformed jaw, according to Trooper Rourke. Plus he wore a pinstriped suit."

Skink returned to a sprawled position. He folded his arms under his head.

Augustine peered over the side of the truck. "Where do we start?" The man could be all the way to Atlanta by now.

"I've got some ideas," said the governor.

Augustine was doubtful. "The cops'll find him first."

"They're all on hurricane duty, double shifts. Even the detectives are directing traffic." Skink chuckled quietly. "It's not a bad time to be a fugitive."

Augustine felt something brush his leg—a neighbor's orange tabby. When he reached to pet it, the cat scooted beneath the pickup.

The governor said, "I'm doing this for Jim. It's not often he asks."

"But there's other reasons."

Skink nodded. "True. I'm not fond of shitheads who beat up women. And the storm has left me, well, unfulfilled. . . ."

It hadn't been the cataclysmic purgative he had hoped for and prophesied. Ideally a hurricane should drive people out, not bring people in. The high number of new arrivals to South Florida was merely depressing; the moral caliber of the fortune-seekers was appalling—low-life hustlers, slick-talking scammers and cold-blooded opportunists, not to mention pure gangsters and thugs. Precisely the kind of creeps who would cave in a lady's face.

"Do not," Skink said, "expect me to control my temper."

"Wouldn't dream of it," said Augustine.

The light in the guest bedroom went on. Augustine found Bonnie Lamb sitting up in bed. For a nightgown she wore a long white T-shirt that she'd found in a drawer: Tom Petty and the Heartbreakers. Augustine had purchased it at a concert at the Miami Arena. The woman whom he'd taken to the show, the psychotic doctor who later tried to filet him in the shower, had bought a black shirt to match her biker boots. At the time, Augustine had found the ensemble fetching, in a faux-trashy way.

"Max call yet?" Bonnie asked.

Augustine checked the answering machine. No messages. He returned to the bedroom and told her.

She said, "I've been married one week and a day. What's the matter with me?" She drew her knees to her chest. "I should be home."

Exactly! thought Augustine. Absolutely right!

"You think my husband's a jerk?"

"Not at all," Augustine lied, decorously.

"Then why hasn't he called." It was not a question. Bonnie Lamb said, "Come here."

She made room under the covers, but Augustine positioned himself chastely on the edge of the bed.

"You must think I'm crazy," said Bonnie.

"No."

"My heart is upside down. That's the only way to describe it."

Augustine said, "Stay as long as you want."

"I want to go along with you and . . . him. The kidnapper."

"Why?"

"Oh, I don't know. Probably goes back to Max, or my dad and his model airplanes, or my wretched childhood, even though my memories are quite wonderful. It's got to be something. Happy normal little girls don't grow up to dump their husbands, do they?" Bonnie Lamb switched off the lamp. "You want to lie down?"

"Better not," said Augustine.

In the dark, her hand found his cheek. She said, "Here's my idea: I think we should sleep together."

"But we *have* slept together, Mrs Lamb." That without missing a beat. Augustine commended himself—a little humor to cut the tension.

Bonnie said, "Come on. You know what I mean."

"Make love?"

"Oh, you're a quick one." She grabbed his shoulders and pulled him down. His head came to rest on a pillow. Before he could get up she was on top, pinning his arms. Impishly she planted her chin on his breastbone. In the light slanting through the window, Augustine was able to see her smile, the liveliness of her eyes and—behind her—the wall of gaping skulls.

Bonnie Lamb said, "Making love with you might clear my thinking."

"So would electroshock therapy."

"I'm very serious."

"And very married," said Augustine.

"Yes, but you're still getting hard."

"Thanks for the bulletin."

She let go of his arms, took his face in both hands. Her smile disappeared, and sadness entered her voice. "Don't be such a smartass," she whispered. "Can't you understand—I don't know what else to do. I tried crying; it doesn't work."

"I'm sorry—"

"I feel closer to you than I've ever felt to Max. That's not a good sign."

"No, it isn't."

"Especially after a week of marriage. My own husband—and already I feel old and invisible when we're together." She took his shirt in her fists. "God, you know what? Forget everything I said."

"Yeah, right."

"Then you've thought about it, too."

"Constantly," said Augustine. Then, in a burst of foolish virtue: "But it would sure be wrong."

Her breasts were lined up just below his rib cage. They rose ever so slightly when she took a breath. Friendship, he reminded himself, could be excruciating.

Bonnie asked, "What happens now?"

"Oh, my erection will eventually go away. Then we can both get some sleep."

She lowered her eyes. Blushing? In the shadows it was hard to tell. She said, "No, I meant with the governor. What're you two guys up to?"

"Hair-raising thrills and high-speed adventure."

Bonnie nestled closer and settled in for the night. Augustine was severely tempted to stroke her hair, or kiss the top of her head, or trace a finger along that famous velvet slope of her neckline. But, with idiotic decency, he held back.

Mrs Max Lamb fell asleep long before he did. Shortly after midnight, the telephone began to ring in the kitchen. Augustine didn't get out of bed to answer it, because he didn't want to wake his new friend. He probably could have moved her gently to one side of the bed, but he didn't even try.

She was sleeping so soundly, and he felt so good.

SEVENTEEN

Bonnie Lamb rolled over at three in the morning, freeing Augustine to rise and answer the phone, which had been ringing intermittently for hours.

Naturally it was Bonnie's husband in New York. Augustine anticipated a lively exchange.

"What's going on!" Max Lamb demanded.

"Bonnie's fine. She's asleep."

"Answer me!"

"She left you several messages. She wasn't up to the airplane trip—"

"Wake her, please. Tell her it's important."

As he waited, Max Lamb reflected over the unalloyed rottenness of his long thankless day. The NIH press conference declaiming the hazards of Bronco cigarets made CNN, MTV and all the networks, followed of course by prominent barbs in the Leno and Letterman monologues. The wiseass MTV coverage was particularly aggravating because it struck directly at young female smokers, a key market component of Bronco's booming sales growth. Front-page stories were expected the following morning in the *Times*, the *Wall Street Journal* and the Washington *Post*. The word "disaster" was insufficient to describe the crisis, as the splenetic chairman of Durham Gas Meat & Tobacco adamantly insisted on a total advertising embargo against all publications reporting the NIH findings—which was to say, all newspapers and magazines in the United States. The atmosphere at Rodale & Burns was sepulchral, due to the many millions of dollars that the agency stood to lose if Bronco's print ads were yanked. Max Lamb had spent the better part of the afternoon attempting to contact DGM&T's chairman in Guadalajara, where he was receiving thrice-daily injections of homogenized sheep semen to arrest the malignant tumors in his lungs. Workers at the clinic said the chairman was taking no calls, and refused to patch Max Lamb through to the old geezer's room.

And if that wasn't enough, Max now had to deal with a flighty, recalcitrant wife in Florida.

Bonnie's voice was husky from sleep. "Honey?" she said.

Max gripped the receiver as if it were the neck of a squirming rattlesnake. "Exactly what's going on down there!"

"I'm sorry. I need a few more days."

"Why aren't you at the motel?"

"I fell asleep here."

"With the skulls? Jesus Christ, Bonnie."

When Max Lamb got highly agitated, he acquired a frenetic rasp that his coworkers likened to that of an asthmatic on amphetamines. Bonnie didn't blame her husband for getting upset that she was with Augustine. Trying to explain was pointless, because she didn't yet comprehend it herself. Her attempted seduction—*that* she understood too well. But the urge to go road-tripping with the governor, the lack of interest in returning home to begin her new marriage . . . confusing emotions, indeed.

"I still don't feel very well, Max. Maybe it's exhaustion."

"You can sleep on the plane. Or in a damn motel."

"All right, honey, I'll get a room."

"Has he tried anything?"

"No!" Bonnie said sharply. "He's been a perfect gentleman." Thinking: *I'm* the one you've got to worry about, buddy boy.

"I don't trust him." Max Lamb's normal vibrant voice had returned, indicating a beneficial drop in blood pressure.

Bonnie decided it was safe to point out that if it weren't for Augustine, Max would still be kidnapped.

That provoked a grinding silence on the other end. Then: "There's something not right about him."

"Oh, and you're perfectly normal, Max. Driving hundreds of miles to take movies of wrecked houses and crying babies."

A movement by Augustine caught Bonnie Lamb's attention. With a mischievous grin, he produced three plump grapefruits and began to juggle, dancing barefoot around the kitchen. Bonnie covered her mouth to keep from giggling into the phone.

She heard Max say, "I'm flying to Mexico tomorrow. When I get back, I expect you to be here."

Bonnie's eyes followed the flying citrus.

"Of course I'll be there." The promise sounded so anemic that her husband couldn't possibly have believed it. Bonnie felt a wave of sadness. Max wasn't stupid; surely he knew something was wrong. She took a slow deep breath. Augustine slipped out of the kitchen and left her alone.

"Bonnie?"

"Yes, honey."

"Don't you want to know why I'm going to Mexico?"

"Mexico," she said, pensively. Thinking: He's going to *Mexico*. Asking: "Will you be gone long, Max?"

And wondering: Who's this strange, reckless woman who has climbed inside my skin!

Avila didn't tell his wife about his harrowing brush with crucifixion, for she would've massaged it into a divine parable and shared it with all the neighbors. Once, Avila's wife had seen the face of the Virgin Mary in a boysenberry pancake, and phoned every TV station in Miami. No telling how far she'd run with a lion story.

Locking himself in the bathroom, Avila bandaged his throbbing hand and waited for his wife to depart for the grocery store. When the coast was clear, he grabbed a shovel from the garage, crept to the backyard and excavated a Tupperware box full of cash that was buried under a mango tree. The money was his wife's brother's share of a small-time marijuana venture. Avila's wife's brother resided in state prison for numerous felony convictions unrelated to the pot, so Avila and his wife had promised to baby-sit the cash until his parole, sometime around the turn of the century. Avila didn't approve of pilfering a relative's life savings, but it was an emergency. If Gar Whitmark didn't get his seven grand immediately he would call the authorities and have Avila thrown in a cell with a voracious pervert. That's how powerful Whitmark was, or so Avila believed.

He dug energetically for the Tupperware, ignoring the pain of the nail wound. He was spurred by the putrid-sweet stench of rotting mangos, and a fear that one of his many in-laws would arrive unannounced—Avila wanted nobody to know he'd been ripped off by one of his own crooked roofers. He unearthed the container without difficulty, and eagerly pried off the lid. He removed seventy damp one-hundred-dollar bills and wadded them into a pocket. But something wasn't right: Money appeared to be missing from his wife's brother's stash. Avila's suspicion was confirmed by a hasty count; the Tupperware box was short by an additional four grand.

Dumb bitches! Avila steamed. They've been losing at Indian bingo again. His wife and her mother were practically addicted.

To confront the women would have given Avila great pleasure, but it also would've exposed his own clandestine filching. Ruefully he reburied the Tupperware, and concealed the disturbed topsoil with a mat of leaves and lawn cuttings. Then he drove to the Gar Whitmark Building, where he was made to wait in the lobby for ninety minutes, like a common peon.

When a secretary finally led him into Gar Whitmark's private office, Avila spoiled any chance for a civil exchange by asking the corporate titan what the hell was wrong with his scalp, was that a fungus or what? Avila, who had never before seen hair plugs, hadn't meant to be rude, but Gar Whitmark reacted explosively. He shoved Avila to the floor, snatched the seven grand from his hand, knelt heavily on his chest and spewed verbal abuse. Whitmark wasn't a large man, but he was fit from many afternoons of country-club tennis. Avila chose not to resist; he was thinking lawsuit. Whitmark's eyes bulged in rage, and he cursed himself breathless, but he did not punch Avila even once. Instead he got up, smoothed the breast of his Italian suit, straightened his necktie and presented the disheveled con man with an itemized estimate from Killebrew Roofing Co. for the staggering sum of $23,250.

Avila was crestfallen, though not totally surprised: Whitmark had selected the best, and most expensive, roofers in all South Florida. Also, the most honest. From his days as a crooked inspector, Avila sourly recalled the few times he'd tried to shake down Killebrew crews for payoffs, only to be chased like a skunk from the construction sites. Killebrew, like Gar Whitmark, had some heavy juice downtown.

Avila pretended to study the estimate while he thought up a diplomatic response.

Whitmark said: "They start work next week. Adjust your finances accordingly."

"Jesus, I don't have twenty-three grand." There—he'd said it.

"You're making me weep." Gar Whitmark clicked his teeth.

With a bandaged hand Avila waved the Killebrew paper in tepid indignation. "I could do this same job for half as much!"

Whitmark snorted. "I wouldn't let you put the roof on a fucking doghouse." He handed Avila a Xeroxed clipping from the newspaper. "You either come up with the money or go to jail. *Comprende*, Señor Dipshit?"

The newspaper article said the Dade State Attorney was appointing a special squad of prosecutors to crack down on dishonest contractors preying on hurricane victims.

"One phone call," said Whitmark, "and you're on your way to the buttfuck motel."

Avila bowed his head. The sight of his blackened fingernails reminded him of the buried Tupperware box. Hell, there was only twelve, maybe thirteen grand left in it. He was screwed.

"My wife's still a wreck from what your people did. You wouldn't believe the goddamn pharmacy bill." Whitmark pointed at the door and told Avila good-bye. "We'll talk," he said, ominously.

On the way home, Avila dejectedly mulled his options. How often could he turn to Chango without offending Him, or appearing selfish? Yet the *santero* priest who trained Avila had mentioned no numerical limit on supernatural requests. Tonight, Avila decided, I'll do a goat—no, *two* goats!

And tomorrow I will hunt that bastard Snapper.

The Church of High Pentecostal Rumination, headquartered in Chicoryville, Florida, attended all natural disasters in the western hemisphere. Earthquake, flood and hurricane zones proved fertile territories for conversion and recruitment of sinners. Less than thirty-six hours after the killer storm smashed Dade County, an experienced team of seven Ruminator missionaries was dispatched in a leased Dodge minivan. Hotel beds were scarce, so they shared a room at a Ramada Inn off the Turnpike. There was no complaining.

Every morning, the missionaries preached, consoled and distributed pamphlets. Then they stood in line for free army lunches at the tent city, and returned to the motel for two hours of quiet contemplation and gin rummy. The Ramada offered free cable TV, which allowed the Ruminators to view a half-dozen different religious broadcasts at any time of day. One afternoon, in the absence of a pure Pentecostal preacher, they settled on Pat Robertson and the *700 Club*. The Ruminators didn't share Robertson's paranoid worldview, but they admired his life-or-death style of fund-raising and hoped to pick up some pointers.

Toward the end of the program, Reverend Robertson closed his eyes and prayed. The Ruminators joined hands—no easy task, since four of them were on one bed and three were on the other. The prayer was not one they recognized from the Scriptures; evidently Reverend Robertson had composed it personally, since it contained several references to his post office box in Virginia. Nonetheless, it was a pretty good prayer, fervently rendered, and the Ruminator missionaries were enjoying it.

No sooner had Reverend Robertson exhaled the word "Amen" when the motel room was rocked by a muffled detonation, and the television set exploded before the missionaries' startled eyes. Reverend Robertson's squinting visage vaporized in a gout of acrid blue smoke, and his whiny beseechment faded in a sprinkle of falling glass. The Ruminators scrambled off the beds, dropped to their knees and burst into a hymn, "Nearer My God to Thee." That's how the manager of the Ramada found them, fifteen minutes later, when he came to apologize.

"Some asshole downstairs shot off a .357," he announced.

All singing ceased. The motel manager pushed the broken television away from the wall and pointed to a ragged hole in the carpet. "From the bullet," he explained. "Don't worry. I kicked 'em out."

"A gun?" cried a Ruminator elder, springing to his feet.

"That ain't the worst of it," the motel manager said. "They had dogs in the room! You believe that? Chewin' up the bed-spreads and God knows *what*." He promised to bring the Rumi-nators another TV set, but warned them to keep their hymn singing at a low volume, so as not to disturb other guests.

"Everybody's on edge," the manager added, unnecessarily.

After he left, the missionaries locked the door and held a solemn meeting. They agreed they'd done all they could for the good people of South Florida, and quickly packed their bags.

"Well, that was brilliant."

Snapper told Edie Marsh to shut up and quit beating it to death. What's done is done.

"No, really," she said, "getting us thrown out of the only hotel room between here and Daytona Beach. Absolute genius."

With a gaseous hiss, Snapper sagged into the BarcaLounger. She had some nerve giving him shit, after the way she'd fucked up his leg with that crowbar. Who wouldn't be in a lousy mood, their goddamn knee all swollen up like a Georgia ham.

He said, "It's your fault, you and them dogs. Hey, get me a Coors."

On the drive back to the Torres house, they had stopped at a 7-Eleven for gas, ice and supplies. Fred Dove had purchased Tylenol and peppermint Tic Tacs before lugubriously departing for a busy afternoon of storm-damage estimates. He drove off with the hollow stare of a man whose life had abruptly gone to ruin.

Edie Marsh pulled a beer from the cooler and tossed it underhanded at Snapper. "We're lucky we're not in jail," she said for the fifth time.

"Dogs wouldn't shut up."

"So you shot a hole in the ceiling."

"Damn straight." Snapper arranged his lower jaw to accommodate the stream of Coors. He reminded Edie of Popeye in the old Saturday cartoons.

"I'm gonna do them fuckin' mutts," he said. "Tonight when you're sleeping. That'll leave me three bullets, too, so don't get no ideas."

"Wow, a math whiz," said Edie, "on top of all your other talents."

"You don't believe me?"

"The dogs are tied outside. They're not bothering anybody."

When Snapper finished the beer, he crumpled the can and tossed it on the carpet. Then he took out the pistol and started spinning the cylinder, something he'd obviously picked up from a movie. Edie Marsh ignored him. She went to the garage to put more gasoline in the generator—they needed electricity to run the TV, without which Snapper would become unmanageable.

Sure enough, by the time she returned to the living room, he was contentedly camped out in front of *Oprah*.

"Hookers," he reported, riveted to the screen.

"Your lucky day."

Edie Marsh felt gummy with perspiration. The hurricane had eviscerated the elaborate ductwork of Tony Torres's air-conditioning system. Even if the unit had worked, there were no doors, windows or roof to keep cooled air in the house. Edie went to the bedroom and changed from her banking dress to a pair of Mrs Torres's expensive white linen shorts and a beige short-sleeved pullover. She would have been inconsolable if the borrowed clothes had fit her, but thank God they didn't; Mrs Torres was easily three sizes larger. The bagginess provided welcomed ventilation in the tropical humidity, and was not entirely unattractive.

Edie Marsh was appraising her new look in the mirror when

the phone started ringing. Snapper hollered for her to pick up, goddammit!

Not given to premonitions, Edie experienced a powerful one that proved true. When she answered the telephone, a long-distance operator asked if she would accept collect charges from a "Neria in Memphis."

Memphis! The witch was heading south!

"I don't know anybody named Neria," Edie said, straining to stay calm.

"Is this 305-443-1676?"

"I'm not sure. See, I don't live here—I was walking past the house when I noticed the phone."

"Ma'am, please—"

"Operator, in case you haven't heard, we had a terrible hurricane down here!"

Neria's voice: "I want to speak to my husband. Ask her if Antonio Torres is around."

Edie Marsh said, "Look, the house is empty. I was walking past and I thought it might be somebody's relative calling. An emergency maybe. The man who stayed here, he's gone. Loaded his stuff in a Ryder truck and moved out Friday. Up to New York, is what he said."

"Thank you," said the operator.

"What! What's your name, lady?" Neria asked excitedly.

"Thank you," the operator repeated, trying to cut the conversation short.

But Edie was rolling. "Him and some young lady had a rental truck. Maybe his wife. She looked twenty-three, twenty-four. Long blond hair."

Neria, exploding: "No, *I'm* the wife! That's my house!"

Sure, thought Edie, now that insurance money is in the air. Dump the granola-head professor and come running back to blimpy old Tony.

"Brooklyn," Edie embellished. "I think he said Brooklyn."

"Sonofabitch," Neria moaned.

Curtly the operator asked Mrs Torres if she wished to try

another telephone number. No reply. She'd hung up. Edie Marsh did, too.

Her heart drummed against her ribs. Unconsciously she rubbed her damp palms on the rump of Mrs Torres's lovely linen shorts. Then she hurried to the garage and located a pair of small green-handled wire cutters.

From the living room, Snapper called: "Who the hell was that? The wife again?" When he heard the garage door, he yelled, "Hey, I'm talkin' to you!"

Edie Marsh didn't hear him. She was sneaking next door to clip the telephone lines, so that Neria Torres could not call Mr Varga to check out the wild story about Tony and the young blonde and the Ryder truck.

The license tag on the black Cherokee was stolen from a Camaro on the morning after the hurricane, in a subdivision called Turtle Meadow. That's where Augustine was headed when Skink directed him to stop at a makeshift tent city, which the National Guard had erected for those made homeless by the hurricane.

Skink bounded from the truck and stalked through rows of open tents. Bonnie and Augustine kept a few steps behind, taking in the sobering scene. Dazed eyes followed them. Men and women sprawled listlessly on army cots, dull-eyed teenagers waded bare-foot through milky puddles, children clung fiercely to new dolls handed out by the Red Cross.

"All these souls!" Skink cried, simian arms waving in agitation.

The soldiers assumed he was shell-shocked from the storm. They let him alone.

At the front of a ragged line, Guardsmen gave out plastic bottles of Evian. Skink kept marching. A small boy in a muddy diaper scurried across his path. With one hand he scooped the child to eye level.

Bonnie Lamb nudged Augustine. "What do we do?"

When they reached Skink's side, they heard him singing in a voice that was startlingly high and tender:

> *It's just a box of rain,*
> *I don't know who put it here.*
> *Believe it if you need it,*
> *Or leave it if you dare.*

The little boy—scarcely two years old, Bonnie guessed—had chubby cheeks, curly brown hair and a scrape healing on his brow. He wore a sleeveless cotton shirt with a Batman logo. He smiled at the song and tugged curiously on a silver sprout of the stranger's beard. A light mist fell from scuffed clouds.

Augustine reached for Skink's shoulder. "Captain?"

Skink, to the boy: "What's your name?"

The reply was a bashful giggle. Skink peered at the child. "You won't ever forget, will you? Hurricanes are an eviction notice from God. Go tell your people."

He resumed singing, in a nasal pitch imposed by tiny fingers pinching his nostrils.

> *And it's just a box of rain,*
> *Or a ribbon in your hair.*
> *Such a long, long time to be gone*
> *And a short time to be there.*

The child clapped. Skink kissed him lightly on the forehead. He said, "You're good company, sonny. How's your spirit of adventure?"

"No!" Bonnie Lamb stepped forward. "We're not taking him. Don't even think about it."

"He'd enjoy himself, would he not?"

"Captain, please." Augustine lifted the boy and handed him to Bonnie, who hurried to find the parents before the wild man changed his mind.

The pewter sky filled with a loud thwocking drone. People in the Evian line pointed to a covey of drab military helicopters, flying low. The choppers began to circle, causing the tents to flutter and snap. Quickly a procession of police cars, government sedans, black Chevy Blazers and TV trucks entered the compound.

Skink said, "Ha! Our Commander in Chief."

Five Secret Service types piled out of one of the Blazers, followed by the President. He wore, over a shirt and necktie, a navy-blue rain slicker with an emblem on the breast. He waved toward the television cameras, then compulsively began to shake the hands of every National Guardsman and Army soldier he saw. This peculiar behavior might have continued until dusk had not one of the President's many aides (also in a blue slicker) whispered in his ear. At that point a family of authentic hurricane refugees, carefully screened and selected from the sweltering masses, was brought to meet and be photographed with the President. Included in the family was the obligatory darling infant, over whom the leader of the free world labored to coo and fuss. The photo opportunity lasted less than three minutes, after which the President resumed his obsessive fraternizing with anyone wearing a uniform. These unnatural affections were extended to a snowy-haired officer of the local Salvation Army, around whom the Commander in Chief flung a ropy arm. "So," he chirped at the befuddled old-timer, "what outfit you with?"

A short distance away, Augustine stood with his arms folded. "Pathetic," he said.

Skink agreed. "Check the glaze in his eyes. There's nothing worse than a Republican on Halcion."

As soon as Bonnie Lamb returned, they left for Turtle Meadow.

EIGHTEEN

Skink had gotten the address from the police report, courtesy of Jim Tile. The mailboxes and street signs were down, so it took some searching to find the house. Because of his respectable and clean-cut appearance, Augustine was chosen to make the inquiry. Skink waited in the back of the pickup truck, singing the chorus from "Ventilator Blues." Bonnie Lamb wasn't familiar with the song, but she enjoyed Skink's bluesy bass voice. She stood by the truck, keeping an eye on him.

Augustine was met at the door by a tired-looking woman in a pink housedress. She said, "The trooper mentioned you'd be by." Her tone was as lifeless as her stare; she'd been whipped by the hurricane.

"It's been, like, three days since I called the cops."

"We're stretched pretty thin," Augustine said.

The woman's entire family—husband, four children, two cats—was bivouacked in the master bedroom, beneath the only swatch of roof that the hurricane hadn't blown away. The husband wore a lime mesh tank top, baggy shorts, sandals and a Cleveland Indians cap. He had a stubble of gray-flecked beard. He tended a small Sterno stove on the dresser; six cans of pork and beans were lined up, the lids removed. The kids were preoccupied with battery-operated Game Boys, beeping like miniature radars.

"We still got no electric," the woman said to Augustine. She told her husband it was the man the Highway Patrol sent about the stolen license plate. The husband asked Augustine why he wasn't wearing a police uniform.

"Because I'm a detective," Augustine said. "Plainclothes."

"Oh."

"Tell me what happened."

"These four kids pulled up and took the tag off my Camaro. I was out'n the yard, burying the fish—see, when the power went off it took care of the aquarium, so we had dead guppies—"

"Sailfin mollies!" interjected one of the kids.

"Anyway, I had to bury the damn things before they stunk up the place. That's when this Jeep comes up, four colored guys, stereo cranked full blast. They take a screwdriver and set to work on the Camaro. Me standin' right there!"

The woman said, "I knew something was wrong. I brought the children inside the bedroom."

Her husband dumped two cans of pork and beans into a small pot, which he held over the royal-blue flame of the Sterno. "So I run over with a shovel and say what do you think you're up to, and one of the brothers flashes a gun and tells me to you-know-what. I didn't argue, I backed right off. Getting shot over a damn license plate was *not* on my agenda, you understand."

Augustine said, "Then what happened?"

"They slapped the tag on the Jeep and hauled ass. You could hear that so-called music for about five miles."

The wife added, "David's got a pistol and he knows how to use it. But—"

"Not over a thirty-dollar license plate," said her husband.

Augustine commended David for being so levelheaded. "Let me double-check the tag number." He took out the folded piece of paper and read it aloud: "BZQ-42F."

"Right," said David, "but it's not on that Jeep no more."

"How do you know?"

"I saw it the other day, goin' down Calusa."

"The same one?"

"Black Cherokee. Mags, tinted windows. I'd bet the farm it's the same truck. I could tell by the mud flaps."

The woman frowned. "Tell him about *those*."

"Mud flaps like what you see on them eighteen-wheelers. You know, fancy, with naked ladies."

"In chrome," the woman said. "That's how we knew it was the same one—"

Augustine said, "Where's Calusa?"

"—only some white guy was driving it."

"What'd he look like?"

"Not friendly," said the husband.

The wife said, "Watch the beans, David. And tell him about the music."

"That's the other thing," David said, stirring the pot. "He had that damn stereo all the way loud, same as the colored kids. Only it wasn't rap music, it was Travis Tritt. I thought it was weird, this guy in a business suit and a niggered-up Jeep, listenin' to Travis Tritt."

"David!" The woman reddened with genuine offense. Augustine liked her. He surmised that she was the strength of the outfit.

Her husband, halfway apologizing for the slur: "Aw, you know what I mean. All that chrome and tint, the guy didn't fit."

Augustine recalled Brenda Rourke's description of the attacker. "You're sure about the suit?"

"Clear as day."

The woman said, "We figured maybe he's the boss. Maybe the kids who stole our license plate work for him."

"It's possible," said Augustine. He sort of enjoyed playing a cop, ferreting fresh trails.

"You say he looked unfriendly. What do you mean?"

David spooned the pork and beans into matching ceramic bowls. "His face," he said. "You wouldn't forget it."

The wife said, "We were on our way to the Circle K for ice. At first I thought he had on a Halloween mask, the man in the Jeep. That's how odd he was—wait, Jeremy, that's too hot!" She intercepted her youngest son, lunging for the beans.

Augustine thanked them, on behalf of the Metropolitan Dade County Police, for their cooperation. He promised to do his best to retrieve the stolen license plate. "I've only got one more question."

"Where's Calusa?" said David, smiling.

"Exactly."

"Margo can do you a map. Use one them napkins."

Avila's wife found him writhing on the floor of the garage, near the Buick. He was bleeding from a large puncture in the groin. One of the sacrificial billy goats, anticipating its fate, had gored him.

"Where are they?" demanded Avila's wife, in Spanish.

Through clenched teeth, Avila confessed that both goats had escaped.

"I tole you! I tole you!" his wife cried, switching to English. She rolled Avila on his back and opened his trousers to examine the injury. "Chew need a tennis shot," she said.

"Take me to the doctor."

"Not in *my* car! I done wanno blood on de 'polstery."

"Then help me to the goddamn truck."

"Chew a mess."

"You want me to die right here on the floor? Is that what you want?"

Avila had purchased the billy goats from the nephew of a *santero* priest in Sweetwater. The nephew owned a farm on which he raised fighting cocks and livestock for religious oblations. The two goats had cost Avila a total of three hundred dollars, and they didn't get along. They'd butted heads and kicked at each other continually on the return trip to Avila's house. Somehow he had managed to wrestle both animals into the open garage, but before he could attach the tethers and shut the door, a liquid wildness had come into their huge amber eyes. Avila wondered if they'd sensed Chango's supernatural presence, or merely smelled the blood and entrails from past *santería* offerings. In any event, the goats went absolutely berserk and destroyed a perfectly good riding mower, among other items. The larger of the two billies gouged Avila cleanly with a horn before clacking off into the neighborhood.

Avila's wife scolded him zealously on the drive to the hospital.

"Three hunnert bucks! Chew fucking crazy!" When swearing she customarily dropped her Spanish for English, due to the richer, more emphatic variety of profanities.

Avila snarled back: "Don't talk to me about money. You and *mamí* been losin' your fat asses at the Miccosukee bingo, no? So don't talk to me about crazy."

He checked the wound in his groin; it was the size of a fifty-cent piece. The bleeding had stopped, but the pain was fiery. He felt clammy and light-headed.

Oh, Chango, Avila thought. What have I done to anger you?

In the emergency room, a businesslike nurse eased him onto a gurney and connected him to a glorious bag of I.V. Demerol. Avila told the doctor that he'd fallen on a rusty lawn sprinkler. The doctor said he was lucky it didn't sever an artery. He asked about the dirty bandage on Avila's left hand, and Avila said it was a nasty golfing blister. Nothing to worry about.

As the pain receded, his mind drifted into a fuzzy free fall. Snapper's lopsided face appeared in a cloud.

I will find you, coño! Avila vowed.

But how?

Dreamily he recalled the night they'd first met. It was in a supper club on LeJeune Road. Snapper was at the bar with two women from an escort service. The women wore caked mascara and towering hair. Avila made friends. He had cash in his pocket, having moments earlier collected a bribe from a fellow who retailed fiberglass roof shingles of questionable durability. The hookers told Avila the name of the escort service was Gentlemen's Choice, and it was open seven days a week. They said Snapper was a regular customer, one of their best. They said he was taking them out on the town to celebrate, on account he was going off to prison for three to five years and wouldn't be getting much pussy, professional or otherwise. Snapper told Avila he'd killed some shithead dope dealer that nobody cared about. Prosecutors had let him cop to a manslaughter-one, and with any luck he'd get out of the joint in twenty months. Avila didn't believe a word the guy was saying, but he thought the manslaughter routine was a pretty good line to use on the babes. He bought several rounds of drinks for Snapper and the prostitutes, in hopes that Snapper might start feeling generous. And that's exactly what happened. When Avila returned from the men's room, the one he liked—a gregarious platinum blonde, Morganna was her name—whispered in his ear that Snapper said it was OK, as long as Avila paid his share. So they'd all gone to a fleabag motel on West Flagler and had quite a time. Morganna proved full of energy and imagination, well worth the shingle money.

Narcotic memories took Avila's mind off the vigorous suturing that was being done on a freshly shaved triangle five inches due southwest of his navel. Then, giddily, it came to him from out of the clouds—one obvious way for Avila to track that cocksucker Snapper and recover the seven grand.

A lead, is what cops would call it.

Not exactly a red-hot lead, but better than nothing.

Another curious neighbor dropped by, asking about Tony. Edie Marsh used the same ludicrous story about being a distant Torres cousin who was watching the place as a favor. She made no effort to explain Snapper, snoring in the recliner, a gun on his lap.

Fred Dove drove up a few minutes later, while Edie was walking Donald and Marla in the front yard. The insurance man looked more cheerless and pallid than ever. From the way he snatched the briefcase off the seat of the car, Edie sensed an urgency to his gloom.

"My supervisor," he announced, "wants to see the house."

"Is he suspicious?"

"No. Routine claims review."

"Then what's the problem, Fred? Show him the house."

He gave a bitter laugh and spun away. Edie tied up the dogs and followed him inside.

"The problem is," Fred Dove said, "Mister Reedy will want to chat with 'Mister and Mrs Torres.'" Loudly he dropped his briefcase on the kitchen counter, rousing Snapper.

Edie said, "Don't panic. We can handle it."

"Don't panic? The company wants to know why I got kicked

out of the motel. My wife wants to know where I'm staying, and with whom. Dennis Reedy will be here tomorrow to interview two claimants that I cannot produce. Personally, I think it's an excellent time to panic."

"Hey, Santy Claus!" It was Snapper, hollering from the living room. "You got the insurance check?"

Edie Marsh went to the doorway and said, "Not yet."

"Then shut him up."

Fred Dove dropped his voice. "I can't stay here with that maniac. It's impossible."

"His leg hurts," said Edie. She had given Snapper the last of her Darvons, which evidently were beginning to wear off. "Look, I'm not thrilled about the setup, either. But it's this or go camp in the woods."

The insurance man removed his glasses and pressed his thumbs against his temples. A mosquito landed on one of his eyelids. He shook his head like a spaniel until it floated away. "We can't go through with this," he said, dolorously.

"Yes we can, sweetie. I'll be Mrs Torres. Snapper is Tony."

Fred Dove sagged. "You don't exactly look Cuban. Neither of you, for God's sake." He punched a cabinet door and cried out, "What was I *thinking*!"

Snapper declared that Fred Dove was on the brink of dismemberment unless he immediately shut the fuck up. Edie Marsh led the distraught insurance man into Neria's bedroom closet. She shut the door and kissed him with expert tenderness. Simultaneously she unzipped his pants. Fred jumped at her touch, warm but unexpected. Edie squeezed gently, until he was calm and quite helpless.

"This Dennis Reedy," she whispered, "what's he like?"

Fred Dove squirmed pleasurably.

"Tough guy? Tightass? What's his deal?"

"He seems all right," the insurance man said. He'd dealt with Reedy only once, in a flooded subdivision outside Dallas. Reedy was gruff but fair. He had approved most of Fred Dove's damage estimates, with only minor adjustments.

Edie's free hand pulled down Fred's pants. She said, "We'll go over the claim papers tonight, in case he makes it a quiz."

"What about Snapper?"

"Let me handle that. We'll have a rehearsal."

"What are you doing?" The insurance man nearly lost his balance.

"What does it look like, Fred. Will Mister Reedy have our check?"

In stuporous bliss, Fred Dove gazed at the top of Edie's head. Fingers explored her silken hair; his own fingers, judging by the familiar gold wedding band and the University of Nebraska class ring. Fred Dove struggled for clarity. It was no time for an out-of-body experience; for this long-awaited moment, he wanted sensual acuity and superior muscle control.

The insurance man struggled to purge his mind of worry and guilt, to make way for oncoming ecstasy. He inhaled deeply. The closet smelled of old gardenias and mildew: Neria Torres's pre-professor wardrobe, damp and musty from the storm. Fred Dove felt stifled, though a vital part of him was not.

Without using her hands, Edie Marsh leaned him against the wall for leverage. He released her hair and rapturously locked a monkey grip on the wooden dowel. His upturned face was obstructed by the silken armpit of somebody's wedding gown.

Suddenly he had a humiliating flashback to what had happened the last time, when Snapper interrupted them on the floor of the living room. To prevent a recurrence, Fred groped for the door-knob and held it shut.

From below, Edie Marsh paused to inquire again: "Will Reedy have the settlement check?"

"N-no. The check always comes from Omaha."

"Shit."

Fred Dove wasn't sure whether he heard her say it, or felt her say it. The important thing was, she didn't stop.

When Augustine came out to the truck, Bonnie Lamb and the governor were gone. He found them a few blocks away, behind a deserted hurricane house. Skink was kneeling next to a swimming pool, scooping chubby brown toads out of the rancid water and slipping them into his pockets. Bonnie was busy fending off the mosquitoes that hovered in an inky cloud around her face.

Augustine related what he'd learned about the black Jeep Cherokee. Skink said, "Where's Calusa Drive?"

"They drew me a map."

"Are we going now?" Bonnie asked.

"Tomorrow," Skink said. "We'll need daylight."

He and Augustine decided to spend the night nearby. They found an empty field and built a campfire from storm debris. Nearby another small fire glowed, flickering from the mouth of a fifty-five-gallon drum—itinerant laborers from Ohio. Two of them wandered over in search of crack. Augustine spooked them off with a casual display of the .38. Skink disappeared with the toads into a scrubby palmetto thicket.

Bonnie said, "What's DMT?"

"A Wall Street drug," Augustine replied. "Before our time."

"He said he dries the toad poison and smokes it. He said it's a chemical strain of DMT."

"I believe I'll stick to beer." Augustine got two sleeping bags from the cab of the truck. He shook them out and spread them near the fire.

She said, "I'm sorry about last night."

"Quit saying that." Like it would have been the worst mistake of her entire life.

"I don't know what's wrong with me," she said.

Augustine arranged some dead branches on the fire. "Nothing's wrong with you, Bonnie. You're so normal it's scary." He sat cross-legged on one of the sleeping bags.

"Come here," he said. When he put his arms around her, she felt completely relaxed and secure. Then he said: "I can take you to the airport."

"No!"

"Because after tonight, you'll be in the thick of it."

Bonnie Lamb said, "That's what I want. Max got his adventure, I want mine."

A reedy howl rose from the palmettos, diffusing into a creepy rumble of laughter.

Bufo madness, thought Augustine. Bonnie stiffened in his embrace. Firmly she said, "I'm not leaving now. No way."

He lifted her chin. "This is not a well person. This is a man who put a shock collar on your husband, a man who gets high off frog slime. He's done things you don't want to know about, probably even killed people."

"At least he believes in *something*."

"Good Lord, Bonnie."

"Then why are *you* here? If he's so dangerous, if he's so crazy—"

"Who said he was crazy."

"Answer the question, Señor Herrera."

Augustine blinked at the firelight. "I'm not so tightly wrapped myself. That should be obvious."

Bonnie Lamb pressed closer. She wondered why she so enjoyed the fact that both of these new men were unpredictable and impulsive—opposites of the man she'd married. Max was exceptionally reliable, but he was neither deep nor enigmatic. Five minutes with Max and you had the whole menu.

She said, "I suppose I'm rebelling. Against what, I don't know. It's a first for me."

Augustine rebuked himself for showing off with the skulls; what woman could resist such charm? Bonnie laughed softly.

"Seriously," he said, "there's a big difference between your situation and mine. You've got a husband and a life. I've got nothing else to do, and nothing to lose by not doing it."

"Your uncle's animals?"

"Long gone," he said. "Anyway, there's worse places than Miami to be for a monkey. They'll make out fine." After a rueful pause: "I do feel lousy about the water buffalo."

Bonnie said there was no point trying to analyze motivation. Both of them were rational, mature, intelligent adults. Certainly they knew what they were doing, even if they didn't know why.

From the thicket, another penetrating wail.

Bonnie stared toward the palmettos. "I get the feeling he could take us or leave us."

"Exactly." Augustine came right out and asked her if she truly loved her husband.

She answered unhesitantly: "I don't know. So there."

Without warning, the governor crashed shirtless out of the trees. He was feverish, drenched in sweat. His good eye was as bright as a radish; the glass one was turned askew, showing yellowed bone in the socket. Bonnie hurried to his side.

"Damn," he wheezed, "was that some bad toad!"

Augustine doubted Skink's technique for removing the toxin and processing it for inhalation. Based on the man's present state, it seemed likely that he'd bungled the pharmacology.

"Sit here by the fire," Bonnie told him.

He held out his hands, which were filled with leathery, lightly freckled eggs. Augustine counted twelve in all. Skink palmed them like golf balls.

"Supper!" he exulted.

"What are they?"

"Eggs, my boy!"

"Of what?"

"I don't have a clue." The governor stalked toward the laborers' camp, returning five minutes later with a fry pan and a squeeze bottle of ketchup.

Regardless of species, the eggs tasted dandy scrambled. Augustine was impressed, watching Bonnie dig in.

When they finished eating, Skink said it was time to hit the rack. "Big day ahead. You take the sleeping bags, I'll be in the scrub." And he was gone.

Augustine returned the fry pan to the Ohio contingent, which was amiably drunk and nonthreatening. He and Bonnie stayed up watching the flames die, sitting close but saying little. At the first onslaught of mosquitoes, they dove into one of the sleeping bags and zipped it over their heads. Like two turtles, Bonnie said, sharing the same shell.

They hugged each other in the blackness, laughing uncontrollably. After Bonnie caught her breath, she said, "God, it's hot in here."

"August in Florida."

"Well, I'm taking off my clothes."

"You aren't."

"Oh yes. And you're going to help."

"Bonnie, we should get some sleep. Big day tomorrow."

"I need a big night to take my mind off it." She got tangled while wriggling out of her top. "Give me a hand, kind sir."

Augustine did as he was told. They were, after all, rational, mature, intelligent adults.

NINETEEN

The death of Tony Torres did not go unnoticed by homicide detectives, crucifixions being rare even in Miami. However, most murder investigations were stuck on hold in the frenetic days following the hurricane. With the roadways in disorder, the police department was precariously shorthanded; every available officer of every rank was put to work directing traffic, chasing looters or escorting relief convoys. In the case of Juan Doe #92–312 (the whimsical caption on Tony Torres's homicide file), the lack of urgency to investigate was reinforced by the fact that no friends or relatives appeared to identify the corpse, which indicated to police that nobody was searching for him, which further suggested that nobody much cared he was dead.

Two days after the body was found, a fingerprint technician faxed the morgue to say that a proper name now could be attached to the crucified man: Antonio Rodrigo Guevara-Torres, age forty-five. The prints of the late Mr Torres were on file because he had, during one rocky stretch of his adult life, written thirty-seven consecutive bum checks. Had one of those checks not been made out to the Police Benevolent Association, Tony Torres likely would have escaped prosecution. To avoid jail, he pleaded guilty and swore to make full restitution, a pledge quickly forgotten amid the pressure of his demanding new job as a junior sales associate at a trailer-home franchise called A-Plus Affordable Homes.

Because the arrest report was old, the home address and telephone number listed for Tony Torres were no good. The current yellow pages showed no listing for A-Plus Affordable.

Three fruitless inquiries sufficiently discouraged the young detective to whom the case of the crucified check-kiter had been assigned. He was relieved when his lieutenant ordered him to put the homicide file aside and drive down to Cutler Ridge, where he parked squarely in the center of the intersection of Eureka Drive and 117th Avenue, in order to block traffic for the presidential motorcade.

The young detective didn't think again of the murdered check-bouncing mobile-home salesman until two days later, when the police department got a call from an agitated woman claiming to be the victim's wife.

Avila phoned the Gentlemen's Choice escort service and asked for Morganna. She got on the line and said, "I haven't used that name in six months. It's Jasmine now."

"OK. Jasmine."

"Do I know you, honey?"

Avila reminded her of their torrid drunken night at the motel on West Flagler Street.

"Gee," she said, "that narrows it down to about ninety guys."

"You had a friend. Daphne, Diane, something like that. Redhead with a tattoo on her left tit."

Jasmine said, "What kinda tattoo?"

"I think it was a balloon or something."

"Don't ring a bell."

Avila said, "The guy you were with, you'd definitely remember. Scary dude with a seriously fucked-up face."

"Little Pepe that got burned?"

"No, it wasn't Pepe with the burns. Man's name was Snapper. His jaws stuck out all gross and crooked. You remember. It was a party before he went upstate."

"Nope, still no bell," said Jasmine. "What're you doing tonight, sweetheart? You need a date?"

What a cold shitty world, thought Avila. There was no such thing as a friendly favor anymore; everybody had their greedy paws out.

"Meet me at Cisco's," he told her tersely. "Nine o'clock at the bar."

"That's my boy."

"You still a blonde?"

"If you want."

Avila arrived twenty minutes late; he had taken a long hot shower following another furtive raid on the buried Tupperware stash. The stitches in his groin still stung from the soaking.

Jasmine sat at the bar, sipping Perrier from the bottle. She wore a subtle scarlet miniskirt and an alarming Carol Channing-style wig. Her perfume smelled like a fruit stand. Avila sat down carefully and ordered a beer. He folded a hundred-dollar bill into Jasmine's empty hand.

She smiled. "I *do* remember you now."

"What about Snapper?"

"You're a squeaker."

"*Cómo?*"

"You squeak when you fuck. Like a happy little hamster."

Avila flushed, and lunged for his beer.

"Don't be embarrassed," Jasmine said. She took his left wrist and examined the beads of his *santería* bracelet. "I remember this, too. Some sorta voodoo."

Avila pulled away. "Has Daphne heard from Snapper lately?"

"It's not Daphne anymore. It's Bridget." Jasmine dug a pack of Marlboros out of her purse. "Matter of fact, she spent the hurricane with him. Drunk as a skunk at some motel up in Broward."

Avila made no move to light her cigaret. He said, "When's the last time she saw him?"

"Just yesterday."

"Yesterday!"

It was too good to be true! Thank you, mighty Chango! Avila was awestruck and humbled.

Jasmine said, "That Snapper calls all the time, ever since he got out of Sumter. She's put her meathooks in that boy. By the way, her tattoo—it's not a balloon, it's a lollipop." Jasmine laughed. "But you were on the money about which tit."

"So where's Snapper?"

"Sugar, how should I know. He's Daphne's trick."

"You mean Bridget."

Jasmine bowed. "Touché," she said, good-naturedly.

Avila produced another hundred-dollar bill. He put it flat on the bar, beneath the Perrier bottle. "Is he at a motel?" he asked.

"A house, I think."

"Where?"

"I gotta ask her," Jasmine said.

"You need a quarter for the phone?"

"She's working tonight. Give me your number."

Avila wrote it in the margin of the damp C-note. Jasmine put it in her purse.

"I'm hungry," she said.

"I'm not."

"What's the matter?" She gave his knee a squeeze. "Oh, I know. I know why you're pissed."

"You don't know a damn thing."

"Yes I do. You're mad 'cause of what I said about the way you are in bed."

Avila shot to his feet and called for the check. Jasmine tugged him back to the barstool. Pressing her chest against his arm, she whispered, "Hey, it's all right. I thought it was cute."

"I don't *squeak*," Avila said coldly.

"You're right," said Jasmine. "You're absolutely right. Come on, honey, couldn't you go for a steak?"

Edie Marsh and Snapper had gotten into a nasty argument over the call girl. Edie had said it was no time for screwing—they needed to practice their husband-and-wife routine for when Fred Dove's boss showed up. Snapper had told her to lighten up or shut her trap. Watching the panel of saucy prostitutes on *Oprah* had made him think about licking the former Daphne's lollipop.

She was delighted to hear from him, the escort service business being slow as molasses after the hurricane. She caught a taxi to the

Torres house, but got there late because the driver got lost in the pitch darkness and traffic confusion.

There was no door on which to knock, so Bridget strolled in unannounced. Edie Marsh and Snapper were glaring at each other by candlelight in the living room.

"Hello again," Bridget said to Edie, who nodded testily.

Bridget scampered to the BarcaLounger and sprawled across Snapper's lap. She scissored her chubby legs in the air and smooched his neck (the disaligned jaws made mouth-kissing problematic).

Snapper said, "You're sittin' on my gun."

Bridget wriggled girlishly as he extricated the pistol. She said, "Baby, what happened to your leg?"

"Ask Little Miss Psychobitch."

Bridget stared at Edie Marsh. "He hit me," Edie said, remorselessly, "so I hit him back."

"With a fucking crowbar."

"Ouch," said the hooker.

Snapper told Edie to go walk the damn dogs for a couple hours.

Bridget said, "You got dogs? Where?" She sat up excitedly. "I love dogs."

"Just take off your clothes," Snapper said. "Where's the Stoli?"

"All the liquor stores were boarded up."

"Mother of Christ!"

Edie Marsh said, "Look, Bridget, nothing personal against you. But we've got a very important meeting tomorrow morning—"

"Wait, now," Snapper cut in. "You're sayin' there's no vodka? Did I hear right?"

"Baby, the storm, remember? Everything's shut down."

"Bullshit. You didn't even try."

"Chill out," said Bridget. "We don't need booze for a party."

Edie Marsh tried once more: "All I'm asking is that you're gone in the morning, OK? There's a man coming to the house, he won't understand."

"No problem, hon."

"Nothing personal."

Bridget laughed. "It's not like I had my heart set on staying over in *this* dump."

Edie said, "You should see the bathrooms. There's mosquitoes *this* big hatching in the toilets!"

Bridget made a face and pressed her knees together. Snapper said: "Edie, I'm countin' to ten. Get your lazy ass in gear."

Donald and Marla began yipping in the backyard.

"Are those your puppies?" Bridget sprang from Snapper's lap and hurried to what once had been French doors. "They sound adorable—what kind?" She peered expectantly into the night.

Snapper gimped to her side. "Fertilizer hounds," he said.

"Fertilizer hounds?"

"When I get done with 'em, yeah. That's the only goddamn thing they'll be good for." He raised the pistol and fired twice at the infernal yowling. Bridget let out a cry and covered her ears. Edie Marsh came up from behind and kicked Snapper in the crook of his bum right leg. He went down with a surprised grunt.

Outside, the volume of doggy racket increased by many decibels. Donald and Marla were hysterical with fear. Edie Marsh hurried outside to untangle the leashes before they garroted each other. Bridget knelt at Snapper's side and scolded him for being such a meanie.

The way Levon Stichler figured it, he had nothing to lose. The hurricane had taken everything, including the urn containing the ashes of his recently departed wife. The life in which he had invested most of his military pension had been reduced to broken glass and razor tinsel. Hours of painstaking salvage had yielded not enough dry belongings to fill a tackle box. Levon Stichler's neighbors at the trailer court were in the same abject fix. Within twenty-four hours, his shock and despair had distilled into high-octane anger. Someone must pay! Levon Stichler thundered. And logically that someone should be the smirking sonofabitch who'd sold them those mobile homes, the glib fat thief who'd promised them that the structures were government certified and hurricane-proof.

Levon Stichler had spotted Tony Torres at the trailer court on the morning after the hurricane, but the mangy prick had fled like a coyote. Levon Stichler had fumed for a few days, gathering what valuables he could find among the trailer's debris until county workers showed up to bulldoze the remains. The old man considered returning to Saint Paul, where his only daughter lived, but the thought of long frigid winters—and sharing space with six hyperactive grandchildren—was more than he could face.

There would be no northward migration. Levon Stichler considered his life to be officially ruined, and considered one man to be morally responsible for the tragedy. He would know no peace until Tony Torres was dead. Killing the salesman might even make Levon Stichler a hero, at least in the eyes of his trailer-court neighbors—that's what the old man convinced himself. He envisioned public sympathy and national headlines, possibly a visit from Connie Chung. And prison wouldn't be such an awful place; a damn sight safer than a double-wide trailer. Haw! Levon Stichler told no one of his mission. The hurricane hadn't actually driven him insane, but that's what he intended to plead at the trial. The Alzheimer's defense was another promising option. But first he had to devise a convincingly eccentric murder.

As soon as he settled on a plan, Levon Stichler called PreFab Luxury Homes. The phone rang over and over, causing the old man to wonder if the storm had put the trailer-home company out of business. In fact, PreFab Luxury was enjoying a banner week, thanks to a massive requisition from the Federal Emergency Management Agency. Uncle Sam, it seemed, was generously providing trailers to homeless storm victims. Many of the miserably displaced souls who'd been living in PreFab Luxury trailers when the hurricane wiped them out would be living in a PreFab Luxury product once again. Neither the company nor the federal government thought it necessary to inform tenants of the irony.

Eventually a receptionist answered the telephone, and made a point of mentioning how busy they all were. Levon Stichler asked to speak to Mr Torres. The woman said that Tony apparently was taking some personal leave after the storm and that nobody knew when he'd return to the office. Levon Stichler gathered that he wasn't the first dissatisfied customer to make inquiries. The receptionist politely declined to divulge the salesman's home number.

From his sodden telephone directory, Levon Stichler carefully removed the page listing the names and addresses of all the Antonio Torreses in Greater Miami. Then he got in the car, filled up the tank and began the hunt.

On the first day, Levon Stichler eliminated from the list three auto mechanics, a scuba instructor, a thoracic surgeon, a palmist, two lawyers and a university professor. All were named Antonio Torres, but none was the scoundrel whom Levon Stichler sought. He was exhausted, but resolute.

On the second day, Levon Stichler continued to winnow the roster of candidates: a stockbroker, a nurseryman, a shrimper, a police officer, two electricians, an optometrist and a greenskeeper. Another Tony Torres, unkempt and clearly impaired, tried to sell him a bag of bootleg Dilaudids; still another threatened to decapitate him with a hoe.

The third day of the manhunt brought Levon Stichler to the Turtle Meadow subdivision and 15600 Calusa Drive. By then he'd seen enough hurricane destruction to be utterly unmoved by the sight of another gutted, roofless home. At least it still had walls, which was more than Levon Stichler could say for his own.

A pretty Anglo woman met him at the open front doorway. She wore baggy jeans and a long lavender T-shirt. Levon Stichler noticed she was barefoot and (unless his seventy-one-year-old eyeballs were mistaken) she was not wearing a bra. Her toenails were the shade of red hibiscus.

He said, "Is this the Torres residence?"

The woman said yes.

"Antonio Torres? The salesman?"

"That's right." The woman held out a hand. "I'm Mrs Torres. Come on in, we've been expecting you."

Levon Stichler jerked and said, "What?"

He followed the barefoot braless woman into the house. She led him to the kitchen, which was a shambles.

"Where's your husband?"

"In the bedroom. Is Mister Dove on the way?"

"I don't know," answered Levon Stichler, thinking: Who the hell is Mr Dove?

"Listen, Mrs Torres—"

"Please. It's Neria." The woman excused herself to tend the generator, which was in the garage. When she returned to the kitchen, she turned on the electric coffeemaker and made three cups.

Levon Stichler thanked her, stiffly, and took a sip. The wife would be a problem; he needed to have Tony Torres alone.

The barefoot woman stirred two spoonfuls of sugar into her coffee. "Is this your first stop of the day?"

"Sure is," said Levon Stichler, hopelessly puzzled. Having never before murdered anybody, he was full of the jitters. He glanced at his wristwatch so often that the woman couldn't help but notice.

She said, "Tony's in the shower. He'll be out very soon."

"That's OK."

"Is the coffee all right? Sorry there's no cream."

Levon Stichler said, "It's fine."

She seemed like a nice enough person. What was she doing with a crooked slob like Torres?

He heard muffled noises from another room, two voices: a man's guttural laughter and a woman's high-pitched giggle. Levon Stichler reached slowly into the right pocket of his windbreaker. His hand tightened on the cool shaft of the weapon.

"Honey?" the barefoot woman called. "Mister Reedy's waiting."

Reedy? Levon Stichler's bold determination began to dissolve in a muddle. Something was awry with this particular Tony Torres. Yet Levon had spied the Salesman of the Year plaque on the wall, *PreFab Luxury Homes*, in raised gold lettering. Had to be the same creep.

Levon Stichler knew he must act swiftly, or lose forever the opportunity to avenge. He removed the concealed weapon from his jacket and raised it, ominously, for the wife to see.

"You better leave," he advised.

Calmly she set her coffee cup on the counter. Her brow furrowed, but not in fear; more as if she were stymied on a crossword puzzle. "What *is* that?" Pointing at the thing in Levon Stichler's hand.

"What's it look like?"

"A giant screw?"

"It's an auger spike, Mrs Torres. It was supposed to anchor my trailer in the storm."

Levon Stichler had choreographed the crime a hundred times in his mind, most recently while sharpening the point of the auger on a whetstone wheel. The fat face of Tony Torres would make an easy target. Either of those cavernous hairy nostrils could be forcibly modified to accept the steel bit, which would (according to Levon's calculation) extrude well beyond the nasal cavity and into the brainpan.

The barefoot woman said, "Excuse me, but are you fucking nuts?"

Before Levon Stichler could respond, the tall shape of a man materialized in the kitchen doorway. Levon Stichler aimed the spike like a lance, and charged. The woman shouted a sharp warning, and the man threw himself backward onto the wet tile floor. The auger impaled itself in the wooden shelf of a cabinet; with both hands Levon Stichler could not pull it free. Frantically he looked down at his intended victim.

"Oh shit," he said. "You're not the one." He released his grip on the spike. "You're not the one who sold me the double-wide!"

Another woman—wild-looking and half dressed—burst from the bedroom. Together she and the barefoot one helped Snapper rise to his feet.

In an accusatory tone, Levon Stichler said, "You are *not* Tony Torres."

"Like hell," Snapper said.

Edie Marsh moved between the two men. "Honey," she said, facing Snapper, "Mister Reedy here appears to be nuts."

"Worse than nuts," Bridget asserted.

"My name's not Reedy."

Edie wheeled on the old man. "Wait a second—you aren't from Midwest Casualty?"

Levon Stichler, who by now had gotten a close-up look at Snapper's feral eyes and disfigured mug, felt his brittle old bones turn to powder. "Where's Mister Torres?" he asked, with noticeably less spunk.

Edie sighed in annoyance. "Incredible," she said to Snapper. "He's not Reedy. Can you believe this shit?"

Snapper wanted to be sure for himself. He leaned forward until he was two inches from the old man's nose. "You're not from the insurance company? You're not Dove's boss?"

Misjudging the situation, Levon Stichler emphatically shook his head no. Edie Marsh stepped out of the way so Snapper could punch him into unconsciousness.

They sat on the rolled-up sleeping bags and waited for the governor to wake up in the palmettos.

Augustine assumed, as men sometimes do when they've had a particularly glorious time, that he should apologize.

Bonnie Lamb said, "For what? It was my idea."

"No, no, no. You're supposed to say it was all a terrible mistake. You got carried away. You don't know what got into you. Now you feel rotten and cheap and used, and you want to rush home to your husband."

"Actually I feel pretty terrific."

"Me, too." Augustine kissed her. "Forgive me, but I was raised Catholic. I can't be sure I've had fun unless I feel guilty afterwards."

"Oh, it's guilt you're talking about? Sure I feel guilty. So should you, allowing yourself to be seduced by a newlywed." She stood up and stretched her arms. "However, Señor Herrera, there's a big difference between guilt and remorse. I don't feel any remorse."

Augustine said, "Me, neither. And I feel guilty that I don't."

Bonnie whooped and climbed on his back. They rolled to the ground in an amorous tangle.

Skink came out of the thicket and smiled. "Animals!" he bellowed, evangelically. "No better than animals, rutting in public!"

Bonnie and Augustine got up and brushed themselves off. The governor was a sight. Twigs and wet leaves stuck to his knotted hair. Gossamer strands of a broken spider's web glistened from his chin.

He tromped melodramatically toward the campfire, shouting: "Fornicators! Fellaters! You ought to be ashamed!"

Augustine winked at Bonnie Lamb. "That's one I hadn't thought of: shame."

"Yeah, that's a killer."

The governor announced he had a tasty surprise for breakfast. "Your carnal frolics awoke me last night," he said, "so I went walking the roads."

From his fatigues he produced two small, freshly skinned carcasses. "Who wants rabbit," he asked, "and who wants the squirrel?"

Later they doused the fire and loaded the truck. Using the hand-drawn map that Augustine had been given by the helpful Margo and David, they located Calusa Drive with no difficulty. The black Jeep Cherokee was parked halfway down the street, in front of a badly damaged house; the bawdy mud flaps were impossible to miss. Skink told Augustine to keep driving. They left the pickup half a mile away and backtracked on foot.

Bonnie Lamb noticed, uneasily, that Augustine wasn't carrying either the pistol or the dart rifle. "Scouting mission," he explained.

They stayed off Calusa and approached on a parallel street, one block north. When they got close, they cut through a yard and slipped into an abandoned house directly across from 15600. From the broken window of a front bedroom, they had a clear view of the front door, the garage, the black Cherokee and two other cars in the driveway.

Margo and David were right. Their stolen license plate had been removed from the Jeep. Skink said: "Here's what happened.

After the guy beat up Brenda, he pulled the tag from the Cherokee and tossed it. What's on there now probably came off that Chevy."

The car parked nearest to the garage was a late-model Caprice. The license plate was missing. The second car was a rusty barge of an Oldsmobile with a lacerated vinyl top and no hubcaps. Augustine said it would be useful to know how many people were inside the house. Skink grunted in assent.

Bonnie tried to guess what the next move would be. Notifying the police, she surmised, was not in the governor's plans. Looking around, she felt a stab of melancholy. The room had belonged to a baby. Gaily colored plastic toys were strewn on the floor; a sodden stuffed teddy bear lay facedown in a dank puddle of rainwater. Mounted on the facing wall were wooden cutouts of popular Disney characters—Mickey Mouse, Donald Duck, Snow White. Oddly, they made Bonnie Lamb think of her honeymoon and Max. The first thing he'd bought at the Magic Kingdom was a Mickey golf cap.

I should've known then and there, she thought. Bless his heart, he probably couldn't help it.

She got up to see the baby's crib. A mobile of tropical butterflies, fastened to the rail, had been snapped at the stem. The mattress was splotched with dark greenish mildew. Shiny red ants trooped across the fuzzy pink blanket. Bonnie wondered what had happened to the infant and her parents. Surely they escaped before the roof blew off.

Augustine waved her back to the broken window. Heart skipping, she knelt between the two men. *What am I doing? Where is this heading?*

Another car drives up to 15600 Calusa. A white compact.

Man gets out. Bony and clerical-looking. Gray hair. Brown windbreaker, loose dark trousers. Reminds Bonnie of her landlord back in Chicago. What was his name? Wife taught piano. What the heck was his name?

Standing by his car, the old man puts on a pair of reading glasses. Looks at a piece of paper, then up at the numerals painted on the house. Nods. Takes off the glasses. Tucks them in the left pocket of his windbreaker. Pats the right pocket, as if checking for something.

Awfully hot for a jacket, Bonnie's thinking. Summertime in Miami, how can a person be chilly?

"Where does *he* fit?" said Augustine.

"Contractor. Utility worker. Something like that," Skink speculated.

Bonnie Lamb watches the old man straighten himself, stride purposefully to the doorway. Into the house he goes.

Augustine said, "I thought I saw a woman."

"Yes." Skink scratched thoughtfully at his beard.

Creedlow! Bonnie thinks. That's the ex-landlord's name. James Creedlow. His wife, the piano teacher, her name was Regina. Chicago wasn't so long ago—Bonnie feels ditzy for not remembering. James and Regina Creedlow, of course.

Augustine said, "What now, captain?"

Skink settled his bristly chin on the windowsill. "We wait."

Two hours later, the old man still hasn't come out of the house at 15600 Calusa Drive. Bonnie's worried.

Then another car pulls up.

TWENTY

Neria Torres had no desire to drive all the way to Brooklyn in search of a thieving husband.

"Then fly," suggested Celeste, the graduate student who shared the Volkswagen van with Neria and Neria's lover, the professor.

The professor's name was Charles Gabler. His field of interest was parapsychology. "Neria won't fly," he said. "She's afraid to death of airplanes."

"Wow," said Celeste, cooking on a portable stove in the back of the van. She was in charge of the macrobiotic menu.

Neria said, "It's not just the flying, it's Brooklyn. How would I find Tony in a place like that?"

"I know how," Celeste piped. "Hire a psychic."

"Great idea. We'll call Kreskin."

The professor said, "Neria, there's no need to be snide."

"Oh yes, there is."

She and Dr Gabler had been sorely low of funds when he'd proposed that young Celeste join them a week earlier as they prepared to depart Eugene, Oregon, for Miami. Young Celeste had been blessed with a comfortable trust fund, a generous heart and handsome gravity-defying breasts. Neria was under no illusions about the professor's motives, but she tried to put aside her concerns. They needed gas money, and young Celeste kept a world of credit cards in her purse. Somewhere near Salina, Kansas, Neria felt the need to inform Dr Gabler that he was paying too much attention to their travel companion, that his behavior was not only rude but disrespectful, and that the Great Plains in the heat of summer was no place to relearn the basics of hitchhiking. The professor seemed to take the warning to heart.

In truth, Neria was growing bored with Dr Gabler and his absurd blue and red crystals. Mystic healing, my ass—a box of Milk Duds starts to look pretty mystical, you smoke enough dope. Which was how the professor spent most of his waking hours, sluggishly bequeathing the driving duties to Neria and Celeste.

"I'd rather go to Miami anyway," Celeste said, measuring out two cups of brown rice. "I'd like to work in one of those tent cities. Cook for the homeless, if they need me."

The professor regarded Neria Torres through bloodshot hound-dog eyes. "Darling, it's entirely up to you. We'll go wherever you wish."

"Wow," said Neria. The mockery was lost on Celeste, who was immersed in a complex recipe. Neria declared she was going for a walk, and exited the van.

They had parked at a public campground off Interstate 20, outside Atlanta, to discuss which way to go—New York or Miami, north or south. Neria Torres replayed in her mind the upsetting conversation with the stranger who'd answered Tony's telephone. The more Neria thought about it, the more doubts she had. Not that her piggy husband wasn't capable of falling for a twenty-four-year-old blonde; rather, it was highly implausible that one would fall for him. And Brooklyn? Hardly a boomtown for the mobile-home trade. The stranger's story didn't add up.

Neria Torres had tried to confirm the lurid details with Varga, the nosy next-door neighbor, but his telephone was out of order. Neria was certain about two things: She was entitled to half the hurricane money for the house in Miami. And her estranged husband was dodging her.

New York was an astronomic long shot. At least in Florida there'd be a trail. Neria decided they should head for Miami, as originally planned.

She thought of a way to widen the net: Why not let the cops search for Tony, too? They were the pros, after all. Neria back-tracked through the campground to a phone booth, where she used her husband's PIN number to call the Metro-Dade police and make a missing-person report.

After a desk officer took the information, he put Neria Torres on hold. She waited several minutes, growing increasingly impatient. The sky began to drizzle. Neria fumed. She thought of Dr Gabler and young Celeste, together in the back of the Volkswagen van. She wondered if the professor was demonstrating his "human Ouija board" exercise, the one he'd worked so charmingly on Neria herself.

Around Neria's neck hung a polished stalk of rose quartz, which Dr Gabler had given her to help channel untapped torrents of "unconditional love." Dickhead! thought Neria. At that very moment he was probably tuning young Celeste's inner chakras. Until she'd met the professor, Neria Torres hadn't known what a chakra was. Celeste undoubtedly did. She and Dr Gabler seemed to operate on the same wavelength.

The drizzle turned to a hard rain. Under Neria's feet, the red Georgia clay turned to slop. A man with a newspaper over his head came up behind her and stood uncomfortably close. He employed noisy, urgent breathing to emphasize his need for the telephone. Neria cursed aloud and slammed down the receiver.

On the other end, at Metro police headquarters in Miami, the desk officer had been diligently cross-checking the missing husband against a list of unclaimed bodies in the morgue. He was surprised to get a possible hit: One dead man had the same name, same date of birth, same extravagant brand of wristwatch.

The officer immediately had transferred Mrs Torres's phone call to the Homicide division. By the time a detective picked up, nobody was on the line.

Max Lamb flew from New York to San Diego to Guadalajara, where he slept for eleven hours. He woke up and called the airport hotel in Miami. Bonnie hadn't checked in. Max lit a Bronco cigaret and fell back on the pillow.

He chewed over a scenario in which his new wife might be cheating on him with one of two certifiable lunatics, or both. He couldn't conceive of it. The Bonnie Brooks he knew wasn't a free spirit—that was one of the things he loved about her. Steady and predictable, that was Bonnie. To Max's knowledge, the most impulsive thing she'd ever done was to hurl a stale pizza, Frisbee style, out the apartment window in Manhattan. When it came to sex, she was practically old-fashioned. She hadn't slept with *him* until their seventh date.

So it took only minutes for Max Lamb to dismiss his worries about Bonnie's fidelity. The ability to delude oneself on such matters was a benefit of owning a grossly inflated ego. Bottom line: Max couldn't imagine that Bonnie would desire another man. Especially *those* types of men: outlaws and psychos. Impossible! He snickered, blowing smoke at the notion. She was punishing him, that was all; obviously she was still ticked off about the hurricane excursion.

Scrubbing in the shower, Max Lamb refocused on the task at hand: the obstreperous Clyde Nottage Jr, ailing chairman of Durham Gas Meat & Tobacco. Max's orders were to talk some sense into the old fart, make him understand the grievous consequences of withdrawing all those expensive advertisements from print. Before Max Lamb had left New York, four Rodale & Burns executive vice presidents had individually briefed him on the importance of the Guadalajara mission. Success, Max knew, would guarantee a long and lucrative career at the agency. A home run, is how one of the honchos had put it. Turning the old man around would be a grand-slam homer in the bottom of the ninth. Clyde Nottage was one crusty old prick.

A cab took Max Lamb to the Aragon Clinic, a two-story stucco building, freshly painted and lushly landscaped, in a residential sub-division of the city. The lobby of the clinic showed evidence of recent remodeling, which unfortunately had not included central air. Max loosened his necktie and took a seat. On a glass table was a stack of informational pamphlets printed in Spanish. Curious, Max picked one up. On the first page was a drawing of a male sheep with an arrow pointing between its hind legs.

Max returned the pamphlet to the table. He wanted a smoke,

but a sign on the wall said "No Fumar." A drop of sweat rolled down his jawline. Max dabbed it away with a handkerchief.

A man wearing a white medical coat came out; a pale-eyed American in his mid-sixties. He introduced himself as Dr Caulk, Mr Nottage's physician.

"When may I see him?" Max Lamb asked.

"In a few minutes. He's finishing his treatment."

"How's he doing?"

"Better, by and large," said Dr Caulk, enigmatically.

The chat turned to the clinic, and cancer. The doctor asked Max Lamb if he was a smoker.

"Just started."

"Started?" The doctor looked incredulous.

"Long story," Max said.

"Mister Nottage smokes four packs a day."

"I'd heard six."

"Oh, we've got him down to four," said the doctor. He gave the impression it was a contest of wills.

Max Lamb inquired about the unusual nature of the tumor treatments. Dr Caulk took full credit.

"We're really onto something," he told Max. "So far, the results have been quite astounding."

"What made you think to try . . . you know—"

"Sheep semen?" Dr Caulk gave a wise smile. "Actually it's quite an interesting story."

As Max Lamb listened, he wondered if the deepening consternation showed on his face. The Caulk therapy was based entirely upon the casual observation that male sheep have a low incidence of lung cancer.

"Compared to . . . ?"

The doctor slyly wagged a finger at Max. "Now you sound just like the FDA." He folded his hands and leaned forward. "I suppose you're curious about how we collect the semen."

"Not in the slightest," said Max, forcefully.

A mountainous nurse appeared at the doctor's shoulder. She said Mr Nottage's afternoon treatment was completed. Dr Caulk took Max to the old man's room.

Outside the door, the doctor dropped his voice. "I'll leave you two alone. Lately he's been a bit cranky with me."

Max Lamb had met Clyde Nottage Jr only once before, on a golf course in Raleigh. The robust, fiery, blue-eyed curmudgeon that he remembered bore no resemblance to the gaunt, gray-skinned invalid in the hospital bed.

Until Clyde Nottage opened his mouth: "The hell you staring at, boy?"

Max pulled a chair to the side of the bed. He sat down and positioned the briefcase on his lap.

"Gimme cigaret," Nottage muttered.

As Max inserted a Bronco in the old man's bloodless lips, he said, "Sir, did the doctor tell you I was coming? How are you feeling?"

Nottage ignored him. He plucked the cigaret from his mouth and eyed it ruefully. "What they say is true, all true. About these goddamn things causing cancer. I know it's a fact. So do you. So does the goddamn guv'ment."

Max Lamb was uneasy. "It's a choice people make," he said.

Nottage laughed, a tubercular snuffle. With a shaky hand he returned the cigaret to his mouth. Max lit it for him.

The old man said, "They got you trained good. Look at me, boy—you heard about the sheep jizz?"

"Yes, sir."

"I got a tumor the size of a Cuban mango in my chest, and I'm down to sheep jizz. My last earthly hope."

"The doctor said—"

"Oh, fuck him." Nottage paused to suck defiantly on the Bronco. "You're here about the ads, right? Rodale sent you to change my mind."

"Sir, the NIH report was news—bad news, to be sure. But they were only doing their jobs, the newspapers and magazines. They *had* to print the story; it was all over television—"

Clyde Nottage laughed until his nose ran. He wiped it with a hairless withered forearm. "Christ, you missed the point. They all did."

The old man's jocular tone gave Max a false burst of hope.

"I yanked those damn ads," Nottage went on, "because I was pissed. That much is true. But I wasn't mad they published the cancer report."

"Then why?"

An inch of dead ash fell from the old man's cigaret onto the sheets. He tried to blow it away, but the exertion of laughing had sapped him; his lungs moaned under the strain. After regaining his breath, he said: "The real reason I was pissed, they're fuckin' hypocrites. They tell the whole world we peddle poison, put it on the front page. Yet they're delighted to take our money and advertise that very same poison. Greedy cocksucking hypocrites, and you may quote me to the boys in New York."

Max Lamb realized the conversation had taken a perilous turn. He said, "It's just business, sir."

"Well, it's a business I'm gettin' out of. Right now. Before I leave this sorry world."

Max waited for a punch line that didn't come. He felt a quaking in his bowels.

Clyde Nottage deposited the smoldering Bronco butt in a plastic cup of orange juice. "As of this morning, Durham Gas Meat & Tobacco is Durham Gas Meat."

"Please," Max Lamb blurted. "Wait on this, please. You're not feeling well enough to make such an important decision."

"I'm dying, you fucking idiot. Three times a day some nurse looks like Pancho Villa shoots sheep cum into my belly. Damn right I don't feel well. Gimme Kleenex."

Max handed him a box of tissues from the bed tray. Nottage snatched one and hacked fiercely into it.

"Mister Nottage, I urge you not to do anything right now."

"Hell, it's already done. Made the call this morning." Nottage spit again. He opened the tissue and examined the contents with a clinical eye. "Last time I checked, I still had fifty-one percent of the company stock. You wasted a perfectly good airplane ticket, boy. The decision's made."

Max Lamb, queasy with despair, began to protest. Nottage hunched forward, cupped his palms to his face and broke into a volcanic spasm of coughing.

Max jumped away from the bed. "Shall I get Dr Caulk?"

The old man gazed into his hands and said, "Oh shit."

Max edged closer. "Are you all right?"

"Considering I'm holding a piece of my own goddamn lung."

"God!" Max turned away.

"Who knows," the old man mused, "it might be worth something someday. Put it in the Smithsonian, like Dillinger's dick."

He drew back his frail right arm and lobbed the rancid chunk of tissue at the wall, where it hung like a gob of salsa.

Max Lamb bolted from the room. Moments later, Clyde Nottage Jr put his head on the pillow and died with a merry wheeze. The expression on his face was purely triumphant.

Dennis Reedy possessed an inner radar for potential trouble. His legendary instincts had saved Midwest Casualty many millions of dollars over the years, so his services as a claims supervisor were prized at the home office in Omaha. Reedy was an obvious choice to lead the Hurricane Crisis Team: South Florida was the insurance-scam capital of the nation, and Reedy knew the territory inside and out.

His radar went on full alert at 15600 Calusa Drive. The injury to the man's jaw was old, and healed. But there was another prospective problem.

"Mister Torres," Reedy said, "how'd you hurt that leg?"

Annoyed, the man looked up from the BarcaLounger. "It was the storm," he said.

Reedy turned stiffly to Fred Dove. "You didn't mention this."

"They're not filing a claim on the injury."

Reedy suppressed the urge to guffaw in young Fred Dove's face. Antonio Torres was a textbook profile of a nuisance claimant. He was disfigured, morose and unsociable—precisely the sort of malcontent who'd have no qualms about defrauding an insurance company. The notion might not have occurred to Torres yet, but it would.

Dennis Reedy asked him how the accident had happened. Mr

Torres shot a look at Mrs Torres, standing next to Fred Dove. Reedy detected nervous animosity in the husband's expression.

Mr Torres began to speak, but his wife cut in to answer: "Tony got hit by a roof beam."

"Oh?"

"While he was walking the dogs. Down the end of the street."

Fred Dove smiled inwardly with relief. Boy, she was good. And quick!

Reedy said, "So the accident didn't happen here on the property?"

"No," replied Edie Marsh, "but I wish it did. Then we'd know who to sue."

They all chuckled, except Snapper. He stared contemptuously at the emblem of a growling badger, stitched to the breast of Dennis Reedy's corporate blazer.

"I hope you don't mind my asking about the accident," said Reedy, "but it's important for us to know all the circumstances — so there's not a misunderstanding later down the road."

Edie Marsh nodded cooperatively. "Well, like I explained to Mister Dove, I told Tony don't you walk those dogs in the storm. It won't kill us if they pee on the carpet or wherever. But would he listen? They're like his little babies — Donald and Marla is what he named them. Spoiled rotten, too. We don't have children, you understand."

She gave Snapper a sad wifely smile. The look he sent back was murderous. She said, "Tony waited till the eye passed over and the wind died before he went outside. 'Fore long it started blowing hard all over again, and before Tony could make it back with the dogs, he got hit by a beam off somebody's roof. Tore up his knee pretty bad."

Reedy nodded neutrally. "Mister Torres, where did this accident occur?"

"Down the end of the street. Like she said." Snapper spoke in a dull monotone. He hated answering questions from pencil dicks like Reedy.

"Do you recall the address, Mister Torres?"

"No, man, the rain was a mess."

"Have you seen a doctor?"

"I'll be OK."

"I think you should go to a doctor."

Fred Dove said, "I suggested the same thing."

"Oh, Tony's stubborn as a mule." Edie Marsh took Dennis Reedy's arm. "Let me show you the rest of the house."

Reedy spent an hour combing through the place. Fred Dove was a jumble of nerves, but Edie stayed cool. Flirting with Reedy was out of the question; she could tell he was an old pro. She steered him away from the hall closet where the crazy geezer with the auger spike was propped, bound and gagged.

Snapper remained sourly camped in front of the television. Edie reminded him that the portable generator was low on gas, but he paid no attention. Donahue was doing a panel on interracial lesbian marriages, and Snapper was riveted in disgust. White chicks eating black chicks! That's what they seemed to be getting at—and there's old Phil, acting like everything's perfectly normal, like he's interviewing the fucking Osmonds!

After inspecting the property, Dennis Reedy settled in the kitchen to work up the final numbers. His fingers were a blur on the calculator keypad. Fred Dove and Edie Marsh traded anticipatory glances. Reedy scratched some figures on a long sheet of paper and slid it across the counter. Edie scanned it. It was a detailed claims form she hadn't seen before.

Reedy said, "Mister Dove estimated the loss of contents at sixty-five. That's a little high, so I'm recommending sixty." He pointed with the eraser end of his pencil. "That brings the total to two hunded and one thousand. See?"

Edie Marsh was baffled. "Contents?" Then, catching on: "Oh yes, of course." She felt like a total fool. She'd assumed the estimate for the house included the Torreses' personal belongings. Fred Dove gave her a sneaky wink.

"One-forty-one for the dwelling," explained Dennis Reedy, "plus sixty for the contents."

Edie said, "Well, I guess that'll have to do." She did a fine job of acting disappointed.

"And we'd like your husband to sign a release confirming that he will not file a medical claim related to his knee injury. Otherwise the settlement process could become quite complicated. Under the circumstances, you probably don't want any delays in receiving your payment."

"Tony'll sign," said Edie. "Let me have it."

She went to the living room and knelt by the BarcaLounger. "We're in great shape," she whispered, and placed both documents—the liability waiver and the claims agreement—on the armrest. "Remember," she said, "it's Torres with an *s*."

Snapper barely took his eyes off the television while he forged Tony's signature. "You believe these perverts?" he said, pointing at Phil's panel. "Bring me a damn beer."

Back in the kitchen, Edie Marsh thanked Dennis Reedy for his time. "How long before we get the money?"

"A couple days. You're at the top of the list."

"That's wonderful, Mister Reedy!"

Fred Dove said, "You've seen our commercials, Mrs Torres. We're the fastest in the business."

Christ, Edie thought, Fred's really overdoing it. But, with the exception of the chatty cartoon badger, she did recall being impressed by Midwest Casualty's TV spots. One in particular showed an intrepid company representative delivering claims checks, by rowboat, to Mississippi flood victims.

"I've got a laptop at the hotel," Dennis Reedy was saying. "We file by modem direct to Omaha, every night."

Edie said, "That's incredible." A couple days! But what about that extra sixty grand?

As soon as Reedy went outside, Fred Dove took her in his arms. When he tried to kiss her, she pushed him away and said, "You *knew*."

"It was supposed to be a surprise."

"Oh, right."

"I swear! Sixty thousand extra, for you and me."

"Freddie, don't screw around."

"How could I steal it, Edie? The check will be made out to 'Mister and Mrs Torres.' That's you guys. Think about it."

Irritably she paced the kitchen. "I'm so stupid," she muttered. "Jesus."

Of course the furnishings would be separate, along with the clothes and appliances and every stupid little doodad inside the place. Fred Dove said, "You never filed a big claim before. You wouldn't know."

"Dwelling *and* contents."

"Exactly."

She stopped pacing and lowered her voice. "Snapper didn't look at the new numbers."

Fred Dove gave her a thumbs-up. "That was my next question."

"I kept my hand over the papers so he wouldn't see."

"Good girl."

"Can we get two checks instead of one?"

"I think so, Edie. Sure."

"One for the dwelling, one for the contents."

"That's the idea," the insurance man said. "An extra sixty for you and me. But don't say a word about this."

"No shit, Sherlock. He's still got three bullets left, remember?" She pecked Fred Dove on the lips and aimed him out the back door.

TWENTY-ONE

Skink and Bonnie Lamb kept watch over the house on Calusa while Augustine returned to the pickup truck for the guns. He wasn't in the mood to shoot at anybody, even with monkey tranquilizer. Making love to Bonnie had left him recklessly serene and sleepy-headed. He resolved to shake himself out of it.

First he attempted to depress himself with misgivings and high-minded reproach. The woman was married, newly married! She was confused, lonely, vulnerable—Augustine piled it on, struggling to feel like a worthless low-life piece of shit. But he was too happy. Bonnie dazzled him with her nerve. Augustine hadn't ever been with a woman who would stoically snack on roadkill, or fail to complain about mosquitoes. Moreover, she seemed to understand the psychotherapeutic benefits of skull juggling. "Touching death," she'd said, "or maybe teasing it."

In the aftermath of passion, zipped naked into a sleeping bag, a lover's groggiest murmurs can be mistaken for piercing insight. Augustine had cautioned himself against drawing too much from those tender exhausted moments with Bonnie Lamb. Yet here he was with a soaring heart and the hint of a goddamn spring in his step. Would he ever learn?

As much as he craved her company, Augustine was apprehensive about Bonnie's joining Skink's expedition. He feared that he'd worry about her to distraction, and he needed his brain to be clear, uncluttered. As long as the governor ran the show, trouble was positively guaranteed. Augustine was counting on it; he couldn't

242

wait. Finally he was on the verge of recapturing, at least temporarily, direction and purpose.

Bonnie was a complication. A week ago Augustine had nothing to lose, and now he had something. Everything. Love's lousy timing, he thought.

Secret moves would be easier with only the two of them, he and Skink. But Bonnie demanded to be in the middle, playing Etta to their Butch and Sundance. The governor didn't seem to care; of course, he lived in a different universe. "'Happiness is never grand,'" he'd whispered to Augustine. "Aldous Huxley. 'Being contented has none of the glamour of a good fight against misfortune.' You think about that."

When Augustine got to the truck, he broke down the dart rifle and concealed the pieces in a gym bag. The .38 pistol he tucked in the gut of his jeans, beneath his shirt. He slung the gym bag over his shoulder and began hiking back toward Calusa, wondering if Huxley was right.

As soon as Dennis Reedy and Fred Dove drove away, Edie Marsh hauled Levon Stichler out of the closet. Snapper wasn't much help. He claimed to be saving his energy.

Edie poked the old man with a bare toe. "So what are we going to do with him?" It was a question of paramount interest to Levon Stichler as well. His eyes widened in anticipation of Snapper's answer, which was:

"Dump him."

"Where?" asked Edie.

"Far away," Snapper said. "Fucker meant to kill me."

"It was a pitiful try, you've got to admit."

"So? It's the thought that counts."

Edie said, "Look at him, Snapper. He's not worth the bullet."

Levon Stichler wasn't the slightest bit insulted. Edie pulled the gag from his mouth, prompting the old man to spit repeatedly on the floor. The gag was a dust cloth that tasted pungently of furniture wax.

"Thank you," he panted.

"Shut up, asshole," said Snapper.

Edie Marsh said: "What's your name, Grampy?"

Levon Stichler told her. He explained why he'd come to assassinate the mobile-home salesman.

"Well, somebody beat you to it." Edie described the visit by the burly fellow with the two dachshunds. "He took your scumbag Tony away. I'm certain he won't be back."

"Oh," said Levon Stichler. "Who are you?"

Snapper gave Edie a cranky look. "See? I told you we gotta kill the fucker."

The old man immediately apologized for being so nosy. Snapper said it didn't matter, they were going to dump him anyway.

Levon said, "That's really not necessary." When he began to plead his case, Snapper decided to gag him again. The old man coughed out the dust rag, crying, "Please—I've got a heart condition!"

"Good." Snapper ordered Edie Marsh to go fetch the auger spike. Levon Stichler got the message. He stopped talking and allowed his mouth to be muffled.

"Cover his eyes, too," said Snapper.

Edie used a black chiffon scarf that she'd found in Neria Torres's underwear drawer. It made for quite a classy blindfold.

"That too tight?" she asked.

Levon Stichler grunted meekly in the negative.

"Now what?" she said to Snapper.

He shrugged unhappily. "You got any more them Darvons? My fucking leg's on fire."

"Honey, I sure don't—"

"Shit!" With his good leg he kicked Levon Stichler in the ribs, for no reason except that the old man was a convenient target. Edie pulled Snapper aside and told him to get a grip, for Christ's sake.

Under her breath: "It's all working out, OK? Reedy signed off on the settlement. All that's left is to wait for the money. Kill this geezer, you'll screw up everything."

Snapper worked his jaw like a steam shovel. His eyes were

shot with pain and hangover. "Well, I can't think of nothin' else to do."

Edie said: "Listen. We put old Levon in the car and haul him out to the boonies. We tell him to take his sweet time walking back, otherwise we'll track down each of his grandchildren and . . . oh, I don't know—"

"Skin 'em like pigs?"

"Fine. Whatever. The point is to scare the hell out of him, and he'll forget about everything. All he wants to do is live."

Snapper said, "My goddamn leg's near to bust open."

"Go watch TV. I'll look for some pills."

Edie searched the medicine cabinets to see if any useful pharmaceuticals had survived the hurricane. The best she could do was an unopened bottle of Midols. She told Snapper it was generic codeine, and pressed five tablets into his hand. He washed them down with a slug of warm Budweiser.

Edie said, "Is there gas in the Jeep?"

"Yeah. After Sally Jessy we'll go."

"And what is today's topic?"

"Boob jobs gone bad."

"How cheery," said Edie. She went outside to walk Donald and Marla.

After days in a morphine fog, Trooper Brenda Rourke finally felt better. The plastic surgeon promised to get her on the operating-room schedule by the end of the week.

Through the bandages she told Jim Tile: "You look whipped, big guy."

"We're still on double shifts. It's like Daytona out there."

Brenda asked if he'd heard what happened. "Some pawnshop off Kendall—the creep tried to hock my mom's ring."

"Same guy?"

"Sounds like it. The clerk was impressed by the face."

Jim Tile said, "Well, it's a start."

But the news worried him. He had unleashed the governor to deal with Brenda's attacker on the assumption that the governor would move faster than police. However, the pawnshop incident freshened the trail. Now it was possible that Skink's pursuit of the man in the black Cherokee would put him on a collision course with detectives. It was not a happy scenario to contemplate.

"I must look like hell," Brenda said, "because I've never seen you so gloomy."

Of course he'd let it get to him—Brenda lying pale and shattered in the hospital. In his work Jim Tile had seen plenty of blood, pain and heartache, yet he'd never felt such blinding anger as he had that first day at Brenda's bedside. Trusting the justice system to deal with her attacker had struck the trooper as laughably naive, certainly futile. This was a special monster. It was evident by what he'd done to her. The guy hated either women, cops or both. In any case, he was a menace. He needed to be cut from the herd.

Now, upon reflection, Jim Tile wished he'd let his inner rage subside before he'd made the move. When Brenda remembered the tag number off the Cherokee, he should've sent it up the chain of command; played it by the book. Turning the governor loose was a rash, foolhardy impulse; vigilante madness. Brenda would recover from the beating, but now Jim Tile had put his dear old friend at dire risk. It would be damn near impossible to call him off.

"I need to ask you something," Brenda said.

"Sure."

"A detective from Metro Robbery came by today. Also a woman from the State Attorney. They didn't know about the black Jeep."

"Hmmm."

"About the license plate—I figured you'd given them the numbers."

"I made a mistake, Bren."

"You forgot?"

"No, I didn't forget. I made a mistake."

Jim Tile sat on the edge of the bed and told her what he'd done. Afterwards she remained quiet, except to make small talk when a nurse came to dress her wounds.

Later, when she and Jim Tile were alone again, Brenda said, "So you found your crazy friend. How?"

"Doesn't matter."

"And he was right here, in this room, and you didn't introduce me?"

Jim Tile chuckled. "You were zonked, darling."

Brenda stroked his hand. He could tell she was still thinking about it. Finally she said, "Boy, you must really love me, to do something like this."

"I screwed up bad. I'm sorry."

"Enough already. I've got one question."

"OK."

"What are the odds," Brenda said, "that your friend will catch up with the asshole who got my mother's ring?"

"The odds are pretty good."

Brenda Rourke nodded and closed her eyes. Jim Tile waited until her breathing was strong and regular; waited until he was certain it was a deep healthy sleep, and not something else. Before leaving, he kissed her cheek, in a gap between bandages, and was comforted by the warmth of her skin. He felt pretty sure he saw the trace of a smile on her lips.

Skink's forehead was propped on the windowsill. He hadn't made a sound in an hour, hadn't stirred when Augustine left to get the guns. Bonnie Lamb didn't know if he was dozing or ignoring her.

"This was the baby's room. Did you notice?" she said.

Nothing.

"Are you awake?"

Still no response.

A yellowjacket flew through the broken-out window and took an instant liking to Skink's pungent mane. Bonnie shooed it away. From across the street, at 15600 Calusa, came the sound of dogs barking.

Eventually the governor spoke. "Oh, they'll be back." He didn't raise his head from the sill.

"Who?"

"Folks who own the baby."

"How can you be sure?"

Silence.

"Maybe the hurricane was all they could take."

"Optimist," Skink grumbled.

Glancing again at the drowned teddy bear, Bonnie thought that no family deserved to have their life shattered in such a harrowing way. The governor seemed to be reading her mind.

He said, "I'm sorry it happened to them. I'm sorry they were here in the first place."

"And you'll be even sorrier if they come back."

Skink looked up, blinking like a sleepy porch lizard. "It's a hurricane zone," he said simply.

Bonnie thought he ought to hear an outsider's point of view. "People come here because they think it's better than where they were. They believe the postcards, and you know what? For lots of them, it *is* better than where they came from, whether it's Long Island or Des Moines or Havana. Life is brighter, so it's worth the risks. Maybe even hurricanes."

The governor used his functional eye to scan the baby's room. He said, "Fuck with Mother Nature and she'll fuck back."

"People have dreams, that's all. Like the settlers of the old West."

"Oh, child."

"What?" Bonnie said, indignantly.

"Tell me what's left to settle." Skink lowered his head again.

She tugged on the sleeve of his camo shirt. "I want you to show me what you showed Max. The wildest part."

Skink clucked. "Why? Your husband certainly wasn't impressed."

"I'm not like Max."

"Let us fervently hope not."

"Please. Will you show me?"

Once more, no reply. Bonnie wished Augustine would hurry back. She returned her attention to the house where the black Cherokee was parked, and thought about what they'd witnessed during the long hot morning.

A half hour after the old man had arrived, a taxi pulled up. Out the doorway of 15600 Calusa had scurried a redheaded woman in a tight shiny cocktail dress and formidable high heels. Augustine and Bonnie agreed she looked like a prostitute. As the woman had wriggled herself into the back of the cab, Skink remarked that her bold stockings would make a superb mullet seine.

A short time later, a teal-blue Taurus had stopped in the driveway. The governor said it had to be a rental, because only rental companies bought teal-blue cars. Two men had gotten out of the Taurus; neither had a disfigured jaw. The younger one was a trim-looking blond who wore eyeglasses and carried a tan briefcase. The older, heavier one had cropped dark hair and carried a clipboard; his bearing was one of authority—probably ex-military, Skink guessed, a sergeant in his youth. The two men had stayed in the house for a long time. Finally the older one had come out alone. He'd sat in the driver's side of the car, with the door open, and jotted notes. Soon the man with the briefcase had appeared around the corner of the house, from the backyard, and together they'd departed.

While the visitors didn't appear to be violent desperadoes, Skink said that one could never be certain in Miami. Augustine got the hint, and went to fetch the guns from the pickup truck.

Now the governor had his forehead on the sill, and he'd begun to hum. Bonnie asked the name of the song.

"'Number Nine Dream,'" he said.

"I don't know that one."

She wanted so much to hear about his life. She wanted him to open up and tell the most thrilling and shocking of true stories.

"Sing it for me," she said.

"Some other time." Skink pointed across the street. A man and a woman were leaving the house.

Bonnie Lamb stared. "What in the world are they doing?"

The governor rose quickly. "Come, child," he said.

*

After the Sally Jessy show ended, Snapper made a couple of phone calls to set something up. Exactly what, Edie Marsh wasn't sure. Evidently he'd gotten a brainstorm about what to do with the old man, short of murder.

"Gimme hand," he said to Edie, and began tearing the living-room drapes off the rods. The drapes were whorehouse pink, heavy and dank from rain. They spread the fabric in a crude square on the floor. Then they put Levon Stichler in the middle and rolled him up inside.

To Edie, it resembled an enormous strawberry pastry. She said, "I hope he can breathe."

Snapper punched the pink bundle. "Hey, asshole. You got air?"

The gagged old man responded with an expressive groan. Snapper said, "He's OK. Let's haul his ass out to the Jeep."

Levon Stichler wasn't easy to carry. Snapper took the heavy end, but each step was agony to his shattered knee. They dropped the old man several times before they made it to the driveway. Each time it happened, Snapper swore vehemently and danced a tortured one-legged jig around the pink bundle. Edie Marsh opened the rear hatch of the Cherokee, and somehow they managed to fold Levon Stichler into the cargo well.

Snapper was leaning against the bumper, waiting for the searing pain in his leg to ebb, when he spotted the tall stranger coming toward them from the abandoned house across the street. The man was dressed in army greens. His long wild hair looked like frosted hemp. At first Snapper thought he was a street person, maybe a Vietnam vet or one of those cracked-out losers who lived under the interstate. Except he was walking too fast and purposefully to be a bum. He was moving like he had food in his stomach, good hard muscles, and something serious on his mind. Ten yards behind, hurrying to catch up, was a respectable-looking young woman.

Edie Marsh said, "Oh shit," and slammed the hatch of the Jeep. She told Snapper not to say a damn word; she'd do the talking.

As the stranger approached, Snapper straightened on both legs.

The pain in his injured knee caused him to grind his mismatched molars. He slipped a hand inside his suit jacket.

"Excuse us," said the stranger. The woman, looking nervous, stood behind him.

Edie Marsh said, helpfully, "Are you lost?"

The stranger beamed—a striking smile, full of bright movie-star teeth. Snapper tensed; this was no interstate bum.

"What a fine question!" the man said to Edie. Then he turned to Snapper. "Sir, you and I have something in common."

Snapper scowled. "The fuck you talkin' about?"

"See here." The stranger calmly pried out one of his eyeballs and held it up, like a polished gemstone, for Snapper to examine. Snapper felt himself keeling, and steadied himself against the truck. The sight of the shrunken socket was more sickening than that of the glistening prosthesis.

"It's glass," the man said. "A minor disability, just like your jaw. But we both struggle with the mirror, do we not?"

"I got no problems in that department," Snapper said, though he could not look the stranger in the face. "Are you some fuckin' preacher or what?"

Edie Marsh cut in: "Mister, I don't mean to be rude, but we've got to be on our way. We've got an appointment downtown."

The stranger had a darkly elusive charm, a dangerous and disorganized intelligence that put Edie on edge. He appeared content at the prospect of physical confrontation. The pretty young woman, tame and fine-featured, seemed an unlikely partner; Edie wondered if she was a captive.

The tall stranger cocked back his head and deftly reinserted the glass eye. Then, blinking for focus, he said, "OK, kids. Let's have a peek in that snazzy Jeep."

Snapper whipped out the .357 and pointed it at a button in the center of the man's broad chest. "Get in," he snarled.

Again the stranger grinned. "We thought you'd never ask!" The young woman clutched one of his arms and tried to suppress her trembling.

*

Augustine noticed a young towheaded boy, rigid in a shredded patio chair outside a battered house. Most of the roof was gone, so a skin of cheap blue plastic had been stapled to the beams for shade and shelter. It puckered and flapped in the breeze.

The towheaded boy looked only ten or eleven years old. He held a stainless-steel Ruger Mini-14, which he raised from his lap as Augustine passed on the sidewalk. In a thin high pitch, the boy yelled: "Looters will be shot!"

The warning matched a message spray-painted in two-foot letters on the front wall: LOOTERS BEWAIR!!

Augustine turned to face the child. "I'm not a looter. Where's your father?"

"Out for lumber. He told me watch the place."

"You're doing a good job." Augustine stared at the powerful rifle. A bank robber had used the same model to shoot down five FBI agents in Suniland, a few years back.

The boy explained: "We had looters, night after the hurrycane. We were stayin' with Uncle Rick, he lives somewheres called Dania. They came through while we's gone."

Augustine slowly stepped forward for a closer look. The clip was fitted flush in the Ruger; all systems Go. The boy wore a severe expression, squinting at Augustine as if he stood a hundred yards away. The boy fidgeted in the flimsy chair. One side of his mouth wormed into a creepy lopsided frown. Augustine half expected to hear banjo music.

The boy went on: "They got our TVs and CD player. My dad's toolbox, too. I'm 'posed to shoot the bastards they come back."

"Did you ever fire that gun before?"

"All the time." The child's hard gray-blue eyes flickered with the lie. The Mini-14 was heavy. His little arms were tired from holding it. "You better go on now," he advised.

Augustine nodded, backing away. "Just be careful, all right? You don't want to hurt the wrong person."

"My dad said he's gone booby-trap everything so's next time they'll be damn sorry. He went to the hardware store. My mom and Debbie are still up at Uncle Rick's. Debbie's my half-sister, she's seven."

"Promise you'll be careful with the gun."

"She stepped on a rusty nail and got infected."

"Promise me you'll take it easy."

"OK," said the boy. A droplet of sweat rolled down a pink, sunburned cheek. It surely tickled, but the boy never took a hand off the rifle.

Augustine waved good-bye and went on up the road. When he arrived at the house where he'd left Bonnie Lamb and the governor, he found it empty. Across the street, at 15600 Calusa, the black Jeep Cherokee was gone from the driveway.

TWENTY-TWO

Augustine sprinted across the street. He pulled the pistol when he reached the doorway. There was no answer when he called Bonnie's name. Cautiously he went through the house. It was empty of life. The air was stale; mildew and sweat, except for one of the bedrooms—strong perfume and sex. A hall closet was open, revealing nothing unusual. A plaque on the living-room wall indicated the house belonged to a salesman, Antonio Torres. The hurricane had done quite a number on the place. In the backyard Augustine saw two miniature dachshunds tied to a sprinkler. They barked excitedly when they spotted him.

He sat down in a Naugahyde recliner and tried to reconstruct what could have happened in the twenty minutes he'd been gone. Obviously something had inspired the governor to make his move. Surely he'd ordered Bonnie to wait across the street, but she'd probably followed him just the same. Augustine had to assume they were now in the Jeep with the bad guy, headed for an unknown destination.

Augustine tore through the house once more, searching for clues. In the rubble of the funky-smelling bedroom was an album of water-stained photographs: the salesman, his spouse, and a multitude of well-fed relatives. Brenda Rourke had not recalled her attacker as an overweight Hispanic male, and the pictures of Antonio Torres showed no obvious facial deformity. Augustine decided it couldn't be the same man. He moved to the kitchen.

Hidden in a large saucepan, in a cupboard over the double sink, was a woman's leather purse. Inside was a wallet containing a Florida driver's license for one Edith Deborah Marsh, white female. Date of birth: 5–7–63. The address was an apartment in West Palm Beach. The picture on the license was unusually revealing: a pretty young lady with smoky, predatory eyes. The photo tech at the driver's bureau had outdone himself. Folded neatly in the woman's purse were pink carbons of two insurance settlements from Midwest Casualty, one for $60,000 and one for $141,000. The claims were for hurricane damage to the house at 15600 Calusa, and bore signatures of Antonio and Neria Torres. Interestingly, the insurance papers were dated that very day. Augustine was intrigued that Ms Edith Marsh would have these documents in her possession, and took the liberty of transferring them to his own pocket.

It was an interesting twist, but Augustine doubted it would help him locate Bonnie and the governor. The key to the mystery was the creep with the crooked jaw. He'd be the one carrying Brenda Rourke's service revolver. He'd be the one at the wheel of the Cherokee. Yet the house yielded no traceable signs.

With every passing moment, the creep was getting farther away. Augustine experienced a flutter of panic, thinking of what might happen. It was inconceivable that the governor would be cooperative during an abduction. Resistance was in the man's blood. A .357 aimed at his forehead would only enhance the challenge. And if he screwed up, Bonnie Lamb would be lost.

Augustine ached with dread. His impulse was to get in the truck and start driving; desperate widening grids and circles, in a wild hope of spotting the Jeep. The creep had only a short head start, but also the considerable advantage of knowing which direction he was going.

Then Augustine thought of Jim Tile, the state trooper. One shout on the police radio and every cop in South Florida would know to keep an eye open for the Cherokee. Augustine had made a point of memorizing the new tag: PPZ–350. Save the Manatee.

He picked up the kitchen phone to get the number for the Highway Patrol. That's when he noticed his old friend, the redial button.

He'd learned the trick while keeping house with the demented surgical intern, the one who ultimately knifed him in the shower. Whenever he found her gone, Augustine would touch the redial button to determine if she'd been phoning around town to score more Dilaudid, or pawn items stolen from his house. Before long he was able to recognize the voices of her various dope dealers and fences, before hanging up. In that way, the redial button had been a valuable tool for predicting his girlfriend's moods and tracing missing property.

So he punched it now, to find out the last number dialed from 15600 Calusa before Skink and Bonnie disappeared. After three rings, a friendly female voice answered:

"Paradise Palms. Can I help you?"

Augustine hesitated. He knew of only one Paradise Palms, a seaside motel down in Islamorada. He gave it a shot. "My brother just called a little while ago. From Miami."

"Oh yes. Mister Horn's friend."

"Pardon me?"

"The owner. Mister Horn. Your brother's name is Lester?"

"Right," said Augustine, flying blind.

"He's the only Miami booking we've had today. Did he want to cancel?"

"Oh no," Augustine said. "No, I just want to make sure the reservation is all set. See, we're supposed to surprise him down there—it's his birthday tomorrow. We're going to take him deep-sea fishing."

The woman at the motel said the dolphin were hitting offshore, and advised him to try the docks at Bud 'n' Mary's to arrange a charter. "Would you like me to call over there?"

"No, that's all right."

"Does Mister Horn know?"

"Know what?" said Augustine.

"That it's Lester's birthday. He'll be so sorry he missed it—he's in Tampa on business."

"Oh, that's too bad," Augustine said. "I meant to ask—what time's my brother getting in? So we can make sure everything's arranged. You know, for the surprise party."

"Of course. He told us to expect him late this afternoon."

"That's perfect."

"And don't you worry. I won't say a word to spoil it."

Augustine said, "Ma'am, I cannot thank you enough."

After a day of inept drinking and arduous self-pity, Max Lamb took a flight from Guadalajara to Miami. There he intended to quit smoking, reclaim his brainwashed spouse and reconstruct his life. Another honeymoon was essential—but, this time, someplace far from Florida.

Hawaii, Max thought. Maybe even Australia.

His head was a cinder block. The tequila hangover fueled vivid, horrific dreams on the plane. Once he awakened clawing at an invisible shock collar, his neck on fire. In the nightmare it was Bonnie and not the kidnapper wielding the Tri-Tronics remote control, diabolically pushing the buttons. An hour later came another dream; again his wife. This time they were making love on the deck of an airboat, skimming across the Everglades under a blue porcelain sky. Bonnie was on top of him with her eyes half open, the sawgrass whipping her cheeks. Clinging to her bare shoulder was a monkey—the same psoriatic pest that Max had videotaped after the hurricane! In the dream, Max couldn't see the face of the airboat driver, but believed it was the quiet young man who juggled skulls. As Bonnie bucked her hips, the vile monkey hung on like a tiny wrangler. Suddenly it rose on its hind legs to display a miniature pink erection. That's when Max screamed and woke up. He was wide-eyed but calmer by the time the plane landed.

Then, at the Miami airport, his tequila phantasms were reignited by a newspaper headline:

Remains in Fox Hollow Identified as Mob Figure; Believed Mauled, Devoured by Escaped Cat

Max bought the paper and read the story in horror. A gangster named Ira Jackson had been gobbled by a wild lion that broke out of a wildlife farm during the storm. The gruesome details heightened the urgency of Max's mission.

He arrived at Augustine's home with a prepared speech and, if necessary, a legal threat. The lights were off. Nobody answered the door. In the absence of confrontation, Max was emboldened to slip around to the backyard.

The sliding glass door on the porch was unlocked. Inside the house, it was stuffy and warm. Max started the air conditioner and turned on every lamp he could find. He wanted to advertise his presence; he didn't want to be found creeping through the halls in darkness, like a common burglar.

Thrilled by his own daring, Max combed the place for signs of his wife. Hanging in a closet was the outfit she'd worn on the day he was kidnapped. Since the rental car had been looted of their belongings, Max reasoned that Bonnie must now be wearing somebody else's clothes, or her folks had wired some cash—or perhaps Augustine had bought her an expensive new wardrobe. Wasn't that what wife-stealers did?

Max Lamb forced himself to enter the guest room. He purposely avoided the wall of skulls, but shuddered anyway under the dissipated stares. He was pleased to find the bed linens rumpled exclusively on the left side—Bonnie's favorite. A depression in the lone pillow seemed, upon inspection, to match the shape of a young woman's head. The bed showed no manifest evidence of male visitation.

An oak dresser yielded an assortment of female clothing, from bras to blue jeans, in an intriguing range of sizes. Relics of Augustine's ex-girlfriends, Max assumed. One of them must have stood six feet two, judging by the Amazonian cut of her black exercise leggings. Max located several petite items that would have fit his wife, including a pair of powder-blue sweat socks in a tidy mound on the hardwood floor. His outlook improved; at least she was wearing borrowed clothes.

He steeled himself for the next survey: Augustine's room.

The man's bed looked like a grenade had been set off under the sheets. Max Lamb thought: He's either having fantastic sex or horrible nightmares. The disarray made it impossible to determine if two persons had shared the mattress; the cast of *A Chorus Line* could have slept there, for all Max could tell.

Uncertainty nibbled at his ego. He got an idea—distasteful but effective. He bent over Augustine's bed and put his nose to the linens, whiffing for a trace of Bonnie's perfume. Uncharacteristically, Max Lamb couldn't recall the brand name of the fragrance, but he'd never forget its orchard scent.

He sniffed in imaginary grids, starting at the headboard and working his way down the mattress. An explosive sneeze announced his findings: Paco Rabanne for men. Max recognized the scent because he wore it himself (in spite of a near-incapacitating allergy) every Monday, for the sixth-floor meetings at Rodale.

Paco and laundry bleach, that's all Max detected on Augustine's sheets.

One more place to check: the wastebasket in the bathroom. Grimly Max pawed through the litter: no used condoms, thank God.

Later, stretched out on Augustine's sofa, Max realized that Bonnie's faithfulness, or possible lack thereof, wasn't the most pressing issue. It was her sanity. Somehow they'd snowed her, those madmen. Like some weird cult—one eats road pizza, the other fondles human skulls.

How could such a bright girl let herself be brainwashed by such freaks!

Max Lamb decided on a bold move. He composed a script for himself and rehearsed it for an hour before picking up the phone. Then he dialed the apartment in New York and left the message for his wandering wife. The ultimatum.

Afterwards Max called back to hear how it sounded on the answering machine. His voice was so steely that he scarcely recognized himself.

Excellent, he thought. Just what Bonnie needs to hear.

If only she calls.

Avila's wife snidely announced that his expensive *santería* goats were in the custody of Animal Control. One had been captured grazing along the shoulder of the Don Shula Expressway, while the other had turned up at a car wash, butting its horns through the grillwork of a leased Jaguar sedan. Avila's wife said it made the Channel 7 news.

"So? What do you want *me* to do?" Avila demanded.

"Oh, forget about! Three hundred dollars, chew jess forget about!"

"You want me to steal the goats back? OK, tonight I'll drive to the animal shelter and break down the fence and kidnap the damn things. That make you happy? While I'm there I'll grab you some kittens and puppies, too. Maybe a big fat guinea pig for your mother, no?"

"I hate chew! I hate chew!"

Avila shook his head. "Here we go again."

"Chew and Chango, your faggot *oricha*!"

"Louder," Avila said. "Maybe you can wake some of your dead relatives in Havana."

The phone rang. He picked it up and turned his back on his wife, who hurled a can of black beans and stormed from the kitchen in a gust of English expletives.

It was Jasmine on the line. She asked, "What's all that noise?"

"Marriage," Avila said.

"Well, love, I'm sitting here with Bridget, and guess where we're going tonight."

"To blow somebody?"

"God, look who's in a piss-poor mood."

"Sorry," Avila said. "It's been a shitty day."

"We're driving to the Keys."

"Yeah?"

"To meet your friend," said Jasmine.

"No shit? Where?"

"Some motel on the ocean. Can you believe he's payin' the both of us to baby-sit some old-timer."

"Who?" Avila couldn't imagine what new scam Snapper was running.

Jasmine said, "Just some yutz, I don't know. We're supposed

to keep him busy for a couple days, take some dirty pictures. Five hundred each is what your friend's giving us."

"Geez, that sucks."

"Business is slow, sweetie. The hurricane turned all our regulars into decent, faithful, God-fearing family men."

Avila heard Bridget's giggle in the background. Jasmine said, "So five hundred looks pretty sweet right about now."

"You can double it if you give up the name of the motel."

"Why do you think we called? Aren't you proud of me?"

Avila said, "You're the best."

"But listen, honey, we need to know—"

"Let me talk to Bridget."

"Nope, we want to know what you got in mind. Because both of us are on probation, as usual—"

"Don't worry," Avila said.

"—and we don't need no more trouble, legally speaking."

"Relax, I said."

"You ain't gonna kill this guy?"

"Which guy—Snapper? Hell, no, he owes me money is all. What time are you meeting him?"

Jasmine said, "Around eight."

Avila checked his wristwatch. "You girls ain't gonna make Key West by eight o'clock unless you got a rocket car."

"Not Key West, honey. Islamorada."

It was seventy-five miles closer, but Avila still wasn't certain he could get there in time. First he had to make an offering; such a momentous trip was unthinkable without an offering.

He said, "Jasmine, what's the name of the motel?"

"Not till you promise me and Bridget won't get in trouble."

"Jesus, I already told you."

She said, "Here's the deal, so listen. You gotta wait till we get our money from your friend Snapper. Then you gotta promise not to shoot anybody in front of us, OK?"

Avila said, "On my wife's future grave."

"Also, you gotta promise to pay us what you said—five hundred each."

"Yep."

"Plus two stone crab dinners. That's Bridget's idea."

"No problem," Avila said. Informing the prostitutes that stone crabs were out of season would only have muddled the negotiation.

"The name," Avila pressed.

"Paradise Palms. I've never been there before. Bridget, neither, but Snapper promised it's really nice."

"Compared to prison, I'm sure it's the fucking Ritz. What's the room number?"

Jasmine asked Bridget. Bridget didn't know.

"Doesn't matter," Avila said. "I'll track you down."

"Remember what you promised!"

"Yeah, I'll try. It's already been at least seven seconds."

"Well, sweetheart, we better cruise."

Avila was about to set the receiver on the cradle when he remembered something. "Hey! Jasmine, wait!"

"Yeah, what."

"Did you tell her about me?"

"Bridget? I didn't tell her nuthin'." Jasmine sounded puzzled. "What's to tell?"

"Nuthin'."

"Oh . . . you mean about—"

"Don't say it!"

Jasmine said, "Honey, I would *never*. That was between you and me. Honest to God."

"'Cause the other night you said I was better." How valiantly Avila had labored to stifle his vocalizing during the lovemaking! What few sounds he'd made were not, by any stretch of the imagination, squeaks.

"The other night you were just great," said Jasmine. "Fantastic, even. Better than I remembered."

Avila said, "Same goes for you, too."

Later, driving to Sweetwater for the chickens, he couldn't stop thinking about the call girl's sultry compliment. Whether she meant a word of it or not wasn't worth speculating on; the concept of sincerity was so foreign to Avila's own life that he felt unqualified to pass judgment on Jasmine. He was just glad she'd quit calling herself Morganna—what a clunker of a name to remember in the heat of passion!

The combined effect of marijuana and methaqualone on Dr Charles Gabler's judgment was not salutary. Never was it more evident than late on the night of September 1, at a roadside motel off Interstate 10 near Bonifay, Florida. Overtaken with desire, the professor slipped out of the twin bed he shared with the sleeping Neria Torres, and slipped into the twin bed occupied by the wakeful young graduate student, Celeste. As he ardently attached himself to one of Celeste's creamy breasts, Dr Gabler was becalmed by a warm, harmonious confluence of physical and metaphysical currents. His timing couldn't have been worse.

Neria Torres had been reevaluating the parameters of her relationship with the professor ever since they'd pulled off a highway outside Jackson, Mississippi, so he could take a leak. Sitting in the driver's seat, watching Dr Gabler try to tinkle in some azaleas, Neria had thought: I don't find this cute anymore.

As the professor had tottered back toward the van, the beams of the headlights dramatically illuminated the ruby-colored crystals dangling from the lanyard around his neck.

"Oh wow," young Celeste had exclaimed, suffused with mystic awe and Humboldt County's finest.

That was the moment when Neria Torres had looked into her future and decided that the professor should share no large part of it; specifically, the insurance settlement from the hurricane. Neria envisioned a scenario in which Dr Gabler might endeavor to sweet-talk her out of a portion of the money—he would probably call it a friendly loan—and then flee in the dead of night with his nubile protégée. After all, that's pretty much what he'd done to his previous lover, a vendor of fine macramés, when Neria Torres entered his life.

Even if the professor harbored no selfish designs on the hurricane booty, Neria had a pragmatic reason to dump him: His appearance in Miami would complicate the duel with her estranged husband over the insurance settlement. Considering the tainted circumstance of her departure from the household, Neria doubted that Tony would be in a mood to forgive and forget. Her inability to make contact in the days following the storm was foreboding— the vindictive bastard obviously intended to pocket her half of the windfall. If the battle went to court, Dr Gabler's bleary presence during the proceedings would not, Neria Torres knew, work in her favor.

These were the thoughts she carried into sleep at the motel in Bonifay. Had it been a deeper sleep, or had the room's Eisenhower-vintage cooling unit been a few decibels louder, Neria Torres might not have been awakened by the muffled suckling and amorous hmmm-hmmms from the nearby bed. But awakened she was.

Except for cracking her eyelids, Neria didn't move a muscle at first. Instead she lay listening in disgusted fascination, struggling to arrange her emotions. On the one hand, she was vastly relieved to have found a solid excuse for jettisoning the professor. On the other hand, she was furious that the sneaky little shit would be so crude and thoughtless. Over the years, Tony Torres undoubtedly had cheated on her now and again—but never while she was sleeping in the same room!

Eventually, it was the immodest giggling of young Celeste that galvanized Neria Torres. She sprang from the bed, turned on all the lights, snatched up the velvet satchel containing Dr Gabler's special healing crystals and began whaling deliriously on the writhing mound of bedsheets. The satchel was heavy and the stones were sharp, taking a toll on the professor's unfirm flesh. With an effeminate cry, he scuttled to the bathroom and chained the door. Meanwhile the graduate student cowered nude and tearful on the mattress. The stubble on Dr Gabler's chin had left a telltale path of abraded, roseate blotches from her neck to her quivering belly. Neria Torres noticed, with fierce satisfaction, a faint comma of a scar beneath each of young Celeste's perfect breasts; an Earth Mother with implants!

Repeatedly she gasped, "I'm sorry, Neria, please don't kill me! Please don't . . ."

Neria threw the satchel of crystals to the floor. "Celeste, you know what I hope for you? I hope that asshole hiding in the john is the highlight of your entire goddamn life. Now where's the keys to the van?"

Hours later, at a busy truck stop in Gainesville, Neria tried another call to Mr Varga, her former neighbor in Miami. This time his phone was working; Varga answered on the third ring. He insisted he knew nothing about Neria's husband and a young blond hussy loading up a rental truck.

"Fact, I haven't seen Tony since maybe two days after the hurricane."

"Are there still strangers at the house?" Neria asked.

"All the time, people come and go. But no blondes."

"Who are they, Leon?"

"I don't know. Friends and cousins of Tony, I heard. They got two dogs bark half the night. I figured Tony's letting 'em watch the place."

Varga shared his theory: Neria's husband was lying low, due to adverse publicity about the mobile-home industry. "Every damn one blew to smithereens in the storm," Varga related. "The papers and TV are making a big stink. Supposedly there's going to be an investigation. The FBI is what they say."

"Oh, come off it."

"That's the rumor," Varga said. "Your Tony, he's no fool. I think he's making himself invisible till all this cools down, these people come to their senses. I mean, it's not *his* fault those trailers fell apart. God's will is what it was. He's testing us, same as He did with Noah."

"Except Noah wasn't insured," said Neria Torres.

Mr Varga was right about one thing: Tony wouldn't stick around if there was heat. His style was to take a nice hotel room and ride things out. In the meantime, he'd have some of his deadbeat relatives or white-trash salesmen pals stay with their bimbos in the house on Calusa. Tony wouldn't be far away; never would he skip town without getting his paws on the Midwest Casualty money.

Neria was buoyed. The story about the young blonde and

Brooklyn obviously was bullshit, a ruse cooked up by her husband. Wishful thinking, too, Neria mused. Talking to Mr Varga validated her decision to return to Miami.

"Are you really heading home?" he asked. "You and the mister give it one more try?"

"Stranger things have happened," said Neria Torres. She made Mr Varga swear on a stack of Holy Bibles not to breathe a word. She said it would ruin everything if Tony found out she was coming.

TWENTY-THREE

Snapper instructed Edie Marsh to take the Turnpike, and watch the damn speedometer. He was pressed against the passenger-side door, keeping the stolen .357 pointed at the freak in the army greens. The young woman was no immediate threat.

The stranger blinked like a craggy tortoise. He said: "How much you get for her ring?"

Snapper frowned. The fucker *knew*—but how?

Edie Marsh didn't take her eyes off the road. "What's he talking about? Whose ring?"

Snapper spied, in the lower margin of his vision, the wandering prow of his jawbone. He said, "Everybody shut the fuck up!"

Leaning forward, the longhair said to Edie: "Your rough-tough boyfriend beat up a policewoman. Ripped off her gun and her mother's wedding band—he didn't tell you?"

Edie shivered. Maybe it was his breath on the nape of her neck, or the slow rumble of his voice, or what he was saying. Meanwhile Snapper waved the police pistol and hollered for the whole world to shut up or fucking die!

He jammed a CD into the dashboard stereo: ninety-five decibels of country heartache. Within minutes his fury passed, soothed by Reba's crooning or possibly the five white pills Edie had given him back at the house.

OK, boy, now *think*.

The original plan was to waylay the nutty old man with the hookers. No problem there. A guy Snapper knew from his Lauderdale days, Johnny Horn, had a small motel down in the Keys. Ideal spot for Levon Stichler to take a short vacation. Snapper's idea was to get one a them cheap disposable cameras, so the hookers could take some pictures, the kind a respectable man wouldn't want his grandkiddies to see. Two or three days tied naked to a motel bed, the old fart wouldn't care to recall he'd ever set foot at 15600 Calusa Drive. If he promised to behave, then possibly the disposable camera would get disposed of. The old man could make his way back to Miami with nothing but a bed rash and a sore cock to show for the experience.

Best of all, Snapper wouldn't have to pay for the motel room in the Keys, because Johnny Horn owed him a favor. Two years back, Snapper had more or less repossessed a Corvette convertible from the freeloading boyfriend of one of Johnny Horn's ex-wives. Snapper had driven the Corvette straight to the Port of Miami and, in broad daylight, parked it on a container ship bound for Cartagena. It was a high-risk deal, and Johnny said for Snapper to call the Paradise Palms anytime he needed a place to crash or hide out or take some girl.

Snapper had dreamed up the plan for old man Stichler all by himself, without Edie's input. He surely didn't want to throw all that cleverness out the window, but he couldn't conceive of how to fit the new intruders into his scheme, and he was too fogged from the pills to improvise. It seemed easier to kill the one-eyed freak and his woman companion—and as long as Snapper was being so bold, why not do loony old Levon as well? That way, Snapper reasoned, he wouldn't have to pay the two whores anything, except for gas money and possibly a seafood dinner.

On the downside: How to get rid of three dead bodies? The logistics were daunting. Snapper suspected that his droopy brain wasn't up to the challenge. Killing took energy, and Snapper all of a sudden felt like sleeping for three weeks solid.

He worked up a pep talk for himself, recalling what a wise guy once told him in prison: *Dumping bodies is like buying real estate—location, location, location.* Snapper thought: Look around, boy. You got your mangrove islands, your Everglades, your Atlantic-mother-fucking-Ocean. What more you want? A fast shot to the head, then let the sharks or the gators or the crabs finish the job. What's so damn difficult about that?

But Jesus, the stakes were high; one measly fuckup and it's back to Raiford for the rest of my life. Probably locked in a ten-by-ten with some humongous horny black faggot weight lifter. Clean and jerk my skinny ass till I walk like Julia Roberts.

And shooting people *is* awful noisy. Edie Marsh wouldn't go for it, Snapper knew for a fact. She'd make quite a stink. And killing Edie with the others was impractical because (a) he didn't have enough bullets and (b) he couldn't cash the insurance checks without her. *Damn.*

"What is it?" Edie shouted over Reba.

Snapper made a sarcastic zipper motion across his lips. He thought: I'm so goddamn tired. If only I could have a nap, it would come to me. A new plan.

The one-eyed stranger began to sing along with the stereo. Snapper scrutinized him coldly. How'd he know about the lady trooper? Snapper's hands had a slight tremor. His lips were as dry as ash. What if the bitch had gone and died? What if first she'd gotten a good look at him, or maybe the Jeep? What if it was already on TV, and every cop in Florida was in the hunt?

Snapper told himself to knock it off, think positive. For the first time in days, his busted-up knee didn't hurt so much. That was something to be glad about.

The young woman in the back seat joined her flaky companion in song. She was winging it with the lyrics, but that was all right with Snapper; her voice was pretty.

Edie Marsh tapped the rim of the steering wheel and acted peeved at the amateur chorus. After about three minutes she reached out and poked the Off button on the CD player. Reba fell silent, and so did the chorus.

Snapper announced that the next selection was Travis Tritt.

"Spare us," Edie said.

"Hell's your problem?"

The woman in the back seat spoke up: "My name's Bonnie. This is the governor. He prefers to be called 'captain.'"

"Skink will be fine," said the one-eyed man. "And I would kill for some Allman Brothers."

Snapper demanded to know what they wanted, why they'd been snooping at the Torres house. The man who called himself Skink said: "We were looking for you."

"How come?"

"As a favor to a friend. You wouldn't know him."

Edie Marsh said, "You're not making a damn bit of sense."

Something shifted in the bed of the Jeep. The sound was followed by a faint quavering moan.

From the woman, Bonnie: "What are your names?"

Edie Marsh rolled her eyes. Bonnie caught it in the rearview.

Snapper said, "Fuckin' idiots, the both of 'em."

"All I meant," said Bonnie Lamb, "is what should we call you?"

"I'm Farrah Fawcett," Edie said. Nodding at Snapper: "He's Ryan O'Neal."

In discouragement, Bonnie turned toward the window. "Just forget it."

A warm hand settled on Edie's shoulder. "Whoever you are," Skink said intimately, "you make a truly lovely couple."

"Fuck you."

Snapper lunged across the seat and stuck the barrel of the .357 in a crease of the stranger's cheek. "You think I don't got the balls to shoot?"

Skink nonchalantly pushed the gun away. He eased back in the seat and folded his arms. His fearless attitude distracted Edie Marsh. Snapper commanded her to pull off at the next exit. He needed to find a bathroom.

Having never been abducted at gunpoint, Bonnie Lamb wasn't as scared as she thought she ought to be. She attributed the unexpected composure to her resolve for adventure and to the governor's implausibly confident air. Based on nothing but blind faith, Bonnie was sure that Skink wouldn't allow them to be harmed by a deformed auto thief. The guy's erratic gun handling was nerve-racking, but somehow not so menacing with another woman in the Jeep. Bonnie Lamb could tell that she wasn't some dull-eyed trailer-park tramp; she was a sharp cookie, and not especially afraid of the dolt with the pistol. Bonnie had a feeling there wouldn't be any killing inside the truck.

She wondered what Max Lamb would think if he could see her now. Probably best that he couldn't. She felt terrible about hurting her husband, but did she miss him? It didn't feel like it. Perhaps she was doing Max the biggest favor of his life. Having waited all of one week to commit adultery with a near-total stranger, Bonnie surmised that she had, in the parlance of pop psychotherapy, "unresolved issues" to confront. Poor eager Max was a victim of misleading packaging. He thought he was getting one sort of woman when he was getting another. For that Bonnie felt guilty.

She vowed not to depress herself by overanalyzing her instant attraction to Augustine. She wished he were there, and wondered how he would ever find them on the road. Bonnie herself had no clue which way they were headed.

"South," the governor reported. "And south is good."

The man with the pistol snarled: "Quiet, asshole."

Suddenly Bonnie got an eerie hologrammic vision of the gunman's naked skull on the wall of Augustine's guest room. The broken mandible caused the bony orb to rest with a sinister tilt on the shelf; a pirate's crooked grin. Then Bonnie had a flash of Augustine, juggling the gunman's skull with the others.

From a pocket Skink withdrew a squirming Bufo toad, which immediately peed on him. The man with the .357 sneered.

The woman who was driving glanced over her shoulder. "What now?" she grumbled.

"Smoke the sweat," Skink said, cupping the toad and its amber piddle in his palm, "and then you see mastodons."

"Get that stinking thing outta here," said the gunman.

"Did you know mastodons once roamed Florida? Eons before your ancestors began their ruinous copulations. Mastodons as big as cement trucks!" Skink put the toad out the window. Then he wiped the toad pee on the sleeve of the gunman's pinstriped suit.

"You fuck!" Snapper took aim at Skink's good eye.

The woman at the wheel told him to cool it—other drivers were staring. She turned off at the next exit and pulled into an abandoned service station. The hurricane had blown down the gas pumps like dominoes. Looters had cleaned out the garage. On the roof lay the remains of a Mazda Miata, squashed upside down like a bright lady-bug.

While the gunman left the Jeep to relieve himself behind the building, the woman reluctantly took charge of the .357. She looked so uncomfortable that Bonnie Lamb felt a little sorry for her; the poor girl could barely hoist the darn thing. Surely, Bonnie thought, now was the moment for Skink to make his move.

But he didn't. Instead he smiled at the woman in the driver's seat and said, "You're truly pretty. And aware of it, of course. The guiding force for most of your life, I imagine—your good looks."

The woman blushed, then toughened.

"Where'd you spend the storm?" Skink asked.

"In a motel. With Mel Gibson there," the woman said, nodding toward Skink, "and a hooker."

"I was tied to a bridge. You should try it sometime."

"Right."

Bonnie Lamb said, "He isn't kidding."

The woman shifted the .357 to her other hand. "What on earth are you people doing? Who sent you to the house—Tony's wife?" She turned around on her knees, bracing her gun arm on the front seat. "Bonnie, dear," she said sharply. "I'd really appreciate some answers."

"Would you believe I'm on my honeymoon."

"You're joking." The woman glanced doubtfully at Skink.

Bonnie said, "Oh, not *him*. My husband's in Mexico."

"Boy, are you ever lost," said the woman.

Bonnie shook her head. "Not really."

The storm had knocked down the traffic signal at Florida City, or what was left of Florida City. A tired policeman in a yellow rainsuit directed traffic at the intersection. Edie Marsh tensed behind the wheel of the Jeep. She told Snapper to make sure the gun was out of sight. As they passed the officer, Bonnie Lamb figured it would be a fine time to poke her head out the window and shout for help, but Skink offered no encouraging signal. His chin had drooped back to his chest.

Most of the street signs remained down from the hurricane, but Bonnie saw one indicating they were about to enter the Fabulous Florida Keys. Snapper was apprehensive about possible checkpoints along Highway One, so he instructed Edie Marsh to use Card Sound Road instead.

"There's a toll," she noted.

"So?"

"I left my purse at the house."

Snapper said, "Jesus, I got money."

"I bet you do." Edie Marsh couldn't stop thinking about what the one-eyed stranger had said: Snapper assaulting a woman cop and swiping her mother's ring.

"How much *did* you get for it?" she asked.

"For what?"

"The ring." Edie stared ahead at the flat strip of road, which stretched eastward as far as she could see.

Snapper muttered obscenely. He fished in his coat and came out with a plain gold wedding band. He held it three inches from Edie's face.

"Happy?" he said.

The sight of the stolen ring affected Edie in an unexpected way: She felt repulsed, then dejected. She tried to picture the policewoman, wondered if she was married or had children, wondered what dreadful things Snapper had done to her.

Lord, Edie thought. What a small, disappointing life I've made for myself. She wanted to believe it would've been different if only she'd talked that shy young Kennedy into the sack. But she was no longer sure.

"I couldn't pawn it," Snapper was saying. "Damn thing's engraved, nobody'll touch it."

"What does it say?" Edie asked quietly. "On the ring."

"Who cares."

"Come on. What does it say?"

The woman in the back seat sat forward, also curious, as Snapper read the inscription aloud: "'For My Cynthia. Always.'" He gave a scornful laugh and hung his bony arm out the window, preparing to toss the ring from the truck.

"Don't do that," Edie said, backing off the accelerator.

"The fuck not? If I can't hock the goddamn thing, I'm gone dump it. Case we get pulled over."

Edie Marsh said, "Just don't, OK?"

"Oops. Too late." He cocked his arm and threw the ring as far as he could. It plopped into a roadside canal, breaking the surface with concentric circles.

Edie saw everything from the corner of her eye. "You lousy prick." Her voice was as hard as marble. The woman in the back seat felt the Jeep gain speed.

Defiantly Snapper waved the heavy black pistol. "Maybe you never heard of somethin' called 'possession of stolen property'— it's a motherfuckin' felony, case you didn't know. Here's another beauty: Vi-o-lay-shun o' pro-bay-shun! Translated: My skinny white ass goes straight to Starke, I get caught. Do not pass Go, do not collect any hurricane money. So fuck the cop's jewelry, unnerstand?"

Edie Marsh said nothing. She willed herself to concentrate on the slick two-lane blacktop, which intermittently was strewn with pine boughs, palmetto fronds and loose sheets of plywood. A regular obstacle course. Edie checked the speedometer: ninety-two miles per hour. Not bad for a city girl.

Snapper, ordering her to slow down, couldn't keep the raw nervousness out of his voice. Edie acted as if she didn't hear a word.

The one who called himself Skink didn't stir from his nap, trance, coma, whatever it was. Meanwhile the young newlywed (Edie noticed in the rearview) carefully removed her own wedding band from her finger.

*

The tollbooth was empty and the gate was up. Edie didn't bother to slow down. Bonnie Lamb held her breath.

When they blew through the narrow lane, Snapper exclaimed, "Jesus!"

As the Jeep climbed the steep bridge, Skink raised his head. "This is the place."

"Where you spent the storm?" Bonnie asked.

He nodded. "Glorious."

Beneath them, broken sunlight painted Biscayne Bay in shifting stripes of copper and slate. Ahead, a bloom of lavender clouds dumped chutes of rain on the green mangrove shorelines of North Key Largo. As the truck crested the bridge, Skink pointed out a pod of bottle-nosed dolphins rolling along the edge of a choppy boat channel. From such a height the arched flanks of the creatures resembled glinting slivers of jet ceramic, covered and then uncovered by foamy waves.

"Just look," said Bonnie Lamb. The governor was right—it was purely spectacular up here.

Even Edie Marsh was impressed. She curbed the Jeep on the downhill slope and turned off the key. She strained to keep the rollicking dolphins in view.

Snapper fumed impatiently. "What *is* this shit?" He jabbed Edie in the arm with the .357. "Hey you, drive."

"Take it easy."

"I said fucking *drive*."

"And I said take it fucking easy."

Edie was livid. The last time Snapper had seen that hateful glare was moments before she'd bludgeoned his leg with the crowbar iron. He cocked the revolver. "Don't be a cunt."

"Excuse me?" One eyebrow arched. "What'd you say?"

Bonnie Lamb feared that Edie was going to lose her mind and go for Snapper's throat, at which point she certainly would be shot dead. Snapper jammed the gun flush against her right breast.

The governor was unaware. He had everted the upper half of his torso out the window to watch the dolphins make their way north, and also to enjoy a fresh sprinkle that had begun to fall.

Bonnie tried to grab his hand, but it was too large. She settled for squeezing two of his fingers. Gradually Skink drew himself back into the Jeep and appraised the tense drama unfolding in the front seat.

"You heard me," Snapper was saying.

"So that *was* you," Edie said, "calling me a cunt."

Violently Snapper twisted the gun barrel, bunching the fabric of Edie's blouse and wringing the soft flesh beneath it. God, Bonnie thought, that's got to hurt.

Edie Marsh didn't let it show.

"Drive!" Snapper told her again.

"When I'm through watching Flipper."

"Fuck Flipper." Snapper raised the .357 and fired once through the top of the Jeep.

Bonnie Lamb cried out and covered her ears. Edie Marsh clutched the steering wheel to steady herself. The pain in her right breast made her wonder briefly if she was shot. She wasn't.

Snapper cheerlessly eyed the hole in the roof of the truck; the acrid whiff of cordite made him sneeze. "God bless me," he said, with a dark chuckle.

A door opened. Skink got out of the Jeep to stretch. "Don't you love this place!" He unfolded his long arms toward the clouds. "Don't it bring out the beast in your soul!"

Glorious, Bonnie agreed silently. That's the word for it.

"Get back in the car," Snapper barked.

Skink obliged, shaking the raindrops from his hair like a sheep dog. Without a word, Edie Marsh started the engine and drove on.

TWENTY-FOUR

"What do you mean, no roosters?"

The owner of the *botánica* apologized. It had been a busy week for fowl. He offered Avila a sacrificial billy goat instead.

Avila said, "No way, José." The sutures from his goring itched constantly. "I never heard anyone running outta roosters. What else you got?"

"Turtles."

"I don't got time to do turtles," Avila said. Removing the shells was a messy chore. "You got any pigeons?"

"Sorry, meng."

"Lambs?"

"Tomorrow morning."

"How about cats?"

"No, meng, hiss no legal."

"Yeah, like you give a shit." Avila checked his wristwatch; he had to hurry, do this thing then get on the road to the Keys. "OK, señor, what *do* you got?"

The shop owner led him to a small storage room and pointed at a wooden crate. Inside, Avila could make out a furry brown animal the size of a beagle. It had shoe-button eyes, an anteater nose, and a long slender tail circled with black rings.

Avila said, "What, some kinda raccoon?"

"Coatimundi. From South America."

The animal chittered inquisitively and poked its velvety nostrils through the slats of the crate. It was one of the oddest creatures Avila had ever seen.

"Big medicine," promised the shop owner.

"I need something for Chango."

"Oh, Chango would love heem." The shop owner had astutely pegged Avila for a rank amateur who knew next to nothing about *santería*. The shop owner said, "*Sí, es muy bueno por Chango.*"

Avila said, "Will it bite?"

"No, my freng. See?" The *botánica* man tickled the coati's moist nose. "Like a puppy dog."

"OK, how much?"

"Seventy-five."

"Here's sixty, *chico*. Help me carry it to the car."

As he drove up to the house, Avila saw the Buick backing out of the driveway; his wife and her mother, undoubtedly off to Indian bingo. He waved. They waved.

Avila gloated. Perfect timing. For once I'll have the place to myself. Quickly he dragged the wooden crate into the garage and lowered the electric door. The coati huffed in objection. From a cane-wicker chest Avila hastily removed the implements of sacrifice—tarnished pennies, coconut husks, the bleached ribs of a cat, polished turtle shells, and an old pewter goblet. From a galvanized lockbox Avila took his newest, and potentially most powerful, artifact—the gnawed chip of bone belonging to the evil man who had tried to crucify him. Reverently, and with high hopes, Avila placed the bone in the pewter goblet, soon to be filled with animal blood.

For sustenance Chango was known to favor dry wine and candies; the best Avila could do, on short notice, was a pitcher of sangria and a roll of stale wintergreen Life Savers. He lighted three tall candles and arranged them triangularly on the cement floor of the garage. Inside the triangle, he began to set up the altar. The coatimundi had gone silent; Avila felt its stare from between the slats. Could it know? He whisked the thought from his mind.

The final item to be removed from the wicker chest was the most important: a ten-inch hunting knife, with a handle carved from genuine elk antler. The knife was an antique, made in Wyoming. Avila had received it as a bribe when he worked as a county building inspector—a Christmas offering from an unlicensed roofer hoping that Avila might overlook a seriously defective scissor truss. Somehow Avila had found it in his heart to do just that.

Vigorously he sharpened the hunting knife on a whetstone. The coati began to pace and snort. Avila discreetly concealed the gleaming blade from the doomed animal. Then he stepped inside the triangle of candles and improvised a short prayer to Chango, who (Avila trusted) would understand that he was pressed for time.

Afterwards he took a pry bar and started peeling the wooden slats off the crate. The sacramental coati became highly agitated. Avila attempted to soothe it with soft words, but the beast wasn't fooled. It shot from the crate and tore crazed circles throughout the garage, scattering cat bones and tipping two of the *santería* candles. Avila tried to subdue the coati by stunning it with the pry bar, but it was too swift and agile. Like a monkey, it vertically scampered up a wall of metal shelves and bounded onto the ceiling track of the electric door-opener. There it perched, using its remarkable tail for balance, squealing and baring sharp yellow teeth. Meanwhile one of the *santería* candles rolled beneath Avila's lawn mower, igniting the gas tank. Cursing bitterly, Avila ran to the kitchen for the fire extinguisher. When he returned to the garage, he was confronted with fresh disaster.

The electric door was open. In the driveway was his wife's Buick, idling. Why she had come back, Avila didn't know. Perhaps she'd decided to pilfer the buried Tupperware for extra bingo money. It truly didn't matter.

Apparently her mother had emerged from the car first. The scene that greeted Avila was so stupefying that he temporarily forgot about the flaming lawn mower. For reasons beyond human comprehension, the overwrought coatimundi had jumped from its roost in the garage, dashed outdoors and scaled Avila's mother-in-law. Now the creature was nesting in the woman's coiffure, a brittle edifice of chromium orange. Avila had always believed that his wife's mother wore wigs, but here was persuasive evidence that her fantastic mop was genuine. She shrieked and spun about the front yard, flailing spastically at the demon on her scalp. The jabbering coati dug in with all four claws. No hairpiece, Avila decided, could withstand such a test.

His wife bilingually shouted that he should do something, for God's sake, don't just stand there! The pry bar was out of the question; one misplaced blow and that would be the end of his mother-in-law. So Avila tried the fire extinguisher. He unloaded at point-blank range, soaping the stubborn animal with sodium bicarbonate. The coati snarled and snapped but, incredibly, refused to vacate the old woman's hair. In the turmoil it was inevitable that some of the cold mist from the fire extinguisher would hit Avila's mother-in-law, who mashed her knuckles to her eyes and began a blind run. Avila gave chase for three-quarters of a block, periodically firing short bursts, but the old woman showed surprising speed.

Avila gave up and trotted home to extinguish the fire in the garage. Afterwards he rolled the charred lawn mower to the backyard and hosed it down. His distraught wife remained sprawled across the hood of the Buick, crying: "*Mami, mami*, luke what chew did to my *mami*!"

Above her keening rose the unmistakable whine of sirens— someone on the block had probably called the fire department. Avila thought: Why can't people mind their own goddamn business! He was steaming as he hurried to his car.

At the very moment he fit the key in the ignition, the passenger window exploded. Avila nearly wet himself in shock. There stood his wife, beet-faced and seething, holding the iron pry bar.

"Chew fucking bastard!" she cried.

Avila jammed his heel to the accelerator and sped away.

"O Chango, Chango," he whispered, brushing chunks of glass from his lap. "I know I fucked up again, but don't abandon me now. Not tonight."

A peculiar trait of this hurricane, Jim Tile marveled on the drive along North Key Largo, was the dramatic definition of its swath. The eye had come ashore like a bullet, devastating a thin corridor but leaving virtually untouched the coastline to the immediate north and south. August hurricanes are seldom so courteous. Its bands had battered the vacation estates of ritzy Ocean Reef and stripped a long stretch of mangrove. Yet two miles down the shore, the mangroves flourished, leafy and lush, offering no clue that a killer storm had passed nearby. A ramshackle trailer park stood undamaged; not a window was broken, not a tree was uprooted.

Phenomenal, thought Jim Tile.

He goosed the Crown Victoria to an invigorating ninety-five; blue lights, no siren. At high speeds the big Ford whistled like a bottle rocket.

Paradise Palms was a lead but not a lock. Augustine had done his best in a tough situation, the trick with the redial button was slick. Maybe the guy who'd beaten up Brenda was in the black Jeep Cherokee. Augustine didn't know for sure. Maybe they were headed to the Keys, maybe not. Maybe they'd stay with the Jeep, or maybe they'd ditch it for another car.

The only certainty was that they were transporting Skink and the tourist woman, Augustine's girlfriend. The circumstances of the abduction, and its purpose, remained a mystery. Augustine had promised to lie back and wait at Paradise Palms, and the trooper told him that was an excellent idea. One-man rescues only worked in the movies.

The old road from Ocean Reef rejoined Highway One below Jew-fish Creek, where it split into four lanes. The traffic thickened, so Jim Tile slowed to seventy miles per hour, weaving deftly between the Winnebagos and rental cars. It was the time of late summer when the setting sun could torment inexperienced drivers, but there was no glare from the west tonight. A bruised wall of advancing weather shaded the horizon and cast sooty twilight over the islands and the water. Lightning strobed high in distant clouds over Florida Bay. Its exquisite sparking was wasted on Jim Tile, who dourly contemplated the prospect of hard rain. A chase was tricky enough when the roads were bone dry.

On Plantation Key the highway narrowed again, and as the traffic merged to two lanes, Jim Tile thought he spotted the black Cherokee not far ahead. Quickly he turned off the blue lights. It had to be the same Jeep; the shiny mud flaps were as preposterous as Augustine had described them.

Four vehicles separated Jim Tile from the Jeep—three passenger cars, and a station wagon towing a fishing boat on a wobbly trailer. The boat was tall and beamy enough to make it hard for those in the Jeep to see the marked police car in the stacked traffic behind them. Already the rain was falling, fat drops popping sporadically on the hood of the Ford. The thickening sky promised a deluge.

The station wagon in front of Jim Tile began an untimely, though predictable, deceleration. Bad omens abounded: Michigan license plates suggested unfamiliarity with local landmarks; the driver and a female passenger were gesticulating heatedly, indicating a marital-type disagreement. Most distressing, from Jim Tile's point of view: A third passenger clearly could be seen unfolding a road map as large as a tablecloth.

They're lost, the trooper thought. Lost in the Florida Keys. Where there was only one way in and out. Amazing.

Now the map was being passed to the front seat, where the driver and his wife pawed at it competitively. The station wagon began snaking back and forth, followed somewhat indecisively by the boat trailer. Two McDonald's bags flew from one of the car's windows, exploding unwanted French fries and ketchup packets on the shoulder of the highway.

"Pigs," Jim Tile said aloud. He scowled at the speedometer: thirty-two damn miles per hour. If he tried to pass, the guy in the Jeep might see him coming. The trooper boiled. As the rain fell harder, he went to his windshield wipers and headlights.

The sluggish station wagon stayed ahead of him for the entire length of Plantation Key, until its sole operative brake light began to flicker. The rig meandered to a dead stop.

Dispiritedly, Jim Tile put the patrol car in Park, thinking: This ain't my day.

Ahead rose the Snake Creek drawbridge. The black Jeep and the three cars behind it easily crossed before the warning gates came down. The moron in the station wagon would have beaten it, too, had he ventured to touch the accelerator.

Now the trooper was stuck. The Jeep was on the other side of the waterway, out of sight. Jim Tile stepped from his car and slammed the door. With raindrops trickling off the brim of his Stetson, he approached the witless driver of the station wagon and asked for a license, registration and proof of insurance. In the eight minutes that passed before the Snake Creek bridge came down, the trooper managed to weigh the bewildered tourist with seven separate traffic citations, at least three of which would inconveniently require a personal appearance in court.

On the way to the Torres house, Fred Dove stopped to buy flowers and white wine. He wanted Edie Marsh to know he was proud of her performance as Neria, devoted wife of Tony.

When the insurance man pulled up to 15600 Calusa, he saw that the Jeep wasn't in the driveway. His heart quickened at the possibility that Snapper was gone, leaving him alone with Edie. Not that she was fussy about privacy, but Fred Dove was. He couldn't perform at full throttle, sexually, as long as a homicidal maniac was watching TV in an adjoining room. Snapper's loud and truculent presence was deflating in all respects.

Nobody answered when the insurance man rapped on the wooden doorjamb. He stepped into the Torres house and called Edie's name. The only reply came from the two miniature dachshunds, barking in the backyard; they sounded tired and hoarse.

The ugly Naugahyde recliner in the living room was unoccupied, and the television was off. Fred Dove was encouraged—no Snapper. Inside the house, the light was fading. When the insurance man flipped a lamp switch, nothing happened. The generator wasn't running; out of gas, probably. He found Snapper's flashlight and peeked in the rooms, hoping to spy Edie napping languorously on a mattress. She wasn't.

Fred Dove saw her purse on the kitchen counter. Her wallet lay open on top. Inside he found twenty-two dollars and a Visa card. Fred Dove was relieved; at least the house hadn't been robbed. He held Edie's driver's license under the flashlight; her expression in the photograph spooked him. It was not a portrait of pure trustworthiness and devotion.

Oh well, he thought, lots of girls look like Lizzie Borden on their driver's license.

The insurance man returned to the living room, lit a candle and sat in the recliner. He wondered where Edie had gone and why she'd left her purse when she knew the streets were crawling with looters. It seemed like she'd departed in a hurry, probably in the Jeep with Snapper.

Fred Dove settled in for a wait. The candle smelled of vanilla. The cozy way it lighted the walls reminded him of the night they nearly made love on the floor, the night Snapper barged in. The humiliation of that moment still stung; it had invested Snapper with indomitable power over the insurance man. That, plus the loaded gun. Fred Dove could hardly wait until the psycho thug was paid off. Then he and Edie would be free of him.

Every so often the insurance man switched on the flashlight and reexamined Edie's picture on the driver's license. The vulturine eyes did not soften. Fred Dove wondered if it was her deviousness that he found so arousing. The notion disturbed him, so he retreated to innocuous diversions. He hadn't known, for example, that her middle name was Deborah. It was a name he liked: plucky, Midwestern and reliable-sounding. He was willing to bet that if you went through every women's prison in America, you wouldn't find a half-dozen Deborahs. Perhaps the name had been taken from one of Edie's grandmothers, or that of a special aunt. In any event, he regarded it as a positive sign.

He wondered, too, about the apartment listed as her address in West Palm: what kind of art Edie had hung on the walls, what color towels were folded in the bathroom, what sort of homey magnets were stuck on her refrigerator door. Linus and Snoopy? Garfield the Cat? If *only*, Fred Dove thought. He thought about Edie's bed, too. He hoped it was king-sized, brass or a big wooden four-poster—anything but a water bed, which negatively affected his thrusting techniques. Fred Dove hoped the sheets on Edie's bed were imported silk, and that one day she would invite him to lie down on them.

The insurance man stayed in the recliner for more than two hours, long after the neighborhood chain saws and hammers had fallen silent. He finally arose to take a position near a windowpane, in glum preparation to witness the vandalism of his rental car by a group of swaggering, loud-talking teenagers. Mercifully they ignored Fred Dove's drab sedan, but minutes after they passed the house he heard a pop-pop that could have been the backfire of an automobile, or gunshots. In the backyard Donald and Marla dissolved in frenzy, striking up an irksome chorus with half a dozen other vigilant dogs on the block. Fred Dove's nerves were fraying fast. He returned Edie's driver's license to the purse. Hurriedly he arranged the flowers in a vase and placed it next to the unopened wine on the dining-room table. Then he blew out the candle and went outside to check on the dachshunds.

Tangled impressively in their leashes, the animals whimpered out of hunger, loneliness and general anxiety. Their low-density memories still twitched from the near-fatal encounter with the prowling bear. The moment Fred Dove set them free, the dachshunds clambered up his lap and licked his chin shamelessly. He was suckered into giving them a short walk.

Admiring the unfettered mirth with which Donald and Marla pranced and peed, the insurance man was bothered by the idea that they might spend the whole night outdoors and unattended. He wrote Edie a note and folded it on top of her purse. Then he led the two wiener dogs to his rented sedan, drove back to the motel and smuggled them in a laundry bag up to his room. It was marginally better than all-night movies on cable.

The motels in the Upper Keys were filling with out-of-town insurance adjusters. The clerk at the Paradise Palms said she felt uncomfortable, profiting off the hurricane.

"But a customer's a customer. Can I have your name?"

Augustine introduced himself as Lester's brother. "I phoned earlier. What's his room number?"

"He's not here yet." The clerk leaned across the counter and whispered: "But your sisters checked in about twenty minutes ago.

Room 255. I mean, I'm assuming sisters, on account of they're Parsons, too."

"Parsons indeed." Augustine nodded and acted pleased. Sisters? He couldn't imagine.

He paid for his room with cash. The clerk said, "Those girls know how to dress for a party, I'll sure say that."

"Oh boy," said Augustine. "What have they done now?"

"Don't you go fussing—let 'em have their fun, all right?" She handed him his key. "You're in 240. I tried to put you in the unit next door, but some wise guy from Prudential, he didn't want to switch."

"That's quite all right."

Once inside his room, Augustine put the loaded .38 on the bureau, near the door. He took the parts of the dart rifle from the gym bag and laid them on the bedspread. The muscles of his neck were in knots. He wished he'd brought a few skulls, for relaxation.

Augustine turned up the TV while he assembled the tranquilizer gun. He was surprised that he'd beaten the black Jeep to Islamorada, hadn't even passed it on the eighteen-mile stretch south of Florida City. He wondered if they'd turned on Card Sound Road, or stopped someplace else—and why. His worst fear, the thing he kept pushing out of his mind, was that the creep with the crooked jaw had already killed Skink and Bonnie, and dumped them. There were only about a hundred ideal locations between Homestead and Key Largo; years might pass before the bodies were found.

Well, he'd know soon enough. If the asshole showed up without them, then Augustine would know.

If the asshole showed up at all. Augustine still wasn't sure if "Lester Parsons" was the man with the crooked jaw.

He stood the dart rifle in a closet and put the pistol in his waistband, under the tail of his shirt. Rain whipped his face as soon as he stepped out the door. He shielded his eyes and hurried along the walkway to Room 255. He knocked seven times in a neighborly cadence—shave-and-a-haircut, two bits—to give the false impression that he was expected.

The door was flung open by a fragrant redheaded woman in high heels and a luminous green bikini. Augustine recognized her as the hooker in fishnets from 15600 Calusa.

An orange sucker was tattooed on the freckled slope of her left breast. In her left hand was a frosty Rum Runner.

She said, "Shit, I thought you were Snapper."

"Wrong room," said Augustine. "I'm sorry."

"Don't be."

Another woman came out of the bathroom, saying, "Goddamn this rain. I wanted to go in the pool." She wore a silver one-piece suit, an explosive white-blonde wig and gold hoop earrings. When she saw Augustine in the doorway, she said, "Who're you?"

"I thought this was my sister's room, but I guess I'm at the wrong motel."

The redhead introduced herself as Bridget. "You wanna come in and dry off?"

"Not if it gets Snapper mad." Augustine was thinking: Snapper—now what the hell kind of name is *that*?

The redhead laughed. "Yeah, he's quite the jealous maniac. Come on in."

The blonde said, "Jesus, Bridget, they're gonna be here any second—"

But Augustine was already inside the room, scouting unobtrusively: an overnight bag, two cosmetic cases, a cocktail dress on a hanger. Nothing out of the ordinary. Bridget tossed him a towel. She said her friend's name was Jasmine. They were from Miami.

"My name's George," said Augustine, "from California." Inanely he shook hands with the hookers.

Bridget held on, examining his ring finger. "Not married?"

"Afraid not." Augustine gently tugged free.

Jasmine told Bridget to forget it, they didn't have enough time. Bridget said they wouldn't need much.

"George looks like a fast starter." She winked somewhat mechanically at Augustine. "You want some fun until the rain stops?"

"Thanks, but I really can't stay."

"Hundred bucks," Bridget suggested. "Double date."

Jasmine pulled a long white T-shirt over her swimsuit. She griped: "Hey, do I get a vote in this? A hundred for what?"

Bridget slipped a milky arm around Augustine's waist and pulled him close. The obvious implant in her left breast felt like a sack of nickels against his rib cage. "Seventy-five," she said, dropping her eyes to the bright tattoo, "and I'll give you a taste of my Tootsie Pop."

"Can't," Augustine said. "Diabetic."

Jasmine gave a biting laugh. "You're both pitiful. Bridget, let 'George from California' go find his sisters." She sat cross-legged on the bed and applied pungent glue to a broken artificial fingernail. "Boy, this weather's suck-o," she muttered, to no one.

Bridget's motivational hug went slack, and slowly she recoiled from Augustine's side. "Our man George has a gun." She announced it with a mix of alarm and regret. "I felt it."

Jasmine, blowing on her glue job, looked up. "Goddamn, Bridget, I knew it! You happy now? We're busted."

"No you're not." Augustine took out the pistol and displayed it in a loose and casual way, hoping to quell their concerns. "I'm not a cop, I promise."

Jasmine's eyes narrowed. "Shit, *now* I know. The squeaker sent you."

"Who?"

"Avila."

"Never heard of him."

Bridget backpedaled to the bed and sat next to her friend. Nervously she crossed her arms over her breasts. "Then who the hell are you, *George*? What is it you're after?"

"Information."

"Yeah, right."

"Really. I just want you to tell me about this 'Snapper,'" said Augustine, "and I also want to know if you two ladies can keep a secret."

TWENTY-FIVE

The professor's VW van ran out of gas two miles shy of the Fort Drum service plaza. Neria Torres stood by the Turnpike and flagged down a truck. It was an old Chevy pickup; three men in the cab, four others sprawled in the bed. They were from Tennessee. Neria wasn't crazy about the odds.

"Looking for work," explained the driver, a wiry, unshaven fellow with biblical tattoos on both arms. He said his first name was Matthew and his middle name was Luke.

Neria was nervous nonetheless. The men stared ravenously. "What do you guys do?" she asked.

"Construction. We're here for the hurricane." Matthew had a spare gas can. He poured four gallons into the van. Neria thanked him.

She said, "All I can give you is three bucks."

"That's fine."

"What kind of construction?"

Matthew said: "Any damn thing we can find." The other men laughed. "We do trees, also. I got chain saw experience," Matthew added.

Neria Torres didn't ask if the crew was licensed to do business in Florida. She knew the answer. The men climbed out of the truck to stretch their legs and urinate. One of them was actually mannered enough to turn his back while unzipping.

Neria decided it was a good time to go. Matthew stood between her and the van. "I dint ketch your name."

"Neria."

"That's Cuban, right?"

"Yes."

"You don't talk with no accent."

She thought: Well, thank you, Gomer. "I was born in Miami," she said.

Matthew seemed pleased. "So you're on the way home—hey, how'd you make out in the big blow?"

Neria said, "I won't know till I get there."

"We do residential."

"Do you really."

"Wood or masonry, it don't matter. Also roofs. We got a helluva tar man." Matthew pointed. "That bald guy doin' his bidness in the bushes—he worked on that new Wal-Mart in Chat'nooga. My wife's cousin Chip."

Neria Torres said, "From what I understand, you won't have a bit of trouble finding jobs when you get to Dade County."

"Hey, what about your place?"

"I don't know. I haven't seen it yet."

"So it could be totaled," Matthew said, hopefully.

Slowly Neria opened the door of the van. Only when it stubbed his shoulder blades did Matthew move out of the way.

Neria got behind the wheel and revved the engine. "Tell you what. When I get home and see how the roof looks, then I'll give you a call. Where you staying?"

The other workers laughed again. "Sterno Hilton," said Matthew. "See, we're campin' out." He said they couldn't afford a motel, no way.

Neria fumbled in the console until she found a gnawed stub of pencil and one of the professor's matchbooks, which reeked of weed. She wrote down a bogus telephone number and gave it to Matthew. "OK, then, you call *me*."

He didn't even glance at the number. "I got a better idea. Since none of us ever been to Miami before . . ."

Oh no! she thought. Please no.

". . . we'll just follow you down. That way, we're sure not to get lost. And if your place needs work, we can git on it rightaways."

Matthew's plan was well received by his crew. Neria said, uselessly: "I don't think that's a good idea."

"We got references."

She was eyeing the pickup truck, wondering if there was a chance in hell that the professor's van could outrun it.

"We kicked some ass over Charleston," Matthew was saying, "after Hurricane Hugo."

Neria said, "It's getting pretty late."

"We'll be right behind you."

And they were, all the way down the Turnpike.

The truck's solitary headlight, stuck on high beam, illuminated the interior of the VW van like a TV studio. Neria stiffened in the harsh brightness, knowing that seven pairs of inbred male eyes were fixed on the back of her head. She drove ludicrously slow, hoping the rednecks would grow impatient and decide to pass. They didn't.

All she could do was make the best of it. Even if the Neanderthals didn't know a thing about construction, they might be helpful in tracking a thieving husband.

Max Lamb cracked the door to poke his head out. He'd never met an FBI man before. This one didn't look like Efrem Zimbalist Jr. He wore a green Polo shirt, tan Dockers and cordovan Bass Weejuns. He also toted a bag from Ace Hardware.

When it came to name brands, Max was nothing if not observant. He believed it was part of his job, knowing who in America was buying what.

The agent said, "Is Augustine home?"

"No, he isn't."

"Who are you?"

"Could I see some ID?" Max asked.

The agent showed him a badge in a billfold. Max told him to come in. They sat in the living room. Max asked what was in the bag, and the agent said it was drill bits. "Storm sucked the cabinets right out of my kitchen," he explained.

"Black and Decker?"

"Makita."

"That's a first-rate tool," said Max.

The agent was exceedingly patient. "You're a friend of Augustine's?"

"Sort of. My name is Max Lamb."

"Really? I'm glad to see you're all right."

Max's eyebrows hopped.

"From the kidnapping," the agent said. "You're the one who was kidnapped, right?"

"Yes!" Max's spirits skied, realizing that Bonnie had been so concerned that she'd called the FBI. It was proof of her devotion.

The agent said, "She played the tape for me, the message you left on the answering machine."

"Then you heard his voice—the guy who snatched me." Max got a Michelob from the refrigerator. The FBI man accepted a Sprite.

"Where's your wife?" he asked.

"I don't know."

Excitedly Max Lamb related the whole story, from his kidnapping on Calusa Drive to the midnight rescue in Stiltsville, up to Bonnie's disappearance with Augustine and the deranged one-eyed governor. The FBI man listened with what seemed to be genuine interest, but took no notes. Max wondered if they were specially trained to remember everything they heard.

"These are dangerous men," he told the agent, portentously.

"Was your wife taken against her will?"

"No, sir. That's why they're so dangerous."

"You say he put a collar on your neck."

"A shock collar," Max said gravely, "the kind used to train hunting dogs."

The FBI man asked if the kidnapper had done the same thing to Bonnie. Max said he didn't think so. "She's very trusting and impressionable. They took advantage of that."

"What's Augustine's role in all this?"

"I believe," said Max, "the kidnapper has brainwashed him, too." He got another beer and tore into a bag of pretzels.

The agent said, "Prosecution won't be easy. It's your word against his."

"But you believe me, don't you?"

"Mister Lamb, it doesn't matter what I believe. Put yourself in the jury box. This is a very weird story you'll be asking them to swallow. . . ."

Max shot to his feet. His cheeks were stuffed with pretzel fragments. "Jeshush Chritht, mahh wife's misshing!"

"I understand. I'd be upset, too." The FBI man was maddeningly agreeable and polite. "And I'm not trying to tell you what to do. But you need to know what you're up against."

Max sat down, glowering.

The agent explained that the Bureau seldom got involved unless a ransom demand was issued. "There was none in your case. There's been none for your wife."

"Well, *I* think her life's in danger," Max said, "and I think you people are in deep trouble if something happens to her."

"Believe me, Mister Lamb, I understand your frustration."

No you don't, Max fumed silently, or you wouldn't talk to me like I was ten years old.

The agent said, "Have you spoken to the police?"

Max told him about the black state trooper who was acquainted with the kidnapper. "He said I was entitled to press charges. He said he'd take me down to the station."

The FBI man nodded. "That's the best way to go, if you've got your mind made up."

Max told the agent there was something he definitely ought to see. He led him to Augustine's guest room and showed him the wall of skulls. "Tell me honestly," he said to the FBI man, "wouldn't you be worried? He *juggles* those damn things."

"Augustine? Yeah."

"You know?"

"He won't hurt your wife, Mister Lamb."

"Gee, I feel so much better."

The agent seemed impervious to sarcasm. "You'll hear from Mrs Lamb sooner or later. That's my guess. If you don't, call me.

Or call me even if you do." He handed his card to Max, who affected hard-bitten skepticism as he studied it. Then he walked toward the kitchen, the agent following.

"I was wondering," the FBI man said, "did Augustine give you a key?"

Max turned.

"To the house," the agent said.

"No, sir. The sliding door was open."

"So you just walked in. He doesn't know you're here?"

"Well . . ." It hadn't occurred to Max Lamb that he was breaking the law. For one infuriating moment, he thought the FBI man was preparing to arrest him.

But the agent said: "That's a swell way to get your head shot off—being in somebody's house without them knowing. Especially here in Miami."

Max, grinding his teeth, realized the impossibly upside-down nature of the situation. He was wasting his breath. A state trooper is friends with the kidnapper, an FBI man is friends with the skull collector.

"You know what I really want?" Max drained his beer with a flourish, set the bottle down hard on the counter. "All I want is to find my wife, put her on a plane and go home to New York. Forget about this fucked-up place, forget about this hurricane."

The agent said, "That's a damn good plan, Mister Lamb."

TWENTY-SIX

Snapper made Edie Marsh pull over at a liquor store in Islamorada.

"Not now," she said.

"I *got* to."

"We're almost there."

A rumble from the back seat: "Let the man have a drink."

She parked behind the store, away from the road. Jim Tile didn't see the black Cherokee as he sped past. Neither did Avila, ten minutes later.

Snapper wouldn't be talked out of his craving, and Edie was worried. She knew firsthand the folly of mixing booze with Midols. Double dosed, Snapper might hibernate for a month.

The woman named Bonnie asked for a cold Coke. "I'm burning up."

"Welcome to Florida," said Edie.

Snapper tossed three ten-dollar bills on her lap. "Johnnie Red," he said.

"Bad idea when you're full of codeines."

"Shit, I've handled ten times worse. Besides, it don't feel like codeine you gave me."

Edie said, "Your knee quit hurting, right? The bottle said 'codeine.'"

Snapper switched the .357 to his left hand. With his right hand he twisted Edie's hair, as if he were uprooting a clump of weeds. When she cried out, he said: "I don't give a fuck if the medicine bottle said turpentine. Go get my Johnnie Walker."

Edie pulled free and jumped out of the Jeep. She flipped him the finger as she went through the door of the liquor store. Snapper said, "Stubborn bitch."

"Feisty," Skink agreed.

Bonnie Lamb felt like her skin was sizzling. She thought it would be glorious to bury herself in fresh snow. "Honest to God, it's so hot. I feel like taking off my clothes."

She couldn't believe she'd said it aloud.

Snapper was startled, and too confused for lust. "Jesus Christ, what's a matter with you people."

Bonnie said, "I'm smothering."

His eyes wandered to the young woman's chest. Nothing like a pair of tits to fuck up the balance of power. He knew that if she flashed those babies, his position instantly would be weakened, his authority diminished. It was a lost advantage that even the .357 could not restore.

"Keep your goddamn shirt on," he told her.

"Don't worry." Bonnie fanned herself in nervous embarrassment. In the back of the Jeep, Levon Stichler mewled inquiringly, trussed in his cocoon of moldy carpet. Skink figured the old man must have been listening, wondering if he was missing something.

Edie Marsh returned from the store. Her hair sparkled with tiny raindrops. She handed Bonnie a can of Dr Pepper. "The Cokes weren't cold. Here, asshole." She shoved a brown paper bag at Snapper. He took out the Johnnie Walker bottle and opened it with one hand. He threw back his head and chugged, as if from a canteen.

"Take it easy," Edie admonished.

Contemptuously he smacked his lips. "I bet you'd look good completely bald," he said to her. "That guy on the new *Star Trek*, Gene Luke—you and him could pass for twins."

Edie said, "Touch my hair again. Just try."

He swung the .357 until the barrel came to rest on the tip of Edie's nose. He cocked the hammer and said: "Come on. Somebody talk me out of it."

Bonnie thought: Oh God, please don't. She shivered in sweat.

Snapper took another sloppy swig of whiskey. The one-eyed

man reminded him of the ammunition shortage. "Shoot her, that'd leave only one bullet for the rest of us."

"There's other ways besides the gun."

Skink let loose an avalanche of laughter. "Son, I'm fairly immune to blunt objects and sharp instruments."

Edie's pitch was more blunt. "Pull the trigger," she said to Snapper, "and kiss your hurricane money good-bye. Forty-seven grand goes out the window with my brains."

Snapper's bad mandible began to creak; a sign, Skink hoped, of possible cogitation. The moron was deciding between the long-term rewards from the money and the short-term satisfaction from shooting her. Apparently it wasn't an easy choice.

Skink said, "Consider it an IQ test, chief."

Impulsively Bonnie Lamb opened the cold Dr Pepper and poured it under her blouse; a fizzing caramel torrent from the cleft of her neck to her tummy.

"Stop!" Snapper yelled. "You stop that crazy shit!"

"I'm suffocating in here—"

"I don't care! I don't fucking care."

Bonnie was so light-headed from the heat that Snapper's fury didn't register. "I'm sorry," she said, "I'm really sorry, but it's a hundred degrees in this stupid truck."

The soda pop soaked through her top, so that Snapper could see the lacy outline of a bra and a pale damp oval of bare belly. Skink asked Edie Marsh to put on the air conditioner.

"I tried. It's broken." Edie's voice was empty.

"Don't even think about getting naked," Snapper warned Bonnie, "or I'll kill you." His head jangled with loud voices, some his own. In exasperation he shouted: "You don't think I'd shoot all you crazy shits? You don't believe me? Check the fuckin' hole in the roof a this Jeep!"

Yeah, Edie thought. Matches the one between your ears.

"Can we get on with this?" she said sourly. "It *is* awfully damn humid."

*

As Bonnie's skin cooled off, she heard herself apologizing repeatedly. Yet it was absurd to be ashamed. Why should she care what two common criminals thought of her?

But she did care. She couldn't help herself. It was the way she'd been raised: A proper young woman did not douse herself with soda pop in front of total strangers, even felons.

"It's all right," Skink said. "You're scared, that's all."

"I guess I am."

Snapper heard her. With a vulgar chuckle, he said, "Good. Scared is damn well what you ought to be." He was halfway to shitfaced.

Edie drove slowly, fretfully. The man was a keeling wreck. *How could they possibly pull this off?* She devised a fantasy scenario: If Snapper passed out drunk, she'd push him from the Jeep. Then she'd tell the eccentric couple in the back seat that she was very, very sorry—it was all a terrible misunderstanding. She'd promise them Snapper's share of the Midwest Casualty settlement if they'd forget the whole dreadful evening. She would drive them back to Miami without delay and (to prove she was basically a decent person) offer to replace the gold ring stolen from the lady trooper. The unconscious Snapper would be run over on the highway by a passing shrimp truck and no longer pose a menace to society, or to Edie's future.

Unfortunately, Snapper wasn't nodding off. The Johnnie Walker bottle lay capped on the dashboard. Now he was playing with the gun, spinning the cylinder and humming mischievously.

Edie Marsh said, "Could you please not do that?"

Snapper gurgled crapulously, his jaw jutting like a window box. "You're so hot and sweaty, Edie, you oughta do what she almost done. Take off your clothes."

"You'd like that, wouldn't you."

"I would *love* it. Wouldn't y'all?" He waggled the .357 at Skink and Bonnie Lamb. "Come on, wouldn't ya like to see Edie's tits? They're cuties."

Bonnie felt crummy that she'd given Snapper the idea.

Skink said, "Speaking for myself, yes, I'm sure they're delightful. But some other time."

Edie Marsh felt herself blush. Nobody spoke. Snapper began to hum again, accompanied by the metered squeak of the windshield wipers. Ahead, on the ocean side of the highway, Edie saw the electric-blue sign for the Paradise Palms Resort Motel.

Skink shook Levon Stichler out of the carpet, dumping him like a sack of flour on the terrazzo. Somebody yanked off the gag and the blindfold.

The old man's eyes watered at the sudden brightness.

A woman's voice: "You again."

Levon blinked until a face came into focus—the redhead from the hurricane house at Turtle Meadow. The chiffon scarf, Levon's blinder, dangled from her festively painted fingernails. Standing next to the redhead was a wild-looking blonde. She said, "What's your name, sweetheart?"

The redhead wore a diaphanous black bustier, fishnet stockings and stiletto heels. The blonde wore a silver lamé teddy that made her shimmer like the hood ornament on a Silver Shadow. The air was sugary with perfume; pure heaven, after three hours of gagging on mildew and carpet fuzz. When Levon Stichler sat up, he found himself in the center of an attentive circle: the two prostitutes, the thug in the pinstriped suit, the pretty long-haired brunette, another young woman, with creamy skin and delicate features, and a large bearded man wearing a flowered shower cap. The bearded man was polishing a glass eye on the sleeve of his jacket. They were gathered in a small motel room.

Levon Stichler said: "What's this all about?"

The prostitutes introduced themselves. Bridget and Jasmine.

Snapper dropped to a crouch. Roughly he pinched the back of the old man's neck. "You tried to kill me, 'member?"

"It was a mistake. I told you."

"Here's the deal: You're gone stay down here two, maybe three days with the girls. They're gone fuck ya and blow ya till you can't walk. Plus they gone take some pitchers."

Levon was skeptical. The man reeked of liquor and spoke as if he had a mouthful of marbles.

"Just shoot me and get it over with."

"We're not shooting anybody." It was the pretty brunette. "Honest," she said, "long as you behave."

Snapper said, "Maybe you're too old to get it up or maybe you like guys—I don't fuckin' care. Point is, you stay here with these girls till I call and say it's OK to leave. Then what you do, you take your sweet time gettin' back to Miami. By that I mean, stand on the highway with your thumb out. Unnerstand?"

Levon stammered and blinked. Snapper swatted him twice across the face.

Edie Marsh said: "I don't think Mister Stichler realizes the alternative. The alternative is we go to the cops and tell how you tried to murder Snapper and rape me with that trailer spike. Your family'll think you've gone senile. The photographs won't help—Grandpa doing pony rides with two call girls."

Levon glanced up at Bridget and Jasmine. They were large and scary. He could tell they'd worked together before.

"Think of it as a vacation," said Edie. "Hey, you're allowed to have fun."

"I wish I could."

"Uh-oh." Bridget knelt beside him. "Prostate?"

The old man nodded somberly. "It was removed last year."

Jasmine told him to cheer up. "We'll think of something."

Skink, fitting his glass eye into its socket, advised Levon Stichler to do what he was told. "It's still better than getting shot."

Bridget said, "Gee, thanks."

Snapper paid the prostitutes from a wad of the stolen roofing money, which they counted, divided and put away. They turned their backs so he wouldn't peek inside their pocketbooks, which bulged with the other cash given to them ten minutes earlier by Avila, and ten minutes before that by the good-looking young man with the .38 Special.

"Is there ice in the bucket?" Bonnie Lamb asked. The hooker named Jasmine told her to help herself Bonnie scooped two handfuls of cubes and pressed them to her cheeks.

The one-eyed man helped the prostitutes lift Levon Stichler to his feet. Snapper poked the old man's Adam's apple with the barrel of the gun. "Don't try nuthin' stupid," he said. "These young girls can crack coconuts in their legs. Killing a skinny old fart like you is no problem whassoever."

Levon Stichler didn't doubt it for a moment. "Don't worry, mister. I'm no hero."

The redhead pinched his butt playfully. "We'll see about that."

Augustine was hiding behind a Dumpster when the black Cherokee with the cheesy mud flaps arrived at the Paradise Palms. His spirits leaped when he saw Bonnie Lamb get out, followed by the governor. The driver was a brown-haired woman in a lavender top; probably the one from the driver's license photo, Edith Deborah Marsh, age twenty-nine. She was the next to get out of the Jeep. From the passenger side: a lanky sallow man in a rumpled suit, no necktie. He carried a gun and a bottle, and seemed unsteady. His crooked jaw was made conspicuous by a street light. Augustine had no doubt. It was him; the one who'd attacked Brenda Rourke, the one the prostitutes had told him about. Snapper in real life, "Lester Parsons" on the motel register.

The man opened the hatch of the Cherokee and barked something at Skink, who removed a long lumpy bundle and hoisted it across his back. Once the procession disappeared into the motel, Augustine ran to the Jeep, climbed in the cargo well and quietly closed the hatch. He flattened himself below the rear window, placing the .38 at his right side. With both hands he held the dart rifle across his chest.

This, he thought, would be something to tell the old man. Make those fat wormy veins in his temples pop up.

Dad wouldn't dream of risking his neck unless vast sums of money were at stake. Love, loyalty and honor weren't part of the dope smuggler's creed. Augustine could hear the incredulity: *A.G., why the hell would you do such a crazy thing?*

Because the man deserved it. He beat up a lady cop and stole her mother's wedding ring. He was scum.

Don't be an idiot. You could've been killed.

He kidnapped the woman I love.

I raised an idiot!

No you didn't. You didn't raise anybody.

Whenever Augustine wrote his father, he made a point of mentioning how much money he'd given away to ex-girlfriends, obscure charities and ultraliberal political causes. He imagined his father's face turning gray with dismay.

You disappoint me, A.G.

This from a dumb shit who ran aground at full throttle with thirty-three kilos in the bilge and the entire Bahamian National Defense Force in pursuit.

"You disappoint me."

Right. Augustine listened to the rain thrumming against the roof of the truck. It made him drowsy.

He hadn't expected to see his father waiting when he awoke from the coma, so he wasn't disappointed. Predominantly he was thrilled to be alive. The person at his bedside was a middle-aged Haitian nurse named Lucy. She told him about the plane crash, the months of slumber. Augustine hugged her tearfully. Lucy showed him a letter from his father, sent from the prison in Talladega; she'd read the letter aloud to Augustine when he was unconscious. She volunteered to read it again.

Son, I hope you are alive to read these words. I'm sorry the way things turned out. Dad should've signed off right there, but grace and decency were never his strong suits.

Everything I did was for you, he wrote. *Every move I made, right or wrong.*

Which was crap, an unnecessary lie. It mildly saddened Augustine but didn't embitter him. He was beyond all that. The airplane accident had pruned his emotions down to the roots. Nothing affected him the way it had before, which was fine. He decided everyone could benefit from a short coma. Wipe the slate clean.

So what if it took him years to come up with a new agenda? Here it was. Here *she* was.

Dad would not approve. Fortunately, Dad was not a factor.

Augustine heard the closing of a door, footsteps slapping in the puddles, voices advancing across the motel parking lot. He took three deep breaths. Checked the safety on the dart rifle.

He was glad for the weather, which misted the Jeep's windows and made him invisible from the outside. The voices grew sharper—two men arguing. Augustine didn't recognize them. Perhaps Snapper and somebody else, but who?

Loud words broke through the whisper of the rain. Augustine decided not to give himself away unless Bonnie Lamb was in trouble. The argument moved closer. Then came a deep huff, the sounds of a clumsy struggle; a bottle shattering on the pavement.

One of the men blurted: "Hold the damn gun while I strangle this fucker."

Snapper's consternation about the two remaining bullets in the .357 was well founded. A crack marksman he was not.

A police report dated July 7, 1989, showed that one Lester Maddox Parsons was arrested for shooting Theodore "Sunny" Shea outside the Satellite Grille in Dania, Florida. The victim was not just a garden-variety crack dealer, as Snapper claimed after the incident. In truth, Sunny Shea was his longtime business partner. The scope of their enterprises extended beyond drugs to stolen guns, jewelry, clothing, patio furniture, stereos, even a shipment of baby food on one occasion. Eventually Sunny Shea came to suspect Snapper of cheating him on the proceeds, and confronted him with the accusation one humid summer night in the doorway of the Satellite Grille, before sixteen eyewitnesses.

Snapper's indignant response was to display a 9mm Glock (swiped from the glove box of an unmarked Coral Springs police car) and attempt to empty said weapon into Sunny Shea. In all, Snapper fired eleven times from a distance of eight feet. Only six rounds struck Sunny Shea, and not one nicked a vital organ—quite a feat, considering that Sunny Shea weighed only one hundred thirty pounds and hadn't an ounce of fat on his body. The hapless shooting exhibition was even more remarkable because Snapper was stone sober at the time.

Sunny Shea never lost consciousness, and was extremely cooperative when police inquired about the identity of his assailant. The two detectives who hauled Lester Maddox Parsons to the

Broward County Jail ridiculed him mercilessly about his lousy aim.

The next morning, when they came to his cell to inform him that the charge of attempted first-degree murder had been upgraded, Snapper glowed with vindication. Then he learned it wasn't one of his shots that had killed his scrawny, obnoxious partner—some bonehead in the emergency room had injected Theodore "Sunny" Shea with an antibiotic to which he was virulently, and fatally, allergic.

Snapper pleaded out to a chickenshit manslaughter and got easy time, but his confidence in the efficacy of handguns was ruined forever. Two bullets in a .357 was scarcely better than no bullets at all.

Which was why he didn't want to waste them on Avila, the whiny spic. He was the last guy on earth that Snapper expected to see at Paradise Palms. He'd materialized like a drowned ghost out of the rainstorm, bitching about the roofing deposit that Snapper had ripped off from Mrs Whitmark.

"You know who she is? You know who she's married to?" Avila was screeching. Skink and the two women retreated to a dry vantage, under the eaves of the motel, while Avila chased Snapper around the parking lot like a terrier. Their conversation was difficult to follow, but Edie Marsh got the substance of it: Snapper had made a seven-thousand-dollar score.

Funny how he'd forgotten to tell her about it. Same as the wedding ring.

The pistol in Snapper's possession worried Avila but didn't deter him. For eighty miles he'd been praying for Chango's protection, and felt moderately imbued. Snapper appeared frazzled and shaky, possibly visited by black spirits.

Avila said, "Gimme the money."

"Eat shit," Snapper growled.

When he turned away, Avila hopped on his back. Snapper shook him off. Avila pounced again, ripping Snapper's suit and knocking the Johnnie Walker from his hand. The two men locked together, spinning in the mist. Ultimately Snapper backed into a sabal palm tree, slamming Avila against the trunk. He made a true squeak as he slid to the ground.

Snapper, panting, weaved toward Edie: "Hold the damn gun while I strangle this fucker."

Halfheartedly she took the pistol and held it on Bonnie and Skink. Snapper fell upon Avila and breathlessly beat him. Avila was surprised by the clarity of the pain. When his nose exploded under Snapper's fist, he realized he'd been foolhardy to count on beatific intervention. Evidently Chango hadn't forgiven him for the aborted coati sacrifice.

As Snapper's grimy fingernails closed upon his throat, Avila inventoried the multiple sources of his agony: the fractured nose, the sliver of broken whiskey bottle in his right thigh, the unhealed crucifixion hole in his left hand, the goat-related goring in his groin and, soon, a crushed larynx.

He thought: Forget the seven grand. Screw Gar Whitmark. It's time to run.

Avila brought his right knee hard to Snapper's crotch. Snapper's eyelids fluttered but he didn't release his grip on Avila's neck. Avila kneed him twice more, ultimately producing the desired result. Snapper moaned and rolled away. Avila struggled to his feet. He took three steps and slipped. When he got up again, he heard Snapper rising behind him. Frantically Avila bolted for the road.

The rain made it hard to discern the details of the two men running along Highway One. Neither was large enough to be the governor, or physically fit enough to be Augustine. From where his Highway Patrol car was parked, a hundred yards away, Jim Tile was unable to see if the tall man had a crooked jaw. He might have been any old Keys drunk in a soggy pinstriped suit.

The black Jeep was still parked at the Paradise Palms. The trooper decided to sit still and wait.

Avila made it half a mile before he ran out of strength. He stopped on the Tea-Table Bridge and doubled over, sucking air.

He tried to flag passing motorists, but none found room in their icy hearts for a bedraggled, saliva-flecked, blood-spattered hitch-hiker. Avila was further dejected to see, framed in the window of a speeding Airstream, a freckle-faced teenaged girl, snapping his photograph.

What a sick world, he thought, when an injured human being becomes a roadside amusement.

Meanwhile, out of the veil of rain came Snapper. He was shambling like a zombie across the bridge. For a weapon he'd selected a rusty axle from an abandoned Jet Ski trailer.

Avila raised both arms in supplication. "Let's forget the whole thing, OK?"

"Don't move." Snapper gripped the axle at one end and brought it high over his head, like a sledgehammer.

With a morose peep, Avila hurled himself sideways off the bridge. The drop was only fourteen feet, but given his dread of heights, it might as well have been fourteen stories. Avila was mildly amazed to survive the impact.

The water was warm and the tide was strong. He let it carry him out the channel toward the ocean, because he wasn't strong enough to swim against it. When the sodden weight of his clothing began to drag him under, he kicked off his shoes and pants, and stripped out of his shirt. Soon the lights from the Overseas Highway were absorbed by darkness and bad weather. Avila could see nothing but the occasional high-altitude flash of heat lightning. When a heavy object thumped him in the small of the back, he was sure it was the snout of a great white shark and that death was imminent.

But it was only a piece of plywood. Avila clung to it like a crippled frog. He thought of a sublime irony—what if the life-saving lumber had blown off one of the roofs that he'd been bribed not to inspect? Perhaps it was Chango's idea of a practical joke.

All night long, adrift in the chop, Avila cursed the hurricane for bringing him such misery: the sadistic doughnut man, Whit-mark and, of course, Snapper. The rainfall stopped at dawn but the sun never broke free of the clouds. It was midafternoon before Avila heard an engine. As he shouted for help, a tall white fishing boat idled within hailing distance. Avila waved. The skipper and his tropically garbed clients waved back.

"Hang in there, *amigo*," the skipper yelled, and trolled away.

Twenty minutes later, a Coast Guard boat arrived and took Avila aboard. The crew gave him dry clothes, hot coffee and homemade chili. He ate in appreciative silence. Afterwards he was led belowdeck to a small briefing room, where he was greeted by a man from the Immigration and Naturalization Service.

In halting Spanish, the immigration man asked Avila for the name of the Cuban port he had fled. Avila laughed and explained that he was from Miami.

"Then what're you doing out here in your underwear?"

Avila said a robber was chasing him down the road, so he jumped off a bridge in Islamorada.

"Tell the truth," the immigration man said sternly. "Obviously you're a rafter. Now where did you come from—Havana? Mariel?"

Avila was about to argue when it dawned on him that there was no faster way to shed his burdens. What could he look forward to in his current life but an unforgiving wife, a traumatized mother-in-law, personal bankruptcy, the wrath of Gar Whitmark and a possible criminal indictment?

He asked the immigration man: "What will happen to me if I confess?"

"Nothing. You'll be processed at Krome and most likely released."

"If I am a political refugee."

"That's the usual procedure."

"*Sí*," Avila said. "*Yo soy balsero*." I am a rafter.

The immigration man seemed so relieved that Avila was left to conclude (as a former civil servant himself) that he'd saved the man mountains of paperwork.

"*Su nombre, por favor?*"

"Juan," Avila replied. "Juan Gómez. From Havana."

"And your occupation in Cuba?"

"I was a building inspector."

TWENTY-SEVEN

They waited in the Jeep—Edie Marsh up front, holding the revolver; Bonnie Lamb pressed against the governor in the back seat.

It was Bonnie who said: "What if he doesn't come back?"

Edie was thinking the same thing. Hoping it. The problem was, Snapper had the damn car keys. She asked the man in the shower cap: "You know how to hot-wire one of these?"

"That would be illegal."

The cinematic smile startled her. She said, "Why aren't you afraid?"

"Of what?"

"The gun. Dying. Anything."

Bonnie said she was frightened enough for all of them. The rain slackened; still no sign of Snapper, or Avila. Edie had difficulty keeping her eyes off the man called Skink.

"What is it," he said. "My hat?"

She lifted the .357. "You could take this away from me anytime you wanted. You know it."

"Maybe I don't want to."

That's what scared her. What was the point of holding a gun on a person like this?

He said, "I won't hurt you." Again with the smile.

Edie Marsh was a sucker for laugh lines around the eyes. She said to Bonnie: "I think I know what you see in this guy."

"We're just friends."

"Really? Then maybe you can tell me," Edie said, "what's he got planned?"

"I honestly don't know. I wish I did."

Edie was all clammy shakes, roiled emotions. In the motel room, depositing Mr Stichler with the two hookers, she'd caught something on the TV that got her daydreaming—a news clip of the President of the United States touring the hurricane damage. At his side was a tall, boyishly attractive man in his thirties, whom the TV newscasters identified as the President's son. When they said he lived in Miami, Edie Marsh got a whimsical flash. So what if he wasn't a Kennedy? And maybe he was too much of a good young Republican to pick up some hot girl in a bar and get raunchy. Or just maybe he'd been waiting his whole repressed life to do exactly that. And he *was* the President's son. It was something to consider, Edie mused, for the future. Particularly if the hurricane scam continued to unravel at its current pace.

She put Snapper's gun on the seat. "Get out of here," she told Skink and Bonnie. "Go on. I'll tell him you pushed me down and got away."

Bonnie looked over at the governor, who said: "Now's your chance, girl."

"What about you?"

He shook his head. "I made a promise to Jim."

"Who the hell's Jim?" asked Edie Marsh.

Bonnie said: "Then I guess we're staying."

Skink encouraged her to make a dash for it. "Go call Augustine. Let him know you're OK."

"Nope," Bonnie said.

"And your husband, too."

"No! Not until it's over."

Edie was exasperated, her nerves worn ragged. Snapper was right; they *are* nuts. "Fine," she said, "you two fruitballs stay if you want, but I'm outta here."

Skink said: "Excellent decision."

"Tell him I went to use the bathroom."

"No problem," said Bonnie.

"I got my period or something."

"Right."

Skink leaned forward. "Could you hand me the gun?"

"Why not," Edie said. Perhaps the smiler would shoot Snapper dead. There were about forty-seven thousand reasons that Edie wasn't upset at the idea, not including the barrel-shaped bruise on her right breast.

She was passing the .357 to Skink when he waved her off, saying: "On second thought—"

Edie turned and let out a gasp. It was Snapper's face, dripping wet, pressed to the window of the Jeep. The bent nose and misshapen mouth made him look like a gargoyle.

"Miss me, bay-beeee?" he crooned, pallid lips wriggling like flatworms against the glass.

Jim Tile was tempted to call for backup, though it would spell the end of the governor's elaborate reclusion.

Long ago they'd made a pact: no cavalry, unless innocent lives were in peril. The trooper was thinking of the tourist woman as more or less innocent. She and Skink might be dead already.

Glumly Jim Tile watched the rain drench the passing cars on Highway One. Again he castigated himself for letting his emotions get the better of his brain. Brenda was alive. He should've thanked God, then let it go.

But he didn't. And the governor had had little trouble talking him out of the license-tag number.

"Pest control" was what Skink had called it, as they were leaving the hospital.

"Whoever did that to Mrs Rourke is not a viable member of the species. Not a welcome donor to the gene pool. Wouldn't Darwin himself agree?"

And the trooper had merely said: "Be careful."

"Jim, we're infested with these mutant shitheads. Look what they've done to the place."

The trooper, locked in some cold distant zone: "The tag's probably stolen off another car. It may lead you nowhere."

The governor, momentarily shaking loose of his friend's firm grip: "They're turning it into a sump hole. Some with guns, some with briefcases—it's all the same goddamn crime."

"Pest control."

"We do what we can."

"Be careful, captain."

Then he'd flashed those movie-star pearlies, the ones that had gotten him elected. And Jim Tile stood back and let him go. Let him stalk the man in the black Jeep Cherokee.

Which was now parked in a windy drizzle outside the Paradise Palms. The trooper counted three figures inside the truck; two of them, he hoped, were Skink and Bonnie Lamb.

A dark shape near the road caught his attention.

The tall man in the suit was hurrying along the gravel shoulder of Highway One. There was a tippiness to his gait; he seemed well challenged to keep a straight course, clear of the speeding cars. He flinched when the high beams of a gasoline tanker caught him in the face.

This time Jim Tile got a good look at the misaligned jaws.

He watched the man pass beneath the bright electric sign in front of the motel. He saw him walk up to the Jeep, lean close to a window. Then the man ran around to the driver's side, opened the door and got in. Smoke puffed from the truck's exhaust pipe. The brake lights flickered.

Jim Tile said, "Hello," and started his engine.

Suddenly, all around, the night was diced into blues and whites.

Snapper was backing the Jeep out, chortling about what had happened to Avila: "Dumb fuck went straight off the bridge, you shoulda seen— Hey! Hey, what the hell . . ."

Bright lights started strobing everywhere. In the reflection of the puddles. On the coral-colored walls of the motel. In the fronds of the sabal palms.

Snapper shoved the Jeep into Neutral. "Fucking cops!"

"No way," Edie said. But she knew he was right.

A figure in gray was approaching the Cherokee. Snapper rolled down the window. It was a state trooper; big black sonofabitch, too. He'd parked his patrol car at an angle, to block the exit.

Snapper's mind raced, half drunk, half wired: Christ Almighty, would Momma and Pappy pitch a fit they ever heard I got taken down by a nigger cop. Momma especially.

In a flash Snapper figured out what must've happened: The lady trooper either was alive, or had survived long enough after the beating to give a description of the Jeep, and maybe even of Snapper himself.

So this was the big black posse.

Snapper knew he should've ditched the Cherokee after it happened. Sure, park the fucker in the nearest canal and call it a deal. But, oh Jesus, how he loved that stereo system! Reba, Garth, Hank Jr., they'd never sounded so sweet. His whole life Snapper had wanted a car with decent speakers. So he'd stayed with the stolen Jeep because of its awesome stereo—and here was the price to be paid.

A big black motherfucker of a cop, coming across the parking lot, drawing his gun.

The one-eyed man tapped him on the shoulder. "Haul ass, chief."

"Huh?"

"That's what I'd do."

"No," murmured Edie Marsh. "We've had it."

Snapper told her to shut up. He snatched the .357 off the seat, pointed it out the window and somehow managed to shoot the trooper in the center of the chest. The man fell backward, landing with a splash.

"Good night, nigger," Snapper said.

Skink went rigid. Bonnie and Edie screamed. Snapper slammed the Jeep into gear and peeled rubber.

"You see thaa-aatt?" he whinnied. "One shot, one nigger cop! Whooheee! One shot!"

In the cargo well of the Cherokee, Augustine popped up on one knee. The stubby dart rifle was at his shoulder, the sights trained on the ragged hairline of Snapper's neck. He was surprised when Skink turned and shoved him back to the floor.

That's when the rear window of the Jeep vaporized.

The explosion caught Snapper furrowed in concentration, as

he labored to steer around the parked Highway Patrol car, lit up like a Mardi Gras float.

Snapper ducked, peering up at the rearview. He saw the black trooper lying in a puddle, his arm waving but not aiming the smoking gun. Then the trooper went limp, and Snapper cackled.

The Cherokee fishtailed on the rain-slicked asphalt as it entered the highway. Edie Marsh hunched like an aged nun, sobbing into her hands. Skink had pulled Bonnie Lamb into his lap, out of the gunfire's path. Huddled in the cargo hatch, Augustine silently plucked nuggets of safety glass from his clothes.

Snapper was loopy on Midols, Johnnie Walker and pure criminal adrenaline. "You see that big nigger go down?" he yammered at the top of his lungs. "You see him go down!"

Christophe Michel spent the night of the hurricane in the safe and convivial atmosphere of Key West. At noon the next morning he put on the television and recognized, with cramps of dread, the bombed-out remains of a luxury housing development called Gables-on-the-Bay. The subdivision had been built by a company called Zenith Custom Homes, which not only employed Christophe Michel as a senior structural engineer but advertised his ecumenical credentials in its sales brochures. Michel had been recruited from one of France's oldest engineering firms, which had not energetically protested his departure. Among the fields in which Michel sorely lacked experience was that of girding single-family structures to withstand the force of tropical cyclones. His new employer assured him there was nothing to it, and FedExed him a copy of the South Florida Building Code, which weighed several pounds. Christophe Michel skimmed it on the flight from Orly to Miami.

He got along fine at Zenith, once he understood that cost containment was higher on the list of corporate priorities than ensuring structural integrity. To justify its preposterously inflated prices, the company had hyped Gables-on-the-Bay as "South Florida's first hurricane-proof community." Much in the same way, Michel later reflected, that the *Titanic* was promoted as unsinkable.

All week the news from Dade County worsened. The newspaper hired its own construction engineers to inspect the storm rubble, uncovering so many design flaws that an unabridged listing was possible only in the tiniest of agate type. One of the engineers sarcastically remarked that Gables-on-the-Bay should have been called Gables-*in*-the-Bay—a quote so colorful that it merited enlargement, in boldface, on the front page.

With home owners picketing Zenith headquarters and demanding a grand jury, Christophe Michel prudently planned his departure from the United States. He closed his bank accounts, shuttered the condo in Key West, packed the Seville and set out for the mainland.

The rain did nothing for his fragile confidence in American traffic. Every bend and rise in the overseas highway was a trial of reflexes and composure. Michel finished his last cigaret while crossing the Bahia Honda Bridge, and by Islamorada had gnawed his forty-dollar manicure to slaw. At the first break in the weather, he stopped at a Circle K for a carton of Broncos, an American brand to which he unaccountably had become devoted.

When he returned to the Seville, four strangers emerged from the shadows. One of them put a gun to his belly.

"Give us your goddamn car," the man said.

"Certainly."

"Don't stare at me like that!"

"Sorry." The engineer's trained eye calculated the skew of the man's jawbone at thirty-five degrees off center.

"I got one bullet left!"

"I believe you," said Christophe Michel.

The disfigured gunman told him to go back in the store and count backward from one hundred, slowly.

Michel asked, "May I keep my suitcase?"

"Fuck, no!"

"I understand."

He was counting aloud as he walked for the second time into the Circle K. The clerk at the register asked if something was wrong. Michel, fumbling to light a Bronco, nodded explicitly.

"My life savings just drove away," he said. "May I borrow the telephone?"

Bonnie Lamb expected Skink to erupt in homicidal fury upon seeing his best friend shot down. He didn't. Bonnie worried about the listless sag to his shoulders, the near feebleness of his movements. He wore the numb, unfocused glaze of the heavily sedated. Bonnie was sorry to see the governor's high spirits extinguished.

Meanwhile Snapper ranted and swore because the Seville had no CD player, only a tape deck, and here he'd gone to all the goddamn trouble of removing his compact discs from the Jeep before they'd ditched it behind the convenience store.

Bonnie squeezed Skink's arm and asked if he was all right. He shifted his feet, and something rattled metallically on the floorboard. He picked it up and asked, "What's this?"

It was a red pronged instrument, with a black plastic grip and a chrome key lock.

Snapper looked over his shoulder and sniggered. "The Club!"

"The what?"

Bonnie Lamb said, "You know. That thing they advertise all the time on TV."

"I watch no television," Skink said.

Snapper hooted. "The Club, for Chrissakes. The Club! See, you lock it across't here"—he patted the steering wheel—"so your car don't get stolen."

"Really?"

"Yeah. Lotta good it did that dickhead back at the Circle K." Snapper's laughter had a ring of triumph.

Edie Marsh was struggling to collect herself after the shooting. Even in the darkness, Bonnie could see fresh tears shining in her eyelashes.

"I had this boyfriend," Edie sniffled, "he put one of those on his new Firebird. They got it anyway. Right out of the driveway, broad daylight. What they did, they iced the lock and cracked it with a hammer."

Snapper said, "No shit? Froze it?"

"Yeah." Edie couldn't come to terms with what had happened at the Paradise Palms, the wrongness and maddening stupidity of it. They'd never get away now. Never. Killing a cop! How had a harmless insurance scam come so unhinged?

Skink was impressed with the ingenious simplicity of The Club. He took special interest in the notched slide mechanism, which allowed the pronged ends to be fitted snugly into almost any large aperture.

"See, that way you can't turn the wheel," Snapper was explaining, still enjoying the irony, "so nobody can drive off with your fancy new Cadillac Seville. 'Less they put a fuckin' gun in your ribs. Ha! Accept no imitations!"

Skink set the device down.

"Accept no imitations!" Snapper crowed again, waving the .357.

The governor's gaze turned out the window, drifting again. Teasingly, Bonnie said: "I can't believe you've never seen one of those."

This time the smile was sad. "I lead a sheltered life."

Edie Marsh wondered if Snapper could have picked a dumber location to shoot a cop—a county of slender, connected islands, with only one way out. She kept checking for blue police lights behind them.

Snapper told her to knock it off, she was making everyone a nervous wreck. "Another half hour we're home free," he said, "back on the mainland. Then we find another car."

"One with a CD player, I bet."

"Damn right."

The Seville got boxed in behind a slow beer truck. They wound up stopped at the traffic light in Key Largo. Again Edie snuck a peek behind them. Snapper heard a gasp.

"What!" He spun his head. "Is it cops?"

"No. The Jeep!"

"You're crazy, that ain't possible—"

"Right behind us," Edie said.

Bonnie Lamb began to turn around, but Skink held her shoulder. The light turned green. Snapper floored the Seville, zipped smartly between the beer truck and a meandering Toyota. He said: "You crazy twat, there's only about a million goddamn black Jeeps on the road."

"Yeah?" Edie said. "With bullet holes in the roof?" She could see a bud of mushroomed steel above the passenger side.

"Jesus." Snapper used the barrel of the .357 to adjust the rearview mirror. "Jesus, you sure?"

The Cherokee was still on their bumper. Bonnie noticed the governor wore a faint smile. Edie picked up on it, too. She said, "What's going on? Who's that behind us?"

Skink shrugged. Snapper said: "How 'bout this? I don't care who's back there, because he's already one dead cocksucker. That's 'zackly how many shots I got left."

In what seemed to Bonnie as a single fluid motion, the governor reached across the seat, wrenched the .357 from Snapper's hand and fired it point-blank into the Cadillac's dashboard.

Then he dropped it on Snapper's lap and said: "Now you've got jackshit."

Snapper labored not to pile the car into a utility pole. Edie Marsh's ears rang from the gun blast, although she wasn't surprised by what had happened. It had only been a matter of time. The smiler had been humoring them.

One thought reverberated in Bonnie Lamb's head: What now? What in the world will he do next?

Snapper, straining not to appear frightened, hollering at Skink over his shoulder: "Try anything, *anything*, I fuckin' swear we're all going off a bridge. You unnerstand? We'll all be dead."

"Eyes on the road, chief."

"Don't touch me, goddammit!"

Skink placed his chin next to the headrest, inches from Snapper's right ear. He said, "That cop you shot, he was a friend of mine."

Edie Marsh's chin dropped. "Tell me it wasn't 'Jim.'"

"It was."

"Naturally." She sighed disconsolately.

"So what?" Snapper said. His shoulders bunched. "Like I'm supposed to know. Fucking cop's a cop."

To Bonnie, the social dynamics inside the carjacked Seville were surreal. Logically the abduction should have ended once Snapper's gun was out of bullets. Yet here they were, riding along as if nothing had changed. They might as well be on a double date. Stop for pizza and milk shakes.

She said: "Can I ask something: Where are we going? Is somebody in charge now?"

Snapper said, "*I* am, goddammit. Long as I'm drivin'—"

He felt Edie jab him in the side. "The Jeep," she said, pointing. "Check it out."

The black truck was in the left lane, keeping speed with the Cadillac. Snapper pressed the accelerator, but the Jeep stayed even.

"Well, shit," he grumbled. Edie was right. It was the same truck they'd abandoned ten minutes earlier. Snapper was totally baffled. Who could it be?

They watched the Cherokee's front passenger window roll down. The ghost driver steered with his left hand. His eyes were locked on the highway. In the oncoming headlights Snapper caught sight of the man's face, which he didn't recognize. He did, however, note that the stranger definitely wasn't wearing a Highway Patrol uniform. The observation gave Snapper an utterly misplaced sense of relief.

Bonnie Lamb recognized the other driver immediately. She gave a clandestine wave. So did the governor.

"What's going on!" Edie Marsh was on her knees, pointing and shouting. "What's going on! Who is *that* sonofabitch!"

She was more dejected than startled when the Jeep's driver one-handedly raised a rifle. By the time Snapper saw it, he'd already heard the shot.

Pfffttt. Like a kid's airgun.

Then a painful sting under one ear; liquid heat flooding down through his arms, his chest, his legs. He went slack and listed starboard, mumbling, "What the fuh, what the fuh—"

Skink said it was a superb time for Edie to assist at the wheel. "Take it steady," he added. "We're coasting."

Reaching across Snapper's body, she anxiously guided the Seville to the gravel shoulder of the highway. The black Jeep smoothly swung in ahead of them.

Edie bit her lip. "I can't believe this. I just can't."

"Me, neither," said Bonnie Lamb. She was out the door, running toward Augustine, before the car stopped rolling.

TWENTY-EIGHT

Jim Tile once played tight end for the University of Florida. In his junior year, during the final home game of the season, a scrawny Alabama cornerback speared his crimson helmet full tilt into Jim Tile's sternum. Jim Tile held on to the football but completely forgot how to breathe.

That's how he felt now, lying in clammy rainwater, staring up at the worried face of a platinum-haired hooker. The impact of the shot had deflated Jim Tile's lungs, which were screaming silently for air. The emergency lights of the patrol car blinked blue-white-blue in the reflection in the prostitute's eyes.

Jim Tile understood that he couldn't be dying—it only felt that way. The asshole's bullet wasn't lodged in vital bronchial tissue; it was stuck in a layer of blessedly impenetrable Du Pont Kevlar. Like most police officers, Jim Tile detested the vest, particularly in the summer—it was hot, bulky, itchy. But he wore it because he'd promised his mother, his nieces, his uncle and of course Brenda, who wore one of her own. Working for the Highway Patrol was statistically the most dangerous job in law enforcement. Naturally it also paid the worst. Only after numerous officers had been gunned down were bulletproof vests requisitioned for the state patrol, whose budget was so threadbare that the purchase was made possible only by soliciting outside donations.

Long before that, Jim Tile's loved ones had decided he shouldn't wait for the state legislature to demonstrate its heartfelt concern for police officers. The Kevlar vest was a family Christmas present. Jim Tile didn't always wear it while patrolling rural parts of the Panhandle, but in Miami he wouldn't go to church without it. He was glad he had strapped it on today.

If only he could remember how to breathe.

"Take it easy, baby," the hooker kept saying. "Take it easy. We called 911."

As Jim Tile sat upright, he emitted a sucking sound that reminded the prostitute of a broken garbage disposal. When she smacked him between the shoulders, a mashed chunk of lead fell from a dime-sized hole in Jim Tile's shirt and plopped into the puddle. He picked it up: the slug from a .357.

Jim Tile asked, "Where'd they go?" His voice was a frail rattle. With difficulty he holstered his service revolver.

"Don't you move," said the woman.

"Did I hit him?"

"Sit still."

"Ma'am, help me up. Please."

He was shuffling for his car when the fire truck arrived. The paramedics made him lie down while they stripped off his shirt and the vest. They told him he was going to have an extremely nasty bruise. They told him he was a very lucky man.

By the time the paramedics were done, the parking lot of the Paradise Palms was clogged with curious locals, wandering tourists and motel guests, a fleet of Monroe County deputies, two TV news vans and three gleaming, undented Highway Patrol cruisers belonging to Jim Tile's supervisors. They gathered under black umbrellas to fill out their reports.

Meanwhile the shooter was speeding up Highway One with the governor and the newlywed.

A lieutenant told Jim Tile not to worry, they'd never make it out of the Keys.

"Sir, I'd like to be part of the pursuit. I feel fine."

"You're not going anywhere." The lieutenant softened the command with a fraternal chuckle. "Hell, Jimbo, we're just gettin' started."

He handed the trooper a stack of forms and a pen.

*

The body of Tony Torres inevitably became a subject of interest to a newspaper reporter working on hurricane-related casualties. The autopsy report did not use the term "crucifixion," but the silhouette diagram of puncture wounds told the whole grisly story. To avert embarrassing publicity, the police made a hasty effort to reignite the investigation, dormant since the aborted phone call from a woman claiming to be the dead man's widow. Within a day, a veteran homicide detective named Brickhouse was able to turn up a recent address for the murdered Tony Torres. This was done by tracing the victim's Cartier wristwatch to a Bal Harbour jeweler, who remembered Tony as an overbearing jerk, and kept detailed receipts of the transaction in anticipation of future disputes. The jeweler was not crestfallen at the news of Señor Torres's demise, and graciously gave the detective the address he sought. While the police department's Public Information division stalled the newspaper reporter, Brickhouse drove down to the address in Turtle Meadow.

There he found an abandoned hurricane house with a late-model Chevrolet and a clunker Oldsmobile parked in front. The Chevy's license plate had been removed, but the VIN number came back to Antonio Rodrigo Guevara-Torres, the victim. The tag on the rusty Olds was registered to one Lester Maddox Parsons. Brickhouse radioed for a criminal history, which might or might not be ready when he got back to the office in the morning; the hurricane had unleashed electronic gremlins inside the computers.

The detective's natural impulse was to enter the house, which would have been fairly easy in the absence of doors. The problem wasn't so much that Brickhouse didn't have a warrant; it was the old man next door, watching curiously from the timber shell of his front porch. He would be the defense lawyer's first witness at a suppression hearing, if an unlawful search of the victim's residence turned up evidence.

So Brickhouse stayed in the yard, peeking through broken windows and busted doorways. He noted a gas-powered generator in the garage, wine and flowers in the dining room, a woman's purse, half-melted candles, an Igloo cooler positioned next to a BarcaLounger—definitive signs of post-hurricane habitation.

Everything else was standard storm debris. Brickhouse saw no obvious bloodstains, which fit his original theory that the mobile-home salesman had been taken elsewhere to be crucified.

The detective strolled over to chat with the snoopy neighbor, who gave his name as Leonel Varga. He told a jumbled but colorful yarn about sinister-looking visitors, mysterious leggy women and insufferable barking dogs. Brickhouse took notes courteously. Varga said Mr and Mrs Torres were separated, although she'd recently phoned to say she was coming home.

"But it's a secret," he added.

"You bet," Brickhouse said. Before knocking off for the evening, he tacked his card to the doorjamb at 15600 Calusa.

That's where Neria Torres found it at dawn.

Matthew's pickup truck had followed her all the way from Fort Drum to the house at Turtle Meadow. The seven Tennesseeans swarmed the battered building in orgiastic wonderment at the employment opportunity that God had wrought. Matthew dramatically announced they should commence repairs immediately.

Neria said, "Not just yet. You help me find my husband, then I'll let you do some work on the house."

"I guess, sure. Where's he at?"

"First I've got to make some calls."

"Sure," Matthew said. "Meantime we should get a jump on things." He asked Neria's permission to borrow some tools from the garage.

"Just hold on," she told him.

But they were already ascending the roof and rafters, like a troop of hairless chimpanzees. Neria let it go. The sight of the place disturbed her more than she had anticipated. She'd seen the hurricane destruction on CNN, but standing ankle-deep in it was different; overwhelming, if the debris once was your home. The sight of her mildewed wedding pictures in the wreckage brought a sentimental pang, but it was quickly deadened by the discovery of flowers and a bottle of wine in the dining room. Neria Torres assumed Tony had bought them for a bimbo.

She fingered the detective's card. She hoped it meant that the cops had tossed her asshole husband in jail, leaving her a clear path toward reclaiming half the marital property. Or possibly more.

She heard a mechanical roar from the garage; the resourceful Tennesseeans had found fuel for the generator. A bare lightbulb flickered on and off in the living room.

Leonel Varga, still in his bathrobe, came over to say hello. He assured her that the police detective was a nice man.

"What did he want? Is it about Tony?"

"I think so. He didn't say." Mr Varga stared up at the busy figures of the men on the roof beams, backlit by the molten sunrise. "You found some roofers?"

Neria Torres said, "Oh, I seriously doubt it."

She dialed the private number that Detective Brickhouse had penciled on the back of the business card. He answered the phone like a man accustomed to being awakened by strangers. He said, "I'm glad you called."

"Is it about Tony?"

"Yeah, I'm afraid it is."

"Don't tell me he's in jail," said Neria, hoping dearly that Brickhouse would tell her precisely that.

"No," the detective said. "Mrs Torres, your husband's dead."

"Oh God. Oh God. Oh God." Neria's mind was skipping like a flat rock on a river.

"I'm sorry—"

"You sure?" she asked. "Are you sure it's Antonio?"

"We should take a ride up to the morgue. You're home now?"

"Yes. Yes, I'm back."

Brickhouse said, "I've got to be in court this morning. How about if I swing by around noon? We'll go together. Give us some time to chat."

"About what?"

"It looks like Antonio was murdered."

"How! Murdered?"

"We'll talk later, Mrs Torres. Get some rest now."

Neria didn't know what she felt, or what she ought to feel.

The corpse in the morgue was the man she'd married. A corpulent creep, to be sure, but still the husband she had once believed she loved. Shock was natural. Curiosity. A selfish stab of fear. Maybe even sorrow. Tony had his piggish side, but even so . . .

Her gaze settled for the first time on the purse. A woman's purse, opened, on the kitchen counter. On top was a note printed in block letters and signed with the initials "F.D." The note said the author was keeping the dogs at the motel. The note began with "My Sexy Darling" and ended with "Love Always."

Dogs? Neria Torres thought.

She wondered if Tony was the same man as "F.D." and, if so, what insipid nickname the initials stood for. Fat Dipshit?

Curiously she went through the contents of the purse. A driver's license identified the owner as Edith Deborah Marsh. Neria noted the date of birth, working the arithmetic in her head. Twenty-nine years old, this one.

Tony, you dirty old perv.

Neria appraised the face in the photograph. A ballbuster; Tony must've had his fat hands full. Neria took unaccountable satisfaction from the fact that young Edith was a dagger-eyed brunette, not some dippy blonde.

From behind her came the sound of roupy breathing. Neria wheeled, to find Matthew looming at her shoulder.

"Christ!"

"I dint mean to scare ya."

"What is it? What do you want?"

"It's started up to rain."

"I noticed."

"Seemed like a good spot for a break. We was headed to a hardware store for some roof paper, nails, wood—stuff like that."

"Lumber," Neria Torres said archly. "In the construction business, it's called 'lumber.' Not wood."

"Sure." He was scratching at his Old Testament tattoos.

She said, "So go already."

"Yeah, well, we need some money. For the lumber."

"Matthew, there's something I've got to tell you."

"Sure."

"My husband's been murdered. A police detective is coming out here soon."

Matthew took a step back and said, "Sweet Jesus, I'm so sorry." He began to improvise a prayer, but Neria cut him off.

"You and your crew," she said, "you *are* licensed in Dade County, aren't you? I mean, there won't be any problem if the detective wants to ask some questions . . . ?"

The Tennesseeans were packed and gone within fifteen minutes. Neria found the solitude relaxing: a light whisper of rain, the occasional whine of a mosquito. She thought of Tony, wondered whom he'd pissed off to get himself killed—maybe tough young Edith! Neria thought of the professor, too, wondered how he and his Earth Mother blow-job artist were getting along with no wheels.

She also thought of the many things she didn't want to do, such as move back into the gutted husk at 15600 Calusa. Or be interviewed by a homicide detective. Or go to the morgue to view her estranged husband's body.

Money was the immediate problem. Neria wondered if careless Tony had left her name on any of the bank accounts, and what (if anything) remained in them. The most valuable item at the house was his car, untouched by the hurricane. Neria located the spare key in the garage, but the engine wouldn't turn over.

"Need some help?"

It was a clean-shaven young man in a Federal Express uniform. He had an envelope for Neria Torres. She signed for it, laid it on the front seat of Tony's Chevy.

The kid said, "I got jumpers in the truck."

"Would you mind?"

They had the car started in no time. Neria idled the engine and waited for the battery to recharge. The FedEx kid said it sounded good. Halfway to the truck, he stopped and turned.

"Hey, somebody swiped your license plate."

"Shit." Neria got out to see for herself. The FedEx driver said it was probably a looter.

"Everybody around here's getting ripped off," he explained.

"I didn't even notice. Thanks."

As soon as he left, Neria opened the FedEx envelope. Her delirious shriek drew nosy Mr Varga to his front porch. He was shirtless, a toothbrush in one cheek. In fascination he watched his neighbor practically bound up the sidewalk into her house.

The envelope contained two checks made out to Antonio and Neria Torres. The checks were issued by the Midwest Life and Casualty Company of Omaha, Nebraska. They totaled $201,000. The stubs said: "Hurricane losses."

Shortly after noon, when Detective Brickhouse arrived at 15600 Calusa, he found the house empty again. The Chevrolet was gone, as was the widow of Antonio Torres. A torn Federal Express envelope lay on the driveway, near the rusty Oldsmobile. Mr Varga, the neighbor, informed the detective that Neria Torres sped off without even waving good-bye.

Brickhouse was backing out of the driveway when a rental car pulled up. A thin blond man wearing round eyeglasses got out. Brickhouse noticed the man had tan Hush Puppies and was carrying a box of Whitman chocolates. High-pitched barking could be heard from the back seat of the visitor's car.

The detective called the man over. "Are you looking for Mrs Torres?"

The man hesitated. Brickhouse identified himself. The man blinked repeatedly, as if his glasses were smudged.

He said, "I don't know anybody named Torres. Guess I've got the wrong address." Speedily he returned to his car.

Brickhouse leaned out the window. "Hey, who's the candy for?"

"My mother!" Fred Dove replied, over the barking.

The detective watched the confused young man drive away, and wondered why he'd lied. Even crackheads know how to find their own mother's house. Brickhouse briefly considered tailing the guy, but decided it would be a waste of time. Whoever crucified Tony Torres wasn't wearing Hush Puppies. Brickhouse would have bet his pension on it.

*

Augustine parked at a phone booth behind a gas station. The governor had them wait while he made a call. He came back humming a Beatles tune.

"Jim's alive," he said.

Edie Marsh leaned forward. "Your friend! How do you know?"

"There's a number where we leave messages for each other."

Bonnie asked if he was hurt badly.

"Nope. He took it in the vest."

Augustine shook a fist in elation. Everybody's mood perked up, even Edie's. Skink told Bonnie she could call her mother, but make it fast. It went like this:

"Mom, something's happened."

"I guessed as much."

"Between Max and me."

"Oh no." Bonnie's mother, laboring to sound properly dismayed, when Bonnie knew how she truly felt. "What'd he do, sweetie?"

"Nothing, Mom. It's all me."

"Did you have a fight?" her mother asked.

"Listen, I've met two unusual men. I believe I've fallen in love with one of them."

"On your honeymoon, Bonnie?"

"I'm afraid so."

"What does he do?"

"He's not certain," Bonnie said.

"These men, are they dangerous?"

"Not to me. Mom, they're totally different from anyone I've ever known. It's a very . . . primitive charisma."

"Let's not mention that last part to your father."

Next Bonnie phoned the apartment in New York. When she got back to the Seville, she told Skink to go on without her.

"Max left a message on the machine." She didn't look at Augustine when she said it. Couldn't look at him.

Bonnie repeated her husband's message. "He says it's over if I don't meet with him."

"It's over regardless," Skink said.

"Please."

"Call back and leave your own message." The governor gave her the details—the place, the time, who would be there.

After Bonnie finished with the phone, Skink made another call himself. When they got back in the car, Augustine punched the accelerator and peeled rubber. Bonnie put her hand on his arm. He gave a tight, rueful smile.

They made the 905 turnoff in the nick of time. Already the northbound traffic was stacked past Lake Surprise; Skink surmised that the police had raised the Jewfish Creek drawbridge for their roadblock. He predicted they'd set up another one at Card Sound, as soon as more patrol cars arrived from the mainland.

Edie Marsh said, "So where are we going?"

"Patience."

The two of them sat together in the back seat. On the governor's lap was a Bill Blass suitcase, removed from the Cadillac's trunk to make space for the blacked-out Snapper.

Skink said, "Driver, dome light! *Por favor.*"

Augustine began pushing dashboard buttons until the ceiling lights came on. Skink broke the locks off the suitcase and opened it.

"What have we here!" he said.

The troopers waited all night at Jewfish Creek. As Jim Tile predicted the black Jeep Cherokee never appeared, nor did the silver Cadillac stolen from a customer at a Key Largo convenience store. The French victim had dryly described the armed carjacker as "a poster boy for TMJ."

At daybreak the cops gave up the roadblock and fanned through the Upper Keys. It would take three days to locate the Seville, abandoned on a disused smugglers' trail off County Road 905, only a few miles from the exclusive Ocean Reef Club. The police would wait another forty-eight hours before announcing the discovery of the vehicle. They omitted mention of the bullet hole in its dashboard, as they didn't wish to unduly alarm Ocean Reef's residents and guests, which included some of the most socially prominent, politically influential and chronically impatient taxpayers in the eastern United States. Many were already in a cranky mood, due to the inconvenient damaging of their vacation homes by the hurricane. News that a murderous criminal might be lurking in the mangroves would touch off heated high-level communiqués with Tallahassee and Washington, D.C. The Ocean Reef crowd didn't mess around.

As it turned out, there was no danger whatsoever.

Most newly married men, faced with unexpected desertion, would have been manic with grief, jealousy and anger. Max Lamb, however, was blessed by a hearty, blinding preoccupation with his career.

A nettlesome thought kept scrolling across his mind, and it had nothing to do with his runaway wife. It was something the nutty kidnapper had told him: *You need a legacy.*

They'd been riding in the back of a U-Haul truck, discussing unforgettable advertising slogans. Max hadn't anything zippy to brag about except the short-lived Plum Crunchies ditty. Since the failure of the cereal campaign, the sixth floor had deployed him more often for billboard concepts and print graphics, and not as much on the verbally creative side.

Which stung, because Max considered himself a genuinely glib and talented wordsmith. He believed it was well within his reach to write an advertising catchphrase that would embed itself in the national lexicon—one of those classics the kidnapper had mentioned. A legacy, if you will.

Now that Bronco cigarets were history, Max was left to review the potential of his other accounts. The hypercarbonated soda served on the plane to Miami put him in mind of Old Faithful Root Beer. Old Faithful's popularity had peaked in the summer of 1962, and since then its share of the global soft-drink market had fizzled to a microscopic sliver. Rodale's mission was to revive Old Faithful in the consciousness of the consumer, and to that end the eccentric Mormon family that owned the company was willing to spend a respectable seven-figure sum.

Around Rodale & Burns, the Old Faithful Root Beer account was regarded as a lucrative but hopeless loser. Nobody liked the stuff because one sixteen-ounce bottle induced thunderous belching that often lasted for days. At a party, Pete Archibald drunkenly offered a joke slogan: "The root beer you'll never forget—because it won't let you!"

Lying there alone in Augustine's house, Max Lamb savored the prospect of single-handedly resuscitating Old Faithful. It was the sort of coup that could make him a legend on Madison Avenue. For inspiration he turned on the Home Shopping Network. Into the wee hours he tinkered determinedly with beverage-related alliterations, allusions, puns, verses and metaphors. Bonnie didn't cross his mind.

Eventually Max struck on a winner, something that sounded like good silly fun to kids, and at the same time titillating to teens and young adults:

"Old Faithful Root Beer—Makes You Tingle in Places You Didn't Know You Had Places!"

Max Lamb was so excited he couldn't sleep. Once more he tried calling the apartment in New York. No Bonnie, but the answering machine emitted a telltale beep. He punched the three-digit code and waited.

Bonnie had gotten his message—and left him a reply that caused him to forget temporarily about the Old Faithful account. The flesh under Max's shirt collar prickled and perspired, and stayed feverish until dawn.

He wasn't surprised by the symptoms. The downside of seeing his wife would be seeing the deranged kidnapper again. Only an idiot wouldn't be scared shitless.

TWENTY-NINE

Snapper regained consciousness with the dreamy impression of being someplace he hadn't been in twenty-two years—a dentist's chair. He sensed the dentist hovering, and felt large deft hands working inside his mouth. The last time Snapper had a cavity filled, he'd reflexively chomped off the top joint of the dentist's right thumb. This time he was becalmed by the ejaculate of the dart rifle.

"Lester Maddox Parsons!" The dentist, attempting to wake him.

Snapper opened his eyes in a fog bank. Looming out of the psychedelic mist was a silvery-bearded grin. A dentist in a plastic shower cap? Snapper squirmed.

"Whhaannffrr?" he inquired.

"Relax, chief."

The dentist's basso chuckle rolled like a freight train through Snapper's cranium. His jaws were wedged wide, as if awaiting the drill. Come on, he thought, get it over with.

He heard buzzing. Good!

But the buzzing wasn't in his mouth; it was in his ears. Bugs. Fucking bugs flying in his ears!

"Hrrrnnnff!" Snapper shook his head violently. It hurt. All of a sudden he was drenched by a wave of salty water. What he didn't cough up settled as a lukewarm puddle in his protruded mandible, which functioned as a natural cistern.

Now he was completely awake. Now he remembered. The fog cleared from his mind. He saw a campfire. Edie, sweaty and barefoot. And the young broad, Bonnie, with her arms around the asshole punk who'd shot him.

"Yo, Lester." It was the giant one-eyed fruitcake, holding an empty bucket. There was no dentist.

But Snapper definitely felt a cold steel object bracing his jaws open, digging into the roof of his mouth, pinching the tender web of flesh beneath his tongue; something so heavy that it caused his head to nod forward, something that extended diagonally upward from his chin to beyond his forehead.

A heavy bar of some type. Snapper crossed his eyes to put it in focus. The bar was red.

Oh fuck.

He wailed, trying to rise. His legs tangled. With rubbery arms he flailed uselessly at the thing locked in his mouth.

Skink held up a small chrome key and said, "Accept no imitations."

"Nnnnngggggoooo!!"

"You shot my friend. You called him a nigger." Skink shrugged in resignation. "You beat up a lady, stole her momma's wedding ring, dumped her on the roadside. What choice have you left me?"

He took Snapper by the hair and dragged him, blubbering, to the shore of a broad milky-green creek.

"What choice?" Skink repeated, softly.

"Unngh! Unnnggghhhh!"

"Sure. *Now* you're sorry."

Edie, Bonnie and Augustine appeared on the bank. Skink crouched in the mud next to Snapper.

"Here's the deal. Most any other species, you'd have been dead long ago. Ever heard of Charles Darwin?"

Mosquitoes tickled Snapper's eyelids as he nodded his head.

"Good," Skink said. "Then you might understand what's about to happen." He turned to the others. "Somebody tell Mister Lester Maddox Parsons where we are."

Augustine said: "Crocodile Lakes."

"Yes indeed." Skink rose. Once more he displayed the chrome key, the only thing that could unlock The Club from Snapper's achingly prolonged jowls.

333

Skink threw it in the water. He said, "Crocodile Lakes Wildlife Refuge. Guess how it got its name."

Mournfully Snapper stared at the circle of ripples where the key had plopped into the creek.

They'd stopped once along County Road 905, so Skink could snatch a dead diamondback off the blacktop.

"Don't tell me," said Edie. "It tastes just like chicken."

The governor, coiling the limp rattlesnake at his feet, pretended to be insulted. He told Edie she was much too pretty to be such a cynic. He snapped off the snake's rattle and presented it to her for a souvenir.

"Just what I always wanted." She dropped it in the ashtray.

After ditching the car, Skink made a torch from a gummy stump of pine. For nearly two hours he led them through a shadowed canopy of buttonwoods, poisonwoods, figs, pigeon plums and mahogany. He'd slung Snapper over his shoulder like a sack of oats. In his right hand he held the torch; in his other was the Bill Blass suitcase. Edie Marsh followed along a path hardly wide enough for a rabbit. Bonnie went next, with Augustine close behind, carrying (at Skink's instruction) the tranquilizer rifle and The Club. The .38 Special was in his belt.

Eventually they entered a small clearing. In the center was a ring of sooty stones; a campfire site. A few yards away sat a junked truck with freckles of rust and a faded orange stripe. Bolted to the roof was a bar of cracked red lights. Bonnie and Augustine stepped closer—it was an old Monroe County ambulance, propped on cinder blocks. Augustine opened the tailgate and whistled appreciatively. The ambulance was full of books.

The governor deposited Snapper on the ground, propped against a scabby tree trunk. He went to a spot on the other side of the clearing and kicked at the leaves and loose twigs, exposing an olive-drab tarpaulin. Rummaging beneath it, he came out with a tin of bread crumbs, a jar of vegetable oil, a five-gallon jug of fresh water and a waxy stick of army insect repellent, which he passed around.

While he collected dry wood for the fire, Edie Marsh came up beside him. "Where are we?"

"Middle of nowhere."

"Why?"

"Because there's no better place to be."

They gathered to watch him skin the rattler. Edie was impressed by his enormous hands, sure and swift and completely at ease with the knife.

As the fire sparked up, Augustine pulled Bonnie closer and buried his face in the silkiness of her hair. He was soothed by the soft crackle of tinder; the owl piping on a distant wire; raccoons trilling and fussing in the shadows; the whoosh of nighthawks scooping insects above the firelit treetops. The sole discordant note was the stuporous snore of Lester Maddox Parsons.

The air tasted fresh; the rain was done for a while. Augustine wouldn't have traded places with another soul. Crocodile Lakes on a warm September night was fine. He kissed Bonnie lightly, having no special plans beyond the moment. He willed himself not to worry about Max Lamb, who would be coming tomorrow on a mission to retrieve his bride.

Skink began spooning out chunks of pan-fried snake. Edie Marsh facetiously said it was impolite not to save some for Snapper. Skink declared that he wouldn't so dishonor the memory of a dead reptile.

That's when he'd asked Augustine for The Club.

He turned his back to the others while he fitted it under Snapper's papery gray lips. Bonnie believed the procedure would have been physically impossible, were it not for the preexisting crookedness of those saurian jawbones. Afterwards nobody said a word, until Snapper made a groggy inquisitive murmur.

Skink bent over him. "Lester?"

"Mmmmmfrrrttthh."

"Lester Maddox Parsons!"

Snapper's eyelids fluttered. The governor asked Augustine to take a bucket down to the creek and get some water to wake up the sorry sonofabitch.

*

The pink-orange parfait of dawn failed to elevate Edie's spirits. She was sticky, scratched, hot, parched, filthy, as wretched as she'd ever been. She wanted to cry and pull at her hair and scream. She wanted to make a scene. Most of all she wanted to escape, but that was impossible. She was trapped on all sides by humming crackling wilderness; it might as well have been a twelve-foot wall of barbed wire. Her hands and feet weren't shackled. The governor held no gun to her head. Nothing whatsoever prevented her from running, except the grim certainty that she'd never find her way out, that she'd become blindly lost in the woods and starve, and that her emaciated body would be torn apart and devoured by crocodiles, rattlers and ravenous tropical ants. The prospect of an anonymous death in the swamps offended Edie's dignity. She didn't want her sun-bleached bones to be found by hunters, fishermen or bird-watchers; pieced together by wisecracking medical students and coroners; identified by X rays from her childhood orthodontist.

She approached the governor. "I want to talk."

He was mumbling to himself, feeling around in his shirt. "Damn," he said. "Out of toad." He glanced at Edie: "You're a woman of the world. Ever smoke Bufo?"

"We need to talk," she said. "Alone."

"If it's about the suitcase, forget it."

"It's not that."

"All right, then. Soon as I finish chatting with Lester."

"No, now!"

Skink cupped her chin in one of his huge, rough palms. Edie Marsh sensed that he could break her neck as effortlessly as twisting the cap off a beer. He said, "You've got shitty manners. Go sit with the others."

Bonnie and Augustine were kneeling in the back of the junked ambulance, poring through Skink's library. Edie couldn't understand how they could seem so unconcerned.

She said, "We've got to do something." It came out like a command.

Augustine was showing Bonnie a first edition of *Absalom,*

Absalom. He glanced up at Edie and said, "It's a ride. When it's over, it's over."

"But who *is* he?" She pointed toward Skink. Then, bracing Bonnie: "Aren't you afraid? God, am I the only one with brains enough to be scared?"

"Last night I was," Bonnie said. "Not now."

Augustine told Edie to quiet down. "It'll be over when he says so. In the meantime, please do your best not to piss him off."

Edie was jarred by the harshness of Augustine's tone. He jerked a thumb toward Snapper, agape by the campfire. "What're you doing with that shitbird, anyway?"

Bonnie cut in: "Let's drop the whole thing."

"No, it's all right. I want to explain," said Edie. "It was just business. We were working a deal together."

"A scam."

"Insurance money," she admitted, "from the hurricane." She caught Bonnie staring. "Welcome to the real world, princess."

"So when's the big payoff?" Augustine asked.

Edie laughed ruefully. "The adjuster said any day. Said it was coming Federal Express. And here I am, lost in the middle of the fucking Everglades."

"It's not the Everglades," said Augustine. "In fact, this is Saint-Tropez compared to the Everglades. But I can see why you're upset, watching two hundred grand fly away."

Edie Marsh was dumbfounded. Bonnie said, "You're joking. Two hundred thousand dollars?"

"Two hundred and one." Augustine chided Edie with a wink.

She asked, almost inaudibly: "How'd you know?"

"You left something in the house on Calusa."

"Oh shit."

He unfolded the pink carbons of the Midwest Casualty claim— Edie recognized the cartoon badger at the top of the page. Augustine ripped the carbons into pieces. He said, "I were you, I'd come up with a clever excuse why your pocketbook might be in that particular kitchen. The police'll be mighty curious."

"Shit."

"What I'm saying is, don't be in such a rush to get back to civilization." He turned back to the governor's books.

Edie bit her lower lip. Lord, sometimes it was tough to stay cool. She felt like breaking down again. "What's this all about—some kind of game?"

"I don't think so," Bonnie said.

"Jesus Christ."

"Ride it out. Hang on till it's over."

Not me, thought Edie. No fucking way.

The Club exaggerated Snapper's pre-exaggerated features. It pushed the top half of his mug into pudgy creases, like a shar-pei puppy; the eyes were moist slits, the nose pugged nearly to his brow. The rest was all maw.

"An authentic mouth-breather," Skink said, studying him as if he were a museum piece.

"Fhhhrrrggaaah," Snapper retorted. His elbows stung from scrapes received when the lunatic had dragged him to the creek.

Now the lunatic was saying: "God, I hate the word 'nigger.' Back at the motel I considered killing you when you said it. Blowing your three pitiful teaspoons of brain matter all over the Jeep. Even if you hadn't shot my friend, the thought would've crossed my mind."

Snapper stopped moaning. Worked at controlling his slobber. Watched gnats and mosquitoes float in and out of his mouth.

"Nothing to be done about that." Skink flicked at the insects. He'd already spread a generous sheen of repellent on his captive's neck and arms. " 'Not to be taken internally.' Says so right on the package."

Snapper nodded submissively.

"Lester Maddox Parsons is the name on your license. Wild guess says you're named after that clay-brained Georgia bigot. Am I right?"

A weaker nod.

"So you started out two strikes against you. That's a shame, Lester, but I expect even if your folks had called you Gandhi, you still would've grown up to be a world-class dickhead. Here, let me show you something."

The governor yanked the Bill Blass suitcase from under his butt. He positioned it in front of Snapper and opened it with a gay flourish. "Drool away," he said.

Snapper rose to his haunches. The suitcase was packed with money: bank-wrapped bundles of twenties.

"Ninety-four thousand dollars," Skink reported. "Plus assorted shirts, socks and casual wear. Two packs of French condoms, a set of gold cuff links, a tube of generic lubricant— what else? Oh yes, personal papers."

He probed in the luggage. "Bank statements, newspaper clippings about the hurricane. And this . . ."

It was a glossy color sales brochure for a real estate project called Gables-on-the-Bay. Skink sat next to Snapper and opened the brochure.

"There's our boy. Christophe Michel. 'Internationally renowned construction engineer.' See, here's his picture."

Snapper recognized him as the dork at the Circle K.

"What would you do," Skink mused, "if you designed all these absurdly expensive homes—and they fell down in the first big blow. I believe a smart person would grab the money and split, before subpoenas started flying. I believe that was Monsieur Michel's plan."

Snapper didn't give two shits about the Frenchman. He was transfixed by the sight of so much money. He would have gaped rapturously even if his jaws weren't bolted open. He remembered a Sally Jessy, or maybe it was a Donahue, with some hotel maid from Miami Beach who'd found like forty-two grand under a bed. The maid, for some reason, instead of grabbing the dough she'd turned it in to the manager! That's how come she'd got on Sally Jessy; the theme that day was "honest people." Snapper remembered shouting at the TV screen: What a dumb cunt! They'd showed a picture of the cash, and he'd almost come in his pants.

And here he was staring at twice as much. In person.

"Whhrrrrooognnn? Whhhaaakkkfff?"

"Good question, Lester."

Without warning, the one-eyed freak stood up, unbuttoned his army trousers, whipped out his unit and—to Snapper's mortification—urinated prodigiously upon the hurricane money.

Woefully Snapper rocked on his heels. He felt sick. Skink tucked himself in and went for the monkey rifle. He opened the chamber, peered inside. Then he strolled over to Snapper, flipped him on his belly and shot a tranquilizer dart into his ass. Right away the fog rolled in and Snapper got drowsy. The last thing he heard came from Skink.

"Who wants to go for a swim?"

Bonnie and Augustine stayed to look at the books while the governor took Edie to the creek. She wanted to talk; Skink wanted to get wet. He stripped, starting with the shower cap.

As he stepped into the water, she said: "What about the crocodiles?"

"They won't bother us. There aren't enough of them left to bother anybody. I wish there were."

Serenely he sank beneath the surface, then burst into the air, shaking bubbles and spray from his beard. He was as brown as a manatee, and so large he seemed to bridge the creek. Edie was unprepared for the sight of his body: the lodgepole arms and broad chest, his bare neck as thick as a cypress trunk. The baggy army fatigues had given none of it away.

"Coming in?"

"Only if we can talk," she said.

"What else *would* we do?"

Edie thought: There's that damn smile again. She asked him to turn around while she took off her clothes.

He heard her slip into the creek. Then he felt her slender arms and legs; she was clinging to his back. As he moved into deeper water, she wrapped herself around his thighs.

"I'm a little scared," she said.

"Haw! You and I are the scariest beasts in the jungle."

Edie's mouth was at his ear. "I want to go back to Miami."

"So go."

"But I don't know the way out."

The governor was treading against the push of a strong tidal current. It cleaved around their bobbing heads as if they were dead stumps in the creek.

Edie's breath quickened from the thrill of being in fast water. She said, "From the minute you and Pollyanna showed up at the house, I knew it was over. Snapper's gun—it meant nothing. We didn't kidnap you; you kidnapped us!"

"Nature imposes hierarchy. Always," Skink said.

Edie, in a taut whisper: "Please. Show me the way out of here."

"And I was so sure you'd be angling for that suitcase."

"No way," she said, although it fleetingly had crossed her mind. Instead she'd decided to concentrate on getting out of the Keys alive.

A small silver fish jumped nearby. Playfully Skink swiped at it. He said, "Edie, your opinion of men—it's not good. That much we share. Christ, imagine what Florida would look like today if women had been in charge of the program! Imagine a beach or two with no ugly high-rises. Imagine a lake without golf courses." He clapped his hands, making a merry splash.

Edie said, "You're wrong."

"Darling, I can dream." He felt her lips feather against his neck. Then a tongue, followed by the unsubtle suggestion of a nibble. He said, "And what was that?"

"What do you think."

When she kissed him again, they went down. The saltiness burned her eyes, but she opened them anyway. He was smiling at her, blowing bubbles. They surfaced together and laughed. Carefully she repositioned herself, climbing around him as if he were a tree—hanging from his rock-hard forearms and shoulders, bracing her knees against his hipbones as she swung to the front. All the time she felt him easing toward a shallower spot in the creek, so he could stand while holding her.

Now they were eye-to-eye, green water foaming up between them. Edie said, "Well?"

"Weren't you the one worried about crocodiles?"

"He'd have to eat both of us, wouldn't he?"

"At the moment, yes."

"That means he'd have to be awfully big and hungry."

Skink said, "We should be quiet, just in case. Certain noises do attract them." He sounded serious.

"How quiet?" Lightly she brushed her nipples along the lines of his ribs.

"Very quiet. Not a sound."

"That's impossible." She felt his hands on the curve of her bottom. He was lifting her, keeping her in a gentle suspension. Then he was inside her. Just like that.

"Hush," he said.

"I can't."

"Yes you can, Edie."

They made love so slowly that often it seemed they weren't moving a muscle. All sense of touch and motion came from the warm summer tide that rushed past and around and between them. In the mangroves an outraged heron squawked. More silver mullets jumped toward the shallows. A long black snake drifted by, indifferently riding the slick of the current as if it were floating on jade-colored silk.

Edie Marsh was good. She hardly made a sound. For quite a while she even forgot the purpose of the seduction.

Afterwards she wanted to dry off and take a nap together, but Skink said there was no time. They dressed quickly. Without a word he led her through the tangled woods. Edie saw no particular trail; at times it seemed they were hiking in circles. Once they reached a paved road, he took her arm. They walked another mile to an intersection with a flashing traffic light. A sign said that one road went to Miami, the other toward Key West.

Skink told her to wait there.

"For what?"

"Somebody's taking you to the mainland. He'll be coming soon."

Edie was caught by surprise. "Who?"

"Relax."

"But I wanted *you* to take me."

"Sorry," said Skink. "This is as far as I go."

"It's going to rain again."

"Yep."

"I heard lightning!" Edie said.

"So don't fly any kites."

"When did you plan this? Dropping me out here . . ." She was angry now. She realized he'd always meant to let her go—which meant the sex-in-the-creek had been unnecessary.

Not that she hadn't enjoyed it, or wouldn't love to try it again, but still she felt tricked.

"Why didn't you tell me last night?"

Skink flashed her the politician's smile. "Slipped my mind."

"Asshole." She picked a leaf out of her wet hair and peevishly flicked it into the wind. Swatted a horsefly off her ankle. Folded her arms and glared.

He leaned down and kissed her forehead. "Look on the bright side, girl. You got over your fear of crocodiles."

THIRTY

At half past noon, a police cruiser stopped at the intersection of Card Sound Road and County Road 905. A broad-shouldered black man in casual street clothes honked twice at Edie Marsh. As he motioned her to the car, she recognized him as the cop whom Snapper had shot outside Paradise Palms.

"You might not believe this," she said, "but I'm really glad you're OK."

"Thanks for your concern." His tone was so neutral that she almost didn't catch the sarcasm. He wore reflector sunglasses and had a toothpick in the corner of his mouth. When he reached across to open the door, Edie glimpsed a white mat of bandage between the middle buttons of his shirt.

"You're Jim, right? I'm Edie."

"I figured."

He took the road toward Miami. Edie assumed she was being arrested. She said, "For what it's worth, I didn't think he would shoot."

"Funny thing about morons with guns."

"Look, I know where he is. I can show you where he is."

Jim Tile said, "I already know."

Then she understood. The trooper had no intention of trying to find Snapper. It was over for Snapper.

"What about me?" she asked, inwardly speculating on the multitude of felonies for which she could be prosecuted. Attempted murder. Fleeing the scene. Aiding and abetting. Auto theft. Not to mention insurance fraud, which the trooper might or might not know about, depending on what the governor had told him.

"So what happens to me?" she asked again.

"Last night I got a message saying a lady needed a ride to the mainland."

"And you had nothing better to do."

From miles behind the sunglasses: "It was an old friend who called."

Edie Marsh kept trying to play tough. It wasn't easy. No other cars were in sight. The guy could rape me, kill me, dump my body in the swamp. Who'd ever know? Plus he was a cop.

She said, "You didn't answer my question."

The toothpick bobbed. "The answer is: Nothing. Nothing's going to happen to you. The friend who left a message put in a good word."

"Yeah?"

"'Jail will not make an impression on this woman. Don't waste your time.' That's a quote."

Edie reddened. "Some good word."

"So you get a free ride to Florida City. Period."

After crossing the Card Sound Bridge, the trooper stopped at Alabama Jack's. He asked Edie if she wanted a fish sandwich or a burger.

"I'm barefoot," she said.

Finally he broke a smile. "I don't believe there's a dress code."

Over lunch, Edie Marsh tried again. "I got sick when Snapper pulled the trigger," she said, "back at the motel, I swear. It's the last thing I wanted."

Jim Tile said it didn't matter one way or the other. To appear friendly, Edie asked how long he'd been assigned to Miami.

"Ten days."

"You came for the hurricane?"

"Just like you," he said, letting her know he had her pegged.

On their way out of the restaurant, he bought her an extra order of fries and a Coke for the road. In the car, Edie tried to keep the conversation moving. She felt more secure when he was talking, instead of staring ahead like a sphinx, working that damn toothpick.

She asked if she could see the bulletproof vest. He said he'd had to turn it in at headquarters, for evidence. She asked if the bullet made a hole and he said no, more of a dimple.

"Bet you didn't think hurricane duty would be so hairy."

Jim Tile fiddled with the squelch on the radio.

Edie said, "What's the craziest thing you've seen so far?"

"Besides your geek partner shooting at me?"

"Yeah, besides that."

"The President of the United States," he said, "trying to hammer a nail into a piece of plywood. Took him at least nine tries."

Edie straightened. "You saw the President!"

"Yeah. We had motorcade duty."

Thoughtfully she munched on a French fry. "Did you see his son, too?"

"They were riding in the same limo."

"I didn't know he lived in Miami, the President's son."

"Lucky him," the trooper said.

Edie Marsh, sipping her Coke, trying not to be too obvious: "I wonder where his house is, somebody like that. Key Biscayne probably, or maybe the Gables. Sometimes I wonder about famous people. Where they eat out. Where they get their cars waxed. Who's their dentist. I mean, think about it: The President's kid, he still has to get his teeth cleaned. Don't you ever wonder about stuff like that?"

"Never." Fat raindrops slapped on the windshield. Still the trooper stayed camped behind the sunglasses.

Edie didn't give up. "You got a girlfriend?" she asked.

"Yes."

Finally, Edie thought. Something to run with. "Where is she?"

"In the hospital," Jim Tile said. "Your buddy beat her to a pulp."

"Oh God, no. . . ."

He saw that she'd spilled the Coke, and that she didn't even know it.

"God, I'm so sorry," she was saying. "I swear, I didn't—will she be all right?"

Jim Tile offered a handful of paper napkins. Edie tried to sop the soda off her lap. Her hands were shaky.

"I didn't know," she said, more than once. She recalled the engraving on the mother's wedding band, the one that Snapper had stolen. "Cynthia" was the name on the ring, the mother of the trooper's girlfriend.

Now Edie felt close to the crime. Now she felt truly sick.

Jim Tile said, "The doctors think she'll be OK."

All Edie could do was nod; she was tapped out. The trooper turned up the volume of the police radio. When they reached the mainland, he stopped at a boarded-up McDonald's. The hurricane had blown out the doors and windows.

A teal-blue compact was parked under a naked palm tree. A man in a green Day-Glo rain poncho was sitting on the hood; from the sharp creases, it appeared that his poncho was brand-new. The man hopped down when he saw the Highway Patrol car.

"Who's that?" Edie asked.

"Watch out for broken glass," Jim Tile said.

"You're leaving me here?"

"Yes, ma'am."

When Edie Marsh got out, the man got in. The trooper told him to shut the door and fasten his seat belt. Edie didn't back away from the car; she just stood there, crossing her arms in a halfhearted sulk. The effect was impaired by the slashing rain, which caused her to blink and squint, and by the stormy wind, which made her hair thrash like a pom-pom.

Through the weather she shouted at Jim Tile: "What am I supposed to do now?"

"Count your blessings," he said. Then he made a U-turn and headed back toward Key Largo.

Bonnie gave Augustine a nervous kiss before she left camp with Skink. Her husband was on his way. They were to meet at the road.

Alone, Augustine tried to read, huddled in the old ambulance to keep the pages dry. But he couldn't concentrate. His imagination was inventing dialogue for Bonnie and Max's reunion. In his head there were two versions of the script; one for a sad good-bye, one for I'm-sorry-let's-try-again.

Part of him expected not to see Bonnie again, expected her to change her mind and fly back to New York. Augustine had accustomed himself to such letdowns.

On the other hand, none of his three ex-fiancées would have lasted so long in the deep woods without a tantrum or a scene. Bonnie Lamb was very different from the others. Augustine hoped she was different enough not to run away.

Despite his emotional distress, Augustine kept a watch on Snapper, still zonked from the monkey tranquilizer. It wouldn't be long before the dumb cracker woke up blathering. Except for the cheap pinstripe suit, he reminded Augustine of the empty-eyed types his father used to hire as boat crew.

Another thing that got him thinking about his old man was the lousy weather. Augustine recalled a gray September afternoon when his father had dumped sixty bales overboard in the mistaken belief that an oncoming vessel was a Coast Guard patrol, when in fact it was a Hatteras full of hard-drinking surgeons on their way to Cat Cay. The marijuana bobbed on seven-foot swells in the Gulf Stream while Augustine's father frantically recruited friends, neighbors, cousins, dock rats and Augustine himself for the salvage. Using boat hooks and fish gaffs, they retrieved all but four bales, which were snatched up by the agile crew of a passing Greek tanker. Later that night, when the load was safe and drying in a warehouse, Augustine's father threw a party for his helpers. Everybody got stoned except Augustine, who was only twelve years old at the time. Already he knew he wasn't cut out for his old man's fishing business.

Augustine climbed out of the ambulance and stretched. A redtailed hawk hunted in tight circles above the campsite. Augustine walked over to the place where Snapper slept. The governor had left the hurricane money lying in the suitcase, reeking of urine.

Augustine nudged Snapper with his shoe. Nothing. He grasped The Club and turned the man's head back and forth. He was as limp as a rag doll. The motion caused a slight stir and a sleepy gargle, but the eyelids remained closed. Augustine lifted one of Snapper's hands and pinched a thumbnail, very hard. The guy didn't flinch.

Dreamland, thought Augustine. No need to tie him up.

He found the sight and sound of Lester Maddox Parsons particularly depressing when married to the fear that Bonnie Lamb wasn't coming back. Sharing camp with a shitbird criminal had no appeal. The smell of fast-moving rain, the high coasting of the hawk, the cool green embrace of the hardwoods—all spoiled by Snapper's sour presence.

Augustine couldn't wait there anymore. It was worse than being alone.

Jim Tile said, "Where's the young man?"

"Library," said Skink.

They were in the trooper's car, near the trail upon which Skink had led Bonnie to the road. She and her husband were sitting side by side on one of the metal rails that ran the perimeter of Crocodile Lakes. The police car was parked seventy-five yards away; it was the best that Jim Tile and Skink could offer for privacy. Even from that distance, in the rain, Max Lamb was highly visible in the neon poncho.

"His old man's in prison." Skink was still talking about Augustine. "You'll love this: She says he was conceived in a hurricane."

"Which one?"

"Donna."

Jim Tile smiled. "That's something."

"Thirty-two years later: another storm, another beginning. The boy's star-crossed, don't you think?"

The trooper chuckled. "I think you're full of it." There was affection in the remark. "What's the story with the father?"

"Smuggler," Skink said, "and not a talented one."

Jim Tile considered that for a moment. "Well, I like the young man. He's all right."

"Yes, he is."

The trooper put on the windshield wipers. They could see—by the movement of the poncho—that Bonnie's husband was up and pacing.

"*Him* I don't envy," Jim Tile said.

Skink shrugged. He hadn't completely forgiven Max Lamb for bringing his Handycam to Miami. He said, "Lemme see where you got shot."

The trooper unbuttoned his shirt and peeled away the bandage. Even with the vest to stop it, the slug had raised a plum-colored bruise on Jim Tile's sternum. The governor whistled and said, "You and Brenda need a vacation."

"They say maybe ten days she'll be out of the hospital."

"Take her to the islands," Skink suggested.

"She's never been to the West. She loves horses."

"The mountains, then. Wyoming."

The trooper said, "She'd go for that."

"Anywhere, Jim. Away from this place is the main thing."

"Yeah." He turned off the wipers. The heavy rain gathered like syrup on the windshield. They did not speak of Snapper.

"Which one is it?" Max Lamb asked.

He hoped it was the kidnapper, the wilder one. That would bolster his theory that his wife had lost her mind; a weather-related version of the Stockholm Syndrome. That would make it easier to accept, easier to explain to his friends and parents. Bonnie had been mesmerized by a drug-crazed hermit. Manson minus the Family.

Bonnie said, "Max, the problem is *me*."

When she knew it wasn't, not entirely. She'd watched him, after stepping from the police car, jump at the sight of a puny marsh rabbit as if it were a hundred-pound timber wolf.

Now he was saying, "Bonnie, you've been brainwashed."

"Nobody—"

"Did you sleep with him?"

"Who?"

"Either of them."

"No!" To cover the lie, Bonnie aimed for a tone of indignation.

"But you wanted to."

Max Lamb rose, raindrops beading on the plastic poncho. "You're telling me that this"—with a mordant sweep of an arm— "you prefer *this* to the city!"

She sighed. "I wouldn't mind seeing a baby crocodile. That's all I said." She was aware of how outrageous it must have sounded to someone like Max.

"He's got you smoking that shit, doesn't he?"

"Oh please."

Back and forth he paced. "I can't believe this is happening."

"Me, neither," she said. "I'm sorry, Max."

He squared his shoulders and spun away, toward the lakes. He was too mad to weep, too insulted to beg. Also, it had dawned on him that Bonnie might be right, that perhaps he didn't know her very well. Even if she changed her mind and returned with him to New York, he constantly would be worrying that she might flip out again. What happened out here had sprained their relationship, probably permanently.

Turning to face her, his voice leaden with disappointment, Max said, "I thought you were more . . . centered."

"Me, too." To argue would only drag things out. Bonnie was determined to be agreeable and apologetic, no matter what he said. She had to leave him with *something*—if not his pride, then his swollen sense of male superiority. She figured it was a small price, to help get him through the hurt.

"Last chance," Max Lamb said. He groped under the bright poncho and pulled out a pair of airline tickets.

"I'm sorry," said Bonnie, shaking her head.

"Do you love me or not?"

"Max, I don't know."

He tucked the tickets away. "This is unbelievable."

She got up and kissed him good-bye. Her eyes were rimmed

with tears, though Max probably didn't notice, with all the raindrops on her face.

"Call me," he said bitterly, "when you figure yourself out."

Alone, he walked back to the patrol car. The kidnapper held the door for him.

Max was quiet on the drive back to the mainland; an accusatory silence. The state trooper was friends with the maniac who'd kidnapped Max and brainwashed his wife. The trooper had a moral and legal duty to stop the seduction, or at least try. That was Max's personal opinion.

When they got to the boarded-up McDonald's, Max told him: "You make sure that nutty one-eyed bastard takes care of her."

It was meant to carry the weight of a warning, and ordinarily Jim Tile would have been amused at Max's hubris. But he pitied him for the bad news he was about to deliver.

"She'll never see the governor again," the trooper said, "after today."

"Then—"

"I think you're confused," said the trooper. "The young fella with the skulls, that's who she fell for."

"Jesus." Max Lamb looked disgusted.

As Jim Tile drove away, he could see him in the rearview—stomping around the parking lot in the rain, kicking at puddles, flapping like a giant Day-Glo bat.

They were a mile from the road when Augustine appeared on the trail. Bonnie ran to him. They were still holding each other when Skink announced he was heading back to camp.

Augustine took Bonnie to the creek. He cleared a dry patch of bank and they sat down. She saw that he'd brought a paperback book from the ambulance.

"Oh, you're going to read me sonnets!" She clasped both hands to her breasts, pretending to swoon.

"Don't be a smartass," Augustine said, mussing her hair. "Remember the first time your husband called after the kidnapping—the message he left on the answering machine?"

Bonnie no longer regarded it as that—a kidnapping—but she supposed it was. Technically.

Augustine said, "The governor had him read something over the phone. Well, I found it." He pointed to the title on the spine of the book. *Tropic of Cancer*, by Henry Miller.

"Listen," said Augustine:

"'Once I thought that to be human was the highest aim a man could have, but I see now that it was meant to destroy me. Today I am proud to say that I am *inhuman*, that I belong not to men and governments, that I have nothing to do with creeds and principles. I have nothing to do with the creaking machinery of humanity—I belong to the earth! I say that lying on my pillow and I can feel the horns sprouting from my temples.'"

He handed the novel to Bonnie. She saw that Skink had underlined the passage in red ink.

"It's him, all right."

"Or me," said Augustine. "On a given day."

The sky was turning purple and contused. Overhead a string of turkey buzzards coasted on the freshening breeze. In the distance there was a broken tumble of thunder. Augustine asked Bonnie what happened with Max.

"He's going back alone," she said. "You know, it's crossed my mind that I'm cracking up." She took out her wedding ring. Augustine figured she was going to either slip it on her finger or toss it in the creek.

"Don't," he said, covering both possibilities.

"I'll send it back to him. I don't know how else to handle it." Her voice was thin and sad. Hurriedly she put the ring away.

Augustine asked, "What do you want to do?"

"Be with you for a while. Is that OK?"

"Perfect."

Brightening, Bonnie said, "What about you, Mister Live-for-Today?"

"You'll be pleased to know I've got a plan."

"That's hard to believe."

"Really," he said. "I'm going to sell Uncle Felix's farm, or what's left of it. And my house, too. Then I intend to find someplace just like this and start again. Someplace on the far edge of things. Still interested?"

"I don't know. Will there be cable?"

"No way."

"Rattlesnakes?"

"Possibly."

"Boy. The edge of the edge." Bonnie pretended to be mulling.

He said, "Ever heard of the Ten Thousand Islands?"

"Somebody counted them all?"

"No, dear. That would take a lifetime."

"Is that your plan?" she asked.

Augustine was familiar with the partner-choosing dilemma. She was deciding whether she wanted an anchor or a sail. He said, "There's a town called Chokoloskee. You might hate it."

"Baloney. Stay right here." Bonnie hopped to her feet.

"Now where are you going?"

"Back to camp for some poetry."

"Sit down. I'm not finished."

She spanked his arm away. "You read to me. Now I'm going to read to you."

What Bonnie had in mind, dashing up the trail, was Whitman. Somewhere in the rusted ambulance was a hardbound volume of "Song of Myself," a poem she'd loved since high school. One line in particular—"In vain the mastodon retreats from its own pow-der'd bones"—reminded her of Skink.

As she entered the campsite, she spotted him motionless on the ground. Snapper craned over him, making throaty snarls. He was coming down from a sulfurous rage. In one hand was a piece of burnt wood that Bonnie recognized as the governor's hiking torch.

She stood rigid, her fists balled at her sides. Snapper wore a contorted expression made no less malignant by the red-and-chrome bar clamped to his face. He was unaware of Bonnie watching from the tree line. He dropped the torch, snatched up the suitcase and began to run.

Insanely she went after him.

THIRTY-ONE

Snapper had been awakened by a cool drizzle. The campsite was still. The one-eyed lunatic was asleep, stretched out in his grubby army duds beneath a tree. There was no sign of Edie Marsh, or the sharpshooter, or the weird broad who'd doused herself with soda pop in the Jeep.

Slowly Snapper sat up. His eyes were crusty and his mouth was ash dry. A clot of black dirt stuck to one eyebrow: For the umpteenth time he tried unsuccessfully to wrench The Club out of his gums. The pain was hideous, as if the bones of his face were spring-loaded to blow apart. He was grateful he couldn't see himself; he must've looked like a fucking circus freak. Bucket-Mouth Man. Dorks lining up to toss softballs down his gullet.

Jesus H. Christ, he thought, I gotta clear the cobwebs.

There on the ground was the suitcase full of cash, yawning, where Skink had left it. The smell pungently reminded Snapper that it hadn't been a nightmare: The asshole had actually pissed on ninety-four thousand perfectly good U.S. dollars.

Snapper tested his legs; left, right, together. Next he clenched his hands, flexed his arms. So far, so good. The second tranquilizer dart finally had worn off.

He rose to his feet. Tenuously he took one step toward the cash. Then another. The iron bar on his jaws was so cumbersome that he almost lost his balance and toppled forward. He tried to hold his breath while he latched the suitcase, but the aroma was unavoidable. Snapper found the water jug and emptied it into his throat. His spluttering failed to disturb the dozing lunatic.

355

Snapper spied a handy weapon—a length of gummy wood, one end charred.

The big dork must've heard him coming, because he tried to roll away when Snapper swung. The blow caught the man in a shoulder instead of the head, but Snapper heard bones crack. He knew it hurt.

"Ahhheeegggnnn!" he brayed, swinging again and again until the fucker quit rolling and just lay there making a faint hiss, like a tire going flat.

Bonnie had always been scrappy for her size. In junior high she had chased down a boy who'd lifted her skirt in the school cafeteria. The boy's name was Eric Schultz. He was almost six feet tall, foul-mouthed and cocky, a star of the basketball team. He outweighed Bonnie by eighty pounds. When he tried to run away, she tackled him, held him down and punched him in the testicles. Eric Schultz missed the first and second rounds of the basketball playoffs. Bonnie Brooks was suspended from class for three days. Her father said it was worth it; he was proud. Bonnie's mother said she overreacted, because the boy Eric had been held back twice for eighth grade. Bonnie's mother said he'd probably done what he had to Bonnie because he didn't know any better. *He does now*, Bonnie had said. She agreed with her father: Stupidity was an overworked excuse.

With his bum knee, Snapper was easy to catch. His speed was further hindered by the unwieldy facial contraption, which snagged in the vines and branches. He went down in the same basic configuration as had Eric Schultz—limbs splayed, nose down. It took only a moment for Snapper to realize it was a woman hanging off his shoulders, and not a large one. The casual manner in which he shook free suggested to Bonnie that her rabbit punches were ineffective. Unlike young Eric Schultz, Lester Maddox Parsons had been to prison, where he'd learned much about dirty fighting. He wasn't about to let a one-hundred-pound girl get a clear shot at his jewels.

With both arms he swung the Frenchman's suitcase, knocking

Bonnie sideways against the gnarled trunk of an old buttonwood. She landed flat on her back, punching frenetically. The red steel bar across Snapper's cheeks blocked her best jabs. He quickly pinned her wrists, but she stopped kicking only when he dug a knee into her pubic bone.

Beneath the dull deadening weight of his torso, she gradually lost sight of the buzzards and the gathering clouds. Her next view was a glistening, pink, fistulous cave—his mouth, stretched in the shape of a permanent scream. He panted from exertion; hot, necrotic gusts. Bonnie wanted to gag. Something wet and wormy settled on the cleft of her chin.

A lip.

She took it in her teeth and bit hard. Snapper yowled and pulled away. A half second later, Bonnie was stunned by a sharp blow to her temple. The Club. The bastard was trying to beat her with it, using frenzied, snorting sweeps of his head. She had no way to protect herself. Snapper wouldn't release her arms because he didn't need his own for the attack; his gourd was doing all the work. Bonnie was dazed by another white burst of pain. She shut her eyes so she wouldn't have to see his goggling wet hole of a face. She made herself go limp, thinking that unconsciousness would be fine and dandy.

Snapper imagined himself a wild bull in the ring; goring at will. The bitch was helpless beneath him, hardly twitching. He paused to catch his breath, spit blood, and congratulate himself for so cleverly converting a handicap to a martial asset. The cop on the TV commercial was right; The Club was indestructible! Despite the stinging of his lip and the burning in his knee and the electric throbbing in the joints of his jaw, Snapper didn't feel so bad. His pride outweighed the pain. Certainly he'd earned the rights to the Frenchman's hurricane money.

That's when a hand moved between his legs; lightly, like a sparrow on a branch.

"Nnnnggggguuuhhh!!"

The bitch grabbed him. Snapper bellowed. He thrashed his head, trying to pummel her with the heavy end of The Club. Then he realized it couldn't be the girl squeezing his balls, because both her wrists remained pinned in the dirt. She wasn't moving a muscle. It had to be somebody else.

Then, from a distance, he heard: "No! Don't do that."

He tried to hold still. Tried to breathe without whimpering. Tried to turn ever so slightly, to see who the fuck had at least one (and possibly both) of his nuts in their fingers.

Again the voice, this time closer: "Don't do it! Don't!"

The one-eyed freak, calling out.

Who's he talking to? Snapper wondered. Don't do *what*?

Then the gun went off at his head, and he knew.

Max Lamb was surprised to find a woman sleeping in the front seat of his rental car. He recognized her as the one whom the state trooper had dropped off in the parking lot earlier that afternoon.

She sat up, brushing her long brown hair from her eyes. "It was raining. I had no place to go." Not the least bit bashful.

"That's OK," Max said. He wormed out of the Day-Glo poncho and tossed it in the back seat.

"My name is Edie." She reached out to shake his hand.

He took it, stiffly. She had a strong grip.

"I'm Max," he said. Then he heard himself saying: "You need a lift back to Miami?"

Edie Marsh nodded gratefully. That's what she'd been counting on. One way or another, all rental cars ultimately returned to Miami.

She said, "I would've tried hitching a ride, but there was lightning."

"Yeah, I heard."

Somehow Max missed the ramp to the Turnpike; it wasn't easy, but he did. Edie didn't complain. A lift was a lift. All the roads went the same direction anyway.

"Where are you from, Max?" He looked perfectly harmless, but still she wanted to get him talking. Silent brooding made her edgy.

"New York. I'm in advertising."

"No kidding."

And off he went. During the next hour, Edie learned a great deal about Madison Avenue. Max was absolutely elated to discover that she'd been a glutton for Plum Crunchies cereal. And she remembered his slogan, word for word!

"What others have you done?" she asked brightly.

Max was tempted to tell her about Intimate Mist but thought better of it. Not everyone felt comfortable on the subject of douches.

"Bronco cigarets," he said.

"Really!"

"Speaking of which, would you mind if I smoked?"

"Not at all," said Edie Marsh.

He offered her a menthol. She declined politely. As smoke filled the car, she rolled down the window and tried not to cough herself blue. "When are you going back to New York?"

"Tomorrow," Max said. He grew quiet again.

Edie said: "If you tell me, I'll tell you."

Max looked perplexed.

She said, "You know—what we were doing with that cop. Me coming, you going."

"Oh." After a pause: "I'm not in any kind of trouble, if that's what you mean."

Dryly she said, "I had a hunch you're no Ted Bundy."

What eyes! Max thought. What an interesting woman! He had reason to believe she was aware of her impact.

He said, "How about this: If you don't tell me, I won't tell you. What's over is over."

"I like that approach."

"Let's just agree we've had a bad day."

"And how."

In South Dade they hit heavy traffic where the storm had blown ashore, taking down everything. Edie Marsh had seen the destruction the day after the hurricane, but it seemed much worse to her now. She was surprised to find herself fighting back tears.

Out of nowhere Max said: "Hey, I bet I can guess what kind of car you drive." Apparently trying to take their minds off what they saw: two unshaven men, on a street corner, fighting over a five-gallon jug of fresh water. Their wives and children watching anxiously from the sidewalk.

"Seriously," Max was saying. "It's a knack I've got. Matching people to their cars."

"Based on . . . ?"

"Intuition, I guess you'd say."

Edie said, "OK, give it a try."

Max, eyeing her up and down, like he was guessing her weight: "Nissan 300?"

"Nope."

"A 280Z?"

"Try an Acclaim."

He winced. "I had you figured for a sports import."

"Well, I'm flattered," Edie said, with a soft laugh.

There was a brutal truth at the heart of Max's silly game. Eligible young Kennedys and even sons of sitting presidents did not customarily flag down women in 1987 Plymouths.

Later, after Max had found the Turnpike extension and made his way downtown, he said: "Where can I drop you?"

"Let me think about that," said Edie Marsh.

"Captain, have you got a mirror?"

"No."

"Good," Bonnie said.

She felt a raw knot rising on her forehead, another on a cheekbone. Augustine assured her that she didn't look as bad as she thought. "But you could use some ice."

"Later." She was watching Skink. "I know somebody who ought to be in a hospital."

"No," said the governor.

"Augustine says your collarbone is broken."

"I believe he's right."

"And several ribs."

"I shall call you Nurse Nightingale."

"Why are you so stubborn?"

"I know a doctor in Tavernier."

"And how do you plan to get there?"

"Walking upright," Skink replied. "One of the few commendable traits of our species."

Bonnie told him to quit being ridiculous. "You're in terrible pain, I can tell."

"The whole world's in pain, girl."

She looked imploringly to Augustine. "Talk to him, please."

"He's a grown man, Bonnie. Now hold still."

He was cleaning her face with his shirt, which he'd wadded up and soaked in the creek. Skink perched on a nearby log, his arms crossed tightly. Moments earlier they'd watched him gobble a dozen Anacins from a plastic bottle he located under the camp tarpaulin. Bonnie boldly swallowed three.

No aspirins were offered to Snapper, who was bound with a corroded tow-truck chain to the buttonwood tree. He was caked with soggy leaves, mulch and dried blood. His cheap suit was filthy and torn. During the struggle, Augustine had made him dig a short trench with his mandible, so his maw was full of stones and loose soil, like a planter. In addition, he was missing an earlobe, which Augustine had shot off at point-blank range. It was inconceivable to Snapper that such a chickenshit wound could be so excruciating.

Skink said to Augustine: "I thought sure you were going to kill him."

"It was tempting."

"My way's better."

"After what he did to Jim's girlfriend?"

"Yes. Even after that." The governor bowed his head. He was hurting.

Augustine was drained. The adrenaline had emptied out in a clammy torrent. He no longer entertained the idea of murdering Snapper, and doubted if he was even capable of it. An hour ago, yes. Not now. It was probably a good time to leave.

Bonnie studied his expression as he tended her cheeks and brow. "You OK?" she said.

"I don't know. The way he hurt you—"

"Hey, I asked for it."

"But you wouldn't be out here if it weren't for me."

Playfully she jabbed a finger in his side. "What makes you so sure? Maybe I'm here because of *him*."

Skink grinned but didn't look up. Augustine had to laugh, too. That's why we're both here, he thought. Because of him.

"Would it be bad manners," Bonnie said to Skink, "if I asked what you plan to do with the money."

His chin came off his chest. "Oh. That." Grimacing, he rose from the log. "Lester, you awake? Yo, Lester!"

"Ghhhnungggh."

The governor used his feet to push the Frenchman's suitcase across the clearing to the buttonwood tree, where he kicked the latches open. Snapper regarded the bundled cash with a mixture of undisguised longing and suspicion. He wondered what sick stunt the fucker was cooking up now.

Only the bills on top were wet. Skink swept them aside with his hands. Bonnie and Augustine walked over to see.

The governor said, "You guys want any of this?" They shook their heads.

"Me, neither," he muttered. "Just more shit to lug around." He addressed Snapper: "Chief, I'm sure there was a time in your sorry-ass life when ninety-four grand would've come in handy. Believe me when I tell you those days are over."

Skink took a matchbook from his pocket. He asked Bonnie and Augustine to do the honors. Snapper spewed dirt and thrashed inconsolably against the chains.

The money gave off a rich, sweet scent as it burned.

Later he unlocked the truck chain holding Snapper to the tree. Plaintively Snapper pointed at the red brace fastened in his mouth. Skink shook his head.

"Here's the deal, Lester. Don't be here when I get back. Do not fuck with my camp, do not fuck with my books. It's about to rain like hell, so lie back and drink as much as you can. You'll need it."

Snapper didn't respond. Augustine stepped up. He took out the .38 Special and said, "Try to follow us out, I'll blow your head off."

Bonnie shuddered. The governor removed a few items from beneath the tarpaulin and placed them in a backpack. Then he lighted the torch and led the others into the trees.

Snapper had no desire to follow; he was glad the crazy fuckers were gone. A gust churned the cinders at his feet, blew a flurry into his lap. He ran his fingers through the ashes, brought a handful to his nose. It didn't even smell like money anymore.

Later he awoke to the hard rustle of leaves. The rain came driving down. Snapper took the man's advice. He filled up on it.

At daybreak he would start his march.

They broke a fresh trail through the hardwoods. Bonnie was worried that Snapper would be able to use it to find his way out. "Not across a lake," Skink said.

She hooked her fingers in Augustine's belt as they swam. The governor hoisted the torch, his boots and the backpack over his head, to keep them dry. Augustine was astounded that the man could swim so well with a fractured collarbone. The crossing took less than fifteen minutes, though it seemed an eternity to Bonnie. She was unable to convince herself that crocodiles shunned firelight.

Afterwards they rested on shore. Skink, struggling into his laceless boots: "If he gets out of here, he deserves to be free."

Augustine said, "But he won't."

"No, he'll go the wrong way. That's his nature."

Then Skink was moving again, an orange flame weaving through the trees ahead of them. Bonnie, hurrying to keep up: "So something'll get him. Panthers or something."

Augustine said, "Nothing so exotic, Mrs Lamb."

"Then what?"

"Time. Time will get him."

"Exactly!" the governor boomed. "It's the arc of all life. For

Lester we merely hasten the sad promenade. Tonight we are Darwin's elves."

Bonnie quickened her pace. She felt happy to be with them, out in the middle of nowhere. Ahead on the trail, Skink was singing to himself. Feeling the horns sprouting from his temples, she supposed.

Two hours later they emerged from the woods. A rip of wind braced them.

"Oh brother," Augustine said, "any second now."

With a grimace, Skink removed the backpack. "This is for your hike."

"It's not that far."

"Take it, just in case."

Bonnie said, "God, your eye."

A stalk of holly berries garnished the empty withered socket. The governor groped at himself. "Damn. I guess it fell out."

Bonnie could hardly look at him.

"It's all right," he said. "I got a whole box of extras somewhere."

She said, "Don't be foolish. Go to the mainland with us."

"No!"

A mud-gray wall of rain came hissing down the road. Bonnie shivered as it hit them. Skink leaned close to Augustine: "Give it a couple three months, at least."

"You bet."

"For what?" Bonnie asked.

"Before I try to find that place again," Augustine said.

"Why go back?"

"Science," said Augustine.

"Nostalgia," said the governor.

The squall doused the torch, which he lobbed into a stand of red mangroves. He tucked his hair under the plastic shower cap and said good-bye. Bonnie kissed him on the chin and told him to be careful. Augustine gave an affable salute.

For a while they could make out his tall shape, stalking south, under violet flashbursts of high lightning. Then he was gone. The weather covered him like a shroud.

They turned and went the other way. Augustine walked fast on the blacktop, the backpack jouncing on his bare shoulders.

"Hey, the scar is looking good," Bonnie said.

"You still like it?"

"Beauty." She could see it vividly whenever the sky lit up. "A corkscrew in the shower—you weren't kidding?"

"God, I wish," said Augustine.

They heard a car behind them. As it approached, the headlights elongated their shadows on the pavement. Augustine asked Bonnie if she wanted to hitch a ride. She said no. They stepped off the road to let the car go by.

Soon they reached the tall bridge at Card Sound. Augustine said it was time to rest. He unzipped the backpack to see what the governor had packed: a coil of rope, two knives, four bandannas, a tube of antiseptic, a waterproof box of matches, a bottle of fresh water, chlorine tablets, some oranges, a stick of bug repellent, four cans of lentil soup and a tin of unidentifiable dried meat.

Augustine and Bonnie shared the water, then started up the bridge.

Needles of rain stung Bonnie's bruises as she climbed the long slope. She tasted brine on the wind, and wasn't embarrassed to clutch Augustine's right arm—the gusts were so strong they nearly lifted her off the ground.

"Maybe it's another hurricane!"

"Not hardly," he said.

They stopped at the top. Augustine threw the pistol as far as he could. Bonnie peered over the concrete rail to watch the splash, a silent punctuation. Augustine placed his hands firmly on her waist, holding her steady. She liked the way it felt, the trust involved.

Far below, the bay was frothed and corrugated; a treacherously different place from the first time Bonnie saw it. Not a night for dolphins.

She drew Augustine closer and kissed him for a long time. Then she spun him around and groped in the backpack.

"What're you doing?" he shouted over the slap of the rain.

"Hush."

When he turned back, her eyes were shining. In her hands was the coil of rope.

"Tie me to the bridge," she said.

EPILOGUE

The marriage of **Bonnie Brooks** and **Max Lamb** was discreetly annulled by a judge who happened to be a skiing companion of Max Lamb's father. Max returned to Rodale & Burns, pouring his energies into a new advertising campaign for Old Faithful Root Beer. Spurred by Max's simpleminded jingle, the company soon reported a 24 percent jump in domestic sales. Max was promoted to the sixth floor and put in charge of an $18 million account for a low-fat malt liquor called Steed.

By the end of the year, Max and **Edie Marsh** were engaged. They got an apartment on the Upper West Side of Manhattan, where Edie became active in charity circles. Two years after the hurricane, while attending a Kenny G concert to benefit victims of a Colombian mud slide, Edie met the same young Kennedy she'd long ago tried so avidly to debauch. She was mildly amazed when, while greeting her, he slipped a tongue in her ear. Max said it surely was her imagination.

Brenda Rourke recovered fully from her injuries and returned to the Highway Patrol. She requested and received a transfer to northern Florida, where she and **Jim Tile** built a small house on the Ochlockonee River. For Christmas he gave her an engraved gold replica of her mother's wedding ring, and two full-grown rottweilers from Stuttgart.

After being rescued in the ocean off Islamorada, **Avila** was taken to

Miami's Krome Detention Center and processed as "Juan Gómez Duran," a rafter fleeing political oppression in Havana. He was held at Krome for nine days, until a Spanish-language radio station sponsored his release. In return, brave "Sēnor Gómez" agreed to share the details of high-seas escape with radio listeners, who were moved by his heart-wrenching story but puzzled by his wildly inaccurate references to Cuban geography. Afterwards Avila packed up and moved to Fort Myers, on the west coast of Florida, where he was immediately hired as a code-enforcement officer for the local building-and-zoning department. During his first four weeks on the job, Avila approved 212 new homes—a record for a single inspector that stands to this day. Nineteen months after the hurricane, while preparing a sacrifice to Chango on the patio of his luxurious new waterfront town house, Avila was severely bitten on the thigh by a hydrophobic rabbit. Too embarrassed to seek medical attention, he died twenty-two days later in his hot tub. In honor of his short but productive tenure as a code inspector, the Lee County Home Builders Association established the Juan Gómez Duran Scholarship Fund.

One day after the state trooper was shot in the parking lot, paramedics again were summoned to the Paradise Palms Motel in the Florida Keys. This time a guest named **Levon Stichler** had suffered a mild myocardial infarction. On the ride to the emergency room, the old man deliriously insisted he'd been held captive at the motel by two bossy prostitutes. Doctors at Mariners Hospital notified Levon Stichler's daughter in Saint Paul, who was understandably alarmed to learn of her father's hallucinations. After hanging up the phone, she informed her children that Grandpa would be coming to stay for a while.

The gnawed remains of **Ira Jackson**, identified by X rays, were cremated and interred at a private ceremony on Staten Island. Several Teamster bosses sent flowers, as did the retired comptroller of the Central States Pension Fund. Three weeks after the hurricane, the African lion that attacked Ira Jackson was captured while foraging in a Dumpster behind a Pizza Hut in Perrine. The tranquilized animal was dipped, vaccinated, wormed and nick-named "Pepperoni." It is now on display at a wildlife park in West Palm Beach.

The murder of **Tony Torres** remains unsolved, although police suspect his wife of arranging the crime so that she could hoard the hurricane money from Midwest Casualty. Detectives seeking to question **Neria Torres** learned that she'd moved to Belize, leased an oceanfront villa and taken up with an expatriate American fishing guide. A court-ordered inspection of her late husband's bank records revealed that before leaving the United States, Mrs Torres moved $201,000 through a single checking account. The house at 15600 Calusa was never repaired and remained abandoned for twenty-two months, until it was finally condemned and destroyed.

Five weeks after the hurricane, **Fred Dove** went home to Omaha and presented his wife with two miniature dachshunds orphaned by the storm. He, **Dennis Reedy** and eight other Midwest Casualty adjusters were honored for their heroic work on the Florida crisis-response team. To publicize its swift and compassionate processing of hurricane claims, the company featured the men in a national television commercial that aired during the Bob Hope Christmas Special. Fred Dove was hopeful that **Edie Marsh** would contact him after the commercial was broadcast, but he never heard from her again.

Faced with a class-action lawsuit by 186 customers whose homes had more or less collapsed in the hurricane, builder **Gar Whitmark** declared bankruptcy and revived his construction companies under different names. He was killed thirteen months later in a freak accident on a job site, when high winds from a tropical storm knocked a bucket of hot tar off a roof and through the windshield of his Infiniti Q45. His troubled widow gave up prescription medicine and joined the Church of Scientology, to which she donated her late husband's entire estate.

*

The body of **Clyde Nottage Jr**. was flown from Guadalajara to Durham, North Carolina, where—at his family's request—an autopsy was performed at the Duke University Medical Center. Four days later, Mexican authorities arrested **Dr. Alan Caulk**, seized his laboratory and deported him to the Bahamas. Oddly, no sheep were ever found at the Aragon Clinic.

Despite contradictory affidavits from two preeminent psychiatrists, attorneys for **Durham Gas Meat & Tobacco** persuaded a judge in Raleigh to declare Clyde Nottage Jr mentally unfit. The posthumous certification was based on disturbing medical evidence supplied by Mexican officials, and sealed forever by the North Carolina courts. Sixty days after Nottage's death, DGM&T resumed production of Bronco cigarets. The advertising contract with Rodale & Burns was not renewed.

Eleven months after the hurricane, a biologist for the US Fish and Wildlife Service made a gruesome find in a remote upland area of the Crocodile Lakes Wildlife Refuge in North Key Largo: a deformed human jaw. Locked to the bone was an adjustable iron bar popularly used to deter auto theft. Dental X rays identified the owner of the mandible as **Lester Maddox Parsons**, a career felon and convicted killer wanted for violent assaults on two Florida Highway Patrol officers. According to the Monroe County Medical Examiner, evidence at the scene indicated that Parsons likely starved to death. A search of the hammocks turned up the remaining pieces of his skeleton, except for the skull.

Augustine Herrera sold his late uncle's wildlife farm and moved with **Bonnie Brooks** to Chokoloskee, a fishing village on the edge of Florida's Ten Thousand Islands. There he bought a crab boat and built a pineboard house with space for a large library, including a wall for his collection of skulls, now numbering twenty.

Bonnie Brooks took up watercolors, cycling and outdoor photography. Her remarkable picture of a pair of bald eagles nesting in the boughs of a cypress made the cover of *Audubon* magazine.

STORMY WEATHER

Most of the wild animals that escaped from **Felix Mojack's** farm during the hurricane were recaptured or, unfortunately, killed by armed home owners. The exceptions include one female cougar, forty-four rare birds, more than three hundred exotic lizards, thirty-eight snakes (venomous and nonvenomous) and twenty-nine adult rhesus monkeys, which have organized into several wily troops that roam Dade County to this day.